William Alexander Clouston

The Book of Sindibad

The Story of the King, his Son, the Damsel and the Seven Vazirs

William Alexander Clouston

The Book of Sindibad
The Story of the King, his Son, the Damsel and the Seven Vazirs

ISBN/EAN: 9783337400705

Printed in Europe, USA, Canada, Australia, Japan

Cover: Foto ©Andreas Hilbeck / pixelio.de

More available books at **www.hansebooks.com**

THE
BOOK OF SINDIBĀD;

OR,

THE STORY OF THE KING, HIS SON, THE DAMSEL, AND THE SEVEN VAZĪRS.

FROM THE PERSIAN AND ARABIC.

WITH INTRODUCTION, NOTES, AND APPENDIX,

BY

W. A. CLOUSTON,

EDITOR OF "ARABIAN POETRY FOR ENGLISH READERS,"
"THE BAKHTYAR NAMA," ETC.

"Alas, women whose love is scorned are worse than poison!"
Somadeva.

PRIVATELY PRINTED.

MDCCCLXXXIV

TO

DR. REINHOLD ROST, LL.D.,

LIBRARIAN TO THE INDIA OFFICE,

THIS WORK,

WHICH, ALIKE AS A FRIEND AND A SCHOLAR, HE WOULD
CRITICISE WITH INDULGENCE,

IS DEDICATED,

BY

THE EDITOR.

PREFACE.

THE present work is, I believe, the first attempt, in this country, to furnish a compendious account of the Eastern and Western groups of romances known respectively under their generic titles of the BOOK OF SINDIBĀD and the BOOK OF THE SEVEN WISE MASTERS. Wright's introduction to his edition, for the Percy Society, of an Early English metrical version of the *Seven Sages* may perhaps be considered as such a work, but he has confounded the Eastern with the Western versions, having been misled by Des Longchamps and other investigators, who, in this field of inquiry, according to Gödeke, "fell into such confusion in essential points that they contributed almost as much to perpetuate old errors and spread them anew as to lay and root out others." Moreover, several important texts have been since discovered, throwing new light upon the history of both groups.—Professor Comparetti's *Ricerche intorno al Libro di Sindibād,* an English translation of which, by Mr. H. C. Coote, forms one of the publications for the Folk-Lore Society, is un-

doubtedly one of the most important contributions to
the history of the romance; but it assumes the reader
to be familiar with the details of the several Eastern
texts, the subordinate stories being mostly referred to
only by their titles, and its usefulness is consequently
confined within a narrow circle, in the absence, for
merely English readers, of the tales themselves. This
want I have now endeavoured to supply, to the best of
my ability, in the following work, which comprises:

(1) An introductory account of the structure of
the Book of Sindibād, and the probable sources of the
several Eastern versions; to which is prefixed a Comparative Table of the Tales in this group, designed to
exhibit, at a glance, the degrees of relationship which
the texts bear towards each other.

(2) An epitome, by Professor Forbes Falconer, of a
Persian text, entitled *Sindibād Nāma*, composed in
1375, of which the only known copy is an imperfect
MS. in the Library of the India Office. Falconer's
work left much to be desired: of some of the Tales he
gave only the titles, and others he presented in a very
abridged form; it has therefore been compared with the
MS.; the abridged and omitted Tales—ten in number,
of which three seem to have altogether escaped his
notice—translated and inserted, and several grave
errors rectified. In foot-notes I have explained such
references and expressions as might be obscure to
some readers, and adduced from the other versions
passages which correspond with, or vary from, this text.

(3) An Arabian version of the *Seven Vazīrs*, translated by Jonathan Scott, with corrections and additions,
and similarly annotated. In my preface to it are some
particulars regarding this and other Arabian texts.

(4) An Appendix, which contains variants of the
Tales in both these texts—forming curious illustrations
of the pedigree of popular fictions and their migrations
and transformations—together with such Tales as do
not occur in them, but are found in the others. Thus
all the Tales of the Eastern Texts, as represented in
the Comparative Table, are now brought together.

It certainly formed no part of my original design
to treat of the Western Texts. These have, in some
measure, preserved—from oral tradition, unquestionably—the leading ideas of the ancient original tale :
the orphanhood of the accused youth; his education
at a distance from his father; his step-mother's malice
against him, and so on;—but, as Comparetti has
observed, "there is no Eastern version which differs
so much from the others as the whole Western group
differs from the Eastern group, whether it be in the
form of the fundamental story, or in the tales inserted
in it, of which scarcely four are common to both
groups." As my work progressed, however, it occurred
to me that abstracts of an Early English metrical version
of the *Seven Wise Masters* and of the oldest European
form of the romance, the Latin original of the old
French metrical version, *Dolopathos*—discovered within
recent years—with variants as found in other collec-

tions, would be acceptable to English students of the history of Fiction, which I have accordingly inserted in the Appendix.

My work is, of course, not free from errors: I trust they will be excused by those who know the difficulties that beset a task of this kind. But however imperfect it may be, it would certainly have been still more so, but for the valuable assistance which I received from several eminent scholars; especially, from Mr. J. W. Redhouse, on whose stores of learning I drew, as on former occasions, perhaps too frequently; Mr. William Platt, to whose erudition I am also much indebted; Mr. E. J. W. Gibb, author of *Ottoman Poems*, etc., whose great kindness of disposition is equalled by his attainments in, and enthusiasm for, Oriental literature; and to Mr. David Ross, Principal of the E.C. Training College, Glasgow, of whose classical and general scholarship I was also happily able to avail myself. That the work should be as comprehensive as possible has been my aim from the first; and, notwithstanding occasional inaccuracies and shortcomings, I venture to hope that it will prove interesting to general readers, and possibly even not altogether without its use to some of those who make a special study of the origin and spread of "old-world tales."

W. A. CLOUSTON

GLASGOW, *May*, 1884.

CONTENTS.

THE SEVEN VAZĪRS.

APPENDIX.

INTRODUCTION.

INTRODUCTION.

———

I N a somewhat extravagant eulogium of the romance
known throughout Europe from mediæval times
as the History, or Book, of the Seven Sages, Görres
says, that "it sprang originally from the Indian mountains, whence from primeval days it took its course as
a little rivulet, and flowed in a westerly direction
through Asia's wide field, and, while it proceeded for
thousands of years through space and time, always
spreading more and more in reaching us. Out of it
whole generations and many nations have drank; and,
having passed to Europe with the great tide of popula-
tion, it is now also in our day and generation supplied
to such a considerable portion of the public, that in
regard to its celebrity and the magnitude of its sphere
of influence, it reaches the Holy Book, and surpasses
all classical works." This account of the romance is
very misleading. The prototype of the Seven Sages was,
no doubt, an ancient Indian work (though surely not
"thousands of years old") called the Book of Sindibād,
from which have sprung two groups of texts, Eastern

b

and Western: the former derived, mediately or immediately, from a common and *written* source; the latter
based upon oral traditions of the romance, brought to
Europe by minstrels and pilgrims from the East, and
preserving little more than the general plan of the
original work. The Eastern group of texts must therefore be considered as having a distinct and separate
history from the Western group. Like so many other
Asiatic collections of fiction, this romance in its several
versions consists of a number of tales and apologues,
strung together by a general story, running throughout
the whole work, of which the following is the outline:

A monarch, powerful, wise, and just, was very unhappy because he had not a son to succeed him on
the throne, and he was now far advanced in years.
After many earnest prayers to Heaven, he is at length
blessed with a son, upon which he assembles the most
skilful astrologers to cast his horoscope (as is still
customary in the East on the birth of a male child),
which is found to portend great danger to his life
when he has attained his twentieth year. The king is
at first greatly alarmed at this intelligence, but ultimately becomes reconciled to the decree of destiny;
and, when the child is old enough, he confides him to
a tutor, under whose instruction, however, in spite of
all his efforts, the young prince makes no progress in
learning during several years. The prince is then
taken in hand by a profound sage, called Sindibād,
but he, too, fails to instruct him—apparently the youth

is hopelessly stupid. The king, on learning this, is
enraged at the philosopher, who, nothing daunted by
his failure, now boldly undertakes to teach the prince
all necessary knowledge in the space of six months, at
the peril of his own life. Having succeeded within
less than the stipulated period, before the prince is to
be presented to his father, in order to exhibit his varied
accomplishments, Sindibād takes an observation of the
prince's star, and discovers that he is threatened with
loss of life should he utter a word during the seven
following days. He communicates this to the prince,
and counsels him, notwithstanding, to appear before his
father, but on no account to speak until the fatal seven
days are passed—for himself, he must hide from the
king's wrath. Accordingly, the prince proceeds to
the palace, and is warmly embraced by his father, but
returns not a word in answer to the questions which
are put to him. One of the king's women, secretly
in love with the prince, now enters the audience-
chamber, and learning that he has been apparently
deprived of the power of speech, requests his Majesty's
permission to try whether she cannot privately induce
the prince to speak, which being granted, she takes the
youth into the harem, where she tells him of her love
for him, and proposes to poison the king, in order that
he may at once ascend the throne. Horrified at the
thought of such a heinous crime, the prince upbraids
her, and flies out of the room. The damsel, fearing
the consequences of her conduct, tears her garments

and scratches her face, and in this condition presents herself before the king, who inquires the cause of her distress. She replies that his son, who had only feigned himself dumb, had no sooner entered her apartment than he made love to her, and proposed to poison his Majesty. Believing this false tale, the king immediately commands the executioner to put the prince to death. But this precipitate sentence coming to the knowledge of the king's Seven Vazírs, or counsellors, they determine to save the life of the prince as long as possible, in hopes that his innocence would be established, by each of them in turn relating to the king instances of the craft and malice of women, and warning him against undue haste in affairs of import-ance. The First Vazír accordingly appears before the king, and relates two stories to show that no reliance should be placed upon the accusation of a woman; after which his Majesty remands the prince to prison in the meantime. At night, however, the Damsel counteracts the effect produced in the king's mind by the vazír's tales, by relating a story designed to ex-emplify the deceitful and wicked disposition of men, with the result of inducing the king to resolve once more to put his son to death. In like manner, the tales of the other vazírs are controverted by the damsel, until the seven days are passed, when the prince, being free to speak again, informs the king of the damsel's atrocious plot against his life, and relates a number of tales, after which the wicked damsel is punished.

The repeated failures to educate the prince, the father's grief and rage, and the sage finally undertaking to instruct the youth in *six months*, correspond exactly with the frame of the *Pancha Tantra* (Five Chapters), a celebrated collection of Hindū fables, in Sanskrit, as old at least as the 6th century; and the resemblance can hardly be merely fortuitous:

"There is a city in the southern country, named Mihilārōpyam, the king of which, learned and munificent, distinguished among princes and scholars, was named Amara Sacti. He had three sons, youths of no capacity or diligence: Vasu Sacti, Bhadra Sacti, and Ananta Sacti. Observing them averse to study, the king called his counsellors, and said to them: 'You are aware that my sons are little inclined to application, and incapable of reflection. When I contemplate them, my kingdom is full of thorns, and yields me no pleasure. It is said by the wise: "Better is a son unborn; better is a dead son, than one who is a fool. The first may cause affliction for a little while, but a fool as long as life endures." Again: "Of what use is a cow who has no milk with her calf? Of what use is a son who has neither knowledge nor virtue? Better it is that a wife be barren, that she bear daughters or dead children, and that the family should become extinct, than that a son, endowed with your form, wealth, and family-credit should want understanding." If, therefore, by any means their minds can be roused, do you declare it.'

"On this a counsellor replied: 'Prince, the study of grammar alone is the work of twelve years, how then is a knowledge of *Dharma, Art'ha, Kāma*, and *Mōksha*[1] to be speedily conveyed?' Another counsellor, named Sumati, observed: 'Prince, the powers of man are limited by his transitory existence; but to acquire a knowledge of language alone demands much time. It is better that we think of some means of communicating the substance of each science in a compendious form; as it is said: "The *Sabda Sāstri* (Philology) is a boundless ocean: life is short, and the difficulties are many; the essence, therefore, is to be taken, as the swan extracts the milk from the water."[2] There is a Brāhman, named Vishnū Sarmā, celebrated for his perfect acquisition of the sciences. To him entrust your sons, and he will render them well-informed.' On hearing this, the king sent for Vishnū Sarmā, and addressed him: 'Venerable Brāhman, confer a favour upon me, by instructing these princes in polite literature, and rendering them superior to the youths, their companions; in recompense of which I promise you lands of large extent.' Vishnū Sarmā replied: 'Hear,

---

[1] The four objects or occupations of human life: Duty, Wealth, Desire, and Final Liberation.

[2] This is a popular notion among the Hindūs: because the bird seems, as they imagine, to extract his food by suction, from solution in water, wherefore a bird of this genus is considered to be an emblem of discrimination, as being capable of separating milk from water.—*Note by H. T. Colebrooke.*

O king, my words. I am not a retailer of knowledge for lands and wealth; but if I do not instruct your sons in the *Nītī Sāstrā* (Polity), I will forego my own name. There is no need to say more. I do not utter this vaunt through any desire of wealth; for wealth is use-less to any one whose passions are mortified and subdued. I wish but to gratify you, and to do the will of Saraswatī. Let it be written, therefore, that if, *in six months from this day,* I do not make the princes more proficient than many people in various branches of knowledge, it shall not be allowed to me, a Brāh-man, to point out the way of God.' The king, highly gratified by this assurance, delivered his sons to him and retired; and Vishnū Sarmā, taking the princes with him, repaired to his own house, where, for their instruction, he composed these five chapters. Reading these, the princes were, in six months, highly accom-plished, and the Five Tantras became famous throughout the world. Whosoever reads this work acquires the whole *Nītī Sāstrā,* and will never be overthrown by Indra himself."

The resemblance between the leading idea of the tale of Sindibād and the biblical story of Joseph and the wife of Potiphar is very obvious. But the incident is found in an Egyptian romance—the oldest extant fairy tale—which dates from the 14th century B.C., "when Pharaoh Ramses Miamun, the founder of Pithom and Ramses, ruled at Thebes, and literature celebrated its highest triumphs at his brilliant court: nine pre-eminent *savans* were attached to the person of the king, the contemporary of Moses."[1] The following is an abstract of the first part of this ancient tale (it is among the papyri in the British Museum):

The story relates to two brothers, of the same mother and father; the name of the elder was Anapou (Anubis), that of the younger was Satou. Anapou, being the head of the house, married, and he treated his younger brother as his son. (Some obliterations here occur, but it appears that Satou was a skilful feeder of cattle, and that he led his brother's herds every day to the pasture, and brought them back at night to their stalls.) "When the season of tillage arrived, the elder brother said to him: 'Let us take the teams and go to plough, for the land appears [*i.e.*, the water of the inundation had subsided], and is fit for culture. When we have ploughed it, you shall fetch the seed.' So the young man proceeded to execute what his elder brother told him." The story goes on to the following effect: The ploughing being finished, the elder brother sends the younger home to fetch seed. On arriving at the house, the young man finds his brother's wife engaged in combing her hair. He asks her for corn, and she bids him go to the granary and help himself, while she completes her toilette. Satou fetches one of the largest baskets, in order to carry back as much corn as possible.

---

[1] Deutsch's *Literary Remains:* Egypt, Ancient and Modern.

On his return from the granary, laden with barley and wheat, the lady compliments him upon his strength, and addresses him in precisely the same fashion as the wife of Potiphar addressed the Hebrew Joseph. Satou indignantly rejects her advances, and departs with his load, promising, however, to observe the strictest silence as to what had occurred. The wife of Anapou determines to be revenged; and when the husband returns in the evening, he is astonished to find his wife stretched on the bed, apparently lifeless, stripped of her clothes, and with all the outward semblance of having been the victim of violent outrage. "Who has been speaking with thee?" he inquires. "No man hath spoken to me," is the reply, "but thy brother, when he came to fetch corn." And she then proceeds to tell the story, *mutatis mutandis*, and concludes with conjuring her husband to take summary vengeance upon the offender. "The elder brother became as furious as a panther; he sharpened his sword, and took it in his hand. Then he went and stood behind the door of the stall, ready to kill his younger brother on his arrival in the evening with his cattle. When the sun set, Satou came back, according to his daily wont. As he approached, the cow which walked first said to her keeper: 'Methinks thy elder brother is yonder, with his sword ready to kill thee when thou comest near him.' He heard the words of the first cow, and then came another and said the same. Then he looked under the door of the stall, and he saw the feet of his brother, who stood behind the door, sword in hand. He threw his load on the ground, and began to run as fast as he could, and his brother pursued him, sword in hand." Satou invokes the aid of the sun-god Ra, who causes a wide river full of crocodiles to flow between the two brothers. The younger calls to the elder to wait until next day, when he will give a full explanation. Accordingly, when the sun rises, he relates the true state of the affair, reproaches his brother with his credulity, and, calling the sun to witness his innocence, he inflicts a grievous mutilation upon himself, and falls fainting on the bank of the river. The elder brother is much afflicted, but is unable to go to his assistance on account of the crocodiles. Satou at length recovers, and announces his intention of quitting his brother's company and of retiring to the valley of the acacia, a remote place, apparently beyond the limits of Egypt.[1]

---

[1] *Cambridge Essays*, 1858 : "Hieratic Papyri," by C. W. Goodman, M.A., pp. 233-235.—Deutsch remarks: "This hieroglyphic document is the only one hitherto known which belongs to the world of fiction. . . Apart from the general literary interest attaching to this relic of more than 3000 years ago—which gains a peculiar significance from the fact that it was first written and read at the very court of Ramses II, at which Moses was educated—it incidentally reveals so much of the manners and customs, the notions and views of that peculiar era of ancient Egypt, that we cannot be too grateful for its almost miraculous preservation." The style, he says, is "lucid and clear, and, though full of poetic fancy, yet simple and unaffected."

Such is the earliest example of the aphorism, "The woman whose love is scorned is worse than poison." Classical legend affords another instance in the tale of Phædra and Hippolytus, and it is probable that the same incident has often actually occurred in different countries and times.—M. Paulin Paris cites the following anecdote, as being historically true, and as having exercised a certain influence on the oldest French form of the romance *(Dolopathos)*, in which the name of the prince, like that of one of the victims in this tragedy, is Lucinian:

Fausta, the daughter of the tyrant Maximian, was the second wife of the great Constantine. For a long time she had the most decisive influence over that prince, and she had stopped at nothing to ensure the success and glory of his reign. She had actually sacrificed to the interests of the emperor the honour and the life of her father. Crispus, son of the first wife, having long appeared to inspire her with an almost maternal love, afterwards Fausta manifested entirely contrary feelings. Whether for the purpose of opening for her own children the path to the throne, or to take revenge of the slight shown to her by her step-son, she accused Crispus of meditating to kill his father, and of wishing to soil the nuptial couch. To give more colour to her imposture, she included in the same accusation the young Lucinian, the son of the hateful Lucinius, and then hardly fourteen years of age. Constantine, too easily persuaded of the crimes of which the two

princes were accused, condemned both to the last
punishment which they would have merited had they
been guilty. But the unhappy father was not long
before he repented himself of his credulity; he learned
at the same time of the misconduct and infidelity of
Fausta, and the execution of that princess was the just
expiation of the death of Crispus and Lucinian.[1]

And Keller has remarked that two pictures by
Dierick Stuerbout (*circa* 1462) exhibit a similar history; the Baron Von Keverberg describes them thus:
These pictures represent a tragic history, told in an
ancient chronicle of the town of Louvain, entitled
√ *Legende Dorée* (Golden Legend), as having happened
in the year 985. It informs us that the Emperor Otho
had caused an illustrious count to be beheaded. The
empress had conceived a violent love for him, and had
falsely accused him of the same crime, because he
would not respond to her adulterous passion. The
tragic end of the count is the subject of the first
picture. In the second his weeping widow is kneeling
before the emperor. Holding in one hand the bleed-
ing head of her husband, and in the other a red-hot
iron, she proves the innocence of the dead count.
Otho, enraged, condemned the empress to the flames,
wherein she paid the penalty of her crime.[2]

---

[1] Paulin Paris: *Étude sur les différents Textes, imprimés et
manuscrits, du Roman des Sept Sages.*

[2] *Dyocletianus Leben*, etc. Von Adelbert Keller. Quedlinburg
und Leipzig, 1841. Einleitung, p. 43.

In the Turkish romance of the *Forty Vazīrs*, it is related (by the 17th Vazīr) that a certain young man, at Mecca, during the season of pilgrimage, and when famine prevailed, went to purchase some wheat of a woman, who at first refused to sell him any, but after-wards promised him a load of wheat on condition that he would make merry with her. But the good youth repelled her advances, upon which she threatened to call her neighbours and complain against him. He then stole into an inner room, intending to mutilate himself (like the Egyptian Satou), when, lo! the wall miraculously opened, and he found outside ten camels laden with wheat—the gift of Allah, as a reward of his piety and virtue.

But the frame of the Book of Sindibād rests (as Professor Benfey has pointed out) on a story out of the life of Asoka, the great defender of Buddhism. After the death of his first wife, Asandhimitra, he made one of his female servants his queen. This second wife had fallen in love with, but had been rejected by, a son of the king by another wife, Pad-mavati, the name of the son being Dharmavivardhana, or (from his beautiful eyes) Kunāla. The son was sent by his father against Takshasila, which was in revolt. During the prince's absence, the king was seized with a dangerous malady, and determined to set Kunāla on the throne. The queen, foreseeing that this would be her ruin, promised to heal the king's disorder. This

she did; and being offered by the king any gift she
might ask, she desired the favour of exercising the
regal power for *seven days*, and employed this time in
sending to Takshasila and having the prince's eyes
put out. The blind son comes before his father as a
lute-player, and is recognised, and the Queen is burnt.[1]

The story has deeply penetrated Indian literature.
In a Telegū palm-leaf manuscript entitled *Sārangdhara Charita*, described by Dr. H. H. Wilson, the
hero, Sārangdhara, is the son of Rājamahendra, king
of Rājamahendri, whose step-mother Chitrāngī falls in
love with him. He rejects her advances, on which she
accuses him to the king of attempting to violate her,
and the king orders him to have his feet cut off, and
to be exposed in the forest to wild beasts. There a
voice from heaven proclaims that the prince in his
former life was Jayanta, minister of Dhaval Chandra,
who, being envious of Sumanta, one of his colleagues,
contrived to hide the slippers of Sumanta under the
bed of the queen. The king, finding them and ascertaining whose they were, commanded Sumanta to be
exposed to wild beasts after having his legs and hands
cut off; in retribution of which Jayanta, now Sārangdhara, suffers the like mutilation. He acknowledges
the justice of the sentence, and his wounds are healed
by a Yogī. A voice from heaven apprises the king of
the innocence of his son, and he takes Sārangdhara

---

[1] *Orient und Occident*, iii, p. 177.

back and puts Chitrāngī to death. Sārangdhara adopts
a religious life.—In the Tamil version, when the prince
has been mutilated and cast into the jungle, his dead
mother's lamentations are heard by the Siddhas, who
restore the prince's limbs, and a voice from heaven
apprises the king of Chitrāngī's guilt.—Again: In the
Kumara Rāma Charita, Ratnangī, one of the wives of
Rāja Kāmpila, became enamoured of Kumara Rāma,
his youngest son, and importuned him to gratify her
desires. Finding him inexorable, her love was changed
to hatred, and she complained to Kāmpila that Rāma
had attempted her chastity. Kāmpila in a rage ordered
Rāma to be put to death instantly, with his four chief
leaders. The minister Bachapa, however, secreted
Rāma and his friends in his palace, and decapitating
five ordinary criminals, produced their heads to the
rāja as those of his intended victims. Kāmpila soon
repented of his haste, and the prince's death was the
subject of universal sorrow. After some time Rāma
reappeared, and the Princess Ratnangī, on hearing of
this, hanged herself, by which Kāmpila was satisfied
of the innocence of his son.[1]

To the sporadic part of the family of the Sindibād
belong the Turkish romance of the *Forty Vazīrs*, the
Persian *Ten Vazīrs* (generally called the *Bakhtyār*

---

[1] *Descriptive Catalogue of the Mackenzie Collection of Oriental
MSS.*, etc. By H. H. Wilson. Calcutta, 1828.

Nāma), and the Hindū *Alakeswara Kathā.*—The
frame of the *Forty Vazīrs* corresponds pretty closely
with that of the Book of Sindibād, but the eighty
subordinate tales, related by the vazīrs and the lady
alternately, are, with but one or two exceptions, quite
different from those found in the several texts of the
Seven Vazīrs, or Wise Men. This romance is said to
have been composed, from an old Arabian work,
entitled, *The Forty Mornings and Forty Evenings,*
early in the 15th century.—The plan of the *Bakhtyār
Nāma* (or the Ten Vazīrs) is essentially different from
the frame of the Sindibād books, in which, as we have
seen, the prince must keep strict silence for seven
days, he is tempted by one of his father's women, who
falsely accuses him, and the vazīrs, or wise men, save
his life from day to day, by relating tales to the king,
until the period of danger to the prince is past. All
this is precisely reversed in the *Bakhtyār Nāma*, the
outline of which is as follows:

A king, flying with his wife from his kingdom, which
is in revolt, is obliged to abandon his newly-born son
near a well. The infant is found by a robber-chief,
who adopts and educates him as his own son. Meanwhile the king recovers his kingdom. It happens that
the robber-chief, at the head of his band, attacks a
large caravan, and is defeated, many of his followers
being killed or taken prisoners, and among the latter
is the robber-chief's adopted son. When the prisoners
are brought before the king, he is struck with the grace

and beauty of the youth—his own son, but, of course, unknown to him—pardons him and takes him into his service. One evening the young man, dazed with wine, wanders into the private apartments of the palace, seeking his way out, and, not knowing what he is doing, lays himself down on the royal couch, and falls asleep. In this condition he is discovered by the king, who, concluding that the queen must be privy to the youth's presence there, is naturally furious, sends for the queen, and accuses her of infidelity, which she denies; and the king causes her and the young man to be confined separately, until he has considered what had best be done. In the morning the prime vazīr, who is envious of the youth's favour with the king, having learned the particulars of the affair of the pre-ceding night, obtains leave to visit the queen, and assures her that his Majesty would not be convinced that she was innocent, and counsels her, if she would save her own life, to accuse the youth (who is only the son of a robber, he reminds her) of having stolen unawares into the harem, and professed love to her. After much persuasion, she at length consents to the vazīr's proposal, and having accused the young man, the king gives orders for him to be brought before him and put to death. But the youth speaks eloquently in his own behalf, and incites the king's curiosity to hear a certain tale in illustration of the evils of pre-cipitation, which, leave being granted, he relates, and is then sent back to prison. Next morning the second

c

vazīr presents himself before the king, and urges him
to put the youth to death. The young man is again
brought forth to be executed, when he obtains leave
to relate another story, showing the deplorable consequences of rashness, after which he is once more
remanded to prison. In this manner, each of the Ten
Vazīrs in turn seeks the youth's destruction, and he
pleads his own cause by means of eloquent speeches
and impressive tales, until the eleventh day, when he
is led out to execution, and his foster-father the robber-
chief, recognises him, hastens to the king, and implores
the life of the youth whom he had found in the wilderness so many years ago; and showing the jewels which
were upon the infant, the king sees with horror that he
was about to murder his own son, and puts the envious
vazīrs to an ignominious death.

✓   It will thus be seen that the frame of the *Bakhtyār
Nāma* is very remotely related to the Sindibād books:
in place of a dumb prince and his seven defenders, we
have an eloquent youth defending himself against his
ten false accusers. I have been at the trouble of
sketching the frame of this romance, because it is
commonly included in the Sindibād cycle, by writers,
too, who ought to know better.[1]

---

[1] Thus Gödeke says (*Orient und Occident*, iii, p. 388): "This form
which gives the power of speech only to the Masters, besides
being found in Nakhshabī [of which I shall have somewhat to
say presently], has been adopted only by the *Ten Vazīrs*, and by
Herbers"—a most preposterous statement, since the Ten Vazīrs

The third romance of the sporadic group, the *Ala-keswara Kathā*, closely resembles the tale of Bakhytār and the Ten Vazīrs: this is a story, written in the Tamil language, of the rāja of Alakapur, and his four ministers, who, "being falsely accused of violating the sanctity of the inner apartments, vindicate their inno-cence and disarm the king's wrath by relating a number of stories," one of which is the familiar tale of the Lost Camel, found also in the Talmud.[1]

MUCH obscurity surrounds the early history of the Book of Sindibād, notwithstanding the important dis-coveries of European scholars during the last thirty years. The work of Des Longchamps is often mis-leading, and his theories regarding the introduction of the romance into Europe and the pedigree of the Eastern texts are now, for the most part, set aside— being superseded by the laborious investigations of such learned and acute men as Baethgen, Benfey, Brockhaus, Comparetti, Gödeke, Keller, Montaiglon, Mussafia, Nöldeke, Paulin Paris, etc.; but when and where the original work was composed, and how it

---

are the accusers, not the defenders, of the young man, and do not relate any tales.

[1] *Descriptive Catalogue of the Mackenzie Collection of MSS.*, etc. By H. H. Wilson. Vol. i, p. 220.

was first spread abroad, are questions which have not yet been satisfactorily answered. True, Ma'sūdī, who has been styled the Herodotus of the Arabs, in his great historical work, *Meadows of Gold and Mines of Gems,* written about A.D. 943-4, speaking of the Indian kings, says: " In the reign of Kūrūsh lived As-Sindibād, who is the author of the Story of the Seven Vazīrs, the Preceptor, the Boy, and the Wife of the King. This is the work," he adds, "which is called the Book of Sindibād." And nearly to the same purpose is the evidence lately found, some sixty years earlier than Ma'sūdī, viz., Al-Ya'qūbī, who wrote about A.D. 880, and who says, also referring to the ancient Indian kings: "To them belongs Kush,[1] who was in the time of Sindibād the Wise; and this Kush composed the Book of the Craft of Women." But from these writers we only learn that, according to tradition, the romance was originally written in India. That either the sage Sindibād or the mythical king Kūrūsh, or Kūsh, was the author is, of course, absurd: there is no more reason to suppose that Sindibād was the author of the work which bears his name than that Vishnū Sarmā composed the *Pancha Tantra,* or Bidpai the *Kalila wa Dimna.* Farther, we see that the romance was well known—and almost certainly in an Arabic form—about A.D. 880. But, according to the *Fihrist,* Abān Lāhiqī, who died A.D. 815-16, composed the tale in rhymed

---

[1] In an astronomical work much used by Ya'qūbī the name is written Karūsh.

couplets, which throws its date back to the early years
of the 9th century, and the prose version from which
it was derived may have been fifty years older—dating
about the middle of the 8th century.

The oldest extant text derived directly from an
Eastern source was until lately assumed to be the
Greek version, entitled *Syntipas*[1] (evidently a corruption of Sindibād), composed, by one Andreopulos, from
the Syriac, as we are informed in his prologue:

" This book which thou seest, (my) friend, is (the
work) of the fabulist Syntipas, according to the Syrians,
nay, rather (according to) the wise prose-writers of
the Persians: which being drawn up in the Syrian
language, I, Andreopulos, worshipper of Christ, the
last [or humblest] of authors, have indited this book,
and translated it into the Greek phraseology of the
present time.   Having been appointed, this work (is)
at the command of Gabriel, the renown of grandees,
the august Duke of the city of Melitene—(he) who is
truly a devout dweller in the house of Christ—who
also decided these (fables) should be set forth, because
they do not exist in the books of the modern Greeks.
For this collection especially denounces evil-doers, and
at the close eulogises deeds admirably achieved."

To Professor Comparetti belongs the honour of
having identified the august Duke Gabriel, at whose

---

[1] This Greek text was published, from two manuscripts in the
King's Library, at Paris, by Boissonade, in 1825 ; and a critical
edition, by Eberhard, was printed at Leipzig, in 1872,

command the work was translated, with the prince of
the same name who ruled in Melitene between 1086
and 1100; the date of the Greek version may thus be
referred to the last decade of the 11th century.[1] In
the preface the book is stated to be translated into
Syriac from the work of "Mousos the Persian." A
unique but, unfortunately, imperfect MS. of the Syriac
text was discovered by Rödiger, and printed, with a
German translation, by Baethgen, in 1879.[2] "There
can be no doubt," says Nöldeke, in a most interesting
and important review in the Journal of the German
Oriental Society, vol. xxxiii, "that this is the Syriac
book translated into Greek by Andreopulos. Both
agree in the general course of the narrative, and also
in the brevity of the introduction. Even in details,
the *Syntipas* shows itself to be, not indeed a literal
translation, but yet a translation tolerably correct as
to the sense. Hence we must conclude that the parts
wanting in the Syriac text stood as they are found in
Syntipas. But the style of the two is very different.
The Syriac narrates plainly and naturally; *Syntipas* is
prolix, ornate, and turgid. . . The greater prolixity
arises simply from the manner of the translator: even

---

[1] *Researches respecting the Book of Sindibād*, by Domenico Com-
paretti, pp. 55-58.—This valuable work was translated by
Mr. Henry Charles Coote, and published for the Folk-Lore
Society, 1882.

[2] *Sindban, oder die Sieben Weisen Meister, Syrisch und Deutsch*,
von Fried. Baethgen. Leipzig, 1879.

his additions are as strong a contrast to the mode of the original as the rest."—The work of Musa the Persian (presumably written in the Arabic, from the Pahlavī) is now apparently lost, but it must have been extant in the middle of the 13th century, since a Castilian rendering, from the Arabic, made in 1253,[1] corresponds in most respects with the Syriac and its Greek derivative. About the same time a Hebrew version[2] was composed, probably also from the Arabic, in which many liberties are taken with the original— stories omitted, others inserted, names given to the seven counsellors, etc.

To recapitulate: the Book of Sindibād was brought from India, its native country, to Persia, where it was translated into Pahlavī (as were the Fables of Bidpai in the 6th century); from Pahlavī, Musa rendered it into Arabic, about the middle of the 8th century; from Arabic it was translated into Syriac, into old Spanish,

---

[1] *Libro de los Engannos et los Asayamientos de las Mugeres:* Book of the Deceits and Tricks of Women.—This text, with a translation into English by Mr. H. C. Coote, is appended to Professor Comparetti's *Researches.*

[2] *Mishlé Sandabar:* Parables of Sandabar. A French translation of this version, by Carmoly, was published at Paris, 1849. In the preface to the edition of Rolland's *Sevin Seages* printed for the Bannatyne Club it is stated that the Hebrew text was "first printed, at Constantinople, in 1516, and afterwards, at Vienna, in 1544, 1568, and 1605." According to Dempster (*Hist. Eccles.*, p. 364), James Bonaventure Hepburn translated the work from Hebrew into Latin.

and into Hebrew; from Syriac into Greek.   Thus far,
satisfactory; but not so, when we inquire into the
source of Persian texts.

According to Daulat Shāh, the tale of Sindibād was
composed in Persian verse by Azraqī, who died at
Herāt, A.D. 1132 (A.H. 537).   This work seems no
longer extant; but it is cited in the Jehangīrī Dictionary (A.D. 1576): "Whoever sees, O king, the
counsels of Sindibād well knows that therein the poet's
art is difficult."   And Saʻdī probably quotes from it in
his *Bustān:* "How charmingly has this subtle remark
been expressed in (the book of) Sindibād, saying:
'Love is a fire, O my son; advice, a wind.' With wind
does fierce fire become more aspiring, (as) by beating
does a leopard become more enraged."

Another Persian poetical version, entitled *Sindibād
Nāma*, was written, by an unknown author, in A.D. 1375,
an epitome of which is contained in the present volume.
The author informs us that his royal patron one day
taxed him with being lazy: "Perform," said the king,
"such an achievement with the sword of the pen as
shall live as long as swords are wielded.   Turn into
verse, during my reign, some prose work, that my
memory may be perpetuated: let it be the Tale of
Sindibād."   To this the poet replied: "If God grant
me his aid, and if my life be spared, I will turn into
verse that celebrated book."   Having stated the year
when his poem was composed (A.H. 776), proceeding
to the tale, he begins: "An Arabian by descent, but

speaking the Persian tongue, has thus informed me, in eloquent language, that there lived in India a sage and mighty monarch," and so on (see pp. 5-7). It thus appears that the Tale of Sindibād was known to our poet and his royal patron only in a prose form, the author of which was an Arab by descent, which Falconer thought might afford ground for conjecture that the Arab had found the tale in the language of his family and translated it from Arabic into Persian : the usual process by which works in Pahlavī were returned in later ages to the Persians was through the Arabic.

But there was a modern Persian prose version in this country some forty years since, purporting to be derived from the Pahlavī through the Darī, which has long escaped notice in the investigation of the gene-alogy of the Book of Sindibād. It is thus referred to by Mr. W. H. Morley, in a letter to Mr. E. W. Lane, dated August, 1841, which is printed in Lane's trans-lation of the *Thousand and One Nights*, vol. iii, p. 681 :

"Some time since the Oriental Translation Com-mittee were kind enough to lend me a manuscript from their library, comprising four volumes and con-taining a collection of tales in the Persian language. Many of these I translated with a view to publication, but one story (occurring in the 4th volume) which is similar in construction to the *Bakhtyār Nāma*,[1] and

---

[1] This is not correct—see outline of that romance, pp. xxxii-xxxiv, above.

is preceded by a very curious preface, I reserved for more particular consideration at a future period. On reading the twenty-third number of your excellent translation of the *Alf Laila wa Laila* I was struck by finding in the Abstract of the Story of the King, and his Son, the Damsel, and the Seven Vazīrs the name of the sage As-Sindibād, and the circumstances related in the introduction coincided with those in the Persian story above alluded to. I suspected that they must be identical, and was fully satisfied that they were so, when on referring to the MS. I found that the same tales occurred in both. The great importance of the Persian version consists in its preface, which is omitted both in your edition and the MS. of the British Museum, and which is exceedingly valuable as an evidence of the Persian origin of the story. The preface states that the book is named the *Kitāb-i Sindi-bād*, and that it was collected from the sages of 'Ajam. It then says: 'This book was originally in the Pahlavī tongue, and till the time of the Amīr Nāsiru-'d-Dawla Abū Muhammad Nūh bin Mansūr Sāmānī, it had not been translated by any person, the Amīr commanded that the Kh'āja Amīd Abū-'l-Fawaris Fatādzarī should translate it and set right the discrepancies and errors he might find therein. In the year 338 [A.D. 949] the aforesaid Kh'āja undertook the task, and con-verted it into the Darī language.' The author of the preface, Muhammad bin 'Alī bin Muhammad bin Husayn Az-Zahīr Al-Kātib As-Samarqandī, then mentions that he has rendered the Darī translation into modern Persian, and dedicates his work to Abū-'l Muzaffar Qilij 'l'amghāh Khāqān."[1]

The Arabic version referred to by Morley as agreeing with his text is that of the *Seven Vazīrs* in the *Thousand and One Nights*—based, of course, upon the old Arabic text derived from the Pahlavī, but composed at a much more recent period than any of the other Eastern versions. The introduction is abridged and garbled; a number of the original tales have been suppressed and others substituted. Morley's statement that the same stories occur in both his text and that of Lane must be understood in a restricted sense, otherwise his text was considerably later than the 12th century. He probably meant that certain stories in Lane's version also occurred in his text.—The approximate date of the modern Persian version of As-Samarqandī is, according to Morley, A.H. 590 (A.D. 1193), when a prince of a somewhat similar name to that of the author's patron, Tamghāh Khāqān, flourished. Azraqī's poem was com-

---

[1] This manuscript seems to have disappeared from the Library of the Royal Asiatic Society, London, many years ago. It is thus described by Morley: "The story in the Persian MS. comprises 117 *folia*, and is written in three different hands: the first part is in very illegible Shikastah, and has been apparently added since the exaration of the other two, which are in the Nastalīk character: the latter portion has been taken from a smaller volume, and inlaid to make it conform in size with the rest, and the other volumes of the collection."

posed about 70 years before that date, and if the foregoing account be accurate, it was doubtless derived from the Darī text. But even had we not good reason to believe that the work existed in Arabic long before the date of the Darī translation, it were almost incredible that it should remain in the Pahlavī till A.D. 949. Possibly, something has been omitted in the preface quoted by Morley—mention of the intermediate Arabic text may have been deliberately suppressed by some copyist, if not indeed by As-Samarqandī himself. Let us rather conclude that from the Arabic the work was translated into the Darī in the 10th century, and suppose that As-Samarqandī was the very "Arabian by descent, but speaking the Persian tongue," whose version furnished the groundwork of the *Sindibād Nāma*. According to this view, the genealogy of the romance would be as follows:

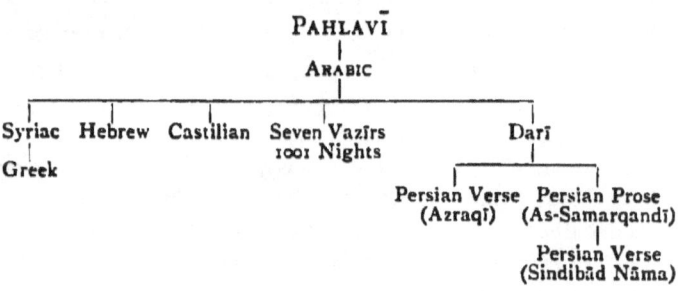

The tale of the Seven Vazīrs occurs in three printed texts of the *Thousand and One Nights:* the text edited by Macnaughtan, at Calcutta; that edited by Habicht

and Fleischer, at Breslau; and the edition printed at
Būlāq (sometimes called the Cairo text), which corresponds pretty nearly with the Calcutta text, and which
was the basis of Lane's translation. It is also found in
the Rich MSS. Nos. 7404, 7405, 7406, an imperfect
copy of the *Nights* brought from Bagdād, of which an
analysis was published in the *Asiatic Journal*, 1839—
the *Seven Vazīrs* is in the third volume of this MS;
and in the fragment of a MS. of the *Nights* procured
in Bengal, now, I believe, in the Bodleian Library at
Oxford.[1] Although these versions are much corrupted
from the original, such as we now possess it in the
oldest Eastern texts, yet, says Professor Nöldeke, "a
few of the stories are fairly preserved in almost the
sequence of words; and it may be asked whether a
careful examination of all the texts of this part of
the *Thousand and One Nights* might not give a considerably better text. At all events, I am disposed to
lay upon this form of the book—which is still *Arabic*
—a somewhat greater value than has hitherto been
done."

Yet another version of the *Seven Vazīrs* is found in
the Persian collection of Nakhshabī, entitled *Tūtī
Nāma*, Parrot-Book, composed early in the 14th century, from an older Persian book of similar character,
based upon a Sanskrit work, of which the *Suka Saptatī*,
Seventy Tales of a Parrot, is a modern redaction. In

---

[1] Jonathan Scott's translation of the *Seven Vazīrs* as found in
this MS. is reprinted in the present volume.

this version,[1] the damsel does not relate any stories, six of the vazīrs have one story each, the seventh has none, but directs, on the 7th day, that the prince be questioned, after which the damsel is condemned to death, and the king abdicates the throne in favour of his son.—Professor Nöldeke thinks that the prose Persian text used by the author of the *Sindibād Nāma* was the same as that from which Nakhshabī derived the tales of his 8th Night, and that it was probably the Sindibād of Muhammad bin 'Alī Daqā'iqī of Hājī Khalīfa, No. 7259. This author is perhaps the same with As-Samarqandi, also a Muhammad bin 'Alī. At all events, Nöldeke's theory of one text having been used for both versions is certainly strengthened by the circumstance, hitherto unnoticed, that the Story of the Father-in-Law is found in both, and in no other known texts of the Sindibād; and, farther, by the fact that the Story of the Libertine Husband, which in the Greek and other texts is fused with the Story of the Go-Between and the She-Dog, appears in both as a separate tale, which it assuredly was originally, and so occurs in the *Suka Saptati*.

Professor Comparetti has attempted, with great ingenuity, to explain the fusion of the stories of the She-Dog and the Libertine Husband. An Arabian writer of the 10th century, Muhammad bin Al-Warraq,

---

[1] The Eighth Night: Story of the Prince and the Seven Vazīrs, and the misfortune which happened to the Prince on account of a Girl.

mentions *two* texts of the Book of Sindibād, a Greater
and a Lesser. According to Comparetti, originally
the vazīrs had but one story each, and a *second* set was
added at a later period, thus constituting the Greater
Sindibād, which he considers is for us represented by
the *Syntipas*, where the *second* tales thus appear:

First Vazīr,	The Parrot
Second Vazīr,	Double Infidelity
Third Vazīr,	Rice Dealer
Fourth Vazīr,	She-Dog
Fifth Vazīr,	Burnt Cloth
Sixth Vazīr,	Bread Elephant
Seventh Vazīr,	Woman's Wiles

Six of this new series were taken from the *Suka Saptati*
(the tale of the Parrot being adapted from the frame),
the fourth forming, as in that collection, two tales,
originally thus:

Fourth Vazīr,	She-Dog
Fifth Vazīr,	Libertine Husband

"There was some one, however, who wished to introduce the tale of the Burnt Cloth, and in order to do
this he united the story of the fifth vazīr with that of
the fourth, and put the new tale in the vacant place."
But in the Persian *Sindibād Nāma* we find not only
the Story of the Burnt Cloth (though in a very different
form), but also the two others still separate; from which
it would appear that this text represents a more ancient
version than that from which the others were derived.
But Comparetti would perhaps be disposed to consider

this deduction as being more specious than sound.
His theory, however, is not favoured by Professor
Nöldeke, who has pointed out that in two MSS. of the
Fihrist is a passage stating that the Larger Sindibād was
translated by Asbagh bin 'Abdu-'l-'Azīz bin Sālim
Sijjistānī, and bore the name of *Aslam and Sindbād*,
and "since in all our existing texts there is not a word
about Aslam·or a similarly written name, we may
pretty confidently conclude that they represent the
lesser book."—The name of Aslam might have been
that of the prince; and the larger work probably disappeared soon after the smaller form of it became
popular—just as Kāderī's abridgment of the *Tūtī
Nāma* seems to have almost wholly superseded the
original work of Nakhshabī. The facility with which
manuscript copies of the smaller work could be multiplied would alone account for the disappearance of
the other.

All the six vazīrs' tales in Nakhshabī occur also in
the *Suka Saptatī*, and five are *second* tales in the Greek,
Syriac, and old Castilian texts—that of the second
vazīr, the Libertine Husband, is in these the concluding
portion of the story of the She-Dog.—Professor Brockhaus regarded Nakhshabī's version of the *Seven Vazīrs*
as the most ancient, from its greater simplicity, only
the vazīrs relating tales on the subject of the deceit of
women. "In this," he remarks, "the oldest of the
French versions, *Dolopathos*, strangely enough, agrees
with this Persian redaction, no doubt by chance." In

the case of *Dolopathos*, the simple form clearly indicates the manner in which the tale came into France,
viz., by oral tradition.   The monkish author of the
original Latin text would probably exercise his own
judgment both in amplifying and embellishing the
frame, and in his choice of the subordinate stories.
Of the eight tales (seven told by the wise men and
one by the tutor), three only, the first two and the
last, are, so far as I am aware, found in later texts,
in which, however, the woman is given stories, and, in
place of the tutor, the prince relates the final tale.[1]

By reference to the Comparative Table of Eastern
Texts, it will be seen that the Persian *Sindibâd Nâma*
has, exclusively, four tales in the introduction.   Of
these, Gödeke has pointed out that the second, third,
and fourth occur, almost exactly in the same forms, in
the *Avadânas*, or Indian apologues, translated by Stan.
Julien from the Chinese, and that "they thus reach
back to a time when the Buddhist teaching had
extended to China, which, according to Chinese state
annals, happened as far back as the first century of the
Christian era."[2]   In a note on this, Comparetti, in p. 30
of his *Researches*, remarks that the fact of these tales
being of Buddhist origin proves nothing—they may
well have been introduced at a recent period.   But
surely not in forms so near the originals?   In the con-

---

[1] See Appendix, Nos. 32 and 33.

[2] *Orient und Occident*, iii, 393.

clusion of this text it has two additional tales, one of which, the Four Liberators, is unquestionably very ancient. It is admitted on all hands that in the Syriac and Greek texts the introduction is considerably abridged. In the Persian, both introduction and conclusion are much more detailed—in short, there is nothing in the plan of the poem to indicate suppression or curtailment, considering the deficiencies in the MS., which are, unfortunately, both numerous and serious.[1] But it will perhaps be contended that in this the poet has used the freedom of enlarging upon his original, and also of suppressing portions and substituting others, or that the author of his original had done

---

[1] Folio 41 is wanting; after fol. 44, a *lacuna;* fol. 57 is wanting; fol. 62, a *lacuna;* fol. 86, a *lacuna,* and the next 40 leaves are displaced: 87-126 should be placed after 155, where another deficiency occurs; fol. 126, a *lacuna:* 127-154 should follow 86, where there is also a deficiency.—Gödeke (in *Orient und Occident,* iii, 394) conjectured that the five tales of the Greek text which are not found in the Persian had been torn out of the MS., "probably owing to something in their contents that was offensive." The tales were certainly not torn out for any such reason, since three of them—the Drop of Honey, the Fox, and Destiny—have nothing whatever offensive in them; of the others, one is nauseous (the Loaves), and one is silly enough (the Bread Elephant). Besides, as we now see, there was no room for three of these, each of the vazīrs having his two tales; the stories of The Fox and Destiny were probably in the MS. originally. No doubt, many of the *lacunæ* are to be explained by the nature of some of the pictures that remain in the MS., of which there are about ninety.

so. Let us see what reasons there are to assume the
Greek text to be the best representative of the Book
of Sindibād as it was translated into Arabic from the
Pahlavī—when, we do not know; but say, the middle
of the 8th century.[1] The only certain date we possess
is that of the Greek text, namely, the latter years of
the 11th century. The Syriac version may have been
composed from the Arabic one hundred years before
the Greek, or about A.D. 990. Now, regarding the
Persian *Sindibād Nāma:* this was written so late
as 1375, from a prose version, "translated from the
Arabic," as is generally assumed, from the author's
statement that "an Arabian *by descent*, but speaking the
Persian tongue," had furnished him with the material
of his poem. But unless we are to consider the preface of As-Samarqandī to his text in the MS. described
by Morley (see above, p. xli) as a tissue of fabrica-
tions, from first to last, it will at least be conceded
that he translated it out of the Darī into modern
Persian, and, if so, the Arabic was certainly the source
of that Darī version; and between A.D. 949, the date of
the Darī, and A.D. 990, the possible date of the Syriac
(and it might have been even later), the Arabic text
may have undergone alterations such as we find in the
Syriac, Greek, and old Castilian versions. The *Sindi-*

---

[1] We are informed of a poetical version having been made by
a man who died A.D. 815, but since we do not know its contents
the fact goes for nothing in dealing with texts which are before
us. It presupposes, however, an earlier prose text.

bād Nāma—poem though it is—may therefore more
faithfully reflect the Book of Sindibād than the older
texts.   All this, of course, is little better than conjecture; a comparison of the Persian prose text described
by Morley with the poem which may have been based
upon it (the *Sindibād Nāma*) would probably satisfactorily settle the whole question, and it is to be hoped
that the missing MS. will yet be discovered.

The name of Sindbād[1] is familiar to every school-
boy in Europe through the fascinating Arabian tale
of the Voyages of the venturous merchant, Sindbād the
Sailor, as he is commonly but erroneously styled.   "It
is singular," says Hole, in his Remarks on that tale,
"that the names of both the narrator and auditor,
Sindbād and Hindbād, are derived, not from the
Arabic, but the old Persian language.   *Bād* [*ābād*]
signifies a city; *Sind* and *Hind* are the territories on
either side of the Indus.   *Sind* indeed is the original
name, as Hind is of those countries which lie between
it and the Ganges."   But this etymology of the name
is rejected by Benfey, who derives it from *Siddhapatī*,
lord of sages, or sorcerers: Siddhi being a Sanskrit
word, signifying "perfection of power," and those

---

[1] Both Lane and Falconer write the name Sindibād, a form
which is retained in the present work, but which is a comparatively recent corruption.   In the *Sheref Nāma*, the oldest
dictionary of Persian extant (though older vocabularies and
glossaries are known), the name is written *Sindbād*.

beings called Siddhas, who are supernaturally endowed, figure frequently in Indian fictions. Applied to a mere mortal, Siddhapati would indicate that such a man was wise beyond all others. The termination *bād* could in no case be identified with *ābād*, a place or an abode.

To what cause, it may be asked, does the Book of Sindibād, as represented more or less closely in Asiatic and European versions, owe its unfailing popularity during so many ages of the world's history? The leading incident, of a youth being in imminent danger of death in consequence of the malice of his step-mother, has, no doubt, ever had a peculiar fascination for readers of all ranks and ages; but it is chiefly, as I think, due to the circumstance that most of the subordinate tales turn upon the wickedness, profligacy, and craft of women. This is not only a characteristic of Muslim tales, inspired probably by the low estimate which the Prophet of Mecca is credited by tradition with having entertained of the female sex, but it also pervades much more ancient Indian fictions. These attributes, as Dr. H. H. Wilson has observed, probably "originate in the feelings which have always pervaded the East unfavourable to the dignity of women. But we are not to mistake the language of satire, or the licentiousness of wit, for truth, or to suppose that

the pictures which are thus given of the depravity
of women owe not much of their colouring to the
malignity of men. The avidity with which this style
of portraiture was adopted and improved upon in
Europe shows that either the women of Christian
Europe were still more vicious than those of India,
or the men were still less disposed to treat them
with deference and esteem. It is in this respect that
stories of domestic manners contrast so remarkably
with the inventions of chivalric romance; and the
homage paid in the latter to the virtues and graces of
the female sex is a feature derived, in all probability,
from that portion of their parentage which comes from
the North, woman being ever held in higher honour
amongst the Teutonic nations than amongst those of
the South of Europe or of the East, and contributing, by
the elevating influence she was permitted to enjoy, to
their moral exaltation and martial superiority."

Our old English jest-books abound in tales of the
levity and perverseness of women, which are paral-
leled in the popular literature of all other European
countries. The well-worn story of the man whose
perverse wife was drowned, and he sought her against
the stream, alleging to his neighbours that she would
be sure to float up the river instead of being carried
with the current, is also domiciled in Germany, Scan-
dinavia, and Russia.—An Eastern anecdote to the same
purpose seems a commentary on a saying ascribed to
Muhammad that a man should always do the opposite

of what his wife advises: A young man once went on
the roof of his house to repair it, and having finished the
task, called to his wife, and asked her how he should
come down. She answered: "You are a young and
active man; what hinders you from jumping down?"
He jumped accordingly, and dislocated his ankle,
which confined him to the house for many months;
and even when able to go about a little, his ankle was
still out of its place. He again had occasion to repair
his roof, and when he had done, he asked his wife how
he should come down this time. "O, by the stairs, to be
sure," quoth she. But when he reflected how he had
come to grief by following his wife's advice formerly,
he resolved to jump down, which he did, and, behold,
his ankle returned to its proper place.

It would appear that collections of "proverbs"
against women were common in England in the days
of Chaucer, if we may credit the Wife of Bath, whose
fifth husband, Jankins, clerk of Oxenforde, we are told,
had a book comprising tales of the wickedness of wives,
which he frequently pored over with pleasure. One
evening he was reading aloud portions of his book,
which so incensed his spouse that she tore three leaves
out of it, and then knocked him backwards into the fire.
Her husband, who was but half her age, bounded up
and felled her to the floor. Lying moaning, as if at
the point of death, she begged him to stoop down,
that she might kiss him in token of her forgiveness.
The husband bent down, when, instead of kissing, she

bit him on the cheek. The end of the brawl was that
he became very penitent and burnt his book.

The sages of ancient Greece were no whit behind
the fablers of India in their bitter sayings about
women. Thus Antiphanes: "In a woman one thing
only I believe, that when she is dead she will not
come to life again; in all else I distrust her until she
is dead;" and Menander: "Of all wild beasts on earth
or in sea, the greatest is woman;" again: "Where are
women there are all kinds of mischief;" and Diogenes,
seeing some women who had been hanged from the
boughs of an olive-tree, said: "I wish all trees bore
that kind of fruit."

Whether Somadeva is to be credited with all the
spiteful remarks upon women in the *Kathā Sarit
Sāgara*, or he has merely versified what he found
ready to hand in the *Vrihat Kathā*, some are conceived in the most malignant spirit; for example:
"Women, like prosperous circumstances, are never
faithful to any one in this world;" again: "A fickle
dame is like a sunset, momentarily aglow for every
one;" and again: "Do not put yourself in the power
of a woman: the heart of a female is a tangled maze."
But he is not always unjust: "Here and there you will
find a virtuous woman, who adorns a glorious family
as the streaks of the moon adorn a broad sky."

THE BOOK OF SINDIBĀD.

EDITOR'S PREFACE.

THE following analytical account of a unique Persian MS.
poem, entitled *Sindibād Nāma*, or the Book of Sindibād,
belonging to the Library of the India Office, was published
by Professor Forbes Falconer in the *Asiatic Journal*, vols.
xxxv and xxxvi, 1841. By the courtesy of Dr Rost, I have
been favoured with a loan of this manuscript, which is beauti-
fully written in the *ta'līq* character, and adorned with numerous
paintings. Unfortunately, several *lacunæ* occur throughout the
volume, and thirty leaves are misplaced. It now comprises
about 170 *folia*, and 5000 couplets. The original numbering
of the leaves seems to have been cut away when it received
its present Oriental binding, as many of the full-page pictures
are imperfect at the top, and the re-numbering is in a different
hand from that of the text, and made consecutive, notwithstanding the displaced and missing leaves. Owing probably to
the defective condition of the MS., Falconer has altogether
overlooked one story (the title of which is written in faint blue
ink at the foot of a page) and the remains of two others; from
which it is evident that in this text, as in all others of the
Eastern group of the *Sindibād*, each of the Seven Vazīrs had
originally two stories. He states that in his analysis he has
" sometimes, for the purpose of giving the reader a better idea
of the work and of the author's style, freely used his own diffuse

and Orientally fanciful expressions and imagery; and sometimes compressed his narrative and trimmed his exuberance (for compression and curtailment were necessary in analysing a work of such extent); and sometimes, especially when the tale was already familiar to readers in other works, or objectionable in its nature, satisfied himself with giving the title, or a reference to the corresponding portion of the Greek version. Those who know the difficulties of Persian poetry," he justly adds, "and the disadvantage of possessing but a single manuscript, will not only excuse, but will even lay their account with meeting, occasional misapprehensions of the sense."

An account of the several Eastern texts of the Book of Sindibād being given in the introductory pages of the present volume, Falconer's preliminary observations on the same subject need not be here reproduced; indeed, they are rather out of date, so many important discoveries regarding this work having been made of recent years. His plan of leaving some of the tales untranslated must be unsatisfactory to students of the genealogy of popular fictions, since it is only by comparing different versions of these stories that their original forms can be ascertained. Stories which are not objectionable are therefore now presented as fully as the state of the manuscript permits, and the additions and corrections printed within square brackets; while such of Falconer's notes as have been retained are distinguished by the letter F from those for which I must be held responsible.

W. A. C.

THE BOOK OF SINDIBĀD.

Introduction.

AFTER the customary opening with an invocation and
address to the Deity, a chapter in praise of the
Prophet, a complaint against fortune, and an exhortation to contentment and abandonment of the world,
the author proceeds, in the fifth chapter, to inform the
reader that he had himself no thought of composing a
poem, no desire to plunge into such a sea of difficulty;
that he was too sensible of his own want of genius to
think of such an undertaking; but that one night his
Majesty—that King whose fortune is awake, and
whose equal the eye of Time beholds not even in
its dreams—addressed him, and, while he complimented him on his talents, complained that he did
not sufficiently exert them. "He observed," says the
poet, "that the nightingale should not sit for ever
songless, nor the parrot mute; that I possessed the
gift of eloquence and sweet discourse; but that I was
lazy, lazy, lazy! 'Perform,' said he, 'such an achievement, with the sword of the pen, as shall live as long
as swords are wielded. Turn into verse, during my

reign, some prose work, that my memory may be
perpetuated: let it be the Tale of Sindibād.' With
downcast looks, I replied: 'If God grant me his aid,
and if my life be spared, I will turn into verse that
celebrated book.'

"I gave ear (for to neglect a commandment is a fault,
especially a supreme command of a king), and when
seventy-six [years] were added to 700,[1] in the reign
of the sultan resembling Jamshīd;[2] the king of the
world; the refuge of the khalifate; the possessor of
the throne, the signet, and the diadem; who plucks
up by the roots violence and oppression; the asylum
of Arabia; the crown-bestower of Persia; the munificent, bold, and dauntless king, before whose prowess

----

[1] A.H. 776, or A.D. 1374-5. The author was therefore a contemporary of Hāfiz, who died A.D. 1389.—Falconer has erroneously rendered this passage: "I had heard that disobedience to
the command of a sovereign is culpable ; and at the time indicated
by the words, *the sublime mandate of the King,* when seventy-six
years had passed beyond 700," for which, on the authority of
Mr. J. W. Redhouse, the above is substituted. A poet never
gives a date in full words and in values also; and he would
certainly not give it both ways when they did not agree—the
supposed chronogram, rendered by Falconer, *sublime mandate of
the King,* would indicate the year 779, while the author, we
have seen, gives the exact date as 776.

[2] Jamshīd was the fifth of the Pīshdādī (or Achæmenian)
dynasty of ancient Persian kings, concerning whom many
extravagant legends are related—amongst which, that he possessed a magical cup, or goblet, that reflected the whole world
and all events and achievements.

lion and tiger flee;—I composed the following work, and thus reared an edifice proof against all the assaults of Time, and not such a structure that any one can designate as the 'house of the spider.'"

The chapter in which the tale commences affords, in the opening couplet, another allusion to the author of the prose work, of which this is a poetical paraphrase, informing us that the poet's original was written in *Persian*, but that its author was an *Arab* by descent. Perhaps this might afford some ground for the conjecture that the Arab had found the tale in the language of his family, and translated it from Arabic into Persian. Loiseleur Des Longchamps, however, who was not acquainted with the existence of the present work, was of opinion that the tale was first translated into Persian (from the Sanskrit), and from Persian into Arabic.

"An Arabian by descent, but speaking the Persian tongue, has thus informed me in eloquent language, that there reigned in India a sage and mighty monarch,[1] the bricks of whose palace were not of stone or marble, but of gold; the fuel of whose kitchen

---

[1] In the Greek version the scene is laid in Persia, and the monarch's name is Cyrus; in the Hebrew translation the scene, as above, is in India, "in the land of Hind," or Hodu, as it is most frequently written in the MS., and the king's name is Bibar; in the old Castilian version, the scene is also in India, and the name of the king is Alcos; in the Breslau (Arabic) text, the scene is in China.

was fresh wood of aloes; who had brought under
the signet of his authority the kingdoms of Rūm
and Abyssinia; and to whom were alike tributary the
Ethiop Mihrāj (Mahārāj) and the Roman Qaysar.
He was distinguished above all monarchs for his
virtue, his clemency and justice.   But, although he
was the refuge of the khalifate, he was not blessed
with an heir: life and the world appeared profitless to
him, because he had no fruit of the heart in the
garden of his soul."

One night, while reclining on his couch, sad and
thoughtful, consumed with grief like a morning taper,
he heaved a deep sigh, upon which one of his favourite
wives (he had a hundred in his harem[1]), advancing
towards him and kissing the ground, inquired the
cause of his distress.   He discloses it.   His wife
consoles him, encourages him to hope, and assures
him that if he prayed, his prayers would be answered;
but that at all events it was his duty to be resigned to
the will of God. "Prayer is the only key that will open
the door of difficulty."   The king fasted for a whole
week, and was assiduous in his devotions.[2]   One night

---

[1] According to *Syntipas*, he had seven wives; the Hebrew
translator assigns him eighty, and calls this one Beria.   In the
old Castilian translation he is said to have had ninety wives.

[2] The Hebrew translation agrees with this version in representing the king as both fasting and praying.   In the Arabian
version, the king requests his nobles and subjects to pray that
God would bless him with a son.—A parallel case is found in

he prayed with peculiar earnestness and self-abasement till morning. The companion of his couch was one of his wives, fairer than the sun, and the envy of ·a perī. He clasped her in his embrace, exclaiming: "There is no strength, no power, save in God!" and he felt assured in his heart that his prayer was granted.

In due time a son is born to .him. Eager to testify his gratitude, he bestows munificent gifts, and lavishes his treasures on all. The babe is entrusted to a nurse. The most distinguished astrologers are commanded to cast his nativity. Among their number was one of the most skilful explorers of the heavens, who, upon completing his observations, intimated to the king that his son would be fortunate above other monarchs; but that a danger awaited him, from which, however, it was likely, thanks to his auspicious fortune, that no injury would accrue.[1] His

---

the Persian romance of the Four Dervishes *(Kissa-i Chehar Darvīsh)*, where King Āzādbakht, having secluded himself through sorrow because he had not a son to succeed him, is advised by his prime vazīr to distribute alms among the poor and needy, and offer up frequent prayers to God—no one ever yet returned hopeless from his threshold.

[1] In the *Mishlé Sandabar*, after the birth of the prince, the king assembles all the sages, and by his order they select a thousand out of themselves, these select a hundred, and they select seven, who draw the horoscope of the prince, and find that he is threatened with some misfortune when twenty years of age. So, too, in the old Castilian translation, we are told, the king "sent for all the wise men of his kingdom to come to

Majesty is filled with anxiety at this information, but at length becomes resigned to the will of Heaven, and acknowledges that the decrees of destiny cannot be countervailed. When the prince had attained his tenth year, his father the sultan confided him to the care of a learned preceptor. "Base copper has by care been transmuted into gold; and a worthless stone converted to a gem." That accomplished and erudite professor devoted his whole time to the education of the prince; but all his exertions were unavailing. "However loudly he shouted, that mountain gave back no echo; however much he sowed, in that soil no grain sprang up." His pupil knew not *ab-u-jadd* (father and grandfather) from *abjad;* could not distinguish *Muhammad* from *Auhad.* When asked how many make *thirty*, he replied, "ten;" and to the question, What is *night?* he answered, "the moon." When asked about the *thorn*, he spoke of "fresh dates;" when desired to say *fire*, he said "fuel." His father was in constant uneasiness about the prince, and made

him and examine the hour and the minute of his son's birth;" and having cast the prince's horoscope, they told the king that "he should have long life and great powers, but at the end of twenty years something should happen between him and his father, through which he should be in danger of death." In the Breslau (Arabic) text, the misfortune was to occur "during his youth." This has been suppressed in *Syntipas*, and also in Scott's *Seven Vazīrs;* in the latter, the danger to the prince is foretold to the king's favourite concubine in a vision.

frequent inquiries as to his progress. When he found him, year after year, in the same state of perfect ignorance, his wrath was kindled against the blameless and unhappy preceptor, whom he reproached for the backwardness of his son.

He then called together the philosophers of the city, each of whom was the Aristotle of his age; and after desiring them to be seated, and showing them the most flattering attentions, he detailed to them all the circumstances connected with his son's history, and the cause of his anxiety. "Wretched," said he, "is he who digs the mine, or rather, who vexes his own soul; who expects to find gold, and grasps but dust! With vows I implored God to grant me this son; I now repent me that I have asked him. How well said the sailor to the captain of the ship: 'Leave the concerns of God to God!' The unleavened mass hath not become leavened; nor hath one spoonful of butter been obtained from ten skins of milk! Tell me," continued the king, "what expedient shall I adopt to remedy this, and who is the person best qualified to carry it into execution? I have none to succeed me in the kingdom save this son. Deliberate, therefore; and when your counsel is matured, a course of conduct may be founded on it."

The sages, who were seven in number, bowed the head in token of obedience, and expressed their wishes for his Majesty's prosperity and happiness. It was then arranged that they should meet for the purpose of discussing the matter together. The learned master, of whom this tale remains as a memorial (says the writer of the poem), thus proceeds: Those experienced sages accordingly one day met in private consultation, and conversed freely on the subject. One of them observed: " O wise men, how can the pulp of colocynth supply the place of sugar? The tree which, when ten years old, has yielded no fruit, the labour of ten years has been entirely thrown away upon it." Another remarked: " Never can the rose spring from the dry willow: how can the musk-willow bear, as its fruit, the musk-bag?"

One of those worthies, who had not his equal, who had no rival among those whom you know (*i.e.*, among the seven), a buzurjmihr,[1] experienced in affairs, a sage resembling Aristotle—his name Sindibād[2]—said, in reply to these observations: " The hawk which has dwelt free and happy in its nest is, nevertheless, subjected to a master; learns from the falconer to soar and seize its prey, and to return when called, and quietly perch on the hand of kings. Why should not the prince, too, be capable of being taught the art of government and the duties of his station? Despair not: everything may be effected by labour and deter-

---

[1] One of great soul.

[2] In the Calcutta and Būlāq printed Arabic texts the name of this sage is also Sindibād; in the Syriac, Sindbān, and (once) Sindbādin; in the Greek, Syntipas; in the Hebrew, Sandabar; and in the old Spanish version, Cendubete.

mination. The fortress of the mine must be stormed ere the ruby can be obtained." The other sages warmly applauded the wisdom of Sindibād, and assured him that they considered him the fittest person to whom the important and difficult charge of the prince's education could be entrusted. Sindibād replied, that he was not to be moved by their compliments and flattery; that he saw as little advantage likely to result to him from such a course as the monkey derived from the stratagem of the old fox. They requested him to tell them the story, upon which he began :

Story of the Old Fox and the Monkey.

ONCE upon a time an old fox was put to great shifts for his subsistence, and resolved to exert all his wits to procure it. After offering up a prayer for success to his endeavours, he set out and ran. When he had advanced some way he saw a fish; he was delighted, and congratulated himself on his good fortune; but, upon reflection, he perceived that the case was one which called for wariness and circumspection; for the place was a dry uncultivated valley, without water, a spot where one sees not a fish, save in his dreams. Neither sea was there nor fishmonger's shop. Advancing two miles, he met a young monkey, upon seeing whom he felt that he had found the key wherewith to unlock his difficulty. He ran up to him,

saluted him, and said: "Well met! The gazelles and
the wild asses send you their salutations through me,
and beg that you will come to their assistance against
the tyranny of the lion, who is never satiated with
shedding innocent blood. Come, that we may bestow
on you the royal crown. They are waiting for your
Majesty farther on the road." The monkey was
deceived by these flattering expressions, and his
ambition threw him into the pitfall. "Advance,"
said he, "and lead the way." When they reached
the spot and saw the fish, "You," said the fox,
"have the first claim to this morsel, for you are my
prince and sovereign." The monkey, blinded by his
cupidity, went forward to seize the fish, and was
instantly caught in a snare from which he was unable
to escape. Upon this, the fox sat down quietly to eat
the fish. "What means this?" inquired the monkey.
"From whose table is this dainty?" "The poor,"
replied the fox, "cannot afford to flee from bread.
Fetters and imprisonment befit the dignity of kings:
make not, O sage, your mind uneasy."

The philosophers were loud in their praises of
Sindibād on his concluding this tale, and compared
him to the sun, and themselves to the motes in the
sunbeam. "If I am not wiser than yourselves,"
replied he, "I am at least not inferior to you in
wisdom. Your case and my own, in this respect,
reminds me of the camel, the wolf, the fox, and the

pumpkin." They requested to hear the story, and Sindibād related it as follows:

Story of the Camel, the Wolf, the Fox, and the Pumpkin.

AN old wolf and a fox, intimate friends, were once travelling together. A short way before them they saw a camel, who joined them, and the three together took the road to the village of the camels. Their only provision for the journey consisted of a pumpkin. They travelled on for a long time, up hill and down dale, till, exhausted by the heat of the road, their eyes became black with thirst. At length they reached a pond full of water, and sat down on its brink. The pumpkin was produced, and after some discussion, it was agreed that this prize should belong to him who was the eldest among them.

First the wolf began: "Indian, Tajik, and Turk, know, that my mother bore me one week before God had created heaven and earth, time and space; consequently, I have the best right to this pumpkin."

"Yes," said the old and crafty fox, "I have nothing to object to this account; for on the night your mother bore you, I was standing by in attendance. That morning it was I that lit the taper, and I burned beside your pillow like a morning taper."

When the camel had heard their speeches to an end, he stalked forward, and, bending down his neck,

snapped up the pumpkin, observing: "It is impossible
to conceal a thing so manifest as this—that with such
a neck, and haunches, and back as mine, it was
neither yesterday nor last night that my mother bore
me." [1][1]

The sages again expressed their admiration of the
wisdom of Sindibād, and all agreed that he alone was
competent to undertake the difficult task. Repairing
into the presence of the king, they acknowledged
that they were but babes in wisdom compared with
Sindibād; upon which his Majesty, addressing the
philosopher, begged him to undertake the management and education of the prince. Sindibād consented, expressing his hope and confidence that his
efforts would be successful. He accordingly applied
himself with zeal to the education of the prince, but
all his efforts were fruitless; all his instructions were
like writing upon water. The king, hearing of this,
was much concerned. Never does a parent wish ill
to his child, but, on the contrary, desires that he may
be better than himself. In anger he said to Sindibād:
"All your boasted care and exertion have proved but
wind; your promises were but the sound of the bell
and the drum. Does not even the wild beast, which
cannot be taken in the net, become tame at last by
persevering efforts? Had due diligence been bestowed

---

[1] The figures within brackets refer to notes in Appendix.

upon my son, the rust would have been effaced from the mirror of his mind."[1] "Sire," replied Sindibād, "I have made every exertion, and tried every art; but when fate seconds not our efforts, we are not to blame." Then, kissing the foot of the throne, he observed: "The situation of myself and the young prince resembles that of the King of Kashmīr with the elephant and the elephant-keeper." The king desiring to hear the story, Sindibād related it as follows:

Story of the King of Kashmir and the Elephant.

IN the time of the Masters of the Elephant,[2] there reigned over Kashmīr a wise and prudent king, who had conquered the whole kingdom of Hindūstān, from

---

[1] Metallic mirrors, such as were used by the ancients, are here alluded to. Thus a Persian poet says: "Many have been melted down in this crucible: when have they made a mirror of every [kind of] iron?"

[2] The miraculous defeat of the host of Abraha, on its approach to Mecca for the purpose of destroying the Ka'ba, occurred in the same year in which Muhammad was born. Abraha and his army are alluded to in the Qur'ān, under the title of Lords, or Masters, of the Elephant, from their bringing with them, according to some, thirteen elephants, which they had obtained from the King of Ethiopia. Others mention but one. See Sale's *Koran*, ch. 105, and note.—F.

Serendil (Ceylon)[1] to Rūm and Syria, and to whom
were subject all the princes of the world. This sovereign had collected elephants instead of steeds, and in
greater numbers than fleas or ants. A certain prince
once sent to his court a wild elephant of prodigious
.size and impetuosity. The king desired the elephant-
keeper to tame him, promising him ample rewards
when he had succeeded. After the labour and constant care of three years, the skilful man had not only
subdued his ferocity, but made him pliable as wax.
He, therefore, brought him to the appointed place,
and exhibited him to the king, who was satisfied with
his success; and the royal litter being adjusted, his
Majesty seated himself in it, by way of trial. No
sooner had he mounted, than, like a demon that leaps
from a bottle[2]—like a lion rushing from a thicket—
the elephant darted off with the monarch, and flew

---

[1] Serendil, or, as it is commonly and more correctly written,
Serendib, being apparently derived from the Sanskrit *Sinhadvīpa*,
Lion Island.—F.

[2] Falconer remarks that this recalls the legend of the Bottle
Imp; and cites, in the original Persian, a couplet from another
part of the text, which may be thus rendered:

" By predominant might he put the demon in the bottle;
  The genii howled and whined on account of him."

This is probably in allusion to the Muslim legend of Solomon's
feat of enclosing the demon Sakhr in a copper vessel, sealing it
with his magical signet, and casting it into the Lake of Tiberias,
where Sakhr is to remain until the day of judgment. According

with the speed of lightning over hill and dale.
The prince, with no guide to control or govern the
animal, abandoned all hope of life, and all expectation
that "the elephant would think again of Hindustan."[1]
Raising his hands to heaven, he prayed for deliverance.
When the divine mandate issues forth, elephant and
ant are alike impotent to resist it. Tired with the
long journey (for it was now evening), and having
eaten nothing, the elephant turned and took his way
homeward. When he reached his stable, he stooped
down, and the prince dismounted unhurt. Enraged
with the keeper, he ordered him to be trodden like
the ant under the feet of the elephant. Fettered and
manacled, he was thrown under the furious animal.

---

to other legends, Solomon treated all the rebellious genii in like
manner. The story of the Fisherman and the Genie *(Jinnī)*
must be familiar to all readers of the *Arabian Nights.* This
notion of demons being confined in bottles is also prevalent in
China. See Mr. Giles' *Strange Stories from a Chinese Studio,* vol. i,
p. 81. The leading idea of *Le Diable Boiteux* was suggested to
Le Sage by that of the Spanish novel *El Diable Cojuelo,* in which
a student accidentally enters the house of a conjuror, and delivers
a demon from a glass bottle where he had been imprisoned.

[1] Compare this passage with the following one from Hāfīz,
which it illustrates: "Either take note of the customs of the
elephant-keeper, or do not bring India into the memory of the
elephant;" and with another, from Mīr Razī, quoted by the
author of the *'Atishkada:* "Take hold of my chain, O friends!
for my elephant brings to mind India." The allusion seems to
have become proverbial.

Finding himself in this situation, he thus reflected:
"The prey that is entangled in the net struggles whether
it will or not; and it is never too late to hope for deliverance." He implored the king to forgive one whose hair
had grown gray in the service; but he refused. Long
he continued to entreat forgiveness, but the king was
still inexorable. At length, again repairing into the
presence of his Majesty, he renewed his entreaties. "I
taught the elephant," said he, "whatever was proper;
but, as fortune favoured me not, it was of no avail.
If the king will spare my life, I will give proof of my
assertion." When his Majesty heard this, and beheld
the poor man's orphan children at his feet, he ordered
him to be unfettered. The keeper then proved the
perfect tameness of the animal by giving it orders to
perform a variety of feats, all which it executed. Then
addressing the king, he said: "I have taught this
animal to perform with its various members the whole
of the feats which are practised; but what avails it
when his heart, which is the sultan of the body,[1]
listens not to my orders?"

"In short," observed Sindibād, "what occurred to
the elephant-keeper arose from certain evil aspects in

---

[1] So in the *Khātima* to the *Rauzatu-'s-Sufa*, the author, in
stating that the Khataians place those whom they wish to
honour on the left hand, assigns this reason: "Because the
heart, which is the sultan of the city of the body, has its mansion
on that side."—F.

his horoscope, and from no fault of his. Thus, O king," continued the sage, "I have examined the horoscope of the prince, and find that all that was evil in it is past; he will henceforward be prosperous. I will now proceed to teach him all I know, to shower upon him all the learning that I have amassed. When six months shall have elapsed from this date, I will have imparted to him the fruit of thirty years' study."[1]

The ministers and courtiers of the king were amazed at such language, and considered his words as an empty boast. "Attempt it not," said one of them: "seeing that your six years' labour has been fruitless, how can this be accomplished in six months?" Another courtier said: "Seeing he learned nothing in his childhood, how can he become a master when he is grown up?"

* * * * *

There is here a deficiency in the manuscript, viz., after fol. 25, probably of one leaf; and two leaves that

---

[1] In the Greek text the sage says: "Having educated him for six months, I will so fill him with all philosophy that none shall be found more learned than he." In the Syriac text the period is "six months and two hours." In the Hebrew version: "I will teach the son of the king in six months so that there shall not be found the like of him in all the land of Hodu [or Hind]." In the old Spanish translation: "I will so teach him in six months that no one shall have more knowledge than he;" and in reply to one of the other sages, who blamed him for his rashness: "Thou shalt see, if God will and I live, that I will

ought to follow are misplaced and incorrectly numbered—fols. 14 and 15.

*   *   *   *   *

The king, now satisfied that Sindibād had not been
wanting in his exertions, continues him in his office of
preceptor to the prince. Sindibād accordingly resumes
his instructions. At fol. 14 the author is describing
the philosopher's preparations for his lectures; the
beginning of the chapter is wanting. Sindibād caused
the walls of a lofty palace to be covered over with
plaster, so smooth as to have the appearance of a
mirror. On one compartment were delineated the
signs of the zodiac, with the divisions into degrees
and minutes; the fixed stars; the planets, with their
courses. On another compartment he drew a map of
the world, and represented the noxious and salutary
qualities of things, of which some are the cause of
disease and others the cure. On a third compartment
were inscribed the principles of commerce, religion,
and morality; and one's duties towards his superiors
and equals. On a fourth were exhibited the principles
of music and melody, and the distinctions of the
musical modes. On a fifth, the rules of justice, the
ceremonial of princely dignity, and the forms of

---

teach him in six months what another would not teach him in
seventy years." In Scott's version the stipulated period is two
years;—this part of the story is much abridged in the other
Arabic texts.

equity.[1] When the whole was completed, Sindibād thus addressed his pupil: "Prince, the time for application has now arrived; be diligent; it is no time for slumber. The virtues that adorn kings come not by inheritance; they must be acquired." The prince listened with attention to the instructions of his master. Much did he study; many a bitter cup of poison did he drink. His mind, clear as a mirror, reflected the knowledge depicted on the walls. His progress was rapid, and in a short time he became deeply learned.

When the appointed period was completed, Sindibād said to his pupil: "Praise be to the Lord and Creator of the world, that, through his grace, I shall not be put to shame before men! When, to-morrow, I take you before the sultan, you will see how they will bite their nails.[2] Rest assured of this, that of all your equals in age not one will be a match for you." Sindibād then during the night took an observation to ascertain the destiny of the prince, and found that an intricate snare threatened his pupil. He was confounded and perplexed by this new difficulty.[3] But it

---

[1] "He built for the son of the king a spacious new house, and embellishing the inside of the house, he narrated on the walls of the house as much as he intended teaching the boy."—*Syntipas.*

[2] Biting the nails, or fingers, is a very common mode in the East of exhibiting anger, grief, or astonishment.

[3] "The philosopher then, having learned from astrological inquiry, was confounded."—*Syntipas.*

is vain to contend against destiny: when it descends,
the eye becomes blind. "Be not cast down," said
he to the prince, "at the caprice of fortune, but
to-morrow, when you appear before the king, whatever
questions you may be asked, answer nothing. Bear
up for this week; the next, your affairs will become
prosperous. If but a word escape your lips, your
life and head will be endangered. Lo! I hasten to
conceal myself, and no one shall see me for one
week, for my life is in peril.[1] I will wait to see
whether the two dice of heaven will turn up three
sixes or three aces."

*   *   *   *   *

The whole of the next chapter is wanting in the
manuscript, but the title of it is given at the end of
fol. 15, as follows: "The king sits in state, and sends
for the prince and Sindibād, but the latter is nowhere
to be found. His Majesty questions the prince, who
makes no reply." The title and commencement of
the next chapter are also wanting. At fol. 26 the
poem proceeds:

---

[1] "Therefore from to-morrow I shall conceal myself," &c.—
Syntipas.—"Said Sandabar to the king's son: 'Behold, I have
sent to thy father to announce that thou shalt go to him
to-morrow, and I have not observed thy constellation.' And
Sandabar observed the stars, and saw that if the son of the king
should open his mouth within seven days, he should instantly be
slain; and Sandabar trembled."—*Mishlé Sandabar.*

A peri-faced moon[1] (one of the wives of his Majesty), fair as a hūrī[2] of Paradise, was secretly enamoured of the prince, but had hitherto found no opportunity of meeting him alone, or of telling him her love. Upon hearing the account of his resolute silence when questioned, she said to herself: "Every occasion has its fitting language;" and repairing to the king, she asked his permission to take the prince to the harem, under pretence of endeavouring to extort from him the secret of his silence. This was granted. But with her also the prince was dumb. At length she declares her passion for him, and offers to put him in possession of the kingdom in return for his confidence. Upon this the prince, forgetting in his surprise his promise to Sindibād, breaks silence by asking her how this was to be done. "Easily," replied she; "by one drop of poison which I will administer to the king." Horror-struck at the idea of such a crime, the prince, after earnestly reprobating it, quits the apartment.

The damsel is alarmed when she reflects on the danger of her situation should the prince reveal the

---

[1] Perīs are good genii, or fairies, of both sexes, though the term is generally applied to females. Amongst us the phrase "moon-faced" is the opposite of complimentary; in Oriental poetry, however, it is the favourite similitude in describing a beautiful girl or boy; and our own poets Spencer and Shakspeare have made use of the same comparison.

[2] Hūrīs (or houris) are the black-eyed beauties promised in the Qur'ān as the companions of the faithful in Paradise.

treachery which she had proposed, when the seven
days shall have passed, and he shall break silence.[1]
Full of these apprehensions, she rushed from her
apartment into the presence of the king, and, in
affected agitation, called loudly for his protection.   In
answer to his inquiries as to the cause of her alarm,
she replied: "My reputation is scattered to the winds!
No sooner had I conducted the prince into the harem
than he began to say: 'The reason of my silence is,
that my heart is ensnared in your tresses, and my soul
slain by the curve of your eyebrows.   Now that fortune
has put it in my power, I entreat you to lend me your
assistance.   I have a secret to impart to you.   I mean
to seize upon the kingdom.   The leaders of the troops
are already secured in my favour.   You can effectually
aid me in my purpose by administering poison to my
father.'"

To this false accusation the king gives credit; and,
believing that the prince thirsted for his blood, commands that he should be ignominiously put to death.

---

[1] The prince must therefore have informed the damsel of his
seven days' silence, and the fact was probably omitted by the
copyist.   In the Greek, Hebrew, and Castilian versions he says
to her: "When seven days are passed I shall be able to give
thee the answer that thou deservest," and there can be no doubt
that this was in the original text of the *Sindibād.*   In Scott's
Seven Vazīrs, the prince is represented as *mentally* addressing
the damsel in these terms—an "improvement" of the translator
or transcriber.

The executioner is ordered to behead him. Meanwhile, the vazīrs,[1] who were met together in council, on hearing this inconsiderate sentence, were greatly concerned. The eldest addresses them on the necessity of warning his Majesty of the danger of precipitation, and of the folly of trusting to the testimony of women; giving it as his conviction that the charge, if inquired into, would be found to be false, and that the innocence of the prince would be ultimately established. Another of the vazīrs was of opinion that, as they had not been consulted on the subject, it was unnecessary for them to interfere, and that silence was their safest course. To this argument the eldest vazīr replied, that if they neglected to listen to his advice, the same thing might happen to them at last as befell the monkeys. The vazīrs requesting to hear what that was, he thus related:

Story of the King of the Monkeys.[2]

WHEN you have quitted Nihāwand, going out by the Lion's Gate, there lies beyond it a village called Būzīna-Gard,[3] the neighbourhood of which is thickly

---

[1] These vazīrs should not be confounded with the seven wise men (see p. 11), one of whom is Sindibād.

[2] This tale, related by the chief vazīr, and the three, told by Sindibād, pp. 13, 15, and 17, are not found in *Syntipas*, or any other version.

[3] Monkey Town.

inhabited by monkeys. There, amid the trees laden
with fruit, and by a running stream, the monkeys used
to congregate. The surrounding forest was full of
them; and there reigned over them a sage monarch,
named Rūz-i-bih,[1] who, in magnanimity and generosity,
was no monkey, but a lion, and who, although aged,
had all the vigour of youth. His cheek like the ruddy
rose, his beard white; he was ever fresh and gay, like
the red willow. Much had he experienced of the
world's red and white; much of its hot and cold. His
subjects were all obedient and loyal, secure and happy.
Their granaries were well stored with figs and walnuts;
and they had herds of goats browsing in the forest—
a paradise—rather, the model of the Garden of Iram[2]
—a place where pleasure was rife and pain unknown!

---

[1] Whose day is good, or excellent.

[2] A fabulous earthly paradise, designed, according to Muslim
legend, by an impious king of El-Yaman (Arabia Felix), named
Shaddād, as a rival to that of the spiritual world. The palace
was constructed of gold and silver bricks in alternate courses,
the walls set with pearls, rubies, emeralds, and other gems; in
the garden were trees of gold and silver, besides others bearing
the most delicious fruits. After five hundred years this paradise
was completed, and Shaddād, with a numerous retinue, in the
utmost pomp and splendour, marched from his capital towards
it. As he was about to enter the gates, the Angel of Death
appeared before him, and seized upon his impure soul; and
instantly the lightnings consumed all his attendants, and the
Rose-Garden of Iram sank into the earth, and became hidden
from the sight of men.

In the forest was a mountain as high as Alwand.[1] Thither this king having on one occasion gone to hunt, and looking towards the town and market which were on it, he saw, at the corner of a street, a goat constantly butting at an old woman. Calling to him the leaders of his army, he desired them to look in that direction, and observe what was going on. The king was himself of opinion that, as the flocks were all his own subjects, it was his duty to interfere; but the general of the army thought the matter too trifling to be noticed. The dispute waxed high, and, as the officers of the army sided with their general, the monarch abdicated, and withdrew to another country, and they chose a new king.

The goat still continued its practice of butting at the old woman; and one day that she had been to ask fire from a neighbour, the goat struck her so violently with his horns when she was off her guard as to draw blood. Enraged at this, she applied the fire which she held to the goat's fleece, which kindled, and the animal ran to the stables of the elephant-keeper, and rubbed his sides against the reeds and willows. They caught fire, which the wind soon spread, and the head and face of the warlike elephants were scorched. When the news reached the sovereign to whom the elephants belonged, he sent for the chief-keeper, and

---

[1] A mountain in Persia, once, if not still, popularly believed to be sixteen miles in height!

asked him what was best to be done for the cure of
the elephants. "I have heard one skilled in such
matters affirm," replied he, "on the authority of an
ancient leech, that when elephants are scorched, the
best remedy is the fat of monkeys rubbed gently over
them with the hand." Upon this the king gave orders
that horsemen should go forth and scour the whole
forest, hunting down every animal they should find of
the monkey tribe. Accordingly, an innumerable band
issued forth, searching mountain and forest; and the
general of the monkeys was made prisoner. He
inquired: "Whose are these troops, and why is this
night attack and slaughter of our race?" He was told
the circumstances in detail, and he then recollected,
but too late, the words of his sage and foreseeing
monarch.

When the eldest vazir had ended, all the others
applauded him, and acknowledged the wisdom of his
counsel. It was therefore agreed that every morning
one of their number should repair into the presence of
the king, and relate tales illustrative of the craft and
deceitfulness of women, in the hope that when one
week had thus passed the fortunes of the prince would
have become prosperous.

Accordingly, the First Vazir, after having gone to
the executioner and desired him to delay till further
orders, waited upon his Majesty, and after humble
prostration, complimented him on his justice, but

warned him of the cunning of women, and cautioned him to avoid precipitation. "The word," said he, "which has once escaped the lips, the arrow which has once left the bow, have ceased to be under your control.[1] Perhaps you may one day repent your rashness, and grieve for what you have done, like the foolish man who slew his parrot without a crime." The king desired him to relate the story, and he began:

Story of the Confectioner, his Wife, and the Parrot.

THERE once lived in Egypt a confectioner, who had a very beautiful wife, and a parrot[2] that performed, as

---

[1] Thus Sa‘dī: "When thou utterest not a word, thou hast thy hand upon it; when thou hast uttered it, it has laid its hand upon thee;" and again: "You may easily separate the soul from the body, but you cannot so readily restore life to the dead; it is a maxim of prudence to be cautious in giving the arrow flight, for let it once quit the bow, and it can never be recalled." So, too, in the *Dictes, or Sayings of Philosophers*, printed by Caxton in 1477, one of the "thre Wysemen" who "cam byfore a King," is represented as saying: "I am mayster of my wordes, or it be pronounced; but when it is spoken, I am servaunt thereto." And in the preface to *Kalila and Dimna* (the Arabian version of the work known in Europe as the Fables of Pilpay) precisely the same "saying" is found: "I am the slave of what I have spoken, but the master of what I conceal."

[2] The Hebrew translator has borrowed the Italian name

occasion required, the office of watchman, guard, policeman, bell, or spy, and flapped his wings did he but hear a fly buzzing about the sugar. This parrot was a great annoyance to the wife, always telling the suspicious husband what took place in his absence. One evening, before going out to visit a friend, the confectioner gave the parrot strict injunctions to watch all night, and desired his wife to make all fast, as he should not return till morning. No sooner had he left, than the woman went for her old lover, who returned with her, and they passed the night together in mirth and feasting, while the parrot observed all. In the morning the lover departed, and the husband, returning, was informed by the parrot of what had taken place; upon which he hastened to his wife's apartment, and beat her soundly. She thought to herself, who could have informed against her, and asked a woman who was in her confidence whether it was she. The woman protested, "by what is hidden and what is open,"[1] that she had not betrayed her; but informed her that in the morning, upon his return, the husband stood some time before the cage, and listened to the talking of the parrot. When the wife heard this, she resolved to plot the destruction of the bird.

---

pappagallo, which he writes most frequently *papĕgáiah*, once *papágáah*, and once *papĕgái*.

[1] "The female slave swore strongly."—*Syntipas.*

Some days after, the husband was again invited to
the house of a friend, where he was to pass the night.
Before departing, he gave the parrot the same injunctions as before.   His heart was free from care, for he
had his spy at home.   The wife and her confidante
then planned how they might destroy the credit of the
parrot with its master.   For this purpose, they resolved
to counterfeit a storm, which they effected by means
of a hand-mill, placed over the parrot's head, which
the lover worked, by a rush of water, by blowing a
bellows, and by suddenly uncovering a taper hid under
a dish.   Thus did they raise such a tempest of rain
and lightning, that the parrot was drenched and immersed in a deluge.   Now rolled the thunder—now
flashed the lightning—the one from the noise of the
hand-mill, the other from the reflection of the taper.
"Surely," thought the parrot to itself, "the deluge has
come on, and such a one as perhaps Noah never
witnessed."   So saying, he buried his head under his
wing, a prey to terror.   The husband, on his return,
hastened to the parrot, to inquire what had happened
during his absence.   The bird replied, that he found
it impossible to convey an idea of the deluge and
tempest of last night; that it would take years to
describe the uproar of the hurricane and storm.   When
the shopkeeper heard the parrot talk of last night's
deluge, he said: "Surely, O bird, you are gone mad.
Where was there—even in a dream—rain or lightning
last night?   You have utterly ruined my house and

ancient family. My wife is the most virtuous woman of the age, and all your accusations of her are false." In anger, he dashed the cage upon the ground, tore off the parrot's head, and threw it from the window. Presently, his friend, coming to call upon him, saw the parrot in this condition, with head torn off, and without wings or plumage. Being informed of the circumstances, he suspected some trick on the part of the wife, and said to the husband: "When your wife leaves home to go to the bath, compel her confidante to disclose the secret." As soon, therefore, as his wife went out, the husband entered his harem, and insisted on the woman telling him the truth. She detailed the whole story, and the husband now bitterly repented having killed the parrot, of whose innocence he had proof.[1]

---

[1] In *Syntipas*, the husband is not undeceived, but ceases to have faith in the parrot. In the Hebrew version, "he slew the parrot, and sent to bring his wife, and gave her presents." In the Arabic, he kills the parrot, and afterwards discovering that his wife is guilty, in Scott's version, he divorces her, but in the Calcutta, Būlāq, and Breslau texts, he kills both the woman and her paramour. In the Syriac and Castilian, as in the Hebrew, he kills the parrot and is reconciled to his wife. The conclusion of the story as found in the Turkish *Forty Vazīrs* agrees with that in *Syntipas*.—In the *Seven Wise Masters*, the old English prose translation of the *Historia Septem Sapientum Romæ*, where the tale is related of a burgess and his magpie (or pye), the husband says to the bird: "Thou liest; thou hast said unto me, that in the same night was hail, and snow, and

"I will now," continued the vazīr, "relate to your Majesty a still pleasanter tale to the same purpose, illustrating the craft of women." The king expressed a wish to hear it, and the vazīr proceeded:

Story of the Officer and his Mistress, his Servant, and the Woman's Husband.[1]

IN the kingdom of Balqīs[2] and city of Sapā, there lived a tailor, of whose wife a young officer became enamoured. When the tailor was from home, the officer sent his servant with a message to the wife.

---

rain, that thou hast near hand lost thy life, which is most false. And therefore from henceforth thou shalt make no more leasings nor discord betwixt me and my wife," and so took the pye and broke her neck. But in the metrical version (Auchinleck MS.—the oldest English text extant) analysed by Ellis, in his *Specimens of Early English Metrical Romances*, the burgess, after killing the bird, discovers the trick that had been practised upon it, and thrusts his wife out of the house.—·The story is also found in John of Capua's *Directorium Humanæ Vitæ*, the *Discorsi degli Animali*, and the *Giorni* of Sansovina.—See Appendix, No. 3.

[1] The MS. has the commencement of the story, but wants a leaf, viz., fol. 41, in the middle of it.—F.

[2] Balqīs, the name of the celebrated Queen of Sheba (Sapā) who visited Solomon, according to the Arabs; she is the 24th in Pocock's list of the sovereigns of Yaman : our author has given her name to the whole province. The city of Sapā (or Sabā) was built by Sabā, the ancestor of the Sabœans, or Himyarites, and was destroyed by the bursting of a great reservoir of water in ancient times.

The slave, being a handsome youth, found favour with her, and stayed so long, that the officer's patience being exhausted, he proceeded himself to the house. Aware of his approach, the woman concealed the slave in an inner apartment. While the officer was with her, the husband was heard knocking at the door. The woman, afraid to hide the officer in the other apartment, lest he should discover his slave there, devised the following escape from her difficulty. She desired her lover to draw his sword, feign to be in a violent passion with her, and, abusing her in opprobrious terms, to rush out of the house past her husband, without saying a word to him. The officer having done so, and the husband entering, the wife hastens to his embrace. " Be thankful," cried she, "that we are delivered from such a calamity! This morning, a lad rushed in here, trembling like a reed, and entreating me to save his life. I concealed him in that apartment. That furious man, whom you saw, burst in upon me, and asked, ' Where is the boy, my slave?' I replied that he was not here, and that I had not seen him; upon which he darted away in a passion. Enter the closet, and quiet the lad's fears. He is an orphan, and without relations." The simple husband did so, and having soothed and consoled the lad, sent him away with good wishes. [4]

"I have related this tale," added the vazír, " to show the cunning of women: believe not their words.

I will vouch for the prince's innocence with my
life." The king reflected for a while, and then,
remanding the youth to prison, retired to his private
apartment.

Next morning, the Damsel, hearing of the impression which had been made upon his Majesty by the
eloquence of one of his vazīrs, and how her plans were
thus overthrown, again presented herself, and, com-
plaining loudly of her wrongs, implored justice. She
reminded his Majesty of a day of retribution; accused
him of protecting one who had looked on his harem
with an eye of sin; denounced the vazīr as corrupt
and a receiver of bribes; and as bent upon bestowing
the sovereignty on the prince by the death of his
master. "If," said she, "your Majesty will not listen
to my advice, the same thing will happen to you which
happened to the washerman through his son." "Relate
it," said the king; and she began:

Story of the Washerman and his Son, who were Drowned in the Nile.

I HAVE heard from an Ethiop washerwoman, who
learned it from her husband, that there once lived in
Egypt, on the banks of the Nile, a washerman, by
name Noah, who was—like an atom—all day in the
sun, and—like a fish—all the year round in the water:
who would have washed with his soap the blackness

from an Ethiop. This man had a darling son, who was headstrong, good-for-nothing, and foolish; and who, as soon as he saw his father in the water, would seat himself on his father's ass, and drive it into the river. The father was in constant terror lest the boy should fall into the water and be drowned, or lest a crocodile should seize him. One day, the boy, as usual, mounted the ass, and rode with such fury into the river, that at once the water reached his head. At one moment he was—like an oyster—under water; the next—like a bubble—on its surface. As soon as the father learned that his son was drowning, he rushed into the water, in the hope of saving him, and caught him by the hand. The lad grasped at his father, and seized him by the hair. Both sank, and were drowned together. [5]

The king, reflecting upon this tale, changes his purpose, and orders the executioner to do his duty.

The Second Vazīr now sends a message to the executioner, desiring him to delay the execution for a short time; he then hastens into the presence of the king, and, after obeisance made, breaks out into invectives against women, and concludes by saying: "If your Majesty listens to the wiles of women, you will repent it, as the partridge did of killing his mate." The king desired to hear the tale, and the vazīr said:

Story of the Two Partridges.

ONCE upon a time two partridges dwelt together in
the closest intimacy—like two souls in one body, or
like two bodies in one shirt; and between them was
neither duality nor separation.   In their vicinity lived
a hawk, that from morning to night preyed on young
partridges, and that occasioned the male bird constant
apprehension, for he was a troublesome and meddle-
some neighbour.   When you buy a house anywhere,
first take care to examine well its neighbourhood.
This hawk was ever on the watch, and never allowed
a young bird to escape, while the parents were in
continual terror, and scarcely ventured to thrust their
heads out of the nest.   One night the male partridge
proposed to his wedded partner that they should leave
their home, saying: "I will go to the confines of Ray
to escape the oppression of this bird of evil omen.
There will I provide a home, and collect corn and
grain.   I have there two relations, who are my friends.
Do thou, too, follow me thither, for this is no home,
but a prison—a net."   His mate shed tears, while he
continued: "Follow after me to those friends; for no
one would, for the sake of his own ease, expose his
family to destruction."

While they were thus conversing, the hoopoe paid
them an unexpected visit.   "What has happened,"
inquired he; "and why is the good-wife weeping?"
They detailed to him their circumstances, the annoy-

ance occasioned by their neighbour, and their resolution of removing. The hoopoe observed: "In Ray there prevails a pestilence; it is the abode of plague, of misery, and woe. I have visited the most distant confines of the earth, and have seen something of every country you can mention. Do not imagine that there is in the whole earth a spot of security and peace like Shīrāz—whose very rubbish and thorns are pleasanter than roses; whose every pebble is a ruby, and whose dust is gold! Musalla,[1] with the stream of Ruknābād flowing through it, is a paradise, with Kauthar[2] in the midst. Sweet, too, is the air of its Ja'farābād,[3] whose breezes perform the work of the Messiah.[4] In the environs of that amber-scented city[5] there is a pleasure-ground like Paradise, in which is a

---

[1] A pleasure-garden near Shīrāz, where Hāfīz is buried.

[2] A river of Paradise, according to Eastern poets.

[3] A suburb of Shīrāz, famous for its gardens and villas.

[4] Muslims believe that the breath of the Messiah had the virtue of restoring the dead to life. In the Persian romance of the Four Dervishes a very skilful physician is named 'Isa (Jesus) in allusion to this notion.

[5] Hāfīz, in one of his beautiful *gazals*, exclaims (according to Mr. S. Robinson's translation:

"Hail Shīrāz! incomparable site! O Lord, preserve it from every disaster!

"God forbid a hundred times that our Ruknābād be doomed, to which the life of Khizar hath given its brightness!

"For between Ja'frābād and Mosella cometh the north wind perfumed with amber."

delightful fountain, resembling the Fountain of Life.
There partridges are abundant, hence it is called the
Fountain of Partridges. Beyond it is another fountain,
which you might suppose to be that of Kauthar. In
that quarter a single ear of corn yields two stacks. A
cousin of mine is the shaykh of the district. Still
further on is the City of the Peacock, where you might
stop a few days."

When the partridge heard this, he smiled, and said
to the hoopoe: "O bird, full of understanding! in this
desert of grief you are the Khizar[1] of my path; well
have you spoken, and you are indeed my friend!"
Then embracing him closely, he bade him adieu, and
set out on his journey, accompanied by his spouse.
The delighted partridge ceased not smiling with joy at
his escape from his bad neighbour. He ate not—
drank not—but travelled on from morn to night—from
even till morn. Thus he proceeded till he reached
the place of security, and beheld from the top of a
mountain the Stream of Birds. Then did his mate

---

[1] According to the Eastern legend, Khizar was despatched by
an ancient Persian king to procure him some of the Water of
Life. After a tedious journey, he reached the Fountain of
Immortality, and having drank of its waters, they suddenly
vanished. It is believed that Khizar still lives, and occasionally
appears to favoured individuals, always clothed in green, and
acts as their guide in difficult adventures—hence the allusion as
above.—Khizar is often confounded with Moses, Elias, and even
St. George. The name Khizar signifies *green.*

exclaim to him: "Gratitude and praise! thanks without bound or limit! It is indeed a blessed abode—a charming spot! In this delightful retreat they fixed their habitation, and sorrow had now given place to happiness. The joy of youth—the season of spring—an affectionate mistress, and the margin of a stream; this is the new-wine of life—and more needs not—happy he who has this within his reach!

The happy day on which the pair arrived at that spot was the night of the middle of the month Āzar (*i.e.* vernal month). On every bush roses were blowing; on every branch a nightingale was plaintively warbling. The tall cypress was dancing in the garden; and the poplar never ceased clapping its hands with joy! With loud voice, from the top of every bough of the willow, the turtle-dove was proclaiming the glad advent of spring! The diadem of the narcissus shone with such splendour, that you would have said it was the crown of the emperor of China! On this side, the north wind, on that, the west were, in token of affection, scattering dirhams at the feet of the rose. The earth was musk-scented; the air musk-laden![1]

---

[1] "There is, I believe," says Dr Johnson, "scarce any poet of eminence who has not left some testimony of his fondness for the flowers, the zephyrs, and the warblers of the spring; nor has the most luxuriant imagination been able to describe the serenity and happiness of the golden age otherwise than by giving a perpetual spring as the highest reward of uncorrupted innocence."

Two affectionate and loving friends find themselves at home wherever they go. The relations of the male partridge and the neighbours heard of his arrival, and hastened to visit him. One kissed his face, another brushed from his plumage the dust of the journey. Such affection did they conceive for each other, that they were never apart: all day, wandering about desert and country; all the year, roaming joyously without a care. I need not say that no cultivated fields or houses were there; that there was no night attack, or plunder, or ravaging; for not even a land-measurer passed that way; no burner of (the herb) alkali came there to give any one a headache. As the father did not wrong the son, the son sought not to take his father's life. As the daughter used not violence towards her mother, brother did not deprive brother of eyesight. Happy that time, those days, that age! when none had a quarrel with his neighbour. The world being then free from the ills of strife, the eye of the arrow saw not the face of the bow.

Thus passed some years over them, during which care or grief visited them not. But triumph not, O friend, in prosperity; still look forward to the evening and the night of grief. Bid the young think of the sorrows of age; let the aged reflect on the sufferings of death. There chanced to come on such a year of drought, that it was impossible to procure a drop of water from the fountains, and a hundred ears of corn yielded not a single grain. Locusts drank from the

cup of every one.   Not merely the store of the poor
was exhausted, but even the granary of kings was
empty.   People went to Egypt and to Syria to procure
corn, as in the time of Joseph (on whom be peace !).
When the eye of the partridge awoke from sleep, he
found himself destitute of provision.   His mate said:
"It matters not; let us practise devotion, and be
satisfied with what little there may be.   It is better to
be content with barley-bread than to carry one's
request before the king."   The male partridge replied:
"You pass your days in difficulty; yet sorrow not, for
grief as well as joy will pass away.   Six days' journey
off is the City of the Peacock; there, perhaps, corn
may be procured.   I have there a friend, by name
Durrāj,[1] from whom I can borrow something."   He
thus spoke, and, embracing his mate, went forth, and
took the way of the mountains.

The male partridge departed; the female remained
behind, and sang her sad songs.   The master is the
stay of the house; when he leaves it, it falls.   He was
absent about five months, for he loitered long upon
the road.   When winter came, and the cloud rained
camphor from the sky, and ice closed fast the eye of
the fountain, suddenly the male partridge returned
from his journey, and entered to take his spouse to
his bosom.   He beheld her changed; her neck slender,

---

[1] Durrāj is not a proper name, but the Persian name of the
francolin, a species of partridge.

her body swollen. When he saw her thus apparently
pregnant, all his affection for her was at an end. "I
see," said he, "that I have involved myself in calamity.
I have left a giddy wife at home! Fine housekeeping
this! A rare husband I! In my absence you were
about your own affairs;—tell me from whose granary
is this grain?" His mate vowed by 'Isa and by
Maryam[1] that he suspected her wrongfully. "No one
has seen my face since you left; no one has beheld a
feather of me. You are my only treasure in life; you
are father, relation, every tie of my soul." The enraged
husband, however, gave her no credit, but tore off the
head of his helpless mate. With her blood they wrote
on her tomb: "Shed not innocent blood; if you wish
not your own disgrace, do it not! He acts wisely who
acts with reflection." The partridge repented of what
he had done, and that he had acted on mere suspicion.
"Where," said he, "can I meet with a companion like
her?—one who was ever contented and accordant, and
who bore patiently with my reproaches!"

The birds of that quarter, hearing of his return,
waited on him to congratulate him on his arrival.
When they saw his wretched mate weltering in her
blood, their hearts burned with compassion for her.
One asked: "Why have you slain your mate? No
one entered this house. I will answer for it that this
poor wretch had no crime." The husband told the

---

[1] Jesus and Mary.

whole story with tears. They assured him with one voice that he had acted precipitately; that he was mistaken grievously; that in that city a disease had been raging for some time, by which the crop was swollen; but that a certain grass was a cure for it. "Why," said they, "did you not tell your case to any one?" The male bird was distracted at hearing this, and reproached himself bitterly. He lit up a fire, and burnt his house and home. He procured poison, which he took, and died. If he deprived another of life, he saved not his own! [6]

"Hence," remarks the vazīr, "your Majesty may see the danger of precipitation." He then relates, in further illustration of the cunning of women, the

Story of the Old Man who sent his Young Wife to the Market to buy Rice.[1]

[THERE was a righteous man in Qandahār, simple and pure of heart, upright, gracious, and exceeding clement. In origin and race he was the leader of men. He was very God-fearing and abstemious; at times standing all night at prayer, and at times fasting. He had a wife, fair-spoken and sweet of speech, who would have carried off the palm amongst a hundred marvels of beauty.

---

[1] Falconer gives only the title of this story, and refers the reader to *Syntipas*, p. 40 [of Boissonade, p. 30 of Eberhard].

She was very young; the good-man was very old: I will not say she was without plans and resources. When the good-man is old, and the wife young, what sayest thou, and seest thou, then, O youth? The youthful wife loved the youthful.

One day the old man took a piece of gold out of his purse, gave it to the woman, and said: "Buy some husked rice[1] with this." Having adorned her person with Chinese brocade, she went out veiled. She proceeded to the bazaar, where she saw a handsome youth, decked in loveliness from head to foot. A balance was hung up in his shop; candy and sugar were poured out. When the woman saw this loveling from afar, she writhed and heaved a sigh from her liver.[2] She brought out the piece of gold and laid it down, saying: "Give me husked rice for this gold."

---

[1] The word in the text is *muqashshar*, which is thus explained in Shakspeare's Hindūstanī Dictionary: "Barked, skinned, peeled, shelled, husked (rice)." In Persian the term may perhaps be equally applicable to shelled nuts or almonds, husked rice, &c. It must be borne in mind, however, that this text seems to have been written in India.

[2] I take the liberty of reproducing the following, from my notes on the Romance of 'Antar (*Arabian Poetry for English Readers*, pp. 456-7):—

The ancients, it is well known, placed the seat of love in the liver. Thus 'Antar says: "Ask my burning sighs that mount on high; they will tell thee of the flaming passion in my liver." An epigram in the seventh book of the *Anthologia* is to the same purpose:

The youth said: "There is no need of the gold; I will give thee presently rice with sugar on the top: do thou rest thyself a moment."—As he was young, and she was young, the (recollection of the) old man could find no room between them. He brought the rice and put it before her; he also put some sugar on the top of it. The woman took off her veil and wrapped both of them therein; then she went into an inner apartment, which had a private way out on that side, and sat down.

＊　　＊　　＊　　＊　　＊

A leaf, fol. 57, is wanting here; but from other versions we may suppose that the story went on to relate that, the grocer having given his servant a secret signal, while he and the lady were conversing together, the lad substituted sand in place of the rice and sugar; that she took up her parcel and returned home; and the old man, on discovering its strange contents,

---

"Cease, Love, to wound my liver and my heart;
　　If I must suffer, choose some other part."

Theocritus, in his 13th Idyll, referring to Hercules, says: "In his liver Love had fixed a wound." Anacreon tells how the god of Love drew his bow, and "the dart pierced through my liver and my heart." Horace (B. I, ode 2) says: "Burning love doth in thy cankered liver rage." But this notion was not peculiar to the ancients. According to our great dramatist:

"Alas! then love may be called appetite;
　　No motion of the liver, but the palate."

naturally inquired what this meant. Perceiving the trick of the grocer, she readily replied (fol. 58):

"When I was making for the bazaar from the street, at that narrow place at the head of the market, a young camel, that had broken away from the rope attached to its nose-ring, had got loose from the file (of camels), like a mountain suddenly sprang to foot, like a rock suddenly moved from its place, roared and so terrified me, that my breath was taken away. In that place where I turned and fled, the piece of gold fell from my hand into the dust.[1] I looked much for it, but could not find it; and as it was drawing late, I took away some of the dust of the road in my veil." The good-man, out of his simplicity of heart, believed her tale, and said: "Who wert thou, to be without fear? Thou knowest gold and dust to be one in my sight." He then gave her another piece of gold, saying: "Buy husked rice at that place thou knowest." So she took the gold, again put on her veil, and returned to the shop of her lover.][2]

---

[1] In the Syriac version, the woman says she was frightened by a *calf;* in the 8th Night of Nakhshabi's *Tūtī Nāma* (where the story is told by the Sixth Vazīr), she says that an *ox*, having got loose, ran at her, and she fell, losing the money among the dust. (This is the 25th tale of Kāderī's abridgment of the *Tūtī Nāma*, of which an English translation, together with the text, was published, at London, in 1801.) In the Hebrew and the Arabic versions, she was jostled by the crowd in the bazaar, and dropped the coin.

[2] This story is also found in John of Capua's *Directorium*

D

The king is induced by these tales and the inter-cession of the vazīr to suspend the execution and remand his son to prison.

The Damsel now returns for the third time,[1] and renews her demand for justice against the prince. "If my counsel be not listened to," says she, "the same thing will happen to you which befell the prince who, yielding to the guidance of his [father's] vazīr, was made prisoner in the haunt of ghūls." His Majesty desires to hear the tale, and the Damsel proceeds:

Story of the Prince and the Ghūl.

A WOMAN of the race of the kings of Persia once related to me that, in the city of Kirmān, a city whose like neither does the earth behold nor space contain, there ruled a brave and just prince, of the family of Kisra, by name Ardashīr,[2] to whose sway were subject

---

Humanæ Vitæ. It is omitted in the old Castilian version of the Book of Sindibād.

[1] That is, including her appearance when she accused the prince, but did not relate a story.

[2] Kisra, or Khusrau, was the general title of Persian kings of the Sāsānī dynasty, hence the Greek forms Cyrus and Chosroes, and perhaps the more modern Cæsar, Kaisar, and Czar. The founder of this dynasty was Ardashīr (Artaxerxes), but there were two other kings of the same name; and since Nūshīrvān the Just (6th century) is often termed Kisra *par excellence* by

fowl, fish, and ant; and whose threshold was kissed
by the sultans of Ghūr. He had but one son, named
Bedr, whom he fondly loved, and who, he hoped,
would succeed him when he should cease to reign:
when the rose should pass away, this rose-water would
remain; when the sun should set, this moon would
arise. One day, in the season of spring, the young
prince, wearied of confinement, asked permission of
his father to go a-hunting for a day or two. "The
master of the hawks," said he, "informs me that in
Rūdbār, and Mushīr, and Nigār there is abundance
of cranes, partridges, and other game, and makes me
eager for the sport."

His aged father replied: "Listen to my counsel, and
do it not, my son. The chase is an evil thing in its
beginning and in its end. In the eye of those endowed
with reflection, it is unlawful that the hawk should
pluck out the eye of the partridge. The antelope, with
all its beauty and grace—is it not a pity that it should
be mangled by the fangs of the dog? The pheasant,
with its delicate and graceful gait—is it not a shame
that it should fall into the power and snare of the
fowler? Those animals cause pain or injury to no one;
are happy amid their thickets and grass, and covet
nothing more. Well said the widowed wife to the

Persian writers, and was called Chosroes I by the Greeks, the
prince above mentioned was probably Ardashīr III, the fourth
successor to Nūshīrvān, and the twenty-fourth king of the
dynasty.

falconer: 'Go, withhold thy hand from this evil occupation. They are all the servants of their Maker; all of them live by his command. What advantage canst thou derive by depriving them of life? What benefit canst thou reap from sacrificing an ant?'"

"Sire," replied the prince, "the law sanctions hunting and the chase; and since it is permitted by the Prophet, whence is this prohibition, and why this severity of rebuke?"

In short, the king, seeing that he was bent on going, cautioned him to be on his guard against evil and danger; and his Majesty's favourite minister, in whom he had the fullest confidence, received instructions to attend and take charge of the prince, but was desired by the king not to conduct him to the desert of Rūdān, as it was infested with ghūls. They set out, and the vazīr proposed that they should proceed to Shemsī Ghūrān, which abounded in wild asses. Another of the vazīrs, however, who had long borne envy towards the premier, and who was secretly the enemy of his sovereign, worked on the prince by his insinuations against the minister, drew him aside from his train, when they were near Shemsī Ghūrān, into a tent, and persuaded him to drink a cup of wine. The prince was then about to repose in the tent, when a cry arose that a wild ass was started.[1] The prince

---

[1] Hunting the wild ass is still a favourite pastime of the Persian nobles. The fleetness of this animal is perhaps only exceeded by that of the antelope.

sprang up, mounted his steed, and rode on in pursuit of the animal, and never reined in until it suddenly disappeared as if the earth had swallowed it up.

The prince looked on every side, and beheld before him a charming lady, beautiful as a perī—her stature straight as a box-tree; her mouth small as the end of a hair; her waist a hair's breadth. One wonders not to find a rose growing by a fountain; but if it is found springing from a salt-marsh, it may well cause surprise. The prince was galloping in pursuit of a wild ass, and if he missed it, he found an antelope; he was in search of a serpent, and found the treasure in its stead.[1] "A table," thought he to himself, "has descended from heaven."—"O envy of hūrī and perī," said he, addressing her, "for human being possesses not such beauty, thou art an angel, and Paradise is thy home; say, what wouldst thou in this world of gloom?"[2] The

---

[1] It is a popular notion among Muslims—borrowed probably from the Hindūs, who have the same superstition—that hidden treasure is guarded by serpents.

[2] "So excessive," remarks Sir William Ouseley, "is the admiration of the amorous Persians for female beauty, that those who possess it in an eminent degree are considered by them as something more than mortal. Of this opinion is the celebrated poet Khusrū, in the beginning of one of his *gazals:*
'Think not that beautiful damsels are of the human race;
They are houris of Paradise, or angels, or superior spirits.'"
Akin to this poetical idea is the following fine passage, from the *King's Quair* (or Book) of James I of Scotland, on seeing Lady Jane Beaufort walking in the garden of Windsor Castle :

damsel replied: "One must not hide one's complaint from the physician. I once beheld thee at a distance, from my terrace. I had ascended to look for the new moon, when, to my unexpected good fortune, the sun appeared. (Thus) one sought the moon, and found the sun; one looked for the Goblet, and found Jamshīd.[1] Since thou art the amber and I the straw, tell me, how can I preserve my heart? O captivating youth, the heart is a source of affliction;—I would not wish even an infidel the misfortune to have his heart enslaved."—The prince was carried away by his desires; for the fountain was in sight, and his lip was parched. The damsel pointed to her abode, and led the way, while the prince rode on after her till they

> "Ah, sweet! are ye a worldly creature,
> Or heavenly thing in likeness of nature?
> Or are ye god Cupid his own princess,
> And coming are to loose me out of band?
> Or are ye very Nature the goddess,
> That have depainted with your heavenly hand
> This garden full of flowers as they stand?"

And the great Persian Sa'dī:
> "Who is walking there—thou, or a tall cypress?
> Or is it an angel in human shape?"

And the Hindū Somadeva: "When the young man saw her, she at once robbed him of his heart, and he was bewildered by love, and no longer master of his feelings. He said to himself: 'Can this be Rati come in person to gather flowers accumulated by spring, in order to make arrows for the god of Love? or is it the presiding goddess of the wood, come to worship the spring?"

[1] See note 2, page 6.

reached a desolate spot.   She entered, and cried out:
"Come and see what I have brought hither by my
contrivance!"[1]   From every corner the black ghūls[2]
rushed out.   The prince, on seeing them, was alarmed
for his life, and conning a prayer,[3] fled to the desert.
He urged on his steed, while the female pursued him,
begging him not to desert her thus cruelly.—"Excuse
me," said the prince; "I am not my own master, but
in the hands of another [*i.e.* his steed].   Whatever I
sew, he undoes; I go not willingly, but he flies with
me."—The damsel continues to entreat; but the prince
persists in not returning.

*   *   *   *   *

Although the pages of the manuscript are numbered
consecutively, a leaf is wanting here.   The conclusion

---

[1] "And behold, the damsel, sporting with the sprites, and
saying to them : 'Behold, I have brought to you a young man,
the son of a king.'"—*Mishlé Sandabar.*

[2] In the Greek version, *lamiæ*, ogresses.—Ghūls (or ghouls)
are a species of demons, believed by Muslims to feed on human
flesh, and to have the power of assuming any form they choose,
to decoy unwary travellers.   In the present case, the ghūl had
first assumed the form of a wild ass, which the prince eagerly
chased, and next that of a beautiful girl.   The ghūls correspond
to the Vetālas, Pisāchas, Yoginis, and Dākinis of Indian mytho-
logy, who play prominent parts in many of the ancient Hindū
fictions.

[3] "And the youth, straightway directing his eyes and hands
to heaven, besought him [*i.e.*, God], saying," &c.—*Syntipas.*

may be guessed from *Syntipas*, where, as soon as the prince had uttered a prayer, the damsel falls powerless on the ground, unable longer to pursue him; while the prince sets off at full speed, and reaches home in safety. [7]

*   *   *   *   *

The commencement of the next chapter is wanting, but it, of course, contained the order of the king for the execution of his son, which is stayed by the Third Vazīr, who, repairing to the foot of the throne, intercedes for the prince. He counsels the king to put no faith in slaves. "If you desire a son," said he, "ask in marriage the daughter of the emperor of China; for whenever you have a son by a slave, he will be of evil disposition, and ill-affected towards you: a beggar will be introduced to your court, and a black seated on your throne. Listen not to the advice of the worthless; slay not your son rashly; otherwise you will repent, as the officer did of killing his cat." The vazīr then relates the

Story of the Snake and the Cat.[1]

[IN a city of Cathay there dwelt a good and blameless woman with her husband. By-and-by she bore him a son, and thereupon died. The man got a nurse to

---

[1] Here presented somewhat more fully than it is given by Falconer.

bring up the child. Now he had a cat, of which he was very fond, and to which his wife had been also much attached.

One day the man went out on some business, and the nurse also had left the house, no one remaining but the infant and the cat. Presently a frightful snake came in, and made for the cradle to devour the child. The cat sprang upon it, and after a desperate fight succeeded in killing it. When the man returned, he was horrified at seeing a mangled mass lying on the floor. The snake had vomited so much blood and poison that its form was hidden, and the man, thinking that the cat, which came up to him, rubbing against his legs, had killed his son, struck it a blow, and slew it on the spot. But immediately after he discovered the truth of the matter, how the poor cat had killed the snake in defence of the boy, and his grief knew no bounds.][1]

---

[1] This story is not found in any of the Arabic texts. In the Syriac, Greek, Hebrew, and old Castilian versions it is a *dog* that kills the snake. In the *Pancha Tantra*, where the same story occurs (B. v, Fab. 2), it is, more appropriately, a *mungūs*— "the fierce hostility of which creature to snakes," remarks Dr. H. H. Wilson, "and its singular power of killing them, are in India so well known as to have become proverbial, and are verifiable by daily observation. It is doubtful," he adds, "if a dog has either any instinctive enmity to snakes, or any charac- teristic dexterity in destroying them." In *Calila and Dimna* and the *Hitopadesa* the snake is killed by a *weasel*, of which the mungūs, or ichneumon, is a species. See Appendix, No. 8.

"Shed not, then, the blood of your innocent son," proceeds the vazír. "If the officer had reflected, he would not have acted so rashly. Slay not a prince on the testimony of a woman. Women are fickle and inconstant, and pray at ten qiblas[1] in one day. I will now, with your Majesty's permission, relate a story, still more entertaining than the last, of the merchant's wife and the old woman who conducted her to a lover."

Story of the Libertine Husband.[2]

An old man had married a young and beautiful wife. The husband used frequently to go to his farm in the country, leaving his wife in town. Upon those occasions she threw off all restraint, and met many lovers; and an old woman acted as her go-between. The husband once, on returning to town, instead of going home, applies to the old woman to introduce him to a mistress; and his own wife, not knowing whom she was to meet, is induced to grant him an assignation. She manages so well to dissemble her own confusion,

---

[1] The term *qibla*, which signifies "the point of adoration," is commonly applied to the *Ka'ba* ("cubical house"), or Temple, in Mecca; and to this point every Muslim must turn his face when he prays.

[2] In *Syntipas*, this forms the conclusion of the story of the Go-Between and the She-Dog. The first portion subsequently appears, in this text, as the second tale of the Fourth Vazír.

and reproaches him so naturally, that he never suspects her guilt, but entreats on his knees to be forgiven his infidelity. [9]

The king's resolution is again shaken by those tales, and he remands his son to prison.

The Damsel now presents herself a fourth time, and demands justice, threatening, if it is refused, to drink a cup of poison which she holds in her hand. She relates the

Story of the Monkey, the Fig-Tree, and the Boar.

AN old monkey, finding himself a burden to his wife and family, takes leave of them, and wanders forth into the world. After suffering much distress, he at last reaches a spot in a forest full of every sort of fruit, and abounding in figs so delicious that you would have supposed them composed of sugar and milk. Here, reposing from the fatigues of travel, he slept long and soundly. When he awoke, he performed his ablutions in the stream, and ate some fruit. Although his heart burned when he thought of his family and relations, of what avail was it to grieve? Having here abundance of provision, he quitted not the spot the whole year. He reserved a quantity of the fruit on the branches for the winter. In the meantime a boar, fleeing from the combat, with his face bathed in blood and the stream flowing from every hair of his body, appeared in the forest, like sudden death entering a door. After lying for a week in feebleness, the wounded boar went about in search of food, but in vain, it being now winter. At length he saw the monkey seated on a fig-tree, every branch of which was laden with figs. He implored the monkey to give him some food; upon which it threw him down a lapful of fresh figs, a *mun* or more. These he quickly devoured, and still demanded more, until he had eaten ten *muns*, and the tree was stripped of fruit. The boar now threatened, and the monkey prayed to heaven for deliverance; upon which the boar, springing upon the tree, fell back, broke its neck, and expired. [10]

"Fear, then, that God by whom this was brought about, and grant me justice," added the Damsel, "remembering that the throne of tyrants shall be overturned."

The king is now more determined than ever on the death of his son, and orders wood to be brought together, that he may be burnt by the executioner; upon which the Fourth Vazir presents himself, and intercedes for the prince. To show the danger of trusting in women, he relates the

Story of the Bathkeeper,

who conducted his wife to the son of the king of
Kanūj.[1]—He next relates the

Story of the Go-Between and the She-Dog.

[IN the city of Shūstar (in Khūzistān, Persia) a gay
young gallant, riding to the chase one day, sees a peri-
faced damsel at a lattice-window, and immediately
falls in love with her. He engages a crafty old woman
to intercede with the lady in his behalf, but she indignantly refuses to entertain any lover, and sends the
go-between away unsuccessful. After some little time
the old woman disguises herself as a devotee, and thus
contrives to obtain admission to the house, soon gains
the confidence of the servants, and ultimately becomes

---

[1] An obscene story of a man whose cupidity induced him to
become a party to the dishonour of his own wife. (See *Syntipas*,
page 48 of Boissonade, page 36 of Eberhard.) This is one of the
four tales which are common to both the Western and the Eastern
groups of the Book of Sindibād. In the Latin text, *Historia
Septem Sapientum Romæ*, as well as in the English prose and
Scottish metrical versions, it is fused with a rather stupid tale of
"Janus and the Defence of Rome." But in the most ancient of
the French versions, *Dolopathos*, and two early English metrical
versions, this story is given separately. (See the *Seven Sages*,
Percy Society Reprints, vol. xvi, page 52.)—A variant, possibly
the original form, is found in the *Hitopadesa*, ch. i, fab. 8 : "The
King's Son and the Merchant's Wife."

the familiar companion of the lady herself. One day this artful and hypocritical old hag secretly feeds the lady's she-dog with cakes strongly seasoned, which cause the creature's eyes to water as though it wept. The lady, observing this, expresses her surprise, and asks the old woman the cause. At first she pretends to be averse to explain the reason why the dog wept, but, after much entreaty, she informs the lady that the dog was once a beautiful damsel, who had been changed into that form as a punishment for rejecting a lover's suit. Alarmed at this tale, the lady confesses that she had refused to receive the addresses of a youth who had professed his love for her through an old woman; but now, lest she should in like manner be transformed into a she-dog, she is willing to grant him an interview. The crafty old go-between hastens to the amorous youth and informs him of the success of her trick; and soon after the lady and her lover are united.][1]

*   *   *   *   *

[There is here a very considerable displacement in the leaves of the MS., and some deficiencies occur throughout the remainder of the volume. The prince

---

[1] Falconer has not given this story, but refers the reader to the version of it in *Syntipas,* p. 51 [of Boissonade, p. 39 of Eberhard]. He does not seem to have observed that the story as found in the Greek and other versions is in this text divided

was doubtless remanded when the fourth vazīr had concluded his second story, as above; and the Damsel, of course, appeared for the fifth time, and urged the king to put his son to death, but it is impossible to say whether she told a story on this occasion, as all this portion of the text is wanting. We must now turn from folio 86 to folio 127 (the intervening leaves being misplaced), where we find but three pages remaining of what is evidently the *first* story of the Fifth Vazīr, from which it can only be conjectured that it relates to a lady who had dissipated, with her paramour, her husband's wealth, during his absence. From what remains, it may be entitled the

Story of the Lady whose Hair was cut off.[1]

WHEN the lady was excited with wine, her lover came into her mind, and she lost her wits, and forgot where she was. The old companion leapt into her suddenly, and with a dagger she cut her hair to the roots. She scratched her cheek with her nails, till her face was

---

into two, the conclusion forming the second tale of the Third Vazīr—page 58.—For variants of this widely-diffused tale, see Appendix, No. 11.

[1] This fragment and the complete story which follows, related by the Fifth Vazīr, are not mentioned in Falconer's analysis; and what he conjectured to be told by this vazīr is the second story of the Seventh Vazīr.

bathed in blood.   At dawn the lady went forth from
the house, confused as her own tresses.   When she
reached home she began to weep; tore her collar and
bared her head—her face all wounds with her nails.
She raised her cries and wail to the moon; twisted her
hairs round her fingers, pulled them out, and strewed
them by handfuls all the way home, so that her path
resembled the Milky Way therewith; saying that her
husband's days were come to an end—a stranger had
unexpectedly told her that news.   The women gathered
in her street, and they all became as disordered as her
hair.   One said: "The poor thing! see how, fair
creature, for the death of her husband, she has cut
off her hair!"   Another said: "See her face, how she
has torn it into wounds!   See what she has done to her
bosom!"   There now befell wailings in that dwelling;
the mansion was filled with the weeping of mourners.
She prepared a worthy wake for her husband, and
gave food.[1]—After a month had elapsed, her lord
came home.   Like fire from iron, the woman leapt
out, and exclaimed: "Take care, O young man—you
outside-cheat!   I knew not if thou wast in the bath
stoke-hole or in the tomb.   For thy death have I cut
off my hair from the roots, and torn all my face with
my nails.   With whom have you been in close converse?
Tell me, with whom have you been in close search?

---

[1] It is customary in Persia to distribute food to friends and the
poor at wakes.

If I had a little once, not an atom now remains;—for
this reason, of thy ten houses not a farthing has been
left. What an evil day was that on which we were
joined!" Thus did she vent her ill-temper. Her lord
said: "O kind companion, what may it all be? Let
no harm come to thy life." He then made up for all
the expenses that had befallen, and paid all the money
she had borrowed.—Thus do women practise sleight-
of-hand; with craft thus do they split hairs. Though
a woman were a phœnix, she were best plucked of
feathers; though she were a noble falcon, she were
best with her head wrung off. None knows the tricks
and spells of women;—make mourning a duty under
her sway, and weep blood.[1]

"If his Majesty," continued the Fifth Vazir, "is not
wearied by these headache-giving tales, I will relate
another example."

Story of the Woman who Outwitted her Father-in-Law.[2]

In days of yore there lived a just and pious husband-
man, who sowed the seeds of goodness and reaped a
hundred-fold. His house was all the year full of corn;
his fields abounded with flocks; and on the poor he

---

[1] See Appendix, No. 12.

[2] "Story of the Woman who brought her Lover by the
Water-Way," etc.

bestowed a portion of his wealth. He had a Baby-
lonish wife; a magician-deceiver—all coquetry and
leering. One day, when he was abroad inspecting the
harvest of his fields, this perī-faced one went up to
the terrace of the mansion, and there, like a fowler,
she spread her snare. A graceful youth was pacing
the plain, and coming near the enclosure of the
harem, he beheld the face of that hūrī—that mail-
haired beauty, of the lasso-tresses—and field and
waste were filled with light. Now his sighs arose
from his heart; now his feet sank in the clay. From
above the perī-faced one shook her head, and stroked
her face and bosom.

In the street of this youth dwelt an aged woman;—
in foxery she was the old wolf of the city; in trickery,
the crafty dissembler of the age. To her the young
man went, and told her what signs the lady had made
to him upon the roof of her house. The old woman
answered: "Thy beloved—thy passionate companion,
thy desired one—indicated thereby: 'Choose a damsel;
seek out a pomegranate-breasted one; if she be fair,
speak with her.'" So the youth sought out such a
girl, and sent her secretly, with a token. When she
had delivered her message, the lady pretended to be
very wroth; spoke harshly to her; made black her
face; and turned her out by the water-way. On
reaching her own house, the young man went to
meet her; and when he saw her plight and heard her
story, he ran along the road to the door of the old

woman. If he had a grief, he told it all; for one must not hide pain from the physician. The past-mistress thus answered him: "Knowest thou what thy beloved hath said?—'When Night draws her pitchy curtain over her head, and the Ethiop king leads his host against Rūm, come thou into the garden by the way of the water, for this indeed is the proper way.'"[1]

By reason of this the youth went off glad and bright. And when it was night he went into the garden. The jasmine-faced one came from the house into the garden, which was (as it were) filled with lamps by (the brightness of) her cheek. In one place were the box-tree and the cypress; the hawk and the pheasant made peace together. Who would think that this night was the night of treachery? . . When it was midnight, sleep bore them off. An aged man, who was father to her husband, chanced to come out of the house. He was confounded at what he saw in the garden, and took away her anklets. Awaking soon afterwards, she perceived what had befallen her, and, having dismissed her companion, went into the house and lay down. And when an hour yet remained of the night, her husband awoke, and she said to him: "O kind comrade, would not the garden be more pleasant than the house? On such a day the garden is a spring-tide. When the rose smiles, the house becomes a prison.

---

[1] The lady having conveyed this message by blackening the girl's face (as the symbol of *night*), and sending her away by the path skirting the pond in the garden.

In the morning, when the nightingale laments from the bough, put forth thy head, like a rose, from the corner of the pavilion. Why liest thou when thou hast slept so long? Now are the walks of garden and orchard pleasant; for the garden is become the place of the nightingale, not of the crow." Then she took her husband by the hand, and with him entered like a nightingale flushed into the rose-bower. In that same place where the anklets had been taken off her feet, she threw down a mat, and lay thus with her husband till the morning. Then said the woman to him: "Ask thy father what he wishes of me. He is neither my uncle nor my aunt;—why does he take off my two anklets?" The young man was angry with his father, saying to her: "Why should he give thee a headache?"

When that experienced man came into the garden from the mansion, he told the whole affair to the youth —told him with displeasure the affair of the anklets. He flared up, and was very wroth with his father, and said to him: "Thou hast beheld all this only in a dream; for this woman was not separated from me this night. Go, master, be shamed before God. It was I who was with her in that place where she lay." When the father heard this tale from his son, he bowed his head and was shamed. Then made he apologies to the woman; he increased her dower, and gave her the half of that garden.[1]

---

[1] See Appendix, No. 13.

The king was grieved at this story; he reflected a
moment, and then commanded the prince to be again
removed to prison.]

The Damsel now presents herself the sixth time,
and demands redress. She inveighs against the.vazīr,
and cautions the king not to trust him. She then
relates the

Story of Sal'ūk the Robber, the Lion, and the Monkey.

IN the happy reign of Farīdūn,[1] a caravan pitched
their tents by the side of a running stream. Thither
a robber of great daring, who would have stolen the
nose from the face of a lion, came by night in
the hope of meeting with some booty, but finding
a sentinel at every corner, and seeing that his art
would be of no avail, he departed. Thinking, however, that he might contrive to steal some of the
fleetest of the horses, he sat down in the midst of
the cattle to watch his opportunity. By chance, a
lion, in search of prey, passed near the caravan,
and fixed his desire on the herds; but from the
outcry raised by the crowd, he could not succeed,
and remained quiet in his place. Sal'ūk, seeing no
other means of safety or escape, suddenly sprang on

---

[1] Farīdūn was the sixth of the Pīshdādī dynasty of ancient
kings of Persia.

the lion's back and held fast. The lion, alarmed, ran off with his rider, and ceased not running the whole night.[1] The robber was exhausted with sitting on the lion's back, yet dared not quit it for almost certain death.

I once heard a traveller in Arabia say, that if you fix a determined gaze on a lion, he will that instant take to flight; while, if you flee from him, he will pursue you. In all cases of danger, courage is the best security. The lion, under his rider, had by this time become timorous as a mouse. Coming to a lofty tree, he went under its shade; upon which Sal'ūk sprang boldly from his seat into the tree. The lion on his part also was glad to escape from his rider, and took to flight with his tail trailing on the ground. Meeting a monkey, he was at first inclined to flee, thinking it might be the man, but observing his humble attitude, he stopped. The monkey, after respectfully saluting him, and inquiring after his royal health, asked him why he was travelling without his train, whither he was going, and on what object—at the same time offering his services. The lion related his adventure, and told him that his enemy was on a

---

[1] In the Syriac text, a party with cattle take up their lodging · in a caravanserai, leaving the gate open. During the night a lion enters in quest of prey, and shortly after a bold thief, who, groping for a fat animal, mistakes the lion for a horse, and mounts him; and the lion, supposing he has got the watchman on his back, rushes off with him in a great fright.

tree not far off. The monkey reproached him for
being afraid of such a foe. The lion then conducted
him to the tree, and the monkey mounted into its
branches, not observing that the robber was concealed
in a cleft of it underneath him. The man suddenly
seized him, and grasped him so powerfully that he
instantly expired. Be not forward or precipitate, and
engage not in a contest with one who is your superior
in strength. The lion, seeing what had taken place,
betook himself to flight. [14]

The king reflects on this tale, and resolves to put
his son to death before his power should increase,
when it might be too late.

The Sixth Vazīr, hearing of his Majesty's change
of determination, comes before him to intercede for
the prince. He inveighs, like the rest, against women,
and advises his Majesty to put no trust in them. In
proof of his assertions, he relates the

*Story of the Perī and the Religious Man; his
learning the Great Name; and his consulting
with his Wife.*

A HOLY man, who spent all his time in devotion, had
a perī for his constant and familiar companion for
many years. At length, the perī is obliged to leave

him,[1] word having been brought her of the illness of one of her children.   On parting, she teaches him the "Three Great Names" (of God), on pronouncing one of which, on any great emergency, his wish will be immediately accomplished.   One night the shaykh communicates the circumstance to his wife, who dictates to him what he is to wish for.   The result shows the folly of consulting with women; but it is unfit to be repeated.   It is sufficient to say that the

---

[1] Falconer cites, in the original Persian, the reflections of the devotee on taking leave of the perī, of which Mr. J. W. Redhouse, the eminent Orientalist, has kindly furnished the following close, line-for-line rendering—the verses have, probably, a mystical (sūfī) signification: "more is meant than meets the ear:"

How happy is he who has no acquaintance,
So that, following on separation, solitude be not.
Like the phœnix, go, be thy own companion;
Thy own associate; thy own confidant be thou:
So that to taste the poison of separation need for thee be not;
So that to bear the pang of separateness need for thee be not.
When the soul for a time has accustomed itself to the body,
See with what difficulty it comes up out of the body.
Happy the man who hath not seen the bazaar of the world,
Nor experienced the sorrow, trouble, bother of the world.
As at first there is in it the pang of being born,
So at last there is in it the pang of giving up the ghost.
The world is the city of grief, the house of woe;
Not a place of rest, but an abode of dragons:
Go not to sleep in the den of dragons;
Cast not thyself into the trap of calamity.
Be it not that the thorn take the habit of [piercing] the rose;
For it is a death to turn away one's affection from a beloved.

tale is similar to that of the "Three Wishes," by
La Fontaine, to Prior's "Ladle," and to that given
in *Syntipas* [p. 84 of Boissonade, p. 66 of Eberhard.][1]

[The vazīr then recounts the stratagem of the old
woman with the merchant's wife and the young man:

Story of the Concealed Robe.[2]

IN old times there was a prince of the city of Ray,
who spent all his time with minstrels, harps, and lutes;
he was never without mirth all the year—a youth
whose lot had never been troubled.   He had no
anxiety for the future, no business save pleasure.   He
never tasted grief, but ever tasted wine.   He had a
hundred lovers in every corner; every eye waited on
his road; his ward thronged with beauties, he was
never a moment without coquetry and drinking.

One night, at the time when he thought to sleep,
when he knew not harp from rebeck, one of his fair
companions said to him: "To-day I saw a beauty,
whose face none ever beheld save the mirror, whose
hair none ever caressed save the comb—a jasmine-
cheeked one from the gardens of Paradise, beside

---

[1] See Appendix, No. 15.

[2] Falconer has omitted this story (which is known through
other versions under the title of "The Burnt Cloth"), because
it is also found in Scott's *Seven Vazīrs*, where, however, it is
told very differently.

whom the hūrīs were ugly as demons." The wine-flushed man was ravished with her locks; all night he slept not for passion of that moon (*i.e.* the damsel); he spoke of nought but her image. When it was day, he arose, and thought to go to her street. He asked for her ward, and he (soon) began to perceive her odour.[1] He inquired regarding her of the neighbours, the eunuchs, and the duennas coming and going. By chance, her fairy-cheek was at the window: the youth had paused at the head of the street; at the same moment came that envy of the perīs—like the petal of the rose for grace and freshness, the perspiration was on the rose of her face, the hyacinths of her hair were in confusion. The youth became intoxicated by the zephyr from her rose; straightway his wits forsook him; suddenly his foot fell into the snare; suddenly his foot slipped from the roof; he flung himself with his own hands into the net, like the fawn that rushes headlong into the lasso. When the fairy-faced hūrī passed quickly away, how shall I tell what passed over him? He no longer knew his head from his foot, through his inebriety (with love); he no longer knew

---

[1] The fragrant odour here alluded to is that arising from perspiration: Eastern poets commonly comparing beautiful girls · to the nymphs of Paradise, whose perspiration is to be odoriferous as musk. Thus, the pre-Islamite Arabian poet Imra'u-'l-Qays, referring to two of his former "flames," says that "when they departed, musk was diffused from them, as the eastern gale sheds the perfume of the clove."

height or depth. He returned helpless from that street
to his own house, where he gave himself up to grief.

The youth had an old woman in the house, who was
a mistress of spells and charms; who had now cleared
her hands from affairs of the world, but had formerly
arranged many such matters. He went to her, and
spoke with her, for the pain of the soul must not be
hidden. When she heard his tale, she began to
consider how to act. She had an old comrade, an
effeminate one; who was fallen into the worst of plights;
whose back was become (bent) like a harp, through
old age; whose voice was like the boom of a drum;
who was altogether hideous;—time had given him
sticks for feet. He signified to the youth that this
business was in his way. So the youth told what was
on his heart, for one must not conceal the secret from
the counsellor. He replied: "Know, O youth, that
that envy of Venus and the moon is the wife of a
great merchant of our city, at whose counter Kārūn[1]
would be a beggar. To-morrow do thou go before his
shop, and buy of him a costly piece of raiment: give
it to me, and thou shalt see how I will manage this
business."

So next day the youth went to the bazaar, and
bought a robe of the merchant, which he gave to the
effeminate one, who proceeded to the street where the

---

[1] Kārūn is the Korah of the Bible, and, according to Muslim
legends, possessed enormous wealth. See the 28th chapter of
Sale's *Koran*, and his note.

moon-faced one dwelt, and by craft managed to get into
the house. When the fairy-face saw his demon-like
form, she laughed and ran before him. After a while
she brought a tray of food, and sat down beside him;
and he made friends with her. And when the girl was
not looking, he slipped the robe under the husband's
pillow, soon after which he left the house. When the
good-man came back, as usual (for he was never a
night absent from the house), he looked at the pillow,
and saw that robe. He was amazed, and tore up the
robe. As this sight was not far from sin, he was disgusted with life and with woman, and he struck the
poor thing's head and face. The woman managed to
escape from him, and went to her mother.

One day the vile hag came forth from her house,
and went to the house where the lady was, and inquired what had befallen her. The lady answered:
" My husband came in and struck me, though I had
done nothing;—I know of nothing wrong that I did; I
said nothing either good or bad. It seems as though
they had cast a spell on him to make him act thus.
What can I do in such a case?" The ill-omened hag
thus answered her: "I know a skilful diviner, than
whom no one better knows secrets; the heavens are to
him as the earth; everything from the moon to the
earth is as wax under his seal; never have I seen any
one who speaks more truly than he;—he will certainly
be able to divine thy case, and annul the enchantment
against thee." With such words she gained her confi-

dence; and returning to the youth's house, she told
him all that had happened, and he was greatly pleased
with what he heard.　In the morning he adorned the
house as for a banquet; made it like a garden when
the roses are in bloom; and collected lutists and
harpers, for they say that wine without music is grief.
When all was ready and he was waiting their coming,
there entered the demon, and after her the fairy, whose
cheek was studded with perspiration, like the rose with
dew in the morning.　She was come to that house in
order that he might draw her out a charm.　The youth
at once came forward to meet her, bowing much and
apologising: the fairy-face saw him whose heart was
distracted for her—saw him whose nights were sleep-
less through longing for her.　That same moment she
forgot the merchant—forgot right and wrong.　The hag
then left the house, for the arrow had struck the mark.
The youth then took her by the hand and seated
her.　.　.　The diviner looked in her face and discovered the state of her mind.　.　.　When the lady
had returned to her mother's house, the youth called
for the hag, and said: "Since thou hast done so well,
and forgotten nothing;—as thou hast done a kindness,
complete it: make peace between these two mates—
speak of the virtue and goodness of the wife."　She
said: "Yes; for such is my work."

In the morning she went to the bazaar, and said to
the merchant: "They have not accepted thy stuff, so I
am disgusted and vexed for shame.　I went on to the

house of prosperity (*i.e.* his own house), and there I
left the stuff. Look, for it is under thy pillow. God
forbid that any should have grieved through this (my
mistake)." She then took the price of the stuff from
the merchant, and returned to her master. When the
merchant heard this story from the old woman, it
seemed to him to be true, and he repented of what he
had done. He took many robes better than that one,
of Khataian, Baghdādī, and Chinese stuffs, and gave
them to his wife, and kissed her, and begged for
pardon, saying: "My wife, the right was with thee."
He rubbed his head against her feet, and so soothed
and did away her displeasure.]¹

The king is again persuaded to suspend the execution, and to remand his son to prison.

The Damsel comes the Seventh Time before the King, rends her Garments, and demands Justice.

When the Damsel learned that her calumnies
were ineffectual, and that the wrath of his Majesty,
and the thirst for his son's blood, which she had
excited, had been dispelled by the counsels of his
sage minister, thinking that she might yet conceal
from him her crime, she approached the throne,
and shedding tears, exclaimed: "O king, whither is

---

¹ See Appendix, No. 16.

departed that justice for which you were renowned?
Dread that God who created the soul, and made
you ruler of the earth. When a son aims, as yours
has done, at the life of his father, he is a curse,
and not a blessing. Trust not your vazīr, who is
attached to other interests than yours, and who seeks
only the aggrandisement of his own family. You
yourself exercise no real sovereignty, but are guided
in everything by him, and have not the liberty of a
common rustic. If I have spoken too freely, consider
for whose interest I am speaking. You are a mighty
sovereign, and honoured with the esteem of other
monarchs. Your son is but an ignorant boy, pleased
with his panther and his hawk;[1] while your vazīr is so
intent on his own ambitious schemes, that he knows
not months from years: entrust not the management
of your kingdom to a foe. You have gained it by the
sword; leave it not to the needle. Since this vazīr is
leagued with your son, choose another minister. What
will it avail you to lament my fate, when I shall be in
my grave? You know what a prince once experienced
from his [father's] vazīr, who acknowledged not the
ties of gratitude, but involved him in dire calamity?
If your Majesty desires it, I will relate the story." The

---

[1] The cheetah, a species of panther, is trained in India and
Persia to hunt the antelope.—Hawking, long a favourite sport
in Europe, is still a common diversion of the Persians and
Arabs. For a graphic description of hunting the antelope with
hawks as well as dogs, see Malcolm's *Sketches of Persia.*

king having expressed a wish to hear it, the Damsel relates the

Story of the Prince who went to hunt, and the stratagem which the Vazir practised on him.

*   *   *   *   *

[The whole of this story, as Falconer has stated, is wanting in the manuscript It is the tale of the prince who was changed into a woman by drinking at an enchanted fountain.—See Scott's version of the *Seven Vazīrs* in the present volume, where it forms the fourth story of the Damsel.

We must now turn back to the displaced leaves —*folia* 87 to 126 inclusive—which should follow the missing story of the Changed Sex. And here is another deficiency; but it may be supposed that, as usual, the king once more gives orders for the execution of his son, upon which the Seventh Vazir presents himself, and, having prevailed upon his Majesty to stay the execution, begins to relate the

Story of the King and the Virtuous Wife,[1]

the commencement of which is also wanting, but it was probably similar to that of the story as found in

---

[1] Or, "The Lion's Track."—This fragment seems also to have escaped Falconer's notice, at least, it finds no place in his analysis.

Syntipas and other old versions: A king, who was very fond of women, chanced one day to see a beautiful lady on the terrace of her house, and immediately became enamoured of her. Having ascertained that she was the wife of one of his officers, or ministers, the king despatched him on a distant expedition, and soon after visited the lady one evening. Now this lady was as virtuous as she was beautiful, and, pretending to accede to the king's desire, she gave him a book to read while she bathed and adorned herself. This book consisted of warnings against the indulgence of illicit passions, and in the first page of what remains of the story, the king seems to be engaged in reading it with great interest, and the narrative thus proceeds: .

When the king reflected on these things, he repented of all he had previously done; and when the lady came in at the door, he looked on her with a different eye. He offered excuses to her; gave her a signet-ring[1] with his name on it, in order that it might be a keepsake for her, and then went to his own palace, with his heart and soul wounded for what he had done. That wine-drinking, beauty-adoring king became by this means a pure devotee, with the sacred volume (the Qur'ān) ever in his hand. He repented of his former wickedness, and never again did he but what was lawful.

---

[1] In the Greek and Arabic versions the king *forgets* his ring; in the Hebrew, his *cane;* in the old Castilian, his *sandals.*

F

One night the lady's husband came home unexpectedly. She had placed beside her the ring, which shone afar, like (the planet) Jupiter. And when he saw it, he was confounded; he examined it, and read the inscription, and recognising the royal name of the king thereon, earth and heaven became black in his eyes. The ring, which was of diamond, became a diamond for the heart of that master—it made him bleed for such a lot, as though there was poison under that signet. He thrust her forth of the house, and said nothing.

The brother of the lady went before the king, and made complaint that "That good-man (his sister's husband) took from us a holding; without cause he has drawn back his hand from it: ask why he has left it." The king demanded of that broken-hearted one: "What is the cause of thy leaving it? If there has arisen a quarrel, on whose account is it?" Then the good-man answered thus: "O king, Defender of the Faith, Issuer of Command, I saw therein the track of the lion's foot;—can one work in the lion's place? Otherwise, there is no complaint against my ground; but it is not prudent to go in the lion's track." The king knew that this was the lady's husband, and the affair of the ring flashed upon him. So he encouraged him, saying: "Make not ill thy heart: thou art mistaken. Do not commit a fault against thyself. The lion that was there did not any harm." On hearing this, the man's heart was set at rest, and he repented the trouble and vexation he had caused his wife; he went at once and begged her forgiveness, and made all things pleasant for her. He sought the content-ment of her heart, for true was her word, and virtuous her condition.[1]

Having thus concluded, the vazīr then proceeds to relate the

Story of the Man who compiled a Book on the Wiles of Women.[2]

IN former days and early times, there was a wise man, active in his affairs; free from stain was his skirt; no sister, or mother, or mother-in-law had he. All his life he had lived in chastity—nought knew he, save prayer. Never in all his life had he seen woman's face; his heart was at peace from the witch, woman; his heart was undisturbed by antimony or collyrium.[3] Even the great ones of the faith, and the lions of the path, have

---

[1] See Appendix, No. 17.

[2] Falconer does not give this story, but refers to the version of it in *Syntipas*, from which, however, as well as from all other versions, it differs materially ; and he conjectured it to be told by the Fifth Vazīr, an error now rectified by the insertion of the two stories proper to that vazīr, which he has not noticed.

[3] It is perhaps hardly necessary to state that Asiatic women stain the edges of their eyelids with a black powder (called *kohl*), to increase the lustre of their naturally expressive eyes; and that antimony was formerly esteemed the best kind of collyrium.

glanced towards women.   Flee thou from aloes-wood
and ambergris,[1] as a child would escape from a lion.
All day he collected (tales of) the wiles of women.
He encompassed the world like the wind; he, the
master, became a disciple.   At length, one day he
arrived at a city, and he saw in that city an experienced
man, who (like himself) had spent his life in the same
work: for forty years he had traversed sea and land,
and finally composed a treatise on this subject,
adorned with the lies and excuses—the tricks and
contrivances of women.   This man became his guest,
and ate at the same table; and when they were done
with bread and tray, they began to converse on various
subjects, and he said that which was on his mind.
When he (the experienced man) saw what was the
object of his guest, he redeemed him from his trouble
and labour, by giving him the collection he had himself made, including the commentary which he had
also composed.   And thus the young man secured
what had been the object of his life from morn till
eve, and his work was completed.   Thereupon, longing for home seized upon his heart.   No evil is worse
than the plight of the poor; nothing is pleasanter than
one's own house.   In truth, when God gives daily
bread, why should the beggar trouble himself? . . .
The wise man desires his own country; for delightful

---

[1] In other words: " Keep far from women," who are, in the
East, addicted to the lavish use of perfumes.

is the sight of an old friend. What is pleasanter than
to return home after a long absence?[1]

He placed his books upon a camel, and proceeded
homeward. In returning he was like a hawk; he sped
in that direction as a falcon. At a village, one day's
journey from his city, one received him as a guest,
with honour, respect, and distinction. He set down
his chests of books outside, for there was no room in
the house sufficient to contain them. Presently some
important business called away the good-man of the
house, who, on leaving, thus commissioned his wife:
"O wise one, be not a moment neglectful of this
man." Having said this, he went off, and left his
wife, who was a rose like the cypress of Paradise.
The blackness (of her eyes) was like the Water of
Life; the sugar of her smile bound up the hand of
the cane. She was a spring-blossom, fresher than the
jasmine-leaf; covered with leaves and flowers fresher
than those in the meadow.

She came to seek an excuse of the youth;—see
what will come of this excuse-seeking! When he

---

[1] This is a favourite theme with poets of all lands and ages.
Thus Rudakī, the Father of Persian Poetry (*circa* A.D. 925),
exclaims, in his eulogium on Bukhara: "The gale cometh from
the stream on whose banks our relations and friends reside, and
with it wafts to us the fragrant information that we are sighed
after by our dear but distant companions. The sandy shore of
the Amū, however painful and disagreeable, shall, in the moment
of our return, feel pleasant to our feet as the softest silk."

beheld her, a torrent poured from his eyes. He fell
into the place of evil. He stumbled, and his face
became pale; his breath became cold as the wind of
autumn. The woman perceived how it was with him
—how her magic had worked on that Sāmirī. She sat
down, and soothed him. She asked, slowly and softly,
her face hidden in her linen veil: "Welcome! whence
hast thou come with joy? Thou hast adorned our
narrow hovel!" She was curious to know whether his
load was gold—she knew not that it was the load of an
ass! "O master," she said to him, "what is your load
—what manner of stuff is in it?" Painfully and slowly,
he gave answer, his heart filled with fire, and his soul
overthrown: "It is a number of books containing all
the wiles and devices of women." When the wanton
beauty heard these words, she tripped out of the
house. The poor wretch remained with his own
griefs;—there was none to draw the thorn from the
wound. He forgot good and bad; he became so that
he forgot himself. The crafty one came back, and
saved him. . . Come, now, and see his case: see
the end of his work and business. The labour of forty
years comes to nothing. His brain was confused, and
he became mad: though he was a friend, he became
a stranger. He washed out all that was in his books.
He ran from door to door like the mad. Now he
smote his breast with a stone, now he tore his collar.
His claims all went to the winds—all his austerity,
asceticism, and piety. At length, in this pain and

stress, he died;—there was none to snatch his soul from the hand of woman's wiles.]¹

The period during which the evil aspects in the prince's horoscope were to prevail having now come to a close, and the seven days during which he was to keep silence being ended, he sent a messenger to the chief vazīr to thank him for the exertions he had made in his behalf.² The vazīr, upon this, waited on the prince, who requested him to beg for him an audience

---

¹ See Appendix, No. 18.

² Professor Comparetti seems to have been misled by the French translator of Falconer's analysis when he states that the Prince, in this text, begins to speak on the seventh day. He certainly did speak to the prime vazīr on the seventh day, but did not appear at court until the day following. The text says : " When the star of the prince became good, that prince became prosperous, of victorious augury. Auspiciousness looked into his case ; inauspiciousness went away from his fortune. Thus the seven days passed over him, in which, like the lily, he never loosed his tongue. He sent to the grand vazīr, that experienced man of wisdom, saying : ' Thy efforts are thanked and approved. From the good comes ever good : who cuts a good branch from a bad root? Thy rights shall never be forgotten ; for the cotton of negligence is not in my ear.' . . This message reached the vazīr's ear, and he thanked God that that sleeping fortune had awakened. To the place where the king's son lay, which was a wretched dwelling, he came." The prince tells the vazīr to summon all the grandees *on the morrow* to the king's court, for then all should be made clear. Accordingly, next morning (the eighth day) the prince appears in court, and speaks in his own defence.

of his Majesty [on the morrow], when the nobles and courtiers should be all assembled. The vazîr joyfully hastened to the king, and announced the request of the prince, expressing his confidence that it would soon appear, before the whole assembly, who was innocent and who was guilty.

The king accordingly assembled his grandees [next day], and when he was seated on his throne, the sage Sindibād entered, and the king desired him to be seated. The prince next presented himself, and, after kissing his father's carpet, raising his head, he gave thanks to God that he was again permitted to appear at the foot of the throne. "When God wills not the destruction of any one," said he, "no ingenuity of man can effect it; and if it be decreed by him, it cannot be countervailed." In illustration of this remark, the Prince relates the

Story of the Poisoned Guests.[1]

[THERE was of old time an ocean-hearted (*i.e.* bountiful) one, by whose hands mines would have been emptied; a noble, of auspicious step and lofty purpose, who never kept his door shut upon guests; to whose mansion was neither door, lock, nor porter. If a poor man asked him for a dirham, he gave him a dînar; if one asked him for a scrap, he gave him an ass-load. Once a party of his friends, great men, relations and

---

[1] Here presented more fully than it is by Falconer.

companions of his, came to him as guests, as of wont;
came to his house and table. He received them after
the fashion of the generous, for this was ever his
custom. A slave-girl went to fetch milk, that he might
feast his guests with sugar and milk—two very good
things. She covered not the top of the milk-dish.
Hearken to these words, and take warning: A stork
was passing in the air, having snatched up an old
snake from the desert. Poison was dropping through
the air from that snake. How can one fly from the
decrees of fate? Saliva dropped from the mouth of
that viper, and that milk was mixed with poison; and
whoever took any of that milk fell down, and there
died forthwith.][1]

"Who was guilty in this instance?" asked the prince;
"and who ought to have been punished?" One said:
"Doubtless, the female slave, because she did not
cover up the milk." Another said: "The stork was to
blame for having the snake in its mouth." Another
said: "The snake, for dropping its venom in the milk."
"Nay, nay," said a fourth; "but the giver of the entertainment, who left it to his slave to bring the milk."—
The prince said: "All these opinions are mistaken.
No one was to blame; it was the decree of God."

"There are four things," continued the prince,
"about which the wise do not distress themselves:
First—One's daily bread; for however scant it may

---

[1] See Appendix, No. 19.

be, it will undoubtedly suffice to conduct one to his grave. *Second*—Death, which none can avert or retard, and which ought, therefore, to be met with resignation. *Third*—One's destiny, which will not cease to attend a man, notwithstanding all his exertions. *Fourth*—Distress, which neither the wise nor the foolish can remedy.

"One is constantly engaged in devotion; another is for ever in the tavern. Who leads the one to the street of the tavern?—who draws the other to the practice of devotion?

"Many a man, though immersed in the water, has reached the shore, while the sailor has not seen it: many an alchemist has gone to his grave poor and naked as he first entered the world; many a grave-digger has found unexpectedly the treasure of Farīdūn.[1] The one and the other events are alike the ordinance of God. Whatever he decrees inevitably happens. If a man undergoes imprisonment and chains, it is not the order of any one, but the decree of destiny."

When the king heard this address of his son, he was filled with admiration of his wisdom; he kissed his face, and took him to his bosom, and all his former love for him returned. He opened the doors of his treasury, and enriched the poor and needy. He set the prisoners free, and the debtors from their confine-

---

[1] Thus Sa'dī : "The alchemist died of grief and distress, while the blockhead found treasure under a ruin."

ment. He now turned his thoughts to the philosopher Sindibād; and when he reflected how he had hazarded his life, his esteem for him increased, and he resolved to reward him munificently. He sent for him, and bestowed ample benefactions on the sage himself, his sons, and dependants.

He then inquired of Sindibād how it happened that the prince was at first averse to learning, and afterwards made such proficiency: how he was at first silent, and afterwards had his mouth opened. Sindibād kissed the hand of his Majesty, and after offering vows for his prosperity, replied: "Your Majesty is aware that everything is restricted to its appointed season. The winds of winter come not in spring. The tree while it is yet but a sapling bears no fruit, but yields it when it has grown tall and affords a shade. The business was at first beset with difficulties. Much did I labour, and the seed which I sowed has sprung up and yielded increase. The prince, O king, has now no equal in this age. On whatever science you question him he will answer with correctness."

The king commended the exertions of Sindibād, and, addressing the prince, requested him to explain his former backwardness. The Prince replies by relating the

Story of the Careless Mother.

[I HAVE heard of a lovely woman in Arabia, that when she grew up to be a fair beauty, she ever sat at her

window or in the alcove. Like the tulip, she hid not
her face from strangers; like the hyacinth, she covered
not constantly her hair. She was wanton, and joyous,
and fond of pleasure, and was never without flute,
harp, or tambourine. She had no care of name, or
thought of fame, but all day listened to the sound
of the harp. She had no fear of brother or thought of
father; and in this manner she passed her days. She
had a little darling (lit. a corner of her liver), very dear
to her heart, from whose mouth the scent of milk
would come to her. One morning she took a cord
and a pitcher, and put the little darling on her
shoulder. She went on to the well, where she saw a
fairy-faced one, like the sun—like the cypress in
figure, like the moon in face, before whom the fame
of Joseph would have fallen into the well. She saw
him, and lost her wits, so that she forgot herself—
forgot all good and bad. In her madness, this
inebriate wanton bound the cord round the child's
neck, and lowered him into the well. The boy cried
out, and a crowd speedily came from the road, and
drew him from the well.]¹

"So thoughtless is youth," said the prince. "Make
not thyself uneasy, then, about the raw stripling, since
time will render him mature. Thus was it with me.
Youth is the season of gaiety and thoughtlessness.
I then cared but for sport and the chase. That

---

¹ Falconer has condensed this story into a few lines.

period is now past, and no one sees it a second time, even in a dream. Reason then became my guide; and when I distinguished right from wrong, my heart was plunged in thought. Virtue and knowledge are the only garments that never grow old.— Sire, I have seen three persons wiser than myself and more experienced in the world: the *first*, an infant at the breast, by the inspiration and aid of the Creator; the *second*, a little child of five years old; the *third*, a blind old man."

At the request of his Majesty, the Prince then relates the

Story of the Infant,

that spoke in its cradle, and reproved an adulterous king, when about to gratify an unlawful passion; on whom its words made so deep an impression, that from that time he became remarkable for his virtue and devotion.[1]

The Prince next relates (fol. 108) the story of the child five years old, that instructed the woman what answer to make to her adversary and the qāzī:[2]

---

[1] See *Syntipas*, p. 115 of Boissonade, p. 91 of Eberhard.

[2] The judge and magistrate in Muslim cities, who performs the rites of marriage, settles disputes, and decides civil and criminal cases, according to the Qur'ān.

Story of the Stolen Purse, and the Child of Five Years.

ONCE on a time three persons agreed among themselves to enter into partnership, have everything in
common, and share one another's secrets.   One was
a farmer, another a merchant, and another a dealer
in grain.   When they had amassed a sum of money,
they agreed to deposit it with an old woman of
approved honesty, but on this condition, that none
should ask it back, unless all the three were present.
One of them was an expert sharper.   Being with his
companions in the street, he pretended that he was
going to ask from the woman some clay and other
necessaries for the bath.   He approached her window,
and begged her to hand him out, not what he had
mentioned, but the purse.   She asked where were his
two partners.   He said: "They are at hand; look from
the window and see that they are both witnesses."   The
woman, seeing them, gave him the purse, while his
companions never suspected any mischief.   The man
immediately on receiving it, fled to the desert, and
went to another kingdom.

The two friends, after waiting some time in the
street, and not finding their companion return, began
to suspect what had happened, and hastening in alarm
to the house of the old woman, demanded the deposit.
She replied that their partner had received the money
by their order and in their presence; upon which they

took her before the qāzī, who commanded her to restore the deposit. She begged a delay of three days,
which was granted. She departed weeping, and a
child of five years of age, whom she met in the street,
inquired the cause of her distress. Upon her relating
it, the child smiled and said: "Tell the qāzī to-morrow
in the court, that when he produces the three partners
before you, you are ready to restore the money."

Next day she did as the child had suggested to her.
The qāzī, in astonishment, asked her "who had pierced
this pearl." She at first claimed the merit to herself;
but as the qāzī would not believe that a woman could
possess such wisdom, she confessed the truth; and
whenever in future a difficulty occurred, the qāzī
referred to that child for a solution.[1]

---

[1] Although this story is omitted in the version of the *Seven
Vazīrs* translated by Scott, it is found in all other texts of the
Book of Sindibād. In *Syntipas*, three merchants leave their gold
and silver, in three purses, with an old woman in whose house
they lodged.—In the Syriac text, three men travelled together
into a foreign land, and, coming to a town, took up their abode
with an old woman. As they were going to bathe, they said to
their hostess: "Put out some bathing linen, and what else we
require." She put out everything for them, but forgot the
comb. Then the men entrusted the old woman with their
money, and told her not to give it to any one of them alone—
only when all three came together to claim it, etc. The old
Castilian translation agrees exactly with the Syriac version.—In
the Arabian texts, *four* merchants, who are partners in trade
and possess a joint capital of a thousand dīnars, in the course of
a journey come to a garden with a running stream, in which

The Prince next relates the

Story of the Sandal-wood Merchant, and the Advice of the Blind Old Man.

THERE was once a young man, a merchant, who wandered about the world like the zephyr or the north wind, and who, like the sun and moon, was on his travels every month and all the year round. Manifold are the advantages of travel, by which a man of enterprise becomes respected. He who has travelled is awake and intelligent; and when an affair of importance occurs, he is powerful; while he who has sat inactive at home can with difficulty procure a livelihood. Travel is the profit and the capital of man; its hardships are his nurse. Through it the raw and inexperienced at length become adepts; through it the great achieve renown. By travel the new moon perpetually becomes the full. What is travel, but a capital by which a fortune may be amassed?[1]   By

---

they agree to bathe, and leave their purse with the woman who had charge of the garden. Three of them had begun to take off their clothes when they discovered that they had no comb, so the fourth, who was still dressed, was requested by his partners to ask the woman for one; but he asked and obtained the purse, and so on, as in the present version.—See Appendix, No. 20.

[1] "Capital is multiplied twice and thrice over, by repeatedly buying and selling, by those who have knowledge and travel to other lands."—*Pancha Tantra.*—For some verses in praise of travel, see Appendix, No. 21.

travel this young man became alert and active; and he who is active attains to wealth. He was now in Khatā, now in Khutan;[1] now in Aleppo, and now in Yaman. He carried the products of Khurasan to Kh,ārazm;[2] he conveyed the stuffs of Ispahan to the emperor of China. As he sold in Bukhara the products of Abyssinia, he necessarily sold them at 1,000 per cent. (lit. one for ten).[3]

Some one having told him that at Kāshgar sandal-wood was of equal value with gold, and was sold for its weight in that metal, he resolved to proceed thither; and accordingly, having converted all his capital into sandal-wood[4], he set out on his journey. When he arrived near Kāshgar, a person of the country, hearing that he had a large supply of sandal-wood (in which he himself dealt), and fearing that that commodity would be depreciated by its abundance, devised the following stratagem.

Going two stages out of the city, he halted at the spot where the foreign merchant was; and having pitched his tent and opened his bales, he lit a fire and piled sandal-wood on ` it for fuel. When the

---

[1] Both Khatā and Khutan were kingdoms, or principalities, in Chinese Tartary.

[2] Kh,ārazm is a region lying along the River Oxus, and extending to the Caspian Sea.

[3] "Of all goods, perfumes are the best: gold is not to be compared to the article which is procured for one, and is parted with for a thousand."—*Pancha Tantra.*

[4] Perfumed woods—spiced woods.—*Syntipas.*

G

merchant smelt the odour of the sandal-wood he
rushed from his tent in amazement and vexation.
The man from the city saluted him, saying: "You
are welcome; may God protect you from evil! Say,
from what country do you come, and what merchandise bring you?" The merchant informed him.
"You have made a sad blunder," remarked the
citizen. "Why have you brought cumin-seed to
Kirmān?[1] The whole timber of this country is sandal-
wood: every casement, roof, and door is composed of it.
If one were to bring common wood hither, it would
be far better than sandal-wood. Who has been so
cruel as to suggest to you this ill-advised scheme?
From whose hand proceeds such a blunder as this?
Does anyone bring the musk-bladder to Chinese
Tartary?"[2]   .

"Alas!" said the young man to himself, "I have
thrown away my capital! Covetousness is an unblest
passion! Alas, for my long journey, and the hardships
I have endured! What have they availed me? He
who is not content with what God allots him, never
prospers."

The man, seeing the merchant now ready for his
purpose, said to him: "The world is never free from
profit and loss. Give this sandal-wood to me, and I

---

[1] Apparently a proverbial expression.—F.

[2] Equivalent to our popular saying, "Coals to Newcastle."
Musk, the perfume so much esteemed in the East, is obtained
from the navel of a species of deer found in Tartary and Thibet.

will give you in return a measure of gold or silver, or
of whatever else you shall ask."[1]   The merchant consented; two witnesses were called, and the bargain was
struck.   The merchant considered that the sum he
should receive was so much gain, and was rejoiced to
be rid of so worthless an article as he had brought.

He thence proceeded to the city of Kāshgar, and
entering that delightful spot, that model of Paradise,
took up his lodging in the house of a virtuous old
woman.   Of her the merchant asked a question, the
reply to which brought him grief and trouble.   He
inquired: "What is the value of sandal-wood in this
kingdom?" and she informed him that it was worth its
weight in gold.[2]   "In this city," said she, "headache
is common; and hence it is in demand."   At this
intelligence the merchant became distracted, for he
saw that he had been duped.   He related his adventure to the old woman, who cautioned him not to trust
the inhabitants of that city, by whose cunning many
had been ruined.

When morning came, he washed his eyes from sleep,

---

[1] "On this account, then, if you are needy, come and sell
your whole business, and what you wish, I shall give you upon
a full plate."—*Syntipas.*—"And the man said, I have great grief
for thee.   Since it is so, I will buy it of thee, and give thee
what thou shalt wish.   And now get up, and give it to me"—
Libro de los Engannos.

[2] Precisely the same answer is made by the old woman both
in the Greek and the old Castilian translations: "It is worth its
weight in gold."

and inquired the way to the market. Thither he bent his course, and wandered through market, street, and field, still solitary, and without a friend or companion. The alien has no portion in enjoyment: he is a martyr wherever he dies. I will suppose him to be but second to Kay-Qubād,[1] and that he has placed on his head the diadem of Farīdūn. Even were he Joseph of Egypt, yet when he calls to mind his home and country, a palace becomes to him a prison.

The young merchant was sad at heart, for his enterprise was entirely at a stand. Suddenly he observed a person playing at draughts in the street. He stopped, and thought to himself: "I will play with this person to dispel my grief;" and sat down beside the player, forgetful of the caution which his landlady had given him. The other agreed to let him play, on condition that whichever of them should lose should be bound to do whatever the winner should desire.[2] The merchant was soon beaten by his crafty opponent, who, upon this, required him to "drink up the waters of the sea," a demand at which the merchant was confounded and perplexed. The report spread through Kāshgar, and a crowd soon collected. Another of the gang had but one eye, which was blue, the colour of the merchant's eyes. "You have stolen my eye," said

---

[1] Kay-Qubād was the founder of the second, or Kayānī, dynasty of ancient Persian kings.

[2] "Otherwise, surrender all his property" must, of course, be understood to be the alternative.

he to the merchant, and he claimed it in the presence of the crowd. A third produced a stone, and said: "Make from this piece of marble a pair of trousers and a shirt."[1]

The story soon spread, and all Kāshgar was in a bustle. The old woman, hearing of it, hastened from her house, and saw her lodger involved in difficulty. She was surety for him, with ten householders, that she would deliver him, when required, to the court of justice. When they reached home, she reproached him, saying: "When a man listens not to advice, fresh calamities will constantly overtake him. Did I not tell you to have absolutely no dealings with the inhabitants of this city—no intimacy with them?"— "It was no fault of yours," replied the youth; "but there is no remedy against the decrees of destiny." He was much dispirited, but she consoled him. "Be not downcast," said she; "for joy succeeds to grief; there can be no cure till there be a complaint. In this city there is a blind old man, with neither power in his feet nor strength in his hands; but a man of great intelligence and acuteness. Those sharpers assemble nightly at his house, and are directed by him how to act. Do you this night dress yourself like them, and repairing to his house sit silent among them. When your adversaries shall enter and relate their

---

[1] As the merchant is not stated to have been engaged in play with this sharper, there is probably something omitted here by the copyist.

adventures of the day, mark his answers and his questions. Be all ear there, like the rose; like the narcissus, be all eye and silent."

The young man did as she desired, and repairing thither at night, quietly seated himself in a corner. The first who entered was the person who had bought the sandal-wood. He related his adventure. "I have bought a quantity of sandal-wood," said he, "for which I am to give one measure of whatever the seller may choose." "O simpleton!" exclaimed the old man, "you have thrown yourself into the net. This crafty merchant has over-reached you, my son. For if he should demand of you neither silver nor gold, but a *sā*[1] of male fleas, with silken housings and jewelled bridles, and all linked together with golden chains, say, how will you be able to extricate yourself from this difficulty?"—"How," replied the sharper, "could that simpleton ever think of such a trick?"—"However that may be," said the old man, "I have given you your answer."

Next entered the draught-player, and related the adventure of the game. "I have beaten him at draughts," said he, "and have bound him to this condition (and there are witnesses to our agreement), that he shall drink up the whole waters of the sea."—"You have blundered," replied the old man, "and

---

[1] The *sā*, according to Falconer, is a measure containing four bushels. Lane says that it is (in Egypt) very nearly equal to six English pints and two thirds.

have involved yourself in difficulty. You thought you
had taken him in; in imagination you had caught
him in a snare from which there was no escape. But
suppose he should say: 'First, pray stop all the
streams and rivers that are flowing into the sea,
before I drink it dry;"[1] what possible answer can
you return?"—"How," said the knave, "could he,
in his whole life, think such a thought?"

Next the other sharper entered—a knave more
shameless than the other two. "I desired him," said
he, "to make with his own hands a pair of trousers
and a shirt from this slab of stone." The crafty old
man replied: "You have managed worse than all.
For if your opponent should say: 'Do you first weave
me from iron the thread to sew it with,'[2] how will you
be able to reply?"—"How should a simpleton like
him think of such an idea?" said the sharper.

---

[1] In the old German folk-book, which recounts the exploits of
Tyl Eulenspiegel, the arch-rogue is commanded to state the
quantity of water in the sea, and returns the same answer as
this suggested by the blind old man. This also occurs in one
of Sacchetti's novels, but the reply is somewhat different.

[2] A jest very similar to this is found in the Talmud. An
Athenian, walking in the streets of Jerusalem one day, saw a
tailor seated on his shop-board, busily plying his needle, and
picking up a broken mortar, he asked him to be so good as put
a *patch* upon it. "Willingly," replied the tailor, taking up a
handful of sand and offering it to the joker; "most willingly,
sir, if you will first have the goodness to make me a few *threads*
of this material."

The man with one eye next came in. "That youth,"
said he, "has blue ·eyes. I said to him: 'This is my
eye; it is evident to every one that you have stolen
it; restore it, and return my other eye its fellow.'"—
"O ignorant of the wiles of the age," replied the old
man; "your fortune is more adverse than that of all
the rest. Suppose he should say: 'Pluck out your one
eye, and then I will pluck out one of mine, that we
may put them both in scales and judge by their weight
whether you are right.' That man will then have one
of his eyes remaining, while you will be quite blind."
"He will never," said the other, "think of such a
trick as that."[1]

---

[1] In the Calcutta, Būlāq, and Breslau Arabic texts, the
merchant, after disposing of his sandal-wood, is accosted by
the one-eyed man, and obtains a day's respite, having provided
surety; his shoe having been torn in the scuffle, he takes it to a
cobbler, saying: "Repair it, and I will give thee what will
content thee;" then he plays at dice with a fourth sharper,
and, losing the game, is required to drink up the sea, or surrender all his property. The blind old man tells the cobbler
that the merchant might say to him: "The sultan's troops have
been victorious, and the number of his children and allies is
increased—art thou content?"—to which he dare not reply in
the negative; and the dice-player might be asked to hold the
mouth of the sea and hand it to him, and he would drink.—In
Syntipas and the *Libro de los Engannos*, as in the present version,
the "stopping of the rivers" is the old man's suggestion; and
the incident of the cobbler is not mentioned.—All that remains
of this story in the unique Syriac MS. text, discovered by
Rodiger, and printed, with a German translation, by Baethgen,

The young man listened, unobserved, to all that had passed, hastened home, and gave the woman a thousand thanks for having put him on a plan of foiling his adversaries. He passed the night in calmness and tranquillity. Next morning, when the parties appeared before the qāzī, the first, who had bought the sandal-wood, seized the merchant by the collar, saying: "Produce your measure, that I may fill it, and give you your due." When the merchant gave him his reply, he was confounded, and sat down mortified in presence of the qāzī. In like manner the merchant made to each of the rest the reply which the old man had suggested. At length, after a hundred difficulties and objections, the merchant consented to take back his sandal-wood, and several bags of gold as compensation; and he availed himself of the first opportunity which offered to escape from the power of those worthless people.[1]

---

is the opening sentence: "There was once a merchant, who bought a scented wood which is called aloe. When he heard " —and here it breaks off.

[1] This tale seems directed by the author of the present text of the *Sindibād* as a satire upon the citizens of Kāshgar. It bears some resemblance to the rabbinical legends of the infamous people of Sodom, who are represented as accomplished sharpers, and their judges as perverters and mockers of justice. For example: if a man were wounded by another to the effusion of blood, the judge would order him to pay the offender the fee for blood-letting; and if one cut off the ear of his neighbour's ass, he was given the ass to keep until its ear grew again!

When his Majesty heard this tale, he blessed heaven that he had such a son; then, turning to his ministers and courtiers, he inquired to whom they considered him indebted for such a blessing. The first said: "To the prince's mother, who attended carefully to his bringing-up." Another ascribed his excellence to his father; another to the attention of Sindibād; "for," said he, "if the sun withhold his glance, how could the stone be converted into a ruby or a turquoise?"[1] Another said: "Nay; but to your Majesty's ministers, who have been a shield interposed between the prince and calamity, so that the shaft of woman hath not taken effect."

Then the eloquent Sindibād opened his mouth like the lily, and said: "There is none worthy of thanks or praise save God—that God who bestows vision and hearing; for nothing proceeds from the blind and deaf. He it is who has bestowed on the prince his capacity and talent."

The king then asked the prince which of these opinions he considered as the best. The Prince replied by relating the

Story of the King's Daughter and her Four Liberators.

A POWERFUL and mighty king, on the confines of Kashmīr, had an only daughter, of great beauty, whom

---

[1] It was believed that rubies were common stones on which the sun had shone for ages.

he fondly loved. One day in spring she obtained permission of her father to visit the gardens which lay without the city. Here her tent was erected, and she sported for some time with her maidens, when suddenly, while she sat on the margin of a tank, there arose a dust and a great cloud, from which a black dīv[1] came forth, and seized and carried her off. Her maidens were frightened, and some tore their hair, others scratched their cheeks. When the king heard of the circumstance, he was filled with grief and affliction. When he had somewhat recovered from the shock, he caused it to be proclaimed that whoever should bring back his daughter should obtain her in marriage, along with half his kingdom.

There were in that city four persons of great ability. One was a guide, who had travelled over the world— in the morning in China, at night in Khatā. The second, a daring freebooter, who would have taken the prey from the lion's mouth. The third, a cavalier like Rustam,[2] the model of Isfandiyār[3] in fight. The fourth, a physician of blessed approach, whose breath possessed the life-giving virtue of the Messiah's.[4] All

---

[1] Dīvs are demons, corresponding in their power and disposition to the *evil* genii (all the genii, or *jinn*, are not bad) of the Arabians, and to the Rakshasas of the Hindūs.

[2] Rustam, the Hercules of the Persians, whose exploits are recorded in the *Shāh Nāma* (Book of Kings), the grand epic, or rather series of epics, of the celebrated poet Firdausī.

[3] Isfandiyār, a renowned warrior, who was slain in battle by Rustam.   [4] See note 4, page 40.

the four were sons of the same father and mother, and each had his peculiar gifts. On hearing the proclamation, they agreed that this was an enterprise suited for them. The guide led the way, and searched everywhere, while his brothers accompanied him. The dīv inhabited a cave in the mountains of Yaman. When they reached it, the robber, who was the most daring of the three, entered it, and brought the damsel out, the dīv being absent at the time. When he returned, and found this Laylī missing, he rushed out, troubled in heart like Majnūn,[1] and despatched a party of demons in their pursuit, bearing ponderous clubs on their shoulders. The warrior put them to flight with his sword. The damsel was dangerously ill, but the physician prescribed for her, and restored her to health.

Having thus achieved their task, they joyfully repaired to court, and each related his own achievement. The king was delighted, and grateful for the recovery of his daughter. He opened his treasury, and bestowed gifts on the poor. He sent for those four persons, to reward them. On the first he bestowed the tribute of the highways; the daring

---

[1] Majnūn and Laylī are the names of two Arabian lovers, whose constancy is celebrated throughout Islām; they are the Romeo and Juliet, the Abelard and Heloise, of Oriental poets and romance writers. The great Persian Nizāmī (13th century) composed a beautiful poem on the Loves of Laylī and Majnūn, which has been translated into English verse by Atkinson.

freebooter he made his kafādār, or protector of his person; [the physician he made his vazīr;] and the cavalier he seated on his throne, and gave him his daughter in marriage, according to his promise.[1]

Thus, every thing has its peculiar quality and re-commendation. Honey possesses sweetness, but is unfit to make vinegar. One robs, another guides; one sells, another buys. Had not the guide led the way, who would have conducted them aright in that intricate research? Had not the robber entered the cave, who would have brought the damsel out? Had not the warrior fought, who would have opposed the army of demons? Had not the physician prescribed, the damsel would not have been restored to health.

["Although this tale is very disordered," adds the Prince, "it is yet an example of the circumstances of this slave (himself). Were hearts without sins, of a certainty the earth would have remained void of God's mercy. (Do thou, then, overlook my short-comings.) Had there not been a counselling master, surely, in the 'A B C' school, things would have been hot. Had I not borne this effort and trouble, the foot of endeavour had not descended to the treasure. Had not my body been healthy—if all remedies for weakness had been weak—how could I have so struggled and kicked?—how had I arrived thus at the desiderated place? All is the 'unmerited goodness'

---

[1] See Appendix, No. 22.

of the Sustainer (God), and enough! For no deed ariseth from the hand of man."

When the Prince concluded, the king and his vazīrs were warm in their applause.[1]

The title of the next chapter is as follows:

The End of the Affair of the Damsel, who was taken in her own Device, and punished by the word of the Prince.[2]   \

Only a page of this chapter remains. The Damsel is made to sit on her knees opposite the Prince, who

---

[1] Professor Comparetti justly complains that, so careless has Falconer been at this part of his work, one does not know from it whether this final tale is told by the Prince or by Sindibād. We are first informed that it is related by the Prince, and after-wards that "when *Sindibād* had concluded," etc. The story, as the title in the manuscript shows, is certainly told by the prince, and the comments upon it seem also to be his, since Sindibād is not mentioned in connection with this tale. Falconer has thus rendered the story-teller's concluding observations, which he puts into the mouth of the sage: "This tale and these remarks are applicable to my own case and that of the prince. Had not I exerted myself, and he possessed talent, all would have been in vain. But everything is due to the goodness of God, without whose aid all human efforts are vain."

[2] *Sar-anjāmi kāri kanīzak, ki ba 'amali kh'ud giriftār shud; wa ta'zīri u ba qawli shah-zāda.*

According to Falconer's rendering, "the Damsel is *pardoned* at the intercession of the Prince." The word *ta'zīr*, however, is in the same posture, before the king's throne. The Prince says: "O king of the world, I have no witness except God! This violence did not proceed from me, for one must needs be ashamed thereof. God knows that his slave (himself) is good;—seek not good from those who know not God." The king treated that sinner (the damsel) with contempt: "This is the time of question and answer. Why hast thou blackened thy own face?[1] Why hast thou done evil against this innocent one? Had he ever done (aught wrong) to thee? Had he injured thee or thine? Thou hast made thyself an example in the world till the judgment day. See what thy deeds have brought to pass! See now, how just is thy retribution! As thou hast mingled the diamond with the draught, drink thou it first, for thou hast poured it out. Drink up the dregs, for it is thy turn. Why should the master of the feast act wrongfully? Seek not that for thyself which thou seekest not for others, for none who does evil sees good." The damsel perspired like the (dew-sprent) rose

does not mean "pardoned," but "punishing by severe stripes;" it also signifies "reproving." From what remains, as follows above, of this important chapter, we cannot say which of the two meanings of the term is the more appropriate.

[1] In other words, "Why hast thou disgraced thyself?" In Persia criminals are often led through the streets with their faces blackened. When an ambassador has returned from a successful mission, or a general from a brilliant campaign, he is said to have "made his face *white* before the king." This, as well as the other phrase, must be familiar to readers of Morier's *Haji Baba.*

for shame. She wept over her plight, and said: "Now
have I no choice therein;—not once, but a hundred
times, have I done it. Order that they tear out my
lily-tongue,[1] if thy slave (herself) has been free and
bold."][2]

*   *   *   *   *

The commencement of the next chapter is wanting.
Sindibād has been making some remarks on the
impossibility of avoiding destiny. The king then
compliments him on the success with which he had
educated the prince. "If I formerly had confidence
in your wisdom and virtue," said his Majesty, "it is
now increased a hundredfold. You are aware what
happy results you have produced, and what accomplishments you have imparted to my son. In return
for your exertions in giving life to this ancient house,

---

[1] The tongue is often, from its shape, likened to the leaf of
the lily.

[2] We are thus, unfortunately, left in ignorance of what was the
end of the Damsel in this text. In the *Mishlé Sandabar*, she is
pardoned at the intercession of the prince; in Nakhshabī's
Persian version (8th night of the *Tūtī Nāma*), she is hanged:
in the Calcutta and Būlāq printed Arabic texts, she is banished
from the city; in the *Libro de los Engannos*, the king orders
her to be burnt in a dry caldron; in *Syntipas*, she is condemned
to be driven through the city upon an ass, with her head shaved
and her face blackened, accompanied by the criers to proclaim
her crimes; in Scott's *Seven Vazīrs*, a large stone is tied to her
feet, and she is thrown into the sea.—See Appendix, No. 23.

I will place your own family in affluence and independence." He then bestowed munificent gifts on the philosopher.

His Majesty next inquired: "Whence did you acquire all this wisdom and excellence, and at whose house did you light your taper?"—Mark how wise an answer the philosopher returned: "Reason, sire, was my instructor," said he. "He who takes reason for his guide will conduct his affairs to a successful issue; for it is a drop from the ocean of God's grace—a key to open—an unerring guide to conduct. I have plucked a rose from the garden of the intelligent; I have profited by the wisdom of the wise.[1] Never was there one like Farīdūn in wisdom, on whom may there be every moment a thousand benedictions! That wise, just, and pious monarch thus addressed the prince who was to succeed him: 'Inscribe on the walls of my palace these counsels, fraught with wisdom, that my words may remain for ever as my memorial after me.'

Counsels which were inscribed around the Hall of the happy Faridun.

If thou possessest wisdom and understanding, lend not thine ear, as far as thou canst avoid it, to a tale-bearer. Such a person has no merit, unless it be

---

[1] Compare Sa'dī: "I have gathered something in each corner; I have gleaned an ear in every harvest."

H

this, that he carries a lie from Khatā to China. Grant not such a one a second audience; admit him not to a confidential interview.

Be not careless of an ill-disposed enemy; for negligence is not excusable under any circumstances, and whilst thou art engaged with other affairs, he is plotting how to injure thee.

Take not compassion on snake or serpent; for the one is a torment, the other a calamity.

If thou hast a friend sincere and accordant, make him thy constant associate.

Take not counsel with any save the wise; turn not from such a straight path.

Beware of the ignorant man and his conversation, schemes, and writing. Beware of the domestic enemy, whose reliance is on his ignorance and folly.

Leave not thorns in the highway, lest perchance thy own foot be wounded unaware.

The person whom thou hast not known all his life —to whom thou hast not given thy confidence— whose companion thou hast not been in travel (for in travel a man is exposed to perils)—to whom thou hast given nothing, and from whom thou hast received nothing—place not reliance on that person, if thou art wise.

A demon whom thou knowest is better than a hūrī whom thou knowest not.

Beware of speaking, except on occasions when thy speaking may be useful.

So speak, that when thou speakest again, thy words may be the same—nay, better.

" How can there be [adds Sindibād] better counsels than those which have the warrant of Farīdūn?"

The king next interrogated the philosopher on the affairs of the world. "Accomplished sage," said he, " who is deserving of sovereignty, and whom does the diadem become?"

" The answer," replied the sage, "is clear as the sun. He deserves to wear a crown, he is worthy of dominion, who knows the worth and dignity of every one, and who pays to each the respect due to him. Entrust not important affairs to the mean man, for he will be impotent under the mighty load."

Again the king asked: " Of monarchs, say, who is the most to be approved?—of the virtues of monarchs, which is the most laudable?"

" He," replied the sage, " who examines an affair in all its bearings, who acts with prudence, and who is neither precipitate nor dilatory."

Various other questions were then put by his Majesty, and answered to his satisfaction by Sindibād; after which he asks the prince to produce some such pearls of advice as those which his tutor had strung. The prince complies, and delivers a series of moral, prudential, and religious maxims, which serve to show that he had improved wonderfully under the tuition of Sindibād, but with which the reader will perhaps dispense. Suffice it to say, that the king was struck with admiration at the wisdom of his son; and being now in his seventieth year, reflected thus:

" How long," said he to himself, " shall the wine-pitcher, the wine, the drum, and the lute engross thee? By thy arm and might didst thou seize the royal crown. Thou hast amassed treasures in abundance by shedding the blood of the weak, not by the hand of toil. Thou hast taken from him who had nothing, and bestowed on him who left behind him. Neither was he from whom those treasures were extorted guilty, nor he who received them deserving. Then what wisdom was there first in taking from such a one, and next in bestowing on the other?

" But thou shalt be seized and receive the penalty of thy misdeeds in that day when every act shall be brought to light. What profit has resulted to thee from this life of seventy years? Go, make blind the eye of thy desire; prepare thy coffin, and benefit at least him who digs thy grave. Long enough have thy thoughts of Rūm, and thy projects on Khatā, engaged thee; go now, prepare thy provision for the journey of eternity. How long wilt thou continue the tormentor of the free-born? How long wilt thou devour the liver of the unfortunate?

" Perhaps thou believest not in a resurrection; perchance thou reckest not of a day of judgment? This delusion proceeds from the clamour of the drum and the bell: but wait until the blowing of the trump, and it will be dispelled. Employ the time that remains to thee in devotion; go, retire to a corner, and be at peace: henceforward seek distinction only as a recluse. Content thee with a barley loaf, and eat not the barley and the wheat of the poor. The time has now arrived to repent of thy misdeeds. Thank God that thou hast a worthy successor in thy son—that darling of thy heart —that pearl of thee, the oyster-shell. In knowledge he is far thy superior; in vigour and energy more powerful. Thy day and night are over: it is now his day. The tree which time has dried up, I should marvel were it to bear fruit. When the branches of the willow are decayed, who looks to it for shade? What can be better for thee than that thy son should succeed thee, and preserve thy name upon the earth?"

He thus spoke, and went, with faltering steps, into the corner of retirement. For a week he beheld not the face of man; gave his courtiers no audience, and assigned not to his vazirs their various duties, but remained alternately engaged in prayer and praise.

The King has a Dream, sends for his Vazirs and Officers of State, bestows in their presence the sovereignty on his Son, and goes into retirement.

WHEN the king awoke from that dream, and was roused from that high intoxication, he comprehended the good and the evil of life, and, on an auspicious day, summoned around his throne the ministers of religion, the nobles, vazīrs, and the generals of his army, and seated beside him on the throne his son and the sage Sindibād. Looking towards his left hand, where was his chief vazīr, he said:

"O worthy and experienced man! the world remains eternally to no one; but the Lord of the world remains, and he alone. In this life of seventy-five years, I have experienced but trouble, and sorrow, and suffering; and should I have yet seventy-five years more to live, would not that time also come to a close? My vision is dull; what was once strong is now weak. When the old man's form is bent like a bow, do not suppose that there is any better course for him than retirement. When the hand that should wield the sword trembles, why should you talk of sword or hanger? Shall I tell you what gray hairs are? They are the heralds of misfortune—the messengers that bid cease to hope.[1]

"Whether I am a king or an athlete, I am not higher in rank than Kay-Khusrau.[2] who resigned the

---

[1] So, too, in the romance of the Four Dervishes, when King Āzādbakht discovered the first white hair in his beard, he exclaimed: "Death has already sent me a messenger!"

[2] Kay-Khusrau (Cyrus), the third king of the Kayānī (Median) dynasty of ancient Persia. He ascended the throne in the lifetime of his grandfather, Kay-Kāūs, who resigned the crown in his favour. He had many battles with Afrāsiyāb, King of Tūrān, who was at last defeated, captured, and slain. Soon afterwards Kay-Khusrau resolved to devote the remainder

sovereignty to Luhrāsp, and his knowledge in affairs to Jāmāsp. The time has arrived for me to retire: when age and its infirmities have come on, the crown and throne yield no pleasure. My sovereignty came to me from my father;[1] I now entrust it, as a deposit, to my son. You know that he is the centre of my hopes. If he be good, you have educated him; if evil, you have made him so."

He then called his son to him, kissed his face, and, taking him by the hand, pressed him for a while in his embrace; after which, removing the crown from his head, he placed it on his son's, seated him on the throne, and came down from it, while the crowd congratulated him with tears in their eyes.

"This," said he, "is the memorial of his father: this

---

of his life to religious retirement; he resigned his throne to Luhrāsp, the son-in-law of Kay-Kāūs, and his own son by adoption and affection. Then he went with many of his nobles to a spring which he had fixed upon as the place of his repose. Here he disappeared (like Arthur and other favourite heroes of romance, he did not die), and all who were with him were overtaken by a great snow-storm and perished.

[1] Yet the damsel is previously represented (page 79) as reminding his Majesty that he had gained his kingdom by the sword; and the king himself says (page 116) that by his arm and might he had seized on the royal crown. Moreover, at the commencement of the tale we are informed that he was a mighty sovereign of India; while in another part of the text (not introduced into the present analysis) he is described as the Chosroes of Rūm and Kashmīr. Such contradictory statements are not uncommon in compositions of this kind.

son is my refuge, and my dispeller of grief. To him do I resign my kingdom, hoping that you will reward me by your loyalty to him, and that you will not allow a stranger to occupy the place of this house." [1]

His son being accepted by the people, the aged king caused an oratory to be built for himself, closed the door against the interruptions of worldly business, and sat down in tranquillity and retirement. Happy fortune! happy end! happy king! happy reign! Henceforward he had no concern but devotion and the duties of religion.

Go,[2] learn from him how to govern—how to cherish thy subjects. Turn not away from the counsels of the wise, but listen to the discourse of venerable worthies.

The Author's Concluding Remarks.

To me, too, the time of retirement has arrived: I, too, must totter to my corner. If he left to his son a kingdom, and betook himself to solitude, I likewise, for my dear and virtuous son, have left this renowned

---

[1] The abdication of the king in favour of his son is omitted in *Syntipas* and the *Libro de los Engannos;* it is, however, in Nakhshabī's *Tūtī Nāma* (8th Night), and in the *Seven Vazīrs* of Scott's and the Breslau texts. In some manuscripts of the *Mishlé Sandabar*, a passage has been added, stating that Sandabar died, at the age of 130, contemporaneously with the king (Bibar), whose son then ascended the throne.

[2] This exhortation seems addressed to the poet's royal patron, by whose command the work was composed.

book, more valuable than treasure and wealth; a book by which, as long as Persian shall exist, as long as earth shall be beneath and heaven above, his name shall be perpetuated, whose end be happy! May the king not withdraw from him his favour; that king whose fortune may it be young, whose life long!

O God! withdraw not thy guidance from me: deprive me not of thy grace at last! My toilsome journey is accomplished: this new work has attained completion!

THE SEVEN VAZÎRS.

EDITOR'S PREFACE.

THE following translation of "The Story of the King, his Son, the Damsel, and the Seven Vazīrs" was made by Jonathan Scott from a fragment of an Arabic MS. of the *Thousand and One Nights*, procured in Bengal, and published by him, in a volume entitled *Tales, Anecdotes, and Letters, translated from the Arabic and Persian*, in 1800. Scott states, in his preface, that in translating these tales, he had omitted a few objectionable expressions: in reprinting the *Seven Vazīrs*, I have taken the liberty of omitting some others which Scott thought fit to be retained; have adopted a more generally approved system of transliteration for the Arabic words and proper names which occur in the stories; and occasionally have made verbal alterations and emendations. Scott's notes are distinguished by the letter S from those which I have added.

It does not appear that Scott was aware that this tale of the *Seven Vazīrs* is an Arabian version, with some stories omitted and others interpolated, of the ancient Book of Sindibād—indeed it may be doubted whether he knew of such a work at all; nor does he seem to have suspected its affinity to the European romance of the *Seven Sages*, with an English rendering of which he was surely acquainted. Although those tales which are foreign to the original work have probably been inserted in the *Seven Vazīrs* at a comparatively recent period, in recasting some version of the Book of Sindibād for the *Thousand and One Nights*, they are yet of very ancient origin, and widely diffused, as will be seen from the variants and parallels presented in the APPENDIX, and therefore serve as interesting illustrations of the genealogy of popular tales and fictions.

In the Calcutta and Būlāq printed Arabic texts of the *Thousand and One Nights* the tale of the *Seven Vazīrs* occupies the 578th to the 606th Nights.   Scott's manuscript seems to have been complete to the 29th Night, after which the division into nights was discontinued, the *Seven Vazīrs* immediately following—probably having been misplaced.   I may add, that while the conclusion of this version is greatly abridged, compared with that of the tale as found in the Calcutta and Būlāq texts, the introduction has been much more fully preserved, and corresponds in many points with the oldest Eastern texts of the Sindibād.

W. A. C.

THE SEVEN VAZĪRS.

Introduction.

THERE lived in ancient days a powerful and mighty sultan, who was a wise sovereign, just to his subjects, bountiful to his dependants, and beloved by the whole empire; but he was become gray-bearded and stricken in years, and there had not been allotted to him a son, who might preserve his memory, and inherit the kingdom after him. On this account uneasiness assailed him, and such depression of spirits, that he secluded himself from society, and passed whole days in his private apartments.

At length his subjects began to murmur concerning him.[1] Some said he was dead; others, that an accident

---

[1] The princes of Asia, except prevented by illness, give public audience twice a day. When this has been neglected by the idle or the dissipated, it has generally proved their ruin, or at least been the cause of troublesome commotions, as the powerful chiefs were left uncontrolled by the interference of the sovereign, who at these audiences received the appeals and petitions of the meanest subjects, and redressed their grievances. One of the chief causes of the fall of the khalifate, the Persian and Mogul empires, was the disuse of frequent public audiences.—S.

had befallen him.   On a certain day his queen entered his chamber, and found him thoughtful, reclining his head towards the earth, like one plunged in sorrow.

She approached, and, kissing his hand, said: " Fortune has not persecuted thee, nor have the evils of chance reached thee.   God has bestowed upon thee enjoyments, and given thee every delight.   What, then, is the cause that I find thee so pensive?"

He replied: " Alas! my years are advanced, my age is drawing to its end, and my kingdom will pass to another family; for I am not blessed with a son, with whom my eyes might be delighted, and who might succeed me in my dominions.   On this account extreme sorrow has overcome me."

The queen said: "God will remove thy grief and thy sorrow.   The same thoughts which afflicted thy heart have afflicted mine, and what had invaded thy mind was invading mine, when, lo! drowsiness overcame me, and I fell asleep.   I dreamt, and saw in my vision a phantom, which revealed to me, saying: ' If the sultan shall be blessed with a son by almighty God, he will with difficulty be preserved from death at a certain period.   After that, prosperity will attend him. But if a daughter is born, her father will not love her; and if she lives, she will occasion the ruin of his kingdom.   He must not, however, think of a child by any other woman than thyself, and thou shalt be the cause of his having one when the moon and the sign Gemini shall be in conjunction.'   I now awoke from sleep, and became thoughtful, reflecting on what I had heard in my vision."

When the sultan heard these words, he said to her: "By God's permission, all will be well;" and the queen did not fail to comfort him until his gloom had passed away. He now quitted his retirement, sat upon the throne of his kingdom, summoned his nobles and his subjects, and entreated their prayers, that God would bless him with a son; when they prayed, and God accepted their prayers.

The night being arrived in which the moon and Gemini entered into conjunction, the queen became pregnant. She informed the sultan of her condition, and he rejoiced with exceeding great joy, and did not refrain, until she had borne her months, and brought forth a son, beautiful as the full moon. Then the sultan made rejoicings from evening till morning, gave alms, and released the prisoners. The infant was suckled nearly two years, when the mother returned to the mercy of God, and they lamented over her with great mourning.

The child did not cease to remain on the bosoms of the nurses and female attendants until he had completed his second year, when his father entrusted him to tutors, that they might teach him what was necessary for princes to acquire.[1] The eighth year of his age

---

[1] The period of ablactation in the East is generally at the end of the second year; but there must have been something omitted by the copyist here.—See below, note, page 134.

passed over, but he had learnt nothing, for every book was to him too difficult. When the tutors represented this to the sultan, he was enraged against his son, and commanded him to be put to death, saying: "This is a disgraceful child, from whom there can no advantage arise."

There was at the court a man of wisdom, learning, and penetration, deeply versed in every science.[1] When he found that the sultan intended to kill his son, he advanced, and kissing the ground before him, said: "O sovereign, be not grieved on account of thy son. Entrust him to me, and I will teach him whatever is necessary in two years.[2] I will not deceive you, but instruct him in the sciences, philosophy, and princely accomplishments."—The sultan exclaimed: "How canst thou make him learn, when every book has been too difficult for him, and his tutors have been wearied out?"—The sage replied: "I pledge myself to do it; and if I do not perfect him in what I have mentioned, act by me as thou shalt think proper."

Upon this the sultan delivered his son to the sage, who took him to his house, prepared for him a chamber, and wrote upon the walls in yellow and white what he wished him to learn. Then he carried to him what was necessary for him of carpets, food, and utensils, and left him alone in the apartment.

[1] In this version the name of the sage does not appear.—See note 2, page 12.

[2] See note, page 21.

He did not permit any person to visit him but himself. Every third day the tutor entered, that he might teach him what was necessary from those books, the contents of which he had written on the walls, and depict for him fresh lessons; after which he placed round him provisions, locked the door upon him, and departed.

Now it came to pass that the boy, when his mind was at a loss for amusement, studied the lessons written on the walls, which he learnt in a short time. When the tutor found his sense and understanding on every point equal to what was necessary for him, he took him from the apartment, and instructed him in horsemanship and archery; after which he sent to his father, and informed him that his son had learnt whatever was becoming his condition in one year.

The sultan rejoiced exceedingly, and informed his vazīrs of it, who were in number seven. Then he wished to examine his son, and commanded the tutor to bring him with him, in order that he might question him. The tutor consulted the horoscope of the youth, and foresaw that if he should speak before there should pass over his head seven days and nights, there would occur to him imminent danger of death. Upon this the sage addressed the prince, saying: "I have inspected thy nativity, and if from this time thou speakest before seven days are expired, great hazard of life will befall thee."—The prince replied: "What can ensure my safety?"—The tutor answered: "Repair to thy father, but when he speaketh to thee, utter not a word."—The youth exclaimed: "I swear by God, that if thou hadst commanded me that I should not breathe, I would have obeyed thee, on account of what thou hast done for me of kindness and favour." The tutor replied: "Go, and speak not, though they beat thee with scourges, for thou wilt recover of thy wounds, there will be in store for thee great glory, and thou shalt rule the kingdom after thy father." Then the prince said: "Remember thy speech to my father before thou lookedst at my nativity." The tutor replied: "What must be must be; further conversation will not profit. Nothing will occur but felicity to thee, whatever may become of me. Be firm, and trust in God; for whoever trusteth in God is secure."

The prince departed, and repaired to his father, when the vazîrs, with the nobles, officers of state, and the men of science met him on his way. They placed before him an herb, that he might describe its genus and properties; but he did not speak. They importuned him to answer, but he would not utter a word.

Upon this the sultan was affected with grief, and sent for the tutor to punish him; when some of the assembly said, the sage had deserted his house in the night; some, that he had taken poison; and others contradicted this last assertion. There was much disputation among them, but still the prince would not speak.[1]   At length the assembly broke up, and there remained only the prince and his father.

The sultan had a concubine, of beautiful person and very young, with the love of whom he was doatingly fascinated. She now entered, and saw the prince sitting near his father, like an affrighted fawn. She approached near, and said to the sultan: "I perceive thee, my lord, overcome with affliction;" when he related to her the conduct of his son. She replied: "I desire that thou wouldst commit him to my charge, for perhaps he will be affable to me and speak, and I shall discover the cause of his silence."[2]

He replied: "Take him with thee." Upon which she led him by the hand, conducted him to her chamber, caressed him, and explained to him her wishes, clasped him to her bosom, and attemped to kiss him; but he rejected her advances. She exclaimed: "I am a young

---

[1] In some of the versions, the assembled sages ascribe the prince's silence to the effect of a drug which his tutor had given him in order that he might learn quickly.

[2] In the Persian text (page 25), the damsel is secretly enamoured of the prince, but had never found an opportunity of telling him her love.   In the Greek, Hebrew, and old Castilian, she tells the king that the prince had been wont, from a boy, to confide in her, and proposes that she should take him with her, to induce him to speak.—Comparetti is in error when he says that in the present text the prince was, "according to the prevailing opinion, taken to the harem." We see that the assembly had "broken up" before the damsel came in, and asked leave to take the prince with her,

damsel, and thou a young man; I will be thine, and
thou shalt be mine. Thy father is become super-
annuated, must soon depart this life, when thou
wilt govern the kingdom after him, and shalt espouse
me; but if thou wilt not comply with my desires, I
will effect thy destruction.   Choose, then, one or the
other—happiness or death." [1]

[1] It is curious that in the other Arabic texts the prince is tempted
by the damsel when he is little more than *ten* years old: and
according to the present version, he could have been only *nine*,
since he was eight when the sage undertook to teach him in two
years, and "he had learnt whatever was becoming his condition
in *one* year." This absurdity is due to the copyist, who has
suppressed a second period of unsuccessful teaching, which is
also omitted in the old Castilian translation.   In the *Sindibād
Nāma*, although the precise age of the prince when he was
tempted by the damsel is not mentioned, he must have been
about twenty years old, since he was ten when first entrusted to
tutors, under whom, "year after year," he made no progress,
and he was afterwards six years in charge of Sindibād before he
finally undertook to teach him in six months.   In the *Mishlé
Sandabar*, the unsuccessful period is twelve years and a half,
after he was seven years old, during which it is not said that his
preceptors were changed; he was, therefore, nineteen and a half
when Sandabar took him in hand for six months, which together
make up the twenty years, when danger to him was predicted
at his birth.   The *Libro de los Engannos* is less exact: although
the danger to the prince was to happen twenty years after his
birth, it actually occurred when he was fifteen and a half years
old; his education having been begun at seven, and unsuccessfully conducted for eight years, after which Cendubete finally
teaches him in six months.   That there was a second unsuccessful

When the prince heard this, he was exceedingly enraged against her, and thought within himself: "I will speedily repay thee for thy crimes, when after seven days I shall be able to speak."[1] The artful damsel, when she perceived his anger, hastened to contrive his ruin. She beat her cheeks, tore her garments, dishevelled her hair, and went before the sultan in that manner. He said: "What can have happened to thee?"—She exclaimed: "He, whom thou seest, hath done this, even thy own son, who has plotted the destruction of thy life, and feigned himself dumb. When I entered with him into my chamber, he declared to me his love; and when I refused him, he said: 'I cannot live without thee, and if thou dost not comply with my desires, I will kill thee, and murder my father.'"[2]

period, during which Cendubete had charge of him, is evident from the question put to the sage when the eight years had passed without result : "Why have you not instructed the prince in those years that he has been with you?"

[1] See note, page 26.

[2] In the Būlāq and Calcutta printed Arabic texts, the introduction to the *Seven Vazīrs* is so much abridged and garbled as to be of no service whatever in showing the original form of this portion of the Book of Sindibād. Nothing is said of the unsuccessful attempts to instruct the prince, or of Sindibād's undertaking the task at the peril of his own life: the prince is entrusted to Sindibād at the age of five, and when he attains his tenth year he is taught horsemanship and warlike exercises; one day Sindibād discovers the threatening aspect of the prince's horoscope, and—so far is he from concealing himself, as in all

When the sultan heard these words, his wrath was violent against his son, and he gave orders to have him put to death. He sent for his vazīrs; but the tutor had informed them of the circumstances, and why the prince was prevented from speaking for seven days. Upon this the vazīrs assembled together, and consulted, saying: "The sultan intends to put his son to death, but there may not be in him any fault, so that when he is dead, our master may repent, when repentance will not avail."—Then the prime vazīr said: "Let us each take charge of him for a day during the seven days, till the whole are expired, and I will be responsible for you all at the conclusion of that period."

The First Vazīr having contrived thus, he repaired to the sultan, kissed the ground, and said: "O sultan, if there were to thee a thousand sons, far be it from thee the death of one of them! Alas, then, when thou hast one only, with whom thou wast blessed after much anxiety and expectation, that thou shouldst

other versions—goes at once before the king and acquaints him of the danger to his son's life should he break silence during the following seven days, and advises him to keep the prince in a secluded place, entertained with mirth and music until the seven days be past. The king accordingly entrusts the young prince to his favourite concubine, with orders to keep him with her for seven days. In the harem were forty apartments, in each of which were ten beautiful slave-girls, all skilled in music: here the prince passed one night; and next day, apparently, he is tempted by the concubine.

command his execution upon the bare assertion of
a woman! God only knoweth whether she hath
spoken truly or accused him falsely; for there are
among the sex women artfully malicious."

Story of Ahmed the Orphan.

I HAVE heard, O my sovereign, that a certain sultan
resolved to educate those unfortunate children who
are sometimes abandoned on the highways. As he
was passing one day, behold, he saw a male infant
upon a heap of rubbish, who appeared beautiful as
the moon at the full. He commanded his attendants
to convey him to the palace; and they took him up,
and committed him to nurses till he grew up, when
they placed him at school. The boy learnt the Qur'ān
and the sciences and languages. When he had finished
his education, the sultan committed to him the care of
his treasury; and it came to pass that at length he did
nothing but with his advice, and the youth attended
in his private chambers.

As he was in waiting one day, the sultan said:
"Go to the apartment of Hayātu-'n-nufūs,[1] and bring
me a medicine from her closet." The youth passed
through the chamber of the concubine, and found
her with a slave. He took up the medicine, but
did not seem to attend to her actions, and returned

[1] Life of the Souls ;—Scott renders the name, Refresher of the
Soul.

with haste to the sultan. The name of this youth was Ahmed Yetīm.[1] Then the sultan said: "What has happened to thee, that I perceive thy colour changed?"—Ahmed replied: "My lord, because I came with hurry and precipitation;" but he did not inform the sultan of what he had discovered.

The concubine Hayātu-'n-nufūs, being convinced that Ahmed must have beheld herself and her paramour, hastily contrived a scheme against him. She scarred her face, and rent her garments. When the sultan entered, and found her in that situation, he said: "What is thy condition?"—She exclaimed: "From him who is the offspring of adultery no good can proceed."—The sultan, understanding her meaning, replied: "Conceal this affair, and within this hour I will bring thee his head." He departed from her, filled with indignation, and ascended his throne.

Ahmed attended, according to custom, but did not suspect what was plotted against him. The sultan beckoned to one of his slaves, and said privately to him: "Go to the house of such a person, and remain there. When any one shall say unto thee: 'Thus saith the sultan, Do that which thou wast commanded to execute,' strike off his head, place it in this basket, and fasten over it the cover. When I shall send to thee a messenger who will say: 'Hast thou performed

---

[1] Orphan Ahmed;—according to Scott, The Good Orphan, thus mis-translating the name Ahmed.

the business?' commit to him the basket." The slave replied: "To hear is to obey," and retired. Soon after, the sultan called to Ahmed Yetīm, and said: "Hasten to a certain house, and say unto such a slave, 'Execute the commands of the sultan.'"

Ahmed departed, but on the way he saw the man who had been criminal with the concubine, with a number of other slaves, sitting down, drinking and feasting. As they saw Ahmed approaching, they stood up; and the guilty slave thought that if he could detain him from the business of the sultan, he might procure his death. He stopped him, paid obeisance to him, and entreated that he would sit down with them a little while. But Ahmed said: "The sultan hath sent me upon business to a certain house, and I cannot stay." Upon this the guilty slave replied: "I will perform the commission." Ahmed answered: "If so, hasten, and say to a slave whom thou wilt find there, that he must execute the orders of the sultan." The slave said: "To hear is to obey," and departed.

Ahmed sat down with the rest, while the other proceeded to the house, and said to the person in waiting: "Thus saith the sultan, 'Complete thy orders.'" He replied: "Most readily," and drawing his scimitar, struck off the head of the guilty slave, washed it from the blood, placed it in the basket, tied the cover on it, and sat down.

When Ahmed had waited some time for the return

of his messenger, he took leave of his company, went
to the house, and said to the slave in waiting: "Hast
thou performed thy orders?" He replied: "Yes," and
committed the basket to Ahmed, who took it up,
and went with it to the sultan; but he did not suspect
what was within the basket, nor did curiosity lead him
to open it.

When the sultan saw him, he said: "Ahmed, I sent
thee upon a commission, but thou hast entrusted it to
another." He replied: "My lord, it is true." The
sultan exclaimed: "Hast thou seen what is contained
in this basket?" Ahmed answered: "No; I swear by
thy head, I do not know what is within it, nor have
I opened it." The king was astonished, and said:
"Take off the covering." He lifted it up, and, behold!
in it was the head of the slave who had done evil with
Hayātu-'n-nufūs.

The sultan exclaimed: "I cannot suppose, Ahmed,
that it should be concealed from thee, whether or not
this slaughtered man was guilty of a crime which rendered him worthy of death." Ahmed replied: "Know,
my lord, when thou didst send me for the medicine to
the chamber of Hayātu-'n-nufūs, I found this slave in
her embraces. I took up the medicine, but did not
disclose what I had beheld. When despatched to the
house, I found on the way this guilty slave, sitting
with his fellows eating and drinking. He stood up,
and entreated me to stay among them. I replied:
'The sultan hath sent me to execute a commission.'

Upon which he said: 'Sit down—I will perform this business,' and departed." He then related the other circumstances, until he was entrusted with the basket.

Then the sultan exclaimed: "O Ahmed! none is discerning but God;" related to him the behaviour of the damsel, and what she had accused him of, and said: "I resign her unto thee." Ahmed replied: "I cannot repay the bounties of the sultan with ingratitude;—I can have no concern with her." When the sultan heard these words, he commanded her to be put to death. [24]

"This, O sultan," continued the vazír, "is only one instance of the deceitfulness of women. Trust not to their declarations, for their artful malice is great. Another example of their arts hath reached me."

Story of the Merchant, his Wife, and the Parrot.

THERE was a merchant, who traded largely, and travelled much abroad; he had a wife whom he loved, and to her he was constant.[1] A journey became necessary for him, and he bought for a hundred dínars a parrot, that could speak like a human being, that it might inform him of what passed in the house.

---

[1] Vatsyayana, in his *Kama Sutra*, says that a man who is much given to travelling does not deserve to be married.

Before he departed upon his journey, he committed to the parrot the charge of watching his wife's conduct. When he was gone, the lady sent to her lover, who was a soldier;[1] and he came, and abode with her during the time of her husband's absence. The parrot observed all that was done. On the merchant's return, he called for the bird, and asked him what had passed, and was informed of his wife's misconduct. When the merchant heard this intelligence, he was enraged against his wife, beat her severely, and kept himself from her. The wife supposed that her neighbours had accused her; but they declared, upon oath, that they had not spoken to him. Then she said: "None can have informed him but the parrot."

Upon a certain night, the merchant went to visit a friend. Then the wife took a coarse cloth, and put it upon the parrot's cage, and placed over it, on the floor above, the grinding-stones; after which she ordered her slave-girls to grind, throw water over the cloth, and raise a great wind with a fan. Then she took a looking-glass, and made it dazzle in the light of the lamp, by a quick motion.

The bird (being in the dark) supposed that the noise of the grinding was thunder; the gleams from the mirror, lightning; the blasts from the fan, wind; and the water, hard rain.[2] In the morning, when the

---

[1] A young Turk, according to the Calcutta text.

[2] In the Turkish version of this story, as found in the *Forty Vazīrs*, a piece of bullock's hide is stretched over the cage, and

merchant returned to his house, the parrot said:
"How fared my lord last night, during the wind,
the rain, and the dreadful lightning?" The merchant
exclaimed: "Villain, thou liest; for I did not see anything of it;" and the parrot replied: "I only tell thee
what I experienced."

The merchant now disbelieved the bird, and put
confidence in his wife. He went to her, and sought
to be reconciled, but she said: "I will not be reconciled, unless you destroy the mischief-making parrot,
who belied me." He killed the bird, and after that
remained some time happy with his wife. At length
the neighbours informed him of her crimes, when he
concealed himself, and detected the soldier with her.
The fidelity of the parrot was apparent, but the merchant repented of putting him to death, when repentance would not avail him. He divorced his wife, and
took an oath never to marry.[1]

"I have thus informed thee, O sultan," added the
vazír, "of the artfulness of women, and proved that
rashness produces only fruitless remorse."—The sultan,
upon this, refrained from the execution of his son.

When night set in, the Damsel came to the sultan,
and said: "Why hast thou delayed doing me justice?

beat from time to time to imitate thunder; water is sprinkled on
the bird through a sieve; and a mirror flashed before it now and
again.

[1] See note, page 34; and Appendix, No. 3.

Hast thou not heard that sovereigns should be obeyed in whatever they command, and that an order not enforced is a sign of weakness? Every one knows what must follow. Do me justice, then, upon thy son, or it will happen to you both, as it happened to the fuller and his son."—Then the king said: "What befell the fuller and his son?" She replied:

Story of the Fuller and his Son.

KNOW, O sultan, that there was a fuller who went daily to wash his cloths on the bank of a river, and with him his son, who used to venture far into the water and swim; which his father forbade, but he would not be prevented. On a certain day, the youth went into a deep part, and his arms became cramped. When the father beheld his situation, he threw himself into the river, hoping to save him; but the youth hung upon his legs, and they were both drowned. [5]

"Do me justice, then, upon thy son. Thy vazīrs pretend that the art of our sex is greater than that of men; but the fact is the contrary, as you will see from the

Story of the Sultan and the Vazīr's Wife.

IT has been related to me, my lord, that there was a certain sultan much addicted to the love of women, of violent passions. Being one day upon the terrace of his palace, he saw a lady upon the platform of her house, beautiful and elegant; his soul desired her, and he was told that she was the wife of his vazīr. Upon this he sent for the minister, and despatched him on a distant expedition, with orders not to return till he had executed his commission. The vazīr attended to his sovereign's commands, and departed.

When the sultan knew of his departure, he was impatient to see the lady, and repaired to her house. She received him standing, and kissed the ground before him; but she was virtuous, and had no inclination to immodesty. She then said: "Why, O my lord, is this auspicious visit?" He replied: "From the excess of my love and passion for thee." Upon which she kissed the ground, and said: "It is not befitting that I should be thy partner; my heart has never aspired to such an honour."

Then the sultan extended his hands upon her, and tempted her; when she cried: "My lord, this must never be." Observing that he was enraged at her refusal, she dissembled, and said: "Wait, O my lord, until I have prepared a supper, which when thou hast partaken of, I shall be honoured with thy commands."

She then seated the sultan upon the sofa of her husband, and brought him a book from which the vazīr was used to read to her. In it were written admonitions and warnings against adultery, and commands to his wife not to admit any one within doors without his orders. On the perusal of it, the sultan's mind was diverted from the pursuit of his guilty passion.

K

At length the lady placed a supper before him, consisting of ninety and nine dishes; when the sultan ate a mouthful from every dish. Each was of a different colour, but all of the same sort of food. Then he said to her: " How is this?"—She replied: " My lord, I have set a parable before thee. In thy palace are ninety and nine concubines, of different stature and complexion; who, however, form but one kind of food."

The sultan was confounded, and did not importune her. Rising up, he went to perform his ablutions, but left his ring under a cushion of the sofa; and on his return to the palace, forgot to take it with him.[1]

When the vazīr returned from his journey, and had visited the sultan, he repaired to his own house, and sat down upon the sofa; and, behold! under the cushion he discovered the sultan's ring, which he knew. Becoming jealous of his wife, he was enraged against her, and secluded himself from her for a whole year; during which he did not go near, nor even inquire after her. When the coolness of her husband became intolerable, the lady complained to her father, and informed him of his neglect of her for a whole year; upon which the father repaired to the sultan, when the vazīr was present, and said:

" May God preserve the sultan! I had an elegant garden, which was formed by my own hand, and I

---

[1] See page 81, and note.

watered it until it was the season of its fruits. Then I presented it to thy vazīr, and he ate of its productions until he was satiated, when he deserted and neglected it; and it was spoiled, and reptiles over-ran it;—its flowers were injured, and its condition was changed."

The sultan said to the vazīr: "How sayest thou?" The vazīr replied: "He speaketh the truth in what he hath related. But one day, when I entered the garden, I saw the track of a lion in it; my mind was alarmed, and I refrained from visiting it."

On hearing this parable, the sultan understood it, recollected that he had forgotten his ring in the house of the vazīr, and knew that by it was meant the track of the lion. He then said: "It is true, O vazīr, that the lion did enter without the consent of the owner's wife; but the lion did not compel her to commit evil. She is a virtuous woman, and of chaste desires."

Then the vazīr said: "To hear is to obey;" and he was now convinced that the sultan had not compelled her to dishonour. He returned to his wife, who related to him all that had passed; and he relied upon her truth, her honour, and her fidelity.

"Had she been vicious," continued the Damsel, "she would have complied with the sultan, when he disclosed his wishes; but know, my lord, that men are more deceitful than women." [17]

Next morning the sultan commanded the execution of his son; when the Second Vazîr entered, and, kissing the ground, said: "Be not rash in executing thy son. Thou wast not blessed with him till after despairing of issue, and could scarcely credit his existence. He may yet prove to thee the preserver of thy kingdom, and a guardian of thy memory. Be patient, then, my lord, until he shall find a proper opportunity to speak for himself. If thou puttest him to death, thou wilt repent when repentance will not avail. I have heard, O sultan, much of the female sex, of their arts and their stratagems, especially in the

Story of the Officer and the Merchant's Wife.

THERE was an officer belonging to the body-guard of his prince, who admired a merchant's wife, and was passionately beloved by her. On a certain day he sent his slave to see whether her husband was at home or absent. When the slave came, not finding her husband, he would have returned; but the lady, on seeing him, would not let him go.

While they were conversing, the officer came up, and she took the slave and locked him in an inner chamber. And, while the officer was with her, suddenly her husband knocked at the door. Upon this the lady said to the officer, who was much alarmed: "Draw thy scimitar, and go down to the entry, abuse me, and revile me, and say: ' He certainly is with thee,

and thou hast concealed him.' When my husband
enters, go out, and pursue thy way."

Her husband, on coming in, saw the officer standing
in the entry, with a drawn sword in his hand, exclaiming: "Thou wretch! thou hast hidden the lad near
thee," and he then hastened home. The merchant
said to his wife: "What has been the matter?" She
replied: "Thou hast this day saved an unfortunate
Mussulman from being murdered." He asked her how
that was, and she replied: "I was sitting, thinking
upon thee, when a young lad rushed in, and cried:
'Save me from death, and God will save thee from
the fire! An officer would murder me without a
fault.' Then I took him, and concealed him in my
chamber; after which the officer entered, and began
to abuse me, and would have killed me, saying, 'He
is with thee.' God be praised that you came in, or
I should have been a corpse."—Her husband said:
"God preserve thee from the fire, for what thou hast
done—I doubt not but he will."

Then she took the lad from the chamber, and he
pretended to weep, and thanked her for her kindness; but the husband did not guess the least of the
disgrace that had befallen his head from his wife's
intrigues. [4]

"This, O sultan, is only one instance of the art of
women; alas, that thou shouldst give credit to their
accusations!"

When the third night was arrived, the Damsel entered, and kissing the ground, wept, and said: "Wilt thou not, my lord, do me justice upon thy son? And wilt thou not refrain from attending to the stories of thy vazīrs? They are full of wickedness. I have heard, O sultan, of a vazīr who would have murdered the son of his master." He inquired: "In what manner?" She replied:

Story of the Prince and the Ghūl.[1]

THERE was a certain sultan who had a son, whom he loved with ardent affection. The prince one day begged permission of his father to hunt; upon which the sultan ordered preparations, commanded his vazīr to attend him, and sent with him slaves, domestics, and troops. They advanced towards the chase, and passed through a. verdant plain, having groves and rivulets, among which the antelopes sported. The prince pursued and ran down much game of various kinds, and remained long, diverting himself with the sport, in great spirits and enjoyment.

As he was returning homewards, there bounded across the plain an antelope, brilliant as the sun shining in a serene sky; and the vazīr said: "Let us pursue this deer, for my heart longs to take her." When the prince heard this, he followed her; and the attendants would have accompanied him, but the vazīr

---

[1] See note 2, page 55.

forbade them. The antelope did not cease to gain
ground, nor the prince to pursue her, till the evening
overshadowed, when she disappeared, and darkness
came on.

The prince would have returned, but could not find
his path, and he fainted with terror; nor could he
move from the thirsty desert until the morning. He
then prayed to God for deliverance, and travelled on,
oppressed with hunger, until mid-day; when, lo! he
came to a ruined town, in which owls and ravens had
their abodes. While he stopped, astonished at their
screamings, a female voice struck his ear, and he beheld a beautiful girl sitting under one of the mould-
ering walls, weeping bitterly. He addressed her, and
said: "Why dost thou lament, and who art thou?"
She replied: "Know that I am the daughter of a
certain sultan of the north. My father espoused
me to the son of my uncle, and detached troops to
escort me to him, and we began our journey. When
we arrived here, I fell from my carriage, as you see,
and my attendants went on, and left me, thinking I
was still upon the camel.[1] I have remained here three

---

[1] In Arabia, Persia, and other Eastern countries women and
children generally travel in litters, of more or less elegant construction according to their rank, secured on the backs of camels
and elephants. The pre-Islamite Arabian poet Labīd, in his
celebrated *Mu'allaqa*, thus describes the litters which bore away
his mistress and her damsels (Lyall's translation):

"The camel-litters of the tribe stirred thy longing, what time
    they moved away

days, famishing and thirsty, and was despairing of life, when I saw thee."—The prince mounted her behind him, and said: "Comfort thy heart, and dry thine eyes, and say, God be praised, for thy deliverance from this desert."

They now proceeded, and besought assistance from the Almighty.[1] When they had journeyed some time, they reached a city, ruinous like the first, and the damsel said to him: "Remain here, while I retire a little; I will soon return." The prince helped her down, and waited with his horse, when, behold! the ghūl (for such was the pretended damsel) cried to two others, saying: "I have brought a prey to feast upon."[2] When the prince heard this, his heart was chilled. The ghūl came out, and found him pale and trembling. She said: "Prince, why do I behold thy colour changed?" He answered: "I was reflecting on the cause of my sorrows." She exclaimed: "Seek a remedy for them in the treasures of thy father." He replied: "They are not to be remedied by treasure or

---

And crept into the litters hung with cotton, as the wooden
    framework creaked—

The litters hung all around, over their frame of wood, with
    hangings, thin veils, and pictured curtains of wool."

An interesting account of the various kinds of litters used in India and Persia is cited by Garcin de Tassy in a note to his translation of the romance of *Kāmarupa*, chap. xxiii.

[1] That is, the *prince* besought, etc.

[2] See page 55, and note 1.

hoards." She said: "Remedy them by your armies
and troops." He replied: "They are not to be remedied by them." She continued: "Ask help of
the God of power and might; for ye pretend that
ye have in the heavens a God who, when ye call upon
him, will be gracious, and that he is absolute over all
things." The prince replied: "It is true; and we have
no other help but him." Then he lifted up his face
towards heaven, and said: "O Lord, I humbly beseech
thee, and implore aid from thee in this crisis, which
grieveth and afflicteth me;"[1] at the same time catching
the pretended princess in his arms. Scarcely had he
concluded his prayer, when an angel descended from
the sky, with a sword of flame, and smote her with it,
and destroyed her.[2] For this miracle may the Almighty
be glorified! The prince after this returned safely to
the capital of his father. [7]

"All this danger," continued the damsel, "occurred
from the schemes of the vazīr; and I inform thee, O
sultan, that thy vazīrs are also treacherous. Be, then,
watchful of their arts."—Upon this the sultan gave
orders for the execution of his son.

On the next day the Third Vazīr entered, kissed
the ground before the sultan, and said: "Know, O

---

[1] See note 3, page 55.

[2] According to the Greek and Syriac texts, and also the old
Castilian translation, when the prince had uttered a prayer she
fell powerless on the ground.

sultan, I would advise thee candidly, and am faithful
to thyself and thy son. Be not violent against thy
child, the light of thine eyes. It is possible the
damsel's desire of his death may proceed from malice;
and I have heard that two great tribes were destroyed
for the sake of a drop of honey." The sultan inquired,
upon what occasion, and the vazír said:

Story of the Drop of Honey.

IT has been related to me that there was a hunter,
who chased every species of wild animals. One
day in his excursion to the mountains, he found a
hollow in the rocks, full of honey, with which he filled
a vessel he had with him, and returned to the city.
He chanced to stop at the door of an oil-merchant,
when a little of the honey happening to drop, the merchant's cat licked it up, and was killed by the hunter's
dog.[1] Upon this, the merchant killed the dog, at
which the hunter was enraged, and having wounded
the merchant, went to his quarter, and raised his

---

[1] In other versions, some flies alight upon the spilled honey, a
bird attacks the flies, the grocer's cat kills the bird, the hunter's
dog worries the cat—thus bearing some resemblance to our
accumulative nursery rhymes of "The House that Jack Built"
and "The Old Woman and the Crooked Sixpence," which
appear to find their indirect original, strange to say, in an
allegorical hymn in the Talmud.—In the Syriac text, a bee
settles on the honey, a weasel seizes the bee, a dog attacks the
weasel, and so on,

friends. The merchant also raised his friends, and
when the parties met, they fought till they were all
destroyed—for the sake of a drop of honey. [25]

[I have also heard, continued the third vazír, among
instances of female artifice, the

Story of the Woman and the Rice-Seller.[1]

A MAN one day gave his wife a dirham[2] to buy rice,
and she went to the shop of the rice-seller, and said to
him: "Give me rice for this dirham." When he saw
that she was possessed of beauty and an elegant form,
he began cajoling her, and said to her: "Rice is not
good unless with sugar; come within, and I will give
. thee some." The woman consented, and the dealer
ordered his slave to measure a quantity of rice and
sugar, but accompanied the order with a private sign,
which the youth understood; and while his master was
engaged with the woman, he filled her towel with earth
and stones. After this the woman took the towel, and
went off, thinking that it contained sugar and rice;
and when she arrived at her house she placed it before
her husband, and went to fetch the caldron. In the
meantime her husband opened the towel, and dis-

---

[1] Omitted by Scott, "it being too indelicate for translation."
After suppressing a few words of the original, the story, as
follows, is certainly not more free than any of those he has
translated.—See also the story in the Persian text, page 46.

[2] About sixpence of our money.

covered the earth and the stones, and when she came back he said to her: "Did I tell thee that we had a house to build, that thou hast brought earth and stones?" She then perceived that the dealer had tricked her, and said: "O my husband, see what I have done in my confusion: I went for the sieve, and have brought the caldron! For the dirham you gave me dropped from my hand in the market-place,[1] and I was ashamed before the people to look around for it; so I brought back earth and stones, that you might sift them." The husband then arose, and took the sieve, and he sat down sifting the earth until his face and his beard were covered with dust; and the poor man knew not what had happened to him.]

On the fourth night the Damsel entered to the sultan, kissed the ground before him, and said: "My lord, you have rejected my cause, delayed my claims, and will not do me justice upon thy son. But God will assist me, as he assisted the son of a certain sultan against his father's vazīr." The sultan inquired in what manner that happened, and she related the

Story of the Transformed Prince.

THERE was a sultan, who had an only son, whom he betrothed to the daughter of a great monarch. She was very beautiful, and passionately beloved by the

---

[1] See note 1, page 49.

son of her uncle; but her father would not consent to give her to him in marriage, on account of his prior engagement to the sultan. When the young man found that his uncle had affianced her to another, he was exceedingly afflicted, and had no other resource but to send rich presents to the vazīr of the intended bridegroom's father, and entreat him that he would deceive the prince by some stratagem, so that the match might be broken off. The vazīr accepted the bribe, and promised compliance.

The father of the princess, after some time, wrote to the sultan, requesting that he would send his son, to celebrate the marriage at his court; after which he might return home with his bride. The sultan consented, and despatched the prince under care of his vazīr, with attendants and slaves, and an escort of a thousand horse; he also sent by him a rich present of camels, and horses, and tents, and valuable curiosities.

The vazīr departed with the prince, but resolved to betray him, on account of the bribes he had received from the cousin of the princess. At length they entered a desert, where the vazīr bethought himself of a fountain, named the White Fountain, of which but few persons knew the properties; these were, that if a man drank of the water, he became a woman; and if a woman drank of it, she became a man. The vazīr encamped at some distance from it, and invited the prince to ride out with him; when he mounted, but did not suspect what the vazīr had devised. They did not cease riding in the wilderness till sunset, when the prince complained that he was overcome with thirst, and unable to converse from the parching of his mouth. The vazīr then brought him to the fountain, and said: "Dismount, and drink."

The prince alighted from his horse, and drank, when lo! he instantly became a woman. On perceiving his condition, he wept aloud, and was overcome with shame, and fainted. On his recovery, the vazīr came up to him with pretended condolements, and said: "What has befallen thee? And whence is this sorrow?" The prince having related what had occurred to him, the vazīr said: "Thy enemies must have done this. A great misfortune and a heavy calamity have certainly come upon thee; for how can the object of our journey be performed when thou art thyself become a bride? I would advise that we return to thy father, and inform him of what has happened." The prince replied: "I swear by the Almighty, that I will not return, until he shall remove from me this affliction, though I should die under it."—The vazīr then returned to his troops, and left the prince; who walked onwards, not knowing whither he should proceed.

On the way there met him a horseman, beautiful as the full moon,[1] who saluted him, and said: "Lady,

---

[1] In the Rich MS. of the 1001 N. (Brit. Mus.), the treacherous vazīr returns to the king, and informs him of what had happened

who art thou, and why behold I thee alone in this
frightful desert? For I perceive upon thee the
marks of distinction, and that thou art sorrowful and
afflicted." When the prince heard these kind expressions from the horseman, he put confidence in him, and
related what had befallen him. The cavalier said:
"Hast thou drank of the White Fountain?" He
answered: "Yes;" and the other rejoined: "Comfort
thyself, and dry thine eyes, for I will attempt thy
delivery." The prince then fell at his feet, and would
have kissed them, but he forbade him; when the
prince said: "I conjure thee by Allah, tell me, how
can relief come to me through thee?" He replied:
"I am a jinnī, but will not injure thee."

They travelled all night, and at dawn reached a
verdant plain, abounding in trees and rivulets, and
upon it lofty edifices; and there they dismounted,
and entered one of the palaces. The jinnī welcomed
him, and they remained all day feasting in mirth and
gladness. At night the jinnī mounted his horse,
and taking the prince behind him, travelled through
the dark until daylight, when, lo! they beheld a black

---

to the prince; and the king, sorely stricken with grief, endeavours
in vain to ascertain the cause of his son's misfortune from masters
of the occult sciences.—The prince remained three days and three
nights, and neither ate nor drank, and his horse was tied, pastur-
ing in the valley, and he weeping over his fate. But when the
fourth day came, behold, a yellow horseman, riding on a yellow
horse, and on his head a yellow diadem, etc.—The Būlāq and
Calcutta texts are to the same purpose.

plain, frightful and gloomy, which might be compared to the confines of hell. The prince inquired the name of the country, and the jinnī replied: "This country is called the Black Region, and is governed by a prince of the jinn, without whose permission no one dare enter it. Remain here, while I ask for leave, and return." The prince remained a little while, when the jinnī appeared, and conducted him onwards; and they did not stop till they came to a stream of water flowing from a rock, of which the jinnī commanded him to drink. He dismounted, and drank, and his sex returned to him as before.

The prince now praised God, and prayed, and he thanked the jinnī and kissed his hands, and inquired the name of the well. The jinnī replied: "This is the Fountain of Women. If a woman drink of it she becomes a man, by the decree of God. Praise the Lord, then, O my brother, for thy welfare and deliverance."

They travelled the remainder of the day, till they arrived at the dwelling of the jinnī, where the prince remained with him in mirth and festivity all that night and the following day; in the evening of which the jinnī said: "Dost thou wish to spend this night with thy bride?" The prince replied: "Certainly; but how, my lord, can I effect it?" The jinnī then called to one of his attendants, whose name was Jāzūr, and said: "Take this youth upon thy back, and do not descend anywhere but upon the terrace

of his father-in-law's palace, near the apartment of his
bride." Jāzūr replied: "To hear is to obey."

When a third of the night remained, Jāzūr appeared.
He was an 'Ifrīt of monstrous size, so that the prince
was alarmed; but the jinnī said: "He will not injure
thee; fear him not." He then embraced the prince,
took leave, and mounting him upon the back of the
'Ifrīt, said: "Bind something over thine eyes." The
prince having done so, the 'Ifrīt soared with him
between heaven and earth; but he perceived no
motion, till he was set down on the terrace of his
father-in-law's palace, when the 'Ifrīt disappeared.
The prince slept till near daylight, when his spirits
revived, and he descended towards the apartments.
The female attendants met him, and saluted him, and
conducted him to the sultan, who knew him, and stood
up and embraced him, and welcoming him, said: "My
son, they usually bring the bridegroom by the gate, but
thou comest from the terrace; truly I am astonished
at thy proceedings." The prince answered: "If that
seems strange, I have still more wonderful events to
detail;" and he then related his adventures from first
to last, at which the sultan was astonished, and praised
God for his deliverance.

The nuptial ceremonies were now commenced, and
when the rites were concluded the prince was admitted
to his bride, and remained with her a whole month.
He then requested leave to return home; upon which
his father-in-law presented him with rich gifts, and

L

furnished him with an escort. The cousin of the princess died of disappointment. The prince arrived with his bride at the capital of his father in safety; and the sultan rejoiced with exceeding great joy, after being in despair for his son. [26]

"I hope," said the Damsel, "that God will also revenge me upon thy vazīrs and upon thy son."—The sultan replied: "I will do thee justice immediately," and issued orders for the execution of the prince.

On the fourth day the Fourth Vazīr came to the sultan, kissed the ground before him, and said: "O sultan, kill not thy son, or thou wilt repent when repentance will not profit thee. A wise man will not act until he hath considered the consequences. I have heard the following anecdote."[1]

*   *   *   *   *

[The vazīr then relates, as an example of the artifice and duplicity of women, the]

Story of the Old Woman and the She-Dog.

THERE was a certain merchant's son, who had a handsome wife, and it happened that a libertine, accidentally

---

[1] This little prefatory address of the fourth vazīr does not refer to the story which follows in Scott's translation, but to the tale of THE BATHMAN, which he has very properly suppressed, and it should also have been omitted.—See note, page 61.

beholding her, fell in love with her. While the husband was absent on a journey of business, the youth went to an old woman of the neighbourhood, who was on intimate terms with the wife, and disclosed to her his passion, offering her ten dinars[1] for her assistance.

The cunning old woman went several times to visit the merchant's wife, and always took with her a little she-dog. One day she contrived the following stratagem. She took flour and minced meat, and kneaded them into a cake, with a good deal of pepper. Then she forced the cake down the animal's throat, and when the pepper began to heat her stomach, her eyes became wet, as if with tears. The merchant's wife, observing this, said to the old woman: "My good mother, this dog daily follows you, and seems as if she wept. What can be the cause?" The old woman replied: "My dear mistress, the circumstance is wonderful; for she was formerly a beautiful girl, straight as the letter *alif*, and made the sun ashamed by her superior radiance. A Jewish sorcerer fell in love with her, whom she refused; and when he despaired of obtaining her, he was enraged, and by magic transformed her into a she-dog, as thou seest. She was a friend of mine; she loved me, and I loved her; so that, in her new form, she took to following me wherever I went, for I have always fed her, and taken care of her, on account of our friendship. She weeps often when reflecting on her unfortunate condition."

---

[1] A gold dinar is equivalent to about ten shillings.

When the merchant's wife heard this, she trembled for herself, and said: "A certain man hath professed love to me, and I did not intend to gratify his criminal passion. But thou hast terrified me with the story of this unhappy damsel, so that I am alarmed lest the man should transform me in like manner."—"My dear daughter," said the wicked old woman, "I am your true friend, and advise you that if any man makes love to you not to refuse him." The wife then said: "How shall I find out my lover?"—"For the sake of thy peace," replied the old wretch, "for the love I bear thee, and for fear lest thou shouldst also be transformed, I will go and seek him."

She then went out, rejoicing that she had gained her ends, and sought the young man, but did not find him at home. So she said to herself: "I will not let this day pass, however, without gaining a reward for my trouble. I will introduce some one else to her, and obtain from him a second present." She then walked through the streets in search of a proper man; when behold! she met the husband just returning from his journey, whom she did not know. She went up to him, and saluted him, and said: "Hast thou any objection to a good supper and a handsome mistress?" He replied: "I am ready;" upon which she took him by the hand, and leading him to his own house, desired him to wait at the door.

When the man reached his own dwelling, jealousy overcame him, and the world became dark to his eyes.

The old woman went to the wife, to inform her of the coming of her lover; whom, when she saw him from the window, she knew, and exclaimed: "Why, mother, thou hast brought my husband!" The old woman, hearing this, replied: "There remains nothing now but to deceive him." The wife took the hint, and said: "I will meet him, and abuse him for his intrigues, and will say, 'I sent this old woman as a spy upon thee.'"

She then began to exclaim against the infidelity of her husband, took a sheet of paper, and descended the staircase, and said to him: "Thou shameless man, there was a promise of constancy between us, and I swore unto thee that I would not love another. Luckily, however, I suspected thy falsehood, and when I knew thou wast returning from thy journey, sent this old woman to watch thee, that I might discover thy proceedings, and whether thou wast faithful to thy agreement or not. It is now clear that thou frequentest the dwellings of courtesans, and I have been deceived. But since I know thy falsehood, there can be no cordiality between us; therefore write me a divorce, for I can no longer love thee."

The husband, on hearing this, was alarmed, and remained for a time in astonishment. He took a solemn oath that he had not been unfaithful to her, and had not been guilty of what she had accused him. He did not cease to soothe her till she was somewhat pacified, when the old woman interfered, and effected a reconciliation between them, for which kindness she was handsomely rewarded. The unfortunate husband little suspected the disgrace he had so narrowly escaped. [11]

"This, O sultan," said the vazīr, "is only one instance of the art and deceit of women."—The sultan then countermanded the execution of his son.

On the fifth evening the Damsel came to the sultan, holding a cup of poison in her hand, and said: "If thou wilt not do me justice upon thy son, I will drink this poison, and my crime will rest upon thy shoulders. Thy vazīrs say that women are cunning and deceitful, but there is no creature in the universe more crafty than man. For instance:

Story of the Goldsmith and the Singing Girl.[1]

I HAVE heard that a goldsmith,[2] who was passionately fond of women, one day entered a friend's house, and saw upon the wall of an apartment the portrait of a beautiful girl, with which he became enraptured; and love so overcame his heart that his friends said to him: "Thou foolish man, how couldst thou think of loving a figure depicted on a wall, of the original of which thou hast never heard or seen?" He replied:

---

[1] In Scott's translation, the hero of this story is a painter, but a goldsmith, or a jeweller, in four other Arabic texts.

[2] In a city of Persia, according to the Calcutta and Būlāq texts.

"A painter could not have drawn this portrait unless he had seen the original." One of his friends observed, that perhaps the painter might have formed it merely from his imagination. He answered: "I hope from heaven comfort and relief; but what you say cannot be proved except by the painter." They then told him that he lived in a certain town; and the young man wrote to inquire whether he had seen the original of the picture he had painted, or had drawn it from fancy. The answer was that the portrait was that of a singing-girl belonging to a vazīr of Ispahān.[1] Encouraged by this intelligence, the young man made preparations for a journey, and having departed, travelled night and day until he reached the city, where he took up his abode.

In a few days he made acquaintance with an apothecary, and became intimate with him. Talking upon various subjects, at length they conversed regarding the sultan of Ispahān and his disposition; when the apothecary said: "Our sovereign bears inveterate hatred to all practitioners of magic, and if they fall into his hands, he casts them into a deep cave without the city, where they die of hunger and thirst." Next they conversed about the famous singing-girl of the vazīr, and the young man learned that she was still with him.

The young goldsmith now began to plan his stratagems. On the first moonlight night he disguised

---

[1] Of Kashmīr, according to four other texts.

himself as a robber, and repairing to the palace of
the vazīr, fixed a ladder of ropes, by which he
gained the terrace, from whence he descended into
the court; when lo! a light gleamed from one of the
apartments. He entered it, and beheld a throne of
ivory, inlaid with gold, on which reposed a lady bright
as the sun in a serene sky. At her head and feet were
placed lamps, the splendour of which her countenance
outshone. He approached, and gazed upon her, and
saw that she was the object of his desires. Near the
pillow was a rich veil, embroidered with pearls and
precious stones. He drew a knife from his girdle,
and wounded her slightly on the palm of her hand.
The pain awakened the lady, but she did not scream
from alarm, believing him to be only a robber in
search of plunder; she said: "Take this embroidered
veil, but do not injure me." He took the veil, and
departed by the same way that he had entered.[1]

When daylight appeared, he disguised himself in
white vestments, like a holy pilgrim; visited the sultan,
and having saluted him, and the sultan having returned
the salutation, he thus addressed him: "O sultan, I
am a pilgrim devoted to religion, from the country of
Khurasan, and have repaired to thy presence because
of the report of thy virtues and thy justice to thy
subjects, intending to remain under the shade of thy
protection. I reached thy capital at the close of day,

---

[1] In some Arabic versions he wounds her in the shoulder, and
takes away part of her ornaments.

when the gates were shut. Then I lay down to repose, and was in slumber, when behold! four women issued from a grove, one mounted upon a hyæna, another upon a ram, a third upon a black she-dog, and the fourth upon a leopard. When I saw them, I knew they must be sorceresses. One of them having approached me, began to kick me with her feet, and to strike me with a whip, which appeared like a flame of fire. I then repeated the names of God, and struck at her hand with my knife, which wounded her, but she escaped from me. There dropped from her this veil, which I took up, and found it embroidered with valuable jewels; but I have no occasion for them, for I have given up the world." Having thus spoken, he laid the veil at the sultan's feet, and departed.

On examining the veil, the sultan recognised it as one which he had presented to his vazīr, of whom he demanded: "Did I not bestow upon thee this veil?" The vazīr replied: "You did, my lord; and I gave it to a favourite singing-girl of my own."—"Let her be sent for immediately," exclaimed the sultan; "for she is a wicked sorceress." The vazīr went to his palace, and brought the girl before the sultan, who, on seeing the slight wound on her hand, was convinced of the pretended pilgrim's assertion, and commanded her to be cast into the cave of sorcerers.

When the goldsmith found that his stratagem had succeeded, and that the girl was thrown into the cave, he took a purse of a thousand dīnars, and went to the keeper of the cave, and said to him: "Accept this purse, and listen to my story." After relating his adventures, the goldsmith said: "This poor girl is innocent, and I am the person who has plunged her into misfortune. If thou wilt release her, it will be a merciful action, and I will convey her privately to my own country. Should she remain here, she will soon be among the number of the dead. Pity, then, her condition and my own, and repay thy generosity with this purse." The keeper accepted the present, and released the girl; and the goldsmith took her with him, and returned to his own city. [27]

"This, O sultan," said the Damsel, "is but one example of the craft of men."—The sultan then gave orders for the execution of his son.

Next day the Fifth Vazîr presented himself before the sultan, and said: "O my lord, reprieve thy son, and be not hasty in his death, lest thou repent, as the man repented, who never afterwards smiled." The sultan inquired his history, and the vazîr proceeded:

Story of the Young Man who was taken to the Land of Women.[1]

THERE was a man, possessed of great wealth and master of many slaves, who died, leaving his estates

---

[1] Scott absurdly entitles this story, "The Ten Old Men and the Decayed Rake." In his time, the term "decayed" was

to an infant son. When he reached manhood, he engaged in pleasure and amusements, in feasting and drinking, in music and dancing, with profusion and extravagance, until he had expended the riches his father had left him. He then took to selling his effects and slaves and concubines, till at length, through distress, he was obliged to ply as a porter in the streets for a subsistence.

As he one day waited for an employer, an old man of portly and respectable appearance stopped, and looked earnestly at him for some time. At length the young man said: "Why, sir, do you so earnestly gaze at my countenance? Have you any occasion for my services?" The old man replied: "Yes, my son. We are ten old men, who live together in the same house,[1] and have at present no person to attend us. If thou wilt accept the office, I trust (God willing) it will afford thee much advantage." The youth replied: "Most willingly and readily." Then said the old man: "You shall serve us, but upon condition that you conceal our situation; and when you see us weeping and lamenting, that you ask not the cause." The young man consented, whereupon his new master took him to a bath, and when he was cleansed, presented

often employed to describe a person who "had seen better days," as a "decayed gentlewoman"—a phrase which seems now-a-days sufficiently ludicrous.—The short title of this story is "Curiosity."

[1] "I have with me ten old men in one house," according to the Būlāq and Calcutta texts—that is, ten besides himself.

him with a handsome dress, and repaired with him to his own house. This proved to be a magnificent palace; its courts surrounded by galleries, and adorned with basins and fountains. All sorts of birds fluttered in the lofty trees which ornamented the gardens, and overshadowed the apartments.

The old man conducted him into one of the pavilions, which was laid over with silken carpets, rich masnads,[1] and superb cushions. In this pavilion sat nine venerable old men, all weeping and lamenting, at which he was astonished, but asked no questions. His master then took him to a large chest, pulled out of it a bag containing a thousand dīnars, and said: "My son, thou art entrusted by God with this treasure, to expend it upon us and thyself with integrity." The young man replied: "To hear is to obey." He now busied himself in providing for their wants, what was necessary for victuals and raiment, during three years. At length one of the old men died, and they washed his corpse, and buried it in the garden of the palace.

The young man continued to serve them, and the old men died one after another, until nine had departed, and he only remained who had hired him. At last he also fell sick, and the young man despaired of his recovery. So he said to himself: "My master will surely die, and why should I not ask him the cause of their bewailings?" Approaching the couch of the old

---

[1] A *masnad* is a kind of counterpane, spread on the carpet where the master of the house sits and receives company.

man, who groaned in the agonies of death, he said:
"O my master, I conjure thee by God to acquaint
me with the reason of your constant lamentations."
"My son," he replied, "there is no occasion for thee
to know it, so do not importune me for what will not
profit thee. Believe me, I have ever loved and com-
passionated thee. I dread lest thou shouldst be
punished as we have been punished, but wish thou
mayest be preserved. Be advised, therefore, my son,
and open not yonder locked door." He then pointed
out the door to him; after which his agonies increased,
and he exclaimed: "I testify that there is no god but
God, and that Muhammad is his servant and prophet!"
Then his soul fluttered, he turned upon his side, and
he was joined to his Lord. The young man washed
the corpse, enshrouded it, and buried him by the side
of his companions.

After this he took possession of the palace, and
diverted himself for some time in examining the
treasures it contained. At length his mind became
restless for want of employment. He reflected upon
the fate of the old men, and on the dying words of his
master, and the charge he had given him. He examined the door; his mind was overcome by curiosity to
see what could be within it, and he did not weigh the
consequences. Satan tempted him to open the door,
and he exclaimed with the poet: "What is not to
happen cannot be effected by human contrivance;
but what is to be will be." He now unlocked the

door. It opened into a long dark passage, in which he wandered for three hours, when he came out upon the shore of the ocean. He was astonished, and gazed with wonder on all sides. He would have returned, but lo! a black eagle of monstrous size darted from the air, and seizing him in her talons, soared for some time between heaven and earth. At length it descended with him upon a small island in the ocean, and fled away.

The young man remained a while motionless with terror; but recovering, began to wander about the island. Suddenly a sail arose to his view on the waters, resembling a fleeting cloud in the heavens. He gazed, and the sail approached, till it reached the beach of the island, when he beheld a boat formed of ivory, ebony, and sandal, the oars of which were made of aloes-wood of Comorin, the sails were of white silk, and it was navigated by beautiful maidens, shining like moons. They advanced from the boat, and kissing his hands, said: "Our souls are refreshed at seeing thee, for thou art the master of our country and of our queen." One of the ladies approached him with a parcel wrapped in rich damask, in which was a royal dress most superbly embroidered, and a crown of gold splendidly set with diamonds and pearls. She assisted him to dress; during which the youth said to himself: "Do I see this in a dream? or am I awake? The old man mentioned nothing of this. He must surely have forbade my opening the door out of envy."

The ladies then conducted him to the boat, which he found spread with elegant carpets and cushions of brocade. They hoisted the sails, and rowed with their oars, while the youth could not divine what would be the end of his adventure. He continued in a state of bewilderment till they reached land, when behold! the beach was crowded with troops and attendants, gallant in appearance, and of the tallest stature. When the boat anchored, five principal officers of the army advanced to the young man, who was at first alarmed, but they paid their obeisance profoundly, and welcomed him in a tone shrill as the sound of silver. Then the drums beat, the trumpets sounded, and the troops arranged themselves on his right hand and on his left. They proceeded till they reached an extensive and verdant meadow, in which another detachment met them, numerous as the rolling billows or waving shadows.

Lastly appeared a young prince, surrounded by the nobles of his kingdom, but all wore veils, so that no part of them could be seen but their eyes. When the prince came near the young man, he and his company alighted, some of them embraced each other, and after conversing a while, remounted their horses. The cavalcade then proceeded, and did not halt till it came to the royal palace, when the young man was helped from his horse,[1] and the prince conducted him into a

---

[1] This is the first intimation that the youth rode on horseback to meet the prince : the copyist had probably omitted to state, what other Arabic texts mention, that, when the boat reached

splendid hall, in which was the royal throne. The seeming prince ascended it and sat down; and on removing the veil from his face, the young man beheld a beautiful damsel in the supposed prince. While he gazed in astonishment, she said: "Young man, this country is mine, the troops are mine, and I am their queen; but when a man arriveth amongst us, he becomes my superior, and governs in my place." The youth, upon hearing this, was wrapt still more in wonder. And while they were conversing, the vazīr entered, who was a stately looking matron, to whom the queen said: "Call the qāzī and the witnesses." She replied: "To hear is to obey."

The queen then said to the young man: "Art thou willing that I should be thy wife, and to be my husband?" Hearing this, and beholding her condescending demeanour, he rose up, and kissing the ground, said (as she would have prevented his prostration): "I am not worthy of such high honour, or even to be one of thy humblest attendants." She replied: "My lord, all that thou hast beheld, and what remains unseen by thee of this country, its provinces, people, and treasures are thine, and I am thy handmaiden. Avoid only yonder door, which thou must not open: if thou dost, thou wilt repent when repentance will not avail."—The vazīr, qāzī, and witnesses, who were all women, now entered, and they were married; after which the

---

the land, four horses of the purest breed were led before him, one of which he selected to ride upon.

courtiers and people were introduced, and congratulated them.

The young man remained for seven months[1] in the
height of enjoyment, when one day he recollected his
old master, and how he had warned him not to open
the door in his palace, which though he had done, yet
from his disobedience such unexpected good fortune
had befallen him. His curiosity and Satan whispered
to him, that within the door which the queen had forbidden him to open, some important scenes must also
be concealed. He advanced, opened it, and entered;
but found a gloomy passage, in which he had not
walked more than twenty steps, when light gleamed
upon him. He advanced, and beheld the same eagle
that had borne him away. He would now have re-
treated, but the monster darted upon him, seized him
in its talons, ascended, and put him down on the spot
where it had first taken him up.

He regretted his lost grandeur, power, and dominion,
exclaiming: "When I rode out, a hundred beautiful
damsels surrounded me, and were flattered by being
permitted to attend me. Alas! I was living in honour,
until I rashly ventured upon what I have committed!"
For two full months he lamented, crying out: "Alas!
alas! if the bird would but once again return!" but in
vain. Night and day, weeping, he would exclaim:
"I was enjoying my ease until my imprudence ruined
me." At length one night, in a restless slumber, he

---

[1] Seven years, according to the Būlāq and Calcutta texts.

heard a voice saying: "Alas! alas! what is past cannot be recovered," upon which he despaired of seeing again his queen or his kingdom. He then entered the palace of his old masters by the dark passage, fatally convinced of what had occasioned their incessant lamentations. He employed himself in praying for their souls; and, like them, wept and lamented, until he died. [28]

"Observe, therefore, O sultan," said the vazīr, "that precipitancy is of ill consequence, and I advise thee from experience."—The sultan then refrained from executing his son.

On the sixth night the Damsel entered with a dagger in her hand, and said: "O sultan, wilt thou revenge me of thy son? If not, I will instantly put myself to death. Thy vazīrs pretend that woman is more artful than man, wishing to destroy my rights; but I assure thee that man is far more deceitful than woman, which is clear from what passed between a prince and a merchant's wife.

Story of the Lover in the Chest.

A MERCHANT, who was exceedingly jealous, had a very beautiful wife. From suspicion of her fidelity, he would not dwell in a city among men, but built a house in a most retired situation, that no one might visit her. It was surrounded by lofty walls, and had a strong gateway. Every morning he locked the door, took the key with him, and proceeded to the city to transact business until the evening.

One day, the sultan's son, riding out for amusement, passed by the house, and cast his eyes on the merchant's wife, who was walking on the terrace. He was captivated by her beauty, and she was no less charmed with his appearance. He tried the gate, but it was securely fastened. At length he wrote a declaration of his love, and fixed it on an arrow, which he shot upon the terrace. The merchant's wife read the letter, and returned a favourable answer. He then took the key of a chest, tied it to a note, in which was written, "I will come to thee in a chest, of which this is the key," and threw it up to her. The prince after this took his leave, and returning to the city, sent for his father's vazír, to whom he communicated what had happened, requesting his assistance. "My son," said the vazír, "what can I do? I tremble for my character in such a business, and what plan can we pursue?" The prince answered: "I only require thy help in what I have contrived. I mean to place myself in a large chest, which thou must lock upon me, and convey at night to the merchant's house, and say to him: 'This chest contains my jewels and treasure, which I am afraid the sultan may seize, and must for a time entrust to thy care.'"

The vazír having consented to the proposal, the prince entered the chest, which was then locked and conveyed privately to the town-house of the merchant.

The vazīr knocked at the door, and the merchant appearing, made a profound obeisance to so honourable a visitant, who requested to leave the chest with him for some days, till the alarm of the sultan's displeasure should be over. The merchant readily consented, and had the chest for security carried to his country house, and placed in the apartments of his wife. In the morning he went about his affairs to the city, when his wife, having adorned herself in her richest apparel, opened the chest. The prince came out, embraced her, and kissed her. They passed the day together in merriment, till the merchant's return, when the prince repaired to his place of concealment.

Seven days had passed in this manner, when it chanced that the sultan inquired for his son, and the vazīr went hastily to the merchant to reclaim the chest. The merchant had returned earlier than usual to his country house, and was overtaken on his way by the vazīr. The lady and the prince, who had been amusing themselves in the court of the house, were suddenly disturbed by a knocking at the gate, and the prince betook himself to the chest, which the wife in her confusion forgot to lock. The merchant entered with his servants, who took up the chest to deliver to the vazīr; when lo! the lid opened, and the prince was discovered, half intoxicated with wine. The poor merchant durst not revenge himself upon the son of his sovereign. He conducted him to the vazīr, who was overwhelmed with shame at the disgraceful discovery. The merchant, convinced of his own dishonour, and that his precautions had been in vain, divorced his wife, and took an oath never to marry again. [29]

"Such is the wiliness of men," added the Damsel; "but thy vazīrs cannot escape my penetration."—After hearing this story, the sultan, who doatingly loved the Damsel, gave orders for the execution of his son.

On the sixth day the Sixth Vazīr came before the sultan, and said: "Be cautious, my lord, in the execution of your son; be not rash, for rashness is sinful, and the artfulness of women is well known, for God has declared, in the Qur'ān, that their craftiness is beyond all measure.

Story of the Merchant's Wife and her Suitors.

It has been reported to me that there was a woman who had a husband accustomed to travel much on business to distant countries. During one of his journeys, his wife became enamoured of a young man, who returned her fondness. It happened one day that this youth, having been engaged in a brawl, was apprehended by the police, and carried before the wālī[1] of the city, when it was proved that he was the transgressor, and the wālī sentenced him to be imprisoned.

---

[1] Chief of police.

When the lady heard of her lover's confinement, her mind was employed from hour to hour devising means for his release.   At length she dressed herself in her richest apparel, repaired to the wālī, made obeisance to him, and complained that her brother having had a scuffle with another youth, hired witnesses had sworn falsely against him, and he had been wrongfully cast into prison.   She added that she could not remain safe without the protection of her brother, and begged that he should be set at liberty.   The lady had a great share of beauty, which when the wālī perceived, he desired her to enter his apartment while he gave orders for her brother's release.   She guessed his design, and said: "My lord, I am an honourable and reputable woman, and cannot enter any apartments but my own.   But if you desire it, you may visit me;" she then mentioned where she resided, and appointed the day when he should come.   The wālī was enraptured, and gave her twenty dīnars, saying: "Expend this at the bath."   She then left him, his heart busy in thinking of her beauty.

The lady next went to the venerable qāzī,[1] and said: "My lord, look upon me," and removed her veil from her face.   "What has happened to thee?" inquired the qāzī.   She replied: "I have a younger brother, and none but him, for a protector, whom the wālī has imprisoned wrongfully, and whom I beseech thee out of thy compassion to release from his confine-

------

[1] See note 2, page 93.

ment." The qāzī said: "Step in, while I order his
release." She answered: "If you mean that, my lord,
it must be at my house;" and she made an assignation
for the same day she had appointed to the wālī. The
qāzī then presented her with twenty dīnars, saying:
"Purchase provisions and sherbets with part of this
sum, and pay for the bath with the remainder."

From the qāzī's house the lady repaired to that of
the vazīr, repeated her story, and besought his interference with the wālī for the release of her brother.
The vazīr also, smitten with her beauty, made proposals
of love, which she accepted, but said he must visit her
at her own house, and fixed the same day she had
named to the wālī and the qāzī. The vazīr then gave
her twenty dīnars, saying: "Expend part of this money
at the bath, and with the rest prepare for us a supper
and wine." She replied: "To hear is to obey."

From the vazīr she proceeded to the hājib,[1] and said:
"My lord, the wālī has imprisoned my brother, who is
but a stripling, on the evidence of false witnesses, and
I humbly beseech thee for his release." The hājib
replied: "Step in, while I send for thy brother." She
suspected his designs, and rejoined: "If my lord has
business with me—in his house is a constant assemblage
of persons—rather let him honour my humble dwelling
with his footsteps." Then she assigned the same day
she had appointed for the others, informing him of the

---

[1] Governor of the city.

situation of her house; and the hājib gave her fifty dīnars, saying: "Prepare a supper for us with part, and lay out the remainder at the bath."

The lady took the gold, and went to a joiner's shop, and said: "I desire that you will make me a large cabinet, with four compartments, so strong that no single person could burst it open. When thou hast finished it, I will pay thee ten dīnars." The joiner agreed, and she hurried him daily till it was finished, when he carried it to her house upon a camel, and set it up in its place. She offered him the price agreed upon, but the joiner refused it, saying: "My dear lady, I will not take anything, and only desire that I may pass an evening with you." She replied: "If that be the case, you must add a fifth compartment to the cabinet." He readily consented, and she fixed the same evening she had appointed for the wālī, the qāzī, the vazīr, and the hājib.

She now went to market, and bought some old garments, which she dyed red, yellow, black, and blue, and made to them whimsical caps of various colours. Then she cooked flesh and fowl, bought wine,[1] and prepared everything for the appointed evening; when she attired herself in her richest apparel, and sat down, expecting her guests.

---

[1] It was formerly the custom at wine-parties in the East for the host and his guests to wear dresses of bright colours, such as red, yellow, and green.—Although wine is prohibited by the Qur'ān, it is often privately drunk by Muslims.

First the wālī[1] knocked at the door, and she rose and opened it, and said: " My lord, the house of your slave is yours, and I am your handmaid." Then, having feasted him till he was satisfied, she took off his robes, and, bringing a black vest and a red cap, said: "Put on the dress of mirth and pleasure;" after which she made him drink wine till he was intoxicated, when lo! there was a knocking at the door, and she said: "My lord, I cannot be cheerful till you have released my brother." He immediately wrote an order to the jailor to give the young man his freedom, which she gave to a servant to deliver, and had no sooner returned to the wālī when the knocking became louder. "Who is coming?" he inquired. "It is my husband," replied the lady; "get into this cabinet, and I will return presently and release thee." Having locked the wālī in the cabinet, she went to the door.

The qāzī now entered, whom she saluted, led in, and seated respectfully. She first filled a cup with wine, and drank to him; and then presented him with meat and wine. The qāzī said gravely: "I have never drunk wine during all my life;" but she per-

---

[1] Here I have made considerable alterations: in Scott's translation (and also in the Calcutta printed text) the qāzī is represented as the first to make his appearance; but we have seen that the first appointment was made with the wālī. It is to be understood that the lady fixed a later hour for each successive suitor, otherwise she might have had two or more on her hands at the same time, which was certainly no part of her plan.

suaded him to drink, saying that company was always dull without wine. After this, she pulled off his magisterial robes, and saying, "My lord, put on the garments of mirth and pleasure," dressed him in a robe of yellow and red, with a black cap. Suddenly the door resounded, and the qāzī, alarmed for his reputation, asked: "Who is at the door? what shall we do?" She replied: "I fear it is my husband. Go into this cabinet, until he goes away, when I will release thee, and we shall pass the evening pleasantly together."

Having locked the qāzī in the cabinet, the lady admitted the vazīr, and, kissing his hand, she said: "Thou hast highly honoured me, my lord, by thy auspicious approach." Then she set supper before him, and cajoled him to drink till he was merry and frolicsome, when she said: "Disrobe yourself, my lord, put on the vesture of pleasure, and leave the habit of the vazīr for its proper offices." Smiling at her playfulness, the vazīr undressed, and put on, at the lady's request, a red vest and a green cap tufted with wool, after which they began to drink and sing, when there was a knocking at the door, and the vazīr, in terror, inquired the cause. "It is my husband," said the lady; "step into this cabinet, till he is gone." The vazīr quickly slipped in, upon which she locked the compartment, and hastened to the door.

The hājib now entered, according to appointment, and having seated him, the lady said courteously: "My lord, you have honoured me by your kindness and condescension." Then she began to undress him, and his robes were worth at least four thousand dīnars. She brought him a parti-coloured vest, and a copper cap set with shells, saying: "These, my lord, are the garments of festivity and mirth." The hājib, having put them on, began to toy and kiss, and she plied him with wine till he was intoxicated. A knocking was again heard at the gate, when the hājib cried out: "Who is this?" and she replied: "My husband; hide in this cabinet, until I can send him away, and I will immediately return to thee."

The poor joiner was next admitted, and the lady plied him so freely with wine, after he had supped, that he was ready for any kind of foolery; so she bade him take off his clothes, and left him, to fetch a dress, when once more the door resounded, and she exclaimed: "Run into this cabinet, even as thou art, for here is my husband." He entered,[1] and having locked him in, the lady then admitted her lover, just released from prison by the wālī's order. She informed him of her stratagem, and said: "We must not remain longer here;" upon which the lover went out and hired camels, and they loaded them with all the effects of the house, leaving nothing but the cabinet, strongly

---

[1] In the Calcutta text, on the arrival of the joiner, she complains that the fifth compartment of the cabinet is too small; he steps into it, to show that there is room for several men, upon which she locks him in, like the others.

secured with five locks, and within it the worthy officers of government and the poor joiner. The lady and her lover set off without further delay, and travelled to another city, where they could be secure from discovery.

Meanwhile the unfortunate lovers in the cabinet were in a woeful condition.[1] At length they became aware of each other's presence, and began to converse, and, notwithstanding their distress, could not refrain from laughing at each other. In the morning the landlord of the house, finding the gate open, entered, but hearing voices from the cabinet, he was alarmed, and summoned a number of the neighbours. Then the landlord exclaimed: "Are you men or jinn that are in this cabinet?" They replied: "If we were jinn, we should not remain here, nor should we want any one to open the doors. We are only men." The neighbours cried out: "Let us not open the cabinet, but in presence of the sultan;" upon which the qāzī exclaimed: "O my people, let us out—'Conceal what God has concealed!'[2] and do not disgrace us. I

---

[1] A short passage, humorous but coarse, is here omitted. Scott states in his preface that he had suppressed "a few expressions rather too plainly descriptive of natural situations;" this is one which he has retained—his notions of "delicacy" being apparently somewhat vague. In the Calcutta text, as well as in Scott's version, the compartments of the cabinet are made "one above the other," in order to introduce the little incident.

[2] A quotation from the Qur'ān.—S.

am the qāzī." They replied: "Thou liest, and it is impossible. For if thou art the qāzī, how camest thou to be confined here? Thou art an impostor; for our worthy qāzī, thou impious wretch, is a man who sub-dueth his passions. Be silent, lest he hear thee, and bring thee to punishment." After this the qāzī durst not speak, and was silent.

Then they brought several porters, who took up the great cabinet, and carried it to the palace of the sultan,[1] who, on being informed of the affair, sent for carpenters and smiths, and caused it to be broken open in his presence, when lo! he discovered the wālī, the qāzī, the vazīr, the hājib, and the poor joiner. "What brought thee here, O reverend qāzī?" inquired the sultan. The qāzī exclaimed: "God be praised, who hath providentially saved thee, O sultan, from what hath befallen us!" He then issued from the cabinet in his coloured vest and fool's cap, as did the rest of his companions in their ridiculous dresses, but the poor joiner in his birth-day habit. The sultan laughed till he almost fainted, and commanded the adventures of each to be written, from first to last. He also ordered search to be made for the merchant's

---

[1] According to the Calcutta text, the suitors were three days in the cabinet before the neighbours broke into the house and released them, when they became the objects of derision; and the woman having taken away all their clothes, they had to send to their own houses for others before they could appear in the streets.

wife, but in vain, for she had escaped with the robes, valuables, and weapons of the foolish gallants.   [30]

"From this story," said the vazīr, "consider, O sultan, how deep is the artifice of women, and how little dependence should be placed upon their declarations."[1]

On the seventh night the Damsel kindled a funeral pile, and affected to cast herself into it, when her attendants prevented her, and carrying her forcibly to the sultan, informed him of her attempt on her own

---

[1] Scott has omitted the second story of the sixth vazīr, "it being too free to bear translation." It is a humorous but very indecent tale of a man who, on the Night of Power (*Al Qadar,* the night on which the whole of the Qur'ān was revealed to Gabriel, who afterwards communicated it to Muhammad piecemeal), was granted THREE WISHES, and acting by his wife's advice, after his third wish was accomplished, found himself no better than before. The story probably suggested the still more obscene fabliau of "Les quatre souhaits de Saint Martin," and is similar in design to one of our nursery tales. (See also pp. 71-73.) An analogous Hindū story is found in the *Panchatantra,* to the following effect: A poor weaver was about to cut down a large sisu-tree, to make a loom, when the spirit of the tree called to him to desist, and he should be granted a boon. Having consulted a friend as to what he should ask and rejected his advice, he applied to his wife, who counselled him to ask an extra head and pair of arms, so that he should be able to do double work. He obtained this boon, and returning to the village was stoned for a goblin by his fellow-villagers. *Moral:* He who neither exercises his own judgment nor follows a friend's advice brings on his own ruin.

life. The sultan exclaimed: "What could have induced thee to such rashness?" She replied: "If thou wilt not credit my assertions, I will certainly throw myself into the fire, when thou wilt be too late regretful on my account, as the prince repented of having unjustly punished the religious woman." The sultan desired to know the particulars, and the Damsel said:

Story of the Devout Woman and the Magpie.

A CERTAIN pious woman, who made pilgrimages to various parts of the world, in the course of one of them came to the court of a sultan, who received her with welcome reverence. One day his queen took the good woman with her to the bath, and handed her a string of jewels, worth two thousand gold dīnars, to take charge of while she bathed. The religious woman placed it upon the sajjāda,[1] and began to say her prayers. Suddenly a magpie alighted from the roof of the palace, and fled away with the string of jewels in its claws, unobserved by the pilgrim, and ascended to one of the turrets.

When the queen came from the bath, she searched for the string of jewels, but not finding it, demanded it of the pilgrim, who said: "It was here this instant, and I have not moved from this place. Whether any of your domestics may have taken it up or not, I cannot tell." The queen was enraged, and complained to the sultan,

---

[1] A prostration cloth, mat, or carpet.

who commanded the pilgrim to be scourged till she should discover the jewels. She was beaten severely, but confessed nothing; after which she was imprisoned, and remained a long time in durance; till one day the sultan, sitting upon the terrace of the palace, beheld a magpie, with the string of jewels twisted round its claws. He commanded the bird to be caught, released the pilgrim, of whom he entreated pardon, kissed her hands, begged forgiveness of God for what he had done, and would have made atonement to her by a valuable present, but she would not accept it. She left the court; and having resolved in her mind, for the remainder of her life, not to enter the house of any one, retired to the mountains, till she died. May God have mercy upon her![1]

The Damsel then related, as an example of the crafty disposition of men, the

Story of Prince Bahram and Princess Ed-Detma.[2]

THERE was formerly a princess, than whom no one of her time was more skilful in horsemanship and throw-

---

[1] This is similar to our popular tale of "The Maid and the Magpie;" only in the latter, with more art, the reader is not informed of the bird's theft until the stolen article is discovered.

[2] "Rumta" in Scott's translation, and no doubt also, by a blunder of the copyist, in the manuscript. The name is Ed-Detmà in all other Arabic texts.—"The Amazon" is the short title by which this story is distinguished.

ing the lance and javelin. Her name was Ed-Detmà. Many powerful princes demanded her in marriage, but she would not consent, having resolved to wed only him who should overcome her in combat, saying: " Whoever worsts me, I will be his; but should I prove victorious, he shall forfeit his weapons and his horse, and I will stamp upon his forehead with a hot iron this inscription: 'The Freedman of Ed-Detmà.'"[1]

Many princes attempted to gain her, but she foiled them, seized their weapons, and marked them as she had signified. At length the prince of Persia, named Bahram, hearing of her charms, resolved to obtain her; for which purpose he quitted his kingdom, and underwent many difficulties on his journey, until he reached his destination. He then entrusted his property to a respectable inhabitant, and visited the sultan; to whom he presented a valuable offering. The sultan seated him respectfully, and inquired the object of his visit. "I am come from a distant country," replied the prince, "anxiously desirous of an alliance with thy daughter." The sultan said: "My son, I have no power over her; for she has resolved not to wed, unless her suitor shall vanquish her in combat." The prince answered: "I accept the conditions;" upon which the sultan informed his daughrer, who accepted the challenge.

---

[1] Scott has "the Slave," etc., but the other texts have, very properly, the "Freedman"—the vanquished losing their arms and steeds, but having their liberty restored them.

On the appointed day a numerous crowd assembled
in the maydan,[1] where the sultan with his nobles appeared in great pomp. Ed-Detmà advanced, arrayed
in dazzling habiliments; and the prince came forth,
elegant in person, and superbly accoutred. They
immediately encountered; the earth vibrated from the
shock of their horses, and violent was the charge of
weapons on both sides. The sultan viewed with
admiration the majestic demeanour of the prince;
and Ed-Detmà, perceiving his superior valour and
agility, dreaded being vanquished. She artfully withdrew her veil, when her countenance appeared as the
resplendent moon suddenly emerging from a dark
cloud. The prince was fascinated with her beauty,
and his whole frame trembled. The princess, observing his confusion, threw her javelin at his breast, and
he fell from his horse, and she returned exulting to
the palace.

The prince rose up, much mortified at his discom-
fiture, and returned to the city, pondering upon the
deceit she had practised, and resolved to try a stratagem upon her. After some days, he fixed to his face
a long white beard, like that of a venerable old man,
clothed himself in the dress of a devotee, and repaired
to a garden which he was informed the princess visited
every month. He formed an intimacy with the keeper
of it, by making him presents, till he had drawn him

---

[1] Open space for martial exercises and sports.

over to his interest. He then pretended to understand the cultivation of a garden, and the management of plants. The keeper therefore entrusted them to his care, and he watered them carefully, so that the shrubs became fresher and the blossoms more beautiful under his management.

At the usual time, the ferashes[1] came, and spread carpets, and made other preparations for the reception of the princess. Bahram, on her approach, took some jewels and scattered them in the walks, when the princess and her attendants, seeing an old man, apparently trembling with age, stopped and inquired what he was doing with the jewels. He replied: "I would purchase a wife with them, and would have her from among you." At this the ladies laughed heartily, and said: "When thou art married, how wilt thou behave to thy wife?" He said: "I would just give her one kiss, and divorce her." Then said the princess jestingly, and pointing to one of her ladies: "I will give thee this girl for a wife," upon which he advanced, kissed the damsel in a tremulous manner, and gave her the jewels. After laughing at him for some time, the princess and her attendants quitted the garden.

The like scene was enacted for several days, the prince every time giving richer jewels to the lady he espoused; till at length the princess thought to her-

---

[1] Servants, who have charge of tents, etc.

self: "Every one of my maidens has obtained from this dotard jewels richer than is in the possession of most sovereigns, and I certainly am more worthy of them than my attendants. He is a decrepid wretch, and can do me no harm." She then went alone to the garden, where she beheld the old man scattering jewels which were invaluable, and said: "I am the sultan's daughter, wilt thou accept me as a wife?" He advanced, and presented her with such a number of jewels that she was delighted beyond measure, and became anxious that he should give her one kiss, and let her depart like the other ladies. The prince, suddenly clasping her in his arms, exclaimed: "Dost thou not know me? I am Bahram, son of the sultan of Persia, whom thou overcamest only by stratagem, and I have now vanquished thee in the same manner. On thy account I exiled myself from my friends and country, but I have now obtained my desires."

The princess rémained silent, not being able to utter a word from confusion. She retired in anger to the palace, but, upon reflection, did not disclose what had passed, through fear of disgrace.[1] She said to herself:

---

[1] "What had passed" is much more explicitly described in the original text; this royal amazon was, in fact, treated by the prince as Dinah the daughter of Jacob was by Shechem, though one would hardly guess so much from Scott's ingenious rendering of the scene.—I shall only add here that the prince's stratagem may be compared with the story in the *Hitopadesa* (i, 8) of "The King's Son and the Merchant's Wife."

"If I have him put to death, what will it profit me? I can now do nothing wiser than marry him, and repair with him to his own country." Having thus resolved, she sent a trusty messenger to inform him of her intentions, and appointed a night to meet him.

At the time fixed upon the prince was ready to receive her; they mounted their horses under cover of the night, and by daylight had travelled a great distance. They did not slacken their speed day or night until they were beyond the reach of pursuit, and arrived at the capital of Persia in safety. The prince then despatched rich presents by an ambassador to the sultan her father, entreating that he would send an envoy to ratify the marriage of his daughter. The sultan having duly complied, the qāzī and proper witnesses attended; and they were married amid the greatest rejoicings, and the prince lived long with her in perfect felicity. [31]

"Such," said the Damsel, "is the artfulness of men." When the sultan had heard these stories, he again gave orders that his son should be put to death.

On the following day the Seventh Vazīr approached the sultan, and, after the usual obeisance, said: "Forbear, my lord, to shed the blood of thy innocent son; for thou hast none but him, and may not have another, when thou hast put him to death. Attend not to the malicious accusations of concubines, for the deceit of bad women is astonishing, and is exemplified in the

Story of the Burnt Veil.

THERE was a certain merchant, very rich, who had an only son, whom he loved exceedingly. One day he said to the young man: "My son, tell me whatever thou desirest of the pleasures of life, that I may gratify thee." The youth replied: "I long for nothing so much as to visit the city of Bagdād, and see the palaces of the khalif and the vazīrs—that I may behold what so many merchants and travellers have so rapturously described." The merchant observed: "I do not approve of such an excursion, because it would occasion your absence from me."—"My dear father," said the young man, "you inquired my wish, and this is it, and I cannot willingly give it up." When the father heard this, being unwilling to vex his son, he prepared for him an adventure of merchandise of the value of thirty thousand dīnars, and recommended him to the care of some eminent merchants, his particular friends.

The youth was amply provided with requisites for the journey, and, attended by many slaves and domestics, he travelled unceasingly till he reached the celebrated capital of Islām, where he hired a handsome house near the grand market. For several days he rode about the city, and beheld such splendid scenes that his mind was bewildered amidst the magnificence of the buildings, the richness of the shops, and the spaciousness of the markets. He admired the dome-crowned palaces, their extensive courts, and regular arcades; the pavements of variously-coloured marbles, the ceilings adorned with gold and azure, the doors studded with nails of silver, and painted in fanciful devices.

At length, he stopped at a mansion of this description, and inquired the rent by the month; and the neighbours told him that the monthly hire was ten dirhams. The young merchant exclaimed in astonishment: "Are ye speaking the truth, or do ye only jeer me?" They replied: "We swear, my lord, that we speak the truth exactly; but it is impossible to reside in that house more than a week or a fortnight, without being in hazard of death—a circumstance well known in Bagdād. The rent originally was twenty gold dīnars monthly, and is now reduced to ten silver dirhams."[1]

The young man was now still more surprised, and said to himself: "There must be some reason for this, which I wish to find out, and am resolved to hire the house." He did so; and, casting all fear from his mind, took possession, brought his goods, and resided some time in it, employed in business and amusement. At length, sitting one day at his gate, he beheld an old woman (may God's vengeance rest upon her!), who was a cunning go-between under a religious garb. When the old jade saw the young man reclining upon

---

[1] Twenty gold dīnars are equivalent to ten pounds, and ten silver dirhams, to five shillings of our money.

a mastaba[1] spread with nice carpets, and that he had
every appearance of affluence around him, she bowed
to him,[2] and he returned her salute. She then gazed
steadfastly at him, upon which he said: "Dost thou
want my services, good mother? Dost thou know me,
or mistake me for one whom I may resemble?" She
answered: "My lord, and my son, I know thee not;
but when I beheld thy beauty and manliness, I thought
upon a circumstance, which, with God's blessing, I
will relate." The youth exclaimed: "God grant it may
be a fortunate one!" She said: "How long hast thou
resided in this house?" On his replying, two months,
she exclaimed: "That is wonderful, my son! For
every one who before resided in it for more than a
week or a fortnight either died or, being taken dangerously ill, gave it up. I suppose thou hast not
opened the prospect-room or ascended the terrace?"
When she had thus spoken, she went away, and left
the young man astonished at her questions.

Curiosity made him immediately examine closely all
the upper apartments of the mansion, till at length he
found a secret door, almost covered with cobwebs,
which he wiped away. He then opened the door,

---

[1] A platform, of stone or brick, built against the front wall of
a house or shop.

[2] The salute in Asia, from men and women, is a gentle inclination of the body, at the same time touching the forehead with
the right hand. For this double action we have no expression;
the Arabic one is *es-salám*.—S.

and, hesitating to proceed, said to himself: "This is wonderful! What if I should meet my death within?" Relying, however, upon God, he entered, and found an apartment having windows on every side, which over-looked the whole neighbourhood. He opened the shutters, and sat down to amuse himself with the pro-spect. His eyes were speedily arrested by a palace more elegant than the others, and while he surveyed it, a lady appeared upon the terrace, beautiful as a hūrī; her charms would have ravished the heart, changed the love of Majnūn,[1] torn the continence of Joseph, overcome the patience of Job, and as-suaged the sorrow of Jacob:[2] the chaste and devout would have adored her, and the abstinent and the pilgrim would have longed for her company.

When the merchant's son beheld her, love took pos-session of his heart. He sank down on the carpet, and exclaimed: "Well may it be said, that whoever resides in this mansion will soon die from hopeless love of this beautiful damsel!" He quitted the apart-ment, locked the door, and descended the staircase. The more he reflected the more he was disturbed, and both rest and patience forsook him. Then he went

---

[1] See note, page 108.

[2] The sorrow of Jacob at the loss of his son Joseph is pro-verbial among the Muslims: according to the Qur'ān, he wept himself blind, but his sight was restored by the virtue of Joseph's upper garment, brought from Egypt on the return of his sons from their second journey to buy corn.

and sat down at his gate, when, lo! after a short
interval, the old woman appeared, devoutly counting
her beads, and mumbling prayers.[1]   When she came
near, he saluted her, and said: "I was at ease and
contented until I looked out of the apartment you
mentioned, and beheld a young lady, whose beauty
has distracted me; and if thou canst not procure me
her company, I shall die with disappointment."[2]   She
replied: "My son, do not despair on her account, for
I will accomplish thy desires."   Then she consoled
him, and he gave her fifty dīnars, with many thanks
for her kindness, saying: "My dear mother, assist me
to the purpose, and you may demand what you
please."   The old woman replied: "My son, go to
the great market, and inquire for the shop of our lord
Abū-'l Fat-h the son of Qaydām, the great silk merchant, whose wife this lady is.   Approach him with
all civility, and say that you want a rich veil,[3] embroidered with gold and silver, for your concubine.
Return with it to me, and your desires shall be grati-

---

[1] It is a custom of Muslim devotees to hang round the neck,
in several circumvolutions, a string of many hundreds of beads.
The object is either to employ these beads in repeating certain
ejaculations in praise of God, or to make others believe that the
wearer is accustomed to so employ them. —*Lane.*

[2] According to *Syntipas*, before the youth engaged the services
of the old woman, he had introduced himself into the lady's
house, and been repulsed.

[3] In *Syntipas* it is a mantle, and in the *Libro de los Engannos,*
"a cloth, which he [the lady's husband] keeps hidden."

fied." The young man hastened to the bazār of the chief merchants, and was soon directed to the person he inquired after, who was also a broker of merchandise to the khalīf Harūnu-'r-Rashīd. He easily found such a veil as he was directed to purchase, for which he paid a hundred gold dīnars, and returned home with it to the old woman, who took a live coal, and with it burned three holes in the veil, which she then took away with her.

She then proceeded to the young lady's house, and knocked at the gate. When the lady inquired who was there, the old woman said: "It is I, Ummu Maryam,"[1] on which the merchant's wife, knowing her to be a humble acquaintance of her mother, said: "My dear aunt,[2] my mother is not here, but at her own house." The old woman said: "Daughter, the hour of prayer approaches, and I cannot reach my house in time to perform my ablutions. I request, therefore, that I may make them in your house, as I am secure of having pure water here."[3]

The door was now opened, and the hypocritical

---

[1] The Mother of Mary. In Arabia, the mother is generally addressed in this way as a mark of respect for having borne children, and the eldest gives the title.—S.

[2] Answering to our obsolete term of aunt, or naunt, by which old women of inferior degree were formerly addressed. See Shenstone's "Schoolmistress."—S.

[3] It is a religious point with Muhammadans to have pure water for their ablutions; and in their law-books many chapters define how it may be defiled.—S.

jade entered, counting her beads, and mumbling her prayers for the welfare of the young lady, her husband, and her mother. She then took off her drawers,[1] girded her vest round her waist, and a vessel of water being brought, performed her ablutions; after which she said: "Show me, good daughter, a pure spot, free from pollution, to pray upon." The young lady replied: "You may pray upon my husband's carpet." The old woman now muttered her prayers, during which, unperceived by the merchant's wife, she slipped the burnt veil under the cushion at the head of the husband's carpet, and then, rising up from her devotions, she thanked the young lady, warned her against meeting the eyes of licentious men, and took her leave.

Soon after this the merchant returned home, sat down upon his carpet to repose himself, and his wife brought him a collation, of which he ate. She then set before him water, and he washed his hands, after which he turned to take a napkin from under his cushion to wipe them, when, lo! he discovered the veil which he had that day sold to the young man, and instantly became suspicious of his wife's fidelity. For some time he was unable to speak. On reflection, he resolved that his disgrace should not become public

---

[1] It is unlawful for the Muhammadans to pray in silk that touches the skin. For this they have, to save trouble, a salvo, namely, a stuff called *mashrū'*, or legal, made of silk and cotton mixed. If the upper garment only be of silk it is of no injury to devotion.—S.

among his brother merchants, or reach the ears of the
khalíf, whose agent and broker he was, lest he should
be dishonoured at court. He kept the discovery of
the veil to himself; but, in a little time, addressing his
wife, desired that she would go and visit her mother.

The lady, supposing from this that she was indis-
posed, put on her veil, and hastened to the house of
her mother, whom, however, she found in good health,
and that no ill had befallen her. The mother and
daughter sat down, and were talking of indifferent
matters, when suddenly several porters entered the
house, loaded with the wife's effects, her marriage
dower, and a writing of divorce. The old lady in
alarm exclaimed: "Knowest thou not, daughter, the
cause of thy husband's displeasure?" The wife replied: "I can safely swear, my dear mother, that I
know not of any fault of which I can have been guilty,
deserving this treatment." The mother wept bitterly
for the disgrace of her daughter, and the wife lamented
her separation from her husband, whom she ardently
loved. She continued to grieve night and day; her
appetite failed her, and her beauty began to decay.

In this manner a month passed away. At the
expiry of this period the old woman Ummu Maryam
came to visit the young lady's mother, and after many
fawning caresses sat down. When she had told the
common news, she said: "I heard, sister, that my lord
Abū-l Fat-h had divorced your daughter his wife, on
which account I have fasted some days and spent the

nights in prayer, in hopes that God may restore her condition." The mother replied: "May God grant us that blessing!" The old woman then inquired after her daughter, and the mother said: "She is grieving for the loss of her husband; her heart is breaking; she feels no pleasure in company, which is disgustful to her, and I fear that, should her lamentations and sorrow continue, they will occasion her death." Then the old woman asked: "Does thy daughter wish to be reconciled to her husband?" The mother replied, that she did. "If so," said the old woman, "let her abide with me for a night or two. She will see proper company; her heart will be refreshed; and society will relieve her depression of mind." The mother assented to the propriety of her observations, gained the consent of her daughter, prevailed upon her to dress herself, and sent her home with Ummu Maryam, who conducted her to the house of the merchant's son.

The young man, when he saw his beloved, rejoiced as if he had gained possession of the world. He ran to her, saluted her, and kissed her between the eyes. The affrighted lady was overcome with shame and confusion; but he addressed her with such tenderness, made such ardent professions, and repeated so many elegant verses, that at length her fears were dispelled. She partook of a collation, and drank of various wines. Every now and then she looked at the young man, who was beautiful as the full moon, and love for him

at length fascinated her mind. She took up a lute,
and played and sang in praise of his accomplishments,
so that he was in such ecstasies that he would have
sacrificed his life and property to her charms.[1]

In the morning the old woman returned, and said:
"My children, how passed you the evening?" The
young lady replied: "In ease and happiness, my dear
aunt, by virtue of your supplications and midnight
prayers." On this the old woman said roughly: "Thou
must now accompany me to thy mother." The young
merchant flattered her, and giving her ten gold dinars,
said: "I pray thee let her remain with me this day."
She took the gold, and then repaired to the mother of
the young lady, to whom, after the usual salutations,
she said: "Sister, thy daughter bids me inform thee
that she is better, and her grief is removed; so that I
hope you will not take her from me." The mother
replied: "Since my daughter is happy, why should I
deny thee, even should she remain a month; for I know
that thou art an honest and pious woman, and that thy
dwelling is auspicious."

After this the young lady remained seven days at
the house of the young merchant, during which on
each morning Ummu Maryam appeared, saying to

---

[1] In *Syntipas* the young man accomplishes his purpose by
force. The Arabian version of the incident may not, perhaps,
be a very great improvement; but Mr Lane gives a still less
objectionable turn to the story at this point.—See his 1001 N.,
vol. iii, p. 161, note 35.

her: "Return with me to thy mother;" and the young man entreated for another day, giving her regularly ten gold dīnars. Having received the present, she always visited the mother, and gave her agreeable tidings of her daughter's health. On the eighth day, however, the mother said to the old woman: "My heart is anxious about my daughter; and truly her long absence seems extraordinary;" and Ummu Maryam, pretending to be affronted, replied: "Sister, dost thou cast reflections upon me?" She then repaired to the house of the young merchant, brought away the lady, and conducted her to her mother, but did not enter the house.

When the mother saw that her health and beauty were restored, she was delighted, and said: "Truly, daughter, my heart was anxious concerning thee; and I began to suspect Ummu Maryam, and treated her unkindly because of thy long absence."—"I was not with her," replied the young lady, "but in pleasure and happiness, and in repose, and safety. I have obtained through her means health and contentment; so that I conjure thee, my dear mother, to ease her mind, and be grateful for her kindness." Hearing this, the mother arose, and went immediately to the house of the old woman, entreated her pardon, and thanked her for her kindness to her daughter. Ummu Maryam accepted her excuses, and the old lady returned home with her mind relieved.

Next morning the wily Ummu Maryam visited the

young merchant, and said: "My son, I wish you to repair the mischief you have done, and to reconcile a wife to her husband."—"How can that be effected?" he asked. "Go to the warehouse of Abū-'l Fat-h the son of Qaydām," she replied, "and enter into conversation with him, till I shall appear before you; then start up, and lay hold of me, abuse me roundly, and say: 'Where is the veil I gave thee to darn, which I bought of my lord Abū-'l Fat-h, the son of Qaydām?' If he asks thee the cause of thy claim upon me, answer him thus: 'You may recollect that I bought a veil of you for a hundred gold dīnars, as a present to my concubine. I gave it to her, and she put it on, but soon after, while she was carrying a lamp, some sparks flew from the wick, and burnt it in three places. This old woman was present, and said that she would take it to the lace-darner, to which I consented, and I have never seen her since till this moment.'"

The young merchant accordingly went to the great market, and coming to the shop of my lord Abū-'l Fat-h, the son of Qaydām, he made him a profound obeisance, which Abū-'l Fat-h returned, but in a gloomy and sulky manner. The youth, however, seated himself, and began to address him on various subjects, when Ummu Maryam appeared, with a long rosary in her hands, the beads of which she counted, while repeating aloud the attributes of the Deity.[1] He

---

[1] See note 1, page 202.

immediately started up, ran and laid hold of her, and began to abuse her, when she exclaimed: "I am innocent, and thou art innocent!" A crowd soon gathered around them, and Abū-'l Fat-h, coming from his shop, seized the young man, and demanded: "What is the cause of this rude behaviour to a poor old woman?" He replied: "You must recollect, sir, that I bought of you a rich veil for a hundred dīnars. I gave it to my concubine, who shortly afterwards dropped some sparks from a lamp, which burnt the veil in three places. This cursed hypocritess was present at the time, and offered to carry it immediately to the lace-darner. She took it, accordingly, and I have not set eyes upon her again till now, though more than a month has elapsed."

Ummu Maryam assented to the veracity of this statement, and said: "My son, I honestly intended to get the veil mended; but, calling at some houses on my way to the darner, I left it behind me, but where I cannot recollect. I am, it is true, a poor woman, but of pure reputation, and have nothing wherewith to make up the loss of the veil. 'Let the owner, then,' said I to myself, 'believe that I have cheated him, for that is better than that I should occasion disturbances among families by endeavouring to recover the veil.' This is the whole matter; 'God knows the truth, and God will release from difficulty the true speaker.'"[1]

---

[1] A quotation from the Qur'ān. —S.

When Abū-'l Fat-h heard these words his countenance changed from sorrowful to glad. He thought tenderly of his divorced wife, and said in his mind: "Truly I have treated her harshly." He then begged pardon of God for his jealousy, and blessed him for restoring to him again his happiness. To his inquiry of the old woman, whether she frequented his house, she replied: "Certainly; and also the houses of your relations. I eat of your alms, and pray that you may be rewarded both in this world and the next. I have inquired for the veil at all the houses I visit, but in vain."—"Did you inquire at my house?" said the merchant. "My lord," replied the old woman, "I went yesterday, but found no one at home, when the neighbours informed me that my lord had for some cause divorced his wife."

Addressing the young man, Abū-'l Fat-h said: "Sir, I pray you, let this poor old woman go, for your veil is with me, and I will take care that it shall be properly repaired;" on which Ummu Maryam fell down before the merchant and kissed his hands, and then went her way. Abū-'l Fat-h now took out the veil in the presence of the young man, and gave it to a darner; and was convinced that he had treated his wife cruelly, which indeed was the case, had she not afterwards erred through the temptations of that wicked old woman. He then sent to his wife, requesting her to return, and offered her what terms she pleased; and she complied with his desire, and was reconciled;—but my lord

Abū-'l Fat-h the son of Qaydām little knew what had befallen him from the arts of Ummu Maryam. [16]

When the vazīr had ended his story, "Consider, O sultan," he said, "the cunning of bad women, their wiles, and their artful contrivances."—The sultan again gave orders to stay the execution of his son.

On the eighth morning, when the impediment was done away against his speaking, the prince sent to the vazīrs and his tutor, who had concealed himself, and desired them to come to him. On their arrival, he thanked them for their services to his father, and what they had done to prevent his own death, adding: " By God's help, I will soon repay you."

The vazīrs now repaired to the sultan, informed him of the cause of his son's obstinate silence, and of the arts of the damsel. The sultan rejoiced exceedingly, and ordered a public audience to be held, at which the vazīrs, the officers of state, and the learned men appeared. The prince entered, with his tutor, and, kissing the ground before his father, prayed eloquently for his welfare and that of his vazīrs and his tutor. The whole assembly were astonished at his fluency of speech, his propriety of diction, and his accomplished demeanour. The sultan was enraptured, and ran to him, kissed him between the eyes, and clasped him to his bosom. He did the same to the tutor, and thanked him for his care of the prince. The tutor said: "I only commanded him to be silent, fearful for his life during these seven days, which were marked in his horoscope as unfortunate, but have ended happily."[1] Then the sultan said: "Had I put him to death, in whom would have been the crime—myself, thee, or the damsel?" On this question the assembly differed much in their opinions, and the prince, observing their altercations, said: "I will solve this difficulty." The assembly with one voice exclaimed: "Let us hear," and the Prince said:

Story of the Poisoned Food.

I HAVE heard of a certain merchant to whom there came unexpectedly a visitor; upon which he sent a female domestic to buy laban[2] in the market. As she was returning with it upon her head in an uncovered vessel, she passed under a tree, on which was a serpent, from whose mouth fell some drops of venom into the laban. Her master and his guest ate of it, and both died. [19]

---

[1] In the Calcutta text, the king asks Sindibād why the prince had kept silence during these seven days, and the sage replies in terms similar to the above, that he had foreseen the danger he should be in if he spoke; yet in the introduction it is stated that the king was warned of this danger by the sage, and took precautions to avert it by secluding the prince in the women's apartments. (See note 2, page 135.)

[2] Sour curds.

"Whose, then, was the fault?" asked the prince: "the girl's, who left the vessel uncovered? or her master's, who gave the laban to his guest?"

Some said it was the master's fault, because he did not examine the laban first. The prince replied: "No one was in fault; their time was come and their residence in this world at an end. Had my death taken place, no one would have been guilty but my father's concubine."

When the assembly heard this, all were astonished at the prince's eloquence and wisdom, and raised their voices in applause, saying: "O sultan, thy son is most accomplished!" Then the sultan commanded a ponderous stone to be tied to the feet of the artful and wicked concubine, and she was cast into the sea. The tutor was rewarded, and invested with an embroidered robe of great value. The sultan delighted in his son, and abdicating his throne, gave it up to the prince, who made all happy by his justice and clemency.

APPENDIX.

APPENDIX.

————

BELIEF in the Asiatic origin of many of the Fables and Tales of domestic life which afforded instruction and entertainment to the Middle Ages has for some time prevailed, and of late years the proofs have been multiplied by the industry of Oriental scholars. The evidence adduced has been of the most positive description. It is not built on probabilities, upon general and indefinite analogies, or on partial and accidental resemblances, but upon actual identities. Although modifications have been practised, names altered, scenes changed, circumstances added or omitted, we can still discover the sameness of the fundamental outline; and, amidst all the mystifications of the masquerade, lay our hands, without hesitation, upon the authentic individual.—*Dr. H. H. Wilson* (1840).

————

No. I—p. 15.

THE CAMEL, THE WOLF, THE FOX, AND THE PUMPKIN.

PROFESSOR E. B. Cowell, of Cambridge, in an interesting paper contributed to the Welsh Society's journal (*Y Cymmrodor*), October, 1882, has adduced a number of variants of this tale, together with its oldest (Buddhistic) form, from which, with his kind permission, I make the following extracts:

" Readers of the *Mabinogion* will remember the curious legend of the oldest known animals, which is found in the story of Kilhwch and Olwen. We read there how Arthur's ambassadors went successively in search of tidings about Mabon the son of Modron, to the ousel of Cilgwri, the stag of Redynvre, the owl of Cwm Cawlwyd, the eagle of Gwern Abwy, and, finally, the salmon of Llyn Llyw, and each in turn gave some fresh proof of

its greater age than its predecessors, but still referred the question to some animal of still more venerable antiquity than itself.
Ap Gwilym, however, alludes to another version of the story,
which, I am inclined to think, preserves an older form of this
wide-spread piece of folk-lore.   In his poem, *Yr Oed*, where he
describes himself as waiting and waiting under the thorn for his
faithless mistress, he says :

> A thousand persons and more liken me
> To him who dwelt in Gwernabwy;
> In truth I should not be an eagle at all,
> Except for my waiting for my fair lady three generations of men ;
> I am exactly like the stag
> In Cilgwri, for my beloved ;
> Of the same colour, gray to my thinking,
> As my bedfellow (the owl) in Cwm Cawlwyd.

Here we have only three animals instead of the five in the
Mabinogi; and, as far as I can trace the story in Eastern literature, three is the usual number given, however the species of
the animals themselves may vary.   The legend itself, like so
many other popular stories, came to Europe originally from
India, and probably passed, together with Buddhism, into other
countries.   Its oldest known form is found in the Culla Vagga
portion of the *Vinayapitaka*, one of the oldest parts of the
Buddhist sacred books; and another version of it is given in
the first volume of the *Jātakas*, lately translated by Mr. T. W.
Rhys Davids.   The former version, a translation of which I
subjoin, can hardly be later than the third century B.C.

The Partridge, the Monkey, and the Elephant.

Long ago there was a great banyan tree on the slope of the
Himálaya mountains, and three friends dwelt near it—a partridge, a monkey, and an elephant.   They were disrespectful
and discourteous to one another, and did not live harmoniously
together.   Then it occurred to them : "Oh, if we could but

know which of us is the eldest, we could honour him and respect him, and show him duty and reverence, and abide by his exhortations." Then the partridge and the monkey asked the elephant: "What is the oldest thing, friend, that you remember?" "Friends," he replied, "when I was a child I used to walk over this banyan tree, keeping it between my thighs, and its topmost shoot touched my belly. This is the oldest thing that I remember." Then the partridge and the elephant asked the monkey: "What is the oldest thing, friend, that you remember?" "Friends, when I was a child I used to sit on the ground and eat the topmost shoot of this banyan. This is the oldest thing that I remember." Then the monkey and the elephant asked the partridge: "What is the oldest thing, friend, that you remember?" "Friends, in yonder place there was once a certain great banyan tree; I ate a fruit from it and voided it in this spot, and from it sprang this banyan. Therefore, friends, I am older than either of you." Then the monkey and the elephant thus addressed the partridge: "You, friend, are the oldest of us all; we will honour and respect you, and will show you duty and reverence, and will abide by your exhortations." Then the partridge stirred them up in the five moral duties, and also took those duties upon himself. They were respectful and courteous to one another, and lived harmoniously together, and after the dissolution of their bodies they were reborn happily in heaven.

"The same apologue occurs in the seventeenth of the *Avadánas*, or Indian apologues, translated by Julien from the Chinese.—A curiously distorted version of the Buddhist legend is found in the *Uttara-kanda* of the Sanskrit *Rámáyana*, the later book which was added to the *Rámáyana* to explain and amplify the brief allusions to earlier events which had been left obscure in the original poem. There we read that a vulture and an owl, who had lived in a certain wood from time immemorial, quarrelled about the possession of a certain cave, each claiming it to be his by ancient right. They eventually agreed to bring the matter before Ráma for his decision. On his asking them how long each claimed to have had the cave as a dwelling, the vulture replied: 'It has been my home ever since this earth was first filled with men newly come into being;' while the owl rejoined: 'It has been my home ever since this earth was first adorned with trees.' Ráma then decided that the cave properly belonged to the owl, as trees and plants were originally produced before the creation of mankind from the marrow of two demons slain by Vishnu, whence the earth was called *Medini* (from *meda*, marrow). Here we have only two animals introduced; Ráma, however, as the umpire, occupies the place of the third. But," adds Professor Cowell, "we find the triad of interlocutors reappearing in the version of the story given in the *Sindibád Náma.* This story reproduces the old dialogue, but the animals are changed, and a new point is added at the end."

But there is another form of the legend, current in Europe since the 12th century, in which men are substituted for animals, and which in one particular closely resembles the version in our text, namely, the well-known story of the Three Dreamers and the Loaf. In this form it seems to have been derived from the Arabian fabulists by Peter Alphonsus, who has related it, in his *Disciplina Clericalis* (fab. 17), as follows:

The Three Travellers and the Loaf.

It is related of two citizens and a countryman, going to Mecca, that they shared provisions till they reached there, and then their food failed, so that nothing remained save so much flour as would make a single loaf, and that a small one. The citizens seeing this said to each other: "We have too little bread, and our companion eats a great deal. Wherefore we ought to have a plan to take away from him part of the loaf, and eat it by

ourselves alone." Accordingly a plan of this sort proved acceptable : to make and bake the loaf, and while it was being baked
to sleep, and whoever of them saw the most wonderful things in
a dream should eat the loaf alone. These words they spoke
artfully, as they thought the rustic too simple for inventions of
this sort. They made the loaf and baked it, and at length lay
down to sleep. But the rustic, more crafty than they thought,
whilst his companions were asleep, took the half-baked loaf, ate
it up, and again lay down. One of the citizens, as if terrified
out of his sleep, awoke, and called his companion, who inquired :
"What is the matter?" He said: "I have seen a wondrous
vision ; for it seemed to me that two angels opened the gates of
Paradise, and led me within." Then his companion said to him :
"That is a wondrous vision you have seen ; but I dreamed that
two angels took me, and, cleaving the earth, led me to the lower
regions." All this the countryman heard, and pretended to be
asleep ; but the citizens, being deceived and wishing to deceive,
called on him to awake. But the rustic replied cunningly, and
as though he were terrified : "Who are they that call me?"
Then they said : "We are your companions." But he replied :
"Have you returned already?" To this they rejoined : "Where
did we go, that we should return?" Then the rustic said : "Now
it seemed to me that two angels took one of you, and opened
the gates of heaven and led him within ; then two others took
the other and opened the earth and took him to hell; and seeing
this, I thought that neither of you would return any more, and
I rose and ate the loaf."

From Alphonsus—who may have obtained it from the *Historia
Jeshuae Nazareni*, a scurrilous life of the Saviour, of Jewish invention, where it also occurs—this version was taken into the
Gesta Romanorum, and at a later period Cinthio, the Italian
novelist, introduced it into his *Hecatommithi*, where the characters are a philosopher, an astrologer, and a soldier. The tale

has long been popular in our own country—a well-worn " Joe Miller," of an Englishman, a Scotchman, and an Irishman who travelled in company; the conventional Irishman "dreamt he was hungry, and got up and ate the loaf."

No. II—p. 27.
THE KING OF THE MONKEYS.

A VARIANT of this tale is found in the *Pancha Tantra*, Sect. v, Fab. 10, to the following effect: The sons of a certain King Chandra used to feed a herd of monkeys. There was likewise at their court a herd of rams. One of the latter, a glutton, was in the habit of going to the kitchen to devour whatever he saw, and the cooks always beat him. The monkey king reflected that the quarrel between the ram and the cooks must lead to the destruction of the monkeys, because, if the cooks some day beat him with a burning log of wood, his wool would catch fire, he would run into the horses' stable close by, set fire to the stable, and cause injury to the horses; and as their wounds can only be healed by monkeys' fat, the monkeys will have to suffer. So he advised his tribe to go to the woods. They refuse, and as their king's prediction is eventually fulfilled, he vows revenge on King Chandra, and induces him to go with his suite to a certain pond where pearl necklaces are to be procured. In that pond all the suite are devoured by a Rákshasa, whereupon the monkey king, climbing on a tree, tells King Chandra of the revenge he has taken on him.

No. III—pp. 31 and 141.
THE MERCHANT, HIS WIFE, AND THE PARROT.

THERE must be few readers who are not familiar with this story through the *Arabian Nights' Entertainments*, but it was popular several centuries before that celebrated collection was rendered

into English from Galland's French translation, as it is one of
the tales of the *Seven Wise Masters* and the *Seven Sages*, old
English prose and metrical versions of the *Historia Septem
Sapientum Romæ*, or of *Dolopathos*, which are Latin and French
adaptations of the Book of Sindibād. In our common version of
the *Thousand and One Nights*, the Story of the Parrot is told
(in the introduction) by King Yunan, when his counsellers urged
him to put the sage Dūbān to death; but in the Būlāq and
Calcutta printed Arabic texts, the king says: "I should repent
after it, as King Sindibād repented of killing his falcon;" then
follows the well-known story of the king who killed his falcon,
under the mistaken idea that it had, from mere wantonness,
repeatedly dashed from his hand the cup of spring water, when
he was about to drink, and afterwards found that a venomous
serpent lay coiled at the spring-head.[1]

The 68th chapter of Swan's *Gesta Romanorum* seems imitated
from the Story of the Parrot: A certain king had a fair but
vicious wife. It happened that her husband having occasion to
travel, the lady sent for her gallant, and rioted in every excess
of wickedness. Now one of her handmaids, it seems, was skilful
in interpreting the song of birds, and in the court of the castle
there were three cocks. During the night, while the gallant
was with his mistress, the first cock began to crow. The lady
heard it, and said to her servant: "Dear friend, what says
yonder cock?" She replied: "That you are grossly injuring
your husband." "Then," said the lady, "kill that cock
without delay." They did so, but soon after, the second
cock crew, and the lady repeated her question. "Madam,"

---

[1] This story also occurs in the *Anvar-i Suhaylí*, or Lights of Canopus, a
Persian version, by Husain Vá'iz, of the work generally known in Europe
as the Fables of Pilpay. Mr Lane thought fit in his admirable translation
to substitute for this tale that of the Merchant and the Parrot, although
in his (the Būlāq) text it is found in its proper place, in the tales of the
Seven Vazirs.

said the handmaid, "he says, 'My companion died for reveal-
ing the truth, and for the same cause I am prepared to die.'"
"Kill him!" cried the lady, which they did. After this, the
third cock crew. "What says he?" asked she again. "Hear,
see, and say nothing, if you would live in peace." "Oh, *don't*
kill him," said the lady.

The frame, or leading story, of the Persian collection of
Nakhshabī, entitled, *Tūtī Nāma*, Parrot-Book, or Tales of a
Parrot, is similar to our tale: A man bought, for a large sum
of money, a wonderful parrot, that could talk eloquently and
intelligently, and shortly afterwards, a sharyk—a species of
nightingale, according to Gerrans, "which imitates the human
voice in so surprising a manner, that, if you do not see the bird,
you cannot help being deceived"—and put it in the same cage
with the parrot. When he was about to set out on a distant
journey, he told his wife, that, whenever she had any important
affair to transact, she must first ask the advice of the parrot and
the sharyk, and do nothing without their sanction. Some months
after he was gone, his wife saw from the roof of her house a very
handsome young prince pass along the street with his attendants,
and immediately became enamoured of him. The prince also
perceived the lady, and sent an old woman to solicit an assignation with her on the same evening. The lady consents to meet
him, and having arrayed herself in her finest apparel, proceeds
to the cage, and first consults the sharyk upon the propriety of
her intended intrigue; but the bird forbade her to go, upon which
the lady in a rage seized the faithful bird, and dashed it on the
ground, so that it instantly died. She then represented her case
to the parrot, who, having witnessed the fate of his unhappy
companion, prudently resolved to temporise with the amorous
dame, and accordingly "commiserated her situation, quenched
the fire of indignation with the water of flattery, and began a
tale conformable to her temperament," which he took care to
protract till morning. In this manner, night after night, the

parrot contrives to keep the lady at home until her husband's
return.—The first story the parrot relates, according to Gerrans
(and also in Kāderī's abridgment; but it is the 5th in MS. No.
2573, in the India Office), is of a merchant, who, having occasion
to travel, left his wife and house in charge of a sagacious parrot
—a cockatoo, according to Gerrans. During his absence his wife
had an intrigue with a young man, who came to the house every
evening; but on the merchant's return, the discreet bird, while
giving a faithful account of all other transactions, said not a word
in reference to the lady's merry pranks. The husband soon
hears of them, however, from his neighbours, and punishes his
wife. Suspecting the parrot to have blabbed, the lady goes at
night to the cage, takes out the bird; plucks off all its feathers,
and throws it into the street. In the morning, when the merchant
misses his favourite bird, she tells him that a cat had carried it
away, but he discredits her story, and thrusts her out of doors.
Meantime the parrot had taken up his abode in a burying-ground,
to which the poor wife now also retires; and the parrot advises
her to shave her head and remain there fasting during forty days,
after which she should be reconciled to her husband. This she
does, and at the end of the prescribed period the parrot goes to
his old master, and upbraids him with his cruel treatment of his
innocent wife, adding that she had been fasting forty days in the
burying-ground. The merchant hastens to seek his wife, asks
her forgiveness, and they live together ever afterwards in perfect
harmony. "In like manner," adds the story-telling parrot,
"I shall conceal your secret from your husband, or make your
peace with him if he should find it out."

The *Tūtī Nāma* of Nakhshabī was composed about A.D. 1320;
it was preceded, according to Pertsch, by a similar Persian work,
by an unknown author, which was based upon a Sanskrit book,
now lost, of which the *Suka Saptatī*, Seventy Tales of a Parrot,
is only an abstract, and other sources. And here the question
is suggested: Was the Sindibād story of the Husband and the

Parrot imitated or adapted from the frame, or leading tale, of the original Sanskrit Parrot-Book, or was the idea of the latter taken from the Book of Sindibād? However this may be, the principal story of the *Tūtī Nāma* presents some points of resemblance to incidents in one of the numerous legends of the famous hero Rasalū, which are current in the Panjāb, namely, the story of Rāja Sirikop and Rasalū, kindly communicated to me by General James Abbott, from a small work which he had printed for private circulation, at Calcutta, in 1851. The conclusion of this legend seems to be the original of our old European tale of the cruel knight who caused the heart of his wife's paramour to be dressed and served up to her for supper. Rasalū, having slain the inhuman Rāja Sirikop, who played at dice for the heads of his guests, took away his infant daughter Kokla, and, when she was of age, married her. The Rana Kokla had seldom the society of her husband, as he was passionately devoted to the chase, but he left behind him, as spies upon her conduct, two birds, which could talk intelligently, a parrot and a mina, or hill starling. While Rasalū was absent on a hunting excursion, his young and lonely bride was seated at her window one day, when the handsome Rāja Hodi chanced to see her as he rode past. "And she saw him, and he took the place which Rasalū had left vacant in her heart. . . So Rana Kokla threw him down a rope, which she tied firmly to the balcony. And Rāja Hodi clambered up to the balcony by this rope, and entered the chamber of Rana Kokla. And the mina exclaimed: 'What wickedness is this?' Then Hodi went straight 'to the mina's cage and wrung its neck. So the parrot, taking warning, said: 'The steed of Rasalū is swift; what if he should surprise you? Let me out of my cage, and I will fly over the palace, and will inform you the instant he appears in sight.' And Kokla said: 'O excellent bird! do even as thou hast said,' and she released the bird from its cage. Then the parrot flew swift as an arrow to Dumtūr, and alighting upon Rasalū's shoulder, as he hunted the stag, exclaimed: 'O Raja, a cat is at your cream!'" The sequel is nearly identical with the catastrophe of the story in Boccaccio's *Decameron*, Day iv, Nov. 9, and the French tradition of Raoul de Coucy and the Lady of Fayel.—It is possible that the two birds of Rasalū may have suggested the frame of the Sanskrit prototype of the *Tūtī Nāma*. At all events, the legends of Rasalū and other ancient Indian heroes have been time out of mind the stock-in-trade of the wandering bards of the Panjāb, from whom General Abbott obtained this wild tale, among many others.[1]

Wonderfully-gifted parrots are the principal characters in many of the Hindū tales. The facility with which this bird imitates human speech, together with the doctrine of metempsychosis—and the allied notion of a person being able by magical power to transfer his own soul into the dead body of any animal or bird, upon which, for example, the romance of King Vikram is based —probably induced the fablers of India to adopt the parrot as the favourite character in their fictions. But apart from the marvellous parrot of Oriental romance, it would appear from the accounts of grave authors, Western as well as Eastern, that the bird is not only capable of repeating words and phrases which it has been taught, but is possessed of considerable intelligence. Locke, in his *Essay on the Human Understanding*, relates a curious anecdote of a parrot which answered rationally several questions which it was asked by Prince Maurice, one of which was: "What do you there (*i.e.* at Marignan)?" The parrot replied: "I look after the chickens." The prince laughed, and said: "*You* look after the chickens!" to which the parrot replied: "Yes, I; and I know well enough how to do it," at the same time clucking in imitation of the noise made by the hen to

---

[1] In August last year (1883) Captain R. C. Temple, Cantonment Magistrate at Ambala, Panjāb, commenced the issue, in monthly parts ('Trubner & Co., London), of "The Legends of the Panjāb," a work which must prove invaluable to students of comparative folk-lore.

call together her young ones.—Willoughby tells of a parrot which, when one said, "Laugh, Poll, laugh," laughed, accordingly, and the instant after screamed out, "What a fool you are to make me laugh!" Rhodiginus mentions a parrot that could recite correctly the whole of the Apostles' Creed, and of another that could repeat a sonnet from Petrarch. But these feats dwindle into insignificance when compared with the accomplishments of parrots referred to by the Arabian historian El-Ishākī (cited by Lane, *1001 Nights*, i, p. 111, note 22), one of which could repeat the 36th chapter of the Qur'ān, the other recited the whole of the Qur'ān!—Goldsmith relates that a parrot belonging to Henry VII, having been kept in a room next to the Thames, in his palace at Westminster, had learned to repeat many sentences from the boatmen and passengers. One day, sporting on its perch, it fell into the water. The bird had no sooner discovered its situation than it called out: "A boat! twenty pounds for a boat!" A waterman, happening to be near the place where the parrot was floating, immediately took it up and restored it to the king, demanding, as the bird was a favourite, that he should be paid the reward it had called out. This was refused; but it was agreed that, as the parrot had offered a reward, the man should again refer to its determination for the sum he was to receive. "Give the knave a groat!" the bird screamed the instant the reference was made.

No. IV—pp. 35 and 148.

The Double Infidelity.

A VARIANT—possibly the original—of this widely-diffused story is found in the *Hitopadesa*, Book ii, Fable, 7, as follows:

"In the town of Dwárávatí a certain farmer had a wife, a woman of loose conduct, who used to amuse herself with the magistrate of the town and with his son. One day, as she sat diverting herself with the magistrate's son, the magistrate himself arrived. When she saw him, she shut his son in the cupboard, and began sporting in the same manner with the magistrate. In the meantime, the herdsman her husband returned from the fold. On seeing him, she said: 'O magistrate, do you, taking your staff, and putting on the appearance of anger, depart with haste.' This was done; and now the herdsman, coming up, asked his wife: 'Wherefore came the magistrate here?' She replied: 'For some cause or other, he is angry with his son, who, running away, came here, and entered the house. Him I have made safe in the cupboard. His father, seeking him, and not finding him in the house, is therefore going off in a rage.' Then having made the youth come out of the cupboard, she showed him to her husband."

The 9th tale of the *Disciplina Clericalis* of Peter Alphonsus is evidently a modification of the story:

"In former times there was a good man, who, on setting out on a distant journey, left his wife in charge of her mother. This old woman brought to the house a young man whom her daughter loved. It happened that, while they were seated at table, the husband returned unexpectedly and knocked at the door. The young woman rose to open the door to her husband. But the mother (who lived with the friend of her daughter) did not know what to do, because there was no place in which to hide him. So, while the daughter was opening the door to her husband, the old woman took a drawn sword and handed it to the youth, and told him to stand with it drawn at the door; and if the husband said anything to him, he should answer nothing. The youth did as the old woman told him; and when the door was opened, the husband of the girl saw him, and he stood quite still, and said: 'Who art thou?' He did not say a word, but held the drawn sword in his hand, and the husband was perplexed at this. The old woman said to him: 'Fair son, be quiet; let none hear you.' Then the husband wondered more than before, and said: 'Fair lady, who is he?' The old woman said to him: 'Three men were following him just now; we opened the door and let him enter here, and because he feared lest you be one of them, he will not answer you.' 'Lady,' said the husband, 'you did well;' and he entered and called to the lover of his wife, and caused him to dine with him.''

This is also one of the Fabliaux; but it must have been from another version, more closely resembling the Sindibād tale, that Boccaccio derived his story of the lady of Florence and her two lovers (*Decameron*, Day vii, Nov. 6): To the one called Leonetto she was much attached; but the other, Lambertuccio, only procured her good-will by the power which he possessed, in consequence of his high rank and influence, of doing her an injury. While residing at a country seat, the husband of this lady left her for a few days, and on his departure she sent for Leonetto to bear her company. Lambertuccio, also hearing of the absence of the husband, came to the villa soon after the arrival of her favoured lover. Scarcely had Leonetto been concealed, and Lambertuccio occupied his place, when the husband unexpectedly knocked at the outer gate. At the earnest entreaty of his mistress, Lambertuccio runs down with a drawn sword in his hand, and rushes out of the house, exclaiming: "If ever I meet the villain again!" Leonetto is then brought forth from concealment, and the husband is informed, and believes, that he had sought refuge in his villa from the fury of Lambertuccio, who, having met him on the road, had pursued him with an intention of putting him to death.—*Dunlop.*

From Boccaccio the story was reproduced in *Tarlton's Newes out of Purgatorie* (a catchpenny book), printed about 1590; and eleven years later Samuel Rowlands turned it into verse, in his *Knave of Clubs*, under the title of "The Cuckold:" the lady's lovers are a courtier and a captain;—the former is hidden away on the arrival of the son of Mars, who, when the lady hears that her husband is coming, is instructed how to comport himself in his retreat:

So downe the staires he goes,
With rapier drawne, such fearefull looks he showes,
The cuckold trembles to behould the sight,
And up he comes, as he had met some spright.
Ah, wife, said he, what creature did I meete?
Hath he done any harme to thee, my sweete?
A verier ruffian I did never see;
The sight of him hath almost distracted me.
My loving husband, as I heere sate sowing,
Thinking no harme, or any evill knowing,
A gentleman comes up the staires amaine,
Crying, Oh, helpe me, or I shall be slaine:
I of compassion, husband (life is deere),
Under your bed in pitty hid him heere;
His foe sought for him with his rapier drawne,
While I with teares did wash this peece of lawne.
But when he saw he could not finde him out
(After he tossed all my things about),
He went downe swaggering even as you met him,
My saving the poore man so much did fret him.
A blessed deede, quoth he; it prooves thee wise:
Alas! the gentleman uneasie lies;
Wife, call him forth; I hope all danger's past;
Good Bettris, looke that all the doores be fast.
Sir, you are welcome to my house, I vow,
I joy it is your sanctuary now,
And count myself most happy in the thing,
That such good fortune did you hither bring.
Sir, said the courtier, hearty thanks I give,
I will requite your kindness if I live.

But the story had found its way into an English jest-book many years before its appearance in *Tarlton's Newes,* even before Boccaccio's tales were translated in Paynter's *Palace of Pleasure.* In *Tales and Quicke Answeres, very Pleasant and Mery to Rede,* 1535, it is told of an innkeeper's wife near Florence. While she was entertaining one lover, another came "up the ladder," and she bade him be off. "But for all her words, he would not go away, but still pressed to come in. So long they stood chiding that the good-man came upon them, and asked them why they bawled so. The woman, not unprovided with a deceitful answer, said : Sir, this man would come in perforce to slay or mischief another that is fled into our house for succour, and hitherto I have kept him back.—When he that was within heard her say so, he began to pluck up his heart, and say he would be revenged on him without. And he that was without made a face as he would kill him that was within.—The foolish man her husband inquired the cause of their debate, and took upon him to set them at one. And so the good silly man spake and made the peace between them, yea, and farther, he gave them a gallon of wine."

In all the Eastern texts, excepting the Persian and Scott's versions, the story of the Double Infidelity is preceded by another, related by the same vazīr :

The Infected Loaves.

A certain man was very particular in his food, and could not eat anything that he suspected to be unclean. In the course of a trading journey he came to a town, and sent his servant to buy some bread. The servant returned with two loaves, which his master relished so much that he told him always to procure him the same bread. This he did for some time (25 days, according to the Breslau text), until one day the servant returned without any bread, saying that the woman of whom he had hitherto bought the loaves had no more to sell. The merchant then sends for the woman, and asks her how the bread she had sold his servant was so pleasantly flavoured. She explains, to the infinite disgust of the man who was so particular in his food— and doubtless the explanation will be not less disgusting to the reader—that her master had suffered from blisters on his back, for which the doctor prescribed a poultice of flour mixed with honey and oil;—she took the poultice each day, when it was removed for a fresh one, and made it into a loaf, which the merchant's servant had bought of her daily. But now that her master was cured (in the Breslau text he was dead), she could supply no more loaves.

———

No. V—pp. 37 and 144.
THE FULLER AND IIIS SON.

IN three other Arabic texts of the *Seven Vazīrs*, this rather pointless story—which, however, belongs to the original Book of Sindibād—is followed by a second related by the Damsel, of

The Blackguard,[1]

who devised a diabolical plan to procure the disgrace of a merchant's wife, whose virtue he had unsuccessfully attempted. The story is very objectionable in its details, and must therefore be passed over.

———

No. VI—p. 39.
THE TWO PARTRIDGES.

THIS is a very different story from that of the Two Pigeons as found in the Syriac, Greek, Hebrew, and old Castilian versions, yet it may—Comparetti's opinion to the contrary notwithstanding—be the older form. The story of the Two Pigeons is omitted in all the Arabic texts of the *Seven Vazīrs*. It reappears, as follows, in the *Anvār-i Suhaylī:*

The Two Pigeons.

They have related that a pair of pigeons had collected some grains of corn in the beginning of summer, and stored them up

———

[1] Alfāsik : a worthless, impudent fellow ; a scoundrel, etc.

in a retired place as a hoard for winter. Now that corn was moist, and when summer drew to a close, the heat of the atmosphere had such an effect upon the corn, that it dried up, and appeared less than it did at first. During these days the male pigeon was absent from home. When he came back and observed that the corn appeared to be less in quantity, he began to reproach his partner, and said : " We had laid up this grain for our food in winter, so that when the cold became excessive, and from the quantity of snow, no corn was to be found on the fields, we might support ourselves with this. At this time, when pickings are to be met with in mountain and plain, why hast thou eaten our supplies? and why hast thou swerved from the path of prudence? Hast thou not heard, pray, that the sages have said :

> Now that thou hast food in plenty,
>   Do thy best it up to store,
> That thou may'st still have abundance
>   When the harvest-time is o'er."

The female pigeon said : " I have eaten none of this grain, nor have I used any of it in any way whatever." As the male pigeon saw that the grain had decreased, he did not believe her denial, and pecked her till she died. Afterwards, in the winter, when the rain fell incessantly, and the marks of dampness were evident on door and wall, the grain imbibed moisture and returned to its former state. The male pigeon then discovered what had been the cause of the apparent loss, and began to lament and to bewail his separation from his affectionate partner. Thus he wept bitterly, and said : " Grievous is this absence of my friend, and more grievous still that repentance is unavailing.

> With prudence act, for haste will cause thee pain
> And loss, and to regret the lost is vain."

And the moral of this story is, that it behoves a wise man not to be precipitate in inflicting punishment, lest, like the pigeon, he suffer from the anguish of separation.

In the Syriac, Greek, and old Castilian versions, the vazīr who relates the story of the Two Pigeons has for his second a rather stupid tale, which may be entitled

The Bread Elephant.

A ploughman's wife was bringing him some bread in a basket when she was met in the forest by a robber, who, having first conversed with her, ate up all her bread, excepting a small portion which he made into the form of an elephant, slipped it into her basket, and then let her go. When she reached the field where her husband was ploughing, and opened the basket, she discovered the robber's trick, and, to excuse herself, told her husband that she had dreamt some evil threatened him, which might be averted by his eating a small image of an elephant made of bread.—The story is also found in the *Suka Saptatī* and Nakhshabī's *Tūtī Nāma.*

No. VII—pp. 50 and 150.

THE PRINCE AND THE GHŪL.

THE pretended damsel's account of herself differs materially in the Persian text from that in the *Seven Vazīrs* and other versions. In the Persian she represents herself as having become enamoured of the prince from seeing his beauty from the terrace of her mansion; then she "points to her abode," and they proceed "till they reach a desolate spot." This is certainly not quite so plausible as what she says in the Arabic texts—that she fell from her litter on the way to be married to a certain prince. The conclusion, too, varies quite as much, so far as we possess it in the Persian MS.—In the old Castilian version the Damsel introduces this tale of the "female devil" by warning the king, most absurdly, that his vazīrs would kill him, "*as a vazīr once killed a king,*" since it relates that the *son* of the king was not killed, but returned in safety to his father.—In the Hebrew version the story of the Changed Sex is fused with this tale.

The Shah's own Story-teller gave Sir John Malcolm the following account of the nature and habits of ghûls, while "the Elchee" and his suite were passing through one of their favourite haunts : "The natural shape of these monsters is terrible, but they can assume those of animals, such as cows or camels, or whatever they choose, often appearing to men as their relations or friends, and then they do not only transform their shapes, but their voices also are altered. The frightful screams and yells which are often heard amid these dreaded ravines are changed for the softest and most melodious notes; unwary travellers, deluded by the appearance of friends, or captivated by the forms, or charmed by the music of these demons, are allured from their path, and after feasting for a few hours on every luxury are consigned to destruction. The number of these ghûls," added the worthy Hajjî, "has greatly decreased since the birth of the Prophet, and they have no power to hurt those who pronounce his name in sincerity and faith." (*Sketches of Persia*, ch. xvi.)—In Russian Folk Tales the Baba Yagas perform the part of Ghûls, Râkshasas, etc. Luckily for their intended victims, they are endowed with but a small store of intellect, and are generally outwitted by the interesting heroes and heroines.

——

No. VIII—p. 56.
THE SNAKE AND THE CAT.

IT is somewhat strange that this story should be omitted in the *Seven Vazîrs*, and yet form one of the four tales of the *Seven Sages* which are common to all the Eastern texts of the Book of Sindibâd. The story is thus related in a black-letter copy (preserved in the Glasgow University Library) of the *Seven Wise Masters*, the old English prose translation, by Copland, of the

Septem Sapientum Romæ, or of a French rendering of it ; where it is told by the First Master :

The Knight and the Greyhound.

There was a valiant knight which had one only son, the which he loved so much, that he ordained for his keepers three nowrishers. The first should give him suck, and feed him. The second should wash him, and keep him clean : and the third should bring him to his sleep and rest. The knight had also a greyhound and a falcon, which he also loved right well. The greyhound was so good, that he never run at any game, but he took it, and held it till his master came. And if his master disposed him to go into any battel, if he should not speed therein, anone as he should mount upon his horse, the greyhound would take the horse-tail in his mouth, and draw backward, and would also cry and howl marvelouslie loud. By these signs, and the due observation thereof, the knight did always understand that his journey should have very ill success. The falcon was so gentle and hardy, that he was never cast off to his prey but he took it.

The same knight had much pleasure in justing and tourney, so that upon a time under his castle he proclaimed a tournament, to the which came many great lords and knights. The knight entered into the tourney, and his ladie went with her maidens to see it : and as they went out, after went the nowrishers, and left the child lying alone there in the cradle, in the hall : where the greyhound lay near the wall, and the hawk or falcon standing upon a perch. In this hall there was a serpent lurking, or hid in a hole, to all them of the castle unknown, the which when he perceived that they were all absent, he put his head out of his hole, and when he saw none but the child lying in the cradle, he went out of his hole towards the cradle, for to have slain the child. The noble falcon perceiving that; and he beholding the greyhound that was sleeping, made such a noise and rustling with her wings presently, that the greyhound awoke, and rose up : and when he saw the serpent nigh the child, anone against him he leapt, and they both fought so long together, until that the serpent had grievously hurt and wounded the greyhound, that he bled so sore, that the earth about the cradle was all bloody. The greyhound, when that he felt himself grievously wounded and hurt, start fiercely upon the serpent, and fought so sore together, and so eagerly, that between them the cradle was overcast with the child, the bottome upward. And because that the cradle had four pomels like feet, falling towards the earth, they saved the childs life and his visage from any hurt. What can be more exprest to make good the wonder in the preservation of the child? Incontinently hereafter, with great pain the greyhound overcame and slew the serpent, and laid him down again in his place, and licked his wounds.

And anon after the justs and tourney was done, the nowrishers came first into the castle, and as they saw the cradle turned the up side down upon the earth, compassed round about with blood: and that the greyhound was also bloody, they thought and said amongst themselves, that the greyhound had slain the child: and were not so wise as to turn up the cradle again with the child, for to have seen what was thereof befallen. But they said, Let us run away, lest that our master should put or lay the blame upon us, and so slay us. As they were thus running away, they met the knight's wife, and she said unto them, Wherefore make ye this sorrow, and whither will ye run? Then said they, O lady, wo and sorrow be to us, and to you. Why, said she, what is there happened? show me. The greyhound, they said, that our lord and master loved so well, hath devoured and slain your son, and lyeth by the wall all full of blood. As the lady heard this, she presently fell to the earth, and began to weep and cry piteouslie, and said, Alace, O my dear son, are ye slain and dead? What shall I now do, that I have mine only son thus lost? Wherewithal came in the knight from the tourney, beholding his lady thus crying and making sorrow, he demanded of her wherefore she made so great sorrow and lamentation. She answered him, O my lord, that greyhound that you have loved so much hath slain your only son, and lyeth by the wall, satiated with the blood of the child. The knight, very exceeding angry, went into the hall, and the grey-hound went to meet him, and did fawn upon him, as he was wont to do, and the knight drew out his sword, and with one stroke smote off the greyhound's head, and then he went to the cradle where the child lay, and found his son all whole, and by the cradle the serpent slain; and then by diverse signs he per-ceived that the greyhound had killed the serpent for the defence of the child. Then with great sorrow and weeping he tare his hair, and said, Wo be to me, that for the words of my wife, I have slain my good and best greyhound, the which hath saved my child's life, and hath slain the serpent : therefore I will put myself to penance : and so he brake his sword in three pieces, and went towards the Holy Land, and abode there all the days of his life.

This story occurs in all the Western texts of the Seven Wise Masters, also in the Anglican *Gesta Romanorum ;*—see Madden's old English versions, edited for the Roxburghe Club [xxvi], p. 86. A wolf takes the place of the snake in the well-known Welsh legend, which Edward Jones, in his *Musical Relics of the Welsh Bards,* vol. i, gives as follows: "There is a general tradition in North Wales that a wolf had entered the house of Prince Llywelyn. Soon after, the prince returned home, and going into the nursery, he met his dog Killhart all bloody and wagging his tail at him. Prince Llywelyn, on entering the room, found the cradle where his child lay overturned and the floor flowing with blood: imagining that the greyhound had killed the child, he immediately drew his sword and stabbed it; then turning up the cradle found under it the child alive and the wolf dead. This so grieved the prince that he erected a tomb over his faithful dog's grave, where afterwards the parish church was built, and goes by the name Bedd Gelhart (the grave of Killhart), in Caernarvonshire. From this incident is derived a very common Welsh proverb : ' I repent as much as the man who slew his greyhound.' Prince Llywelyn ab Jowerth," adds Jones, "married Joan, a daughter of King John by Agatha, daughter of Robert Ferrers Earl of Derby, and this dog was a present to the prince from his father-in-law, about the year 1205."—A curious instance, surely, of the transformation of an ancient Indian tale!

The Dog and Snake version reappears in the Italian novels of Sansovino (Day ix, N. 1), in *Dolopathos* and *Erasto*, and also in the *Facétieuses Journées*, and its oldest form is perhaps found in the *Pancha Tantra*, section v, fable 2 :

The Snake and the Ichneumon.

There was a Bráhman, named Déva Sarmá, whose wife had one son ; she had also a favourite ichneumon that she brought up with the infant, and cherished like another child. At the same time, she was afraid that the animal would, some time or other, do the child a mischief, knowing its treacherous nature, as it is said: "A son, though ill-tempered, ugly, stupid, and wicked, is still the source of delight to a father's heart." One day the mother, going forth to fetch water, placed the child in the bed, and desired her husband to guard the infant, especially from the ichneumon. She then departed, and after a while the Bráhman himself was obliged to go forth to collect alms. When the house was thus deserted, a black snake came out of a hole, and crawled towards the bed where the infant lay; the ichneumon, who saw him, impelled by his natural animosity, and by regard for his foster-brother, instantly attacked him, and, after a furious encounter, tore him to pieces. Pleased with his prowess and the service he had rendered, he ran to meet his mistress on her return home, his jaws and face besmeared with blood. As soon as the Bráhman's wife beheld him, she was convinced that he had killed her child, and in her rage and agitation she threw the water-jar at the ichneumon with all her force, and killed him on the spot. She then rushed into the house, where she found the child still asleep, and the body of a venomous snake torn in pieces at the foot of the bed. She then perceived the error she had committed, and beat her breast and face with grief for the unmerited fate of her faithful little favourite. In this state her husband found her on his return. When he had told her the cause of his absenting himself, she reproached him bitterly for that greedy desire of profit, which had caused all the mischief.

In the *Hitopadesa*, the woman goes to make her ablutions after childbirth, and while she is absent the rája sends for the Bráhman to perform for him a certain religious rite. The version in the *Pancha Tantra* is the only one in which the woman slays the faithful animal, and the Persian version is peculiar in representing the infant's mother as having died in giving it birth. The story as found in *Calila and Dimna* agrees with that in the *Hitopadesa.*

———

No. IX—p. 58.
THE LIBERTINE HUSBAND.

IN all other texts, with the exception of Nakhshabí, this story is fused with that of the Go-Between and the She-Dog, but they certainly formed separate tales originally, as they are so found in the Sanskrit collection entitled *Suka Saptatí*, or Seventy Tales of a Parrot. According to Nakhshabí, when the wife is introduced to her own husband by the old procuress, she recognises him under her veil, throws it off, seizes hold of him, declares that she had adopted this device to entrap him, and accuses him of infidelity to the assembled neighbours. She then takes him before the qází, and obtains a divorce.

Q

No. X—p. 59.

THE MONKEY, THE FIG-TREE, AND THE BOAR.

A STORY in the *Kathá Sarit Ságara*,[1] of the Monkey and the Porpoise, is sometimes cited as a parallel to this tale, but I can-not see any resemblance between them. An old monkey, having strayed from his troop into a forest on the sea shore, contracts a friendship with a porpoise, whose mate becomes jealous, and feigning illness, tells him that the only thing which could cure her is the heart of a monkey. With great reluctance the porpoise sets off to induce his friend the monkey to visit his dwelling; and as he carries him on his back through the water the monkey inquires the cause of his evident disquietude. The porpoise confesses that his wife longs for a monkey's heart, upon which the monkey informs him that his heart is upon a tree in the forest, and that if the porpoise would return with him he should be made welcome to it. The porpoise accordingly conveys him back, and the monkey no sooner touches the land than he leaps into a tree, and calls the porpoise a fool for believing that any animal keeps his heart outside his body.

In *Syntipas* and the *Libro de Los Engannos*, the boar waited in expectation of having more figs thrown him, with his head raised, until the veins of his neck burst and he died therefrom. The story as told in the *Anvār-i Suhaylī* is identical with the Persian version. The *Mishlé Sandabar* is the only Eastern text in which, in this tale, a man is substituted for the monkey, and from it the story in this form was taken into the *Septem Sapien-tum:* it is thus related in the black-letter copy of the *Seven Wise Masters* belonging to the Glasgow University Library:

The Boar and the Herdsman.

There was sometime an emperor, the which had a great forest,

---

[1] "Ocean of the Rivers of Story," by Somadeva, 11th century; a poetical version of the Sanskrit prose work, *Vrihat Katha* (Great Story), written by Gunadhya, in the 6th century.

wherein was a wild boar, which was so cruel and so fierce, that he killed and devoured men going through the forest. The emperor therefore being right heavy, proclaimed throughout all his dominions, that whosoever he was that could slay the boar, should have his only daughter to wife, and therewith his empire after his death : and as this was in places proclaimed, there was not one man found that durst give this adventure. But there was a shepherd who thought in himself : Might I the boar overcome and slay, I should not only advantage myself, but also my genera- tion and kindred. So then he took his shepherd's staff in his hand and went to the forest : and as the boar had of him a sight, he drew towards the herdsman, but he for fear climbed upon a tree, and then the boar began to bite and gnaw the tree. So the herd thought shortly that he would have overthrown it. This tree was loaden with great plenty of fruit, and the herd gathered and plucked thereof, and cast them to the boar, inso- much that when he was filled therewith, he laid him down to sleep : the which when the herd perceived, by little and little descended the tree, and with the one hand he clawed the boar, and with the other held him upon the tree, and seeing that the boar slept very soundly, he drew out his knife, and smote the boar to the heart, and killed him. And so shortly after he wedded the emperor's daughter : and after the death of her father, he was made emperor.

Then said she [the empress], My lord, wot ye not what I have said? He said, Right well. Then said she, This mighty boar betokeneth your most noble person, against whom may no man withstand, neither by wisdom nor with strength. This shepherd, with his staff, is the person of your ungracious son, who with his staff of cunning, beginneth to play with you, as the herdsman clawed the boar, and made him to sleep and after killeth him. In the same manner the masters of your son, by their false fables and narrations claw you, and glose with you, until the time that your son slay you, that he may reign. Then said the emperor, God forbid that they should do to me as he did to the wild boar: and he said unto her, This day my son shall die: and she answered, If you do so, then do ye wisely.

The story of the Wild Boar is not found in any of the texts of the *Seven Vazirs.*

No. XI—pp. 61 and 162.
The Go-Between and the She-Dog.

It is very significant that in this story as related in the *Disciplina Clericalis* of Alphonsus (A.D. 1106), the fabliau of *La vielle qui séduisit la jeune fille*, the *Gesta Romanorum* (13th century), and the collection of mediæval tales written in Latin, edited, for the Percy Society, by Wright (No. xiii, *De dolo et arte vetularum*), the incident of the Libertine Husband does not occur; but—as in the Sanskrit *Suka Saptati* and our Persian *Sindibād Nāma*— the scruples of the virtuous matron are done away by the old hag's device, and the lover is introduced to her. In the *Suka Saptati* the lady is the wife of a prince; a young man becomes enamoured of her, and his mother, seeing him fading away because of his love, adopts the expedient of the dog, and persuades her to grant her son an interview.

The oldest form of the story is probably that of the Cunning Siddhikari, in the *Kathá Sarit Ságara:* A Buddhist priestess has been employed by four young merchants to corrupt Devasmitá, the wife of a merchant, and with this object she pays a visit to the virtuous lady. The narrative thus proceeds:

"As she approached the private rooms of Devasmitá, a she-dog, that was fastened there with a chain, would not let her come near, but opposed her entrance in the most determined way. Then Devasmitá, seeing her, of her own accord sent a maid, and had her brought in, thinking to herself: 'What can this person be come for?' After she had entered, the wicked ascetic gave Devasmitá her blessing, and, treating the virtuous

woman with affected respect, said to her: 'I have always had a
desire to see you, but to-day I saw you in a dream, therefore I
am come to visit you with impatient eagerness; and my mind
is afflicted at beholding you separated from your husband, for
beauty and youth are wasted when one is deprived of the
society of one's beloved.' With this and many other speeches
of the same kind she tried to gain the confidence of the virtuous
woman in a short interview, and then, taking leave of her, she
returned to her own house. On the second day she took with
her a piece of meat full of pepper-dust, and went again to the
house of Devasmitá, and there she gave that piece of meat to
the she-dog at the door, who gobbled it up, pepper and all.
Then, owing to the pepper-dust, the tears flowed in profusion
from the animal's eyes, and her nose began to run. And the
cunning ascetic immediately went into the apartment of Devasmitá, who received her hospitably, and she began to cry. When
Devasmitá asked her why she shed tears, she said, with affected
reluctance: 'My friend, look at this dog weeping outside here.
This creature recognised me to-day as having been its companion
in a former birth, and began to weep; for that reason my tears
gushed through pity.' When she heard that, and saw that
she-dog outside apparently weeping, Devasmitá thought for a
moment to herself: 'What can be the meaning of this wonderful
sight?' Then the ascetic said to her: 'My daughter, in a former
birth, I and that dog were the two wives of a certain Bráhman.
And our husband frequently went about to other countries on
embassies by order of the king. Now while he was away from
home I lived with other men at my pleasure, and so did not
cheat the elements of which I was composed, and my senses,
of their lawful enjoyment. For considerate treatment of the
elements and senses is held to be the highest duty. Therefore
I have been born in this birth with a recollection of my former
existence. But she, in her former life, through ignorance, confined all her attention to the preservation of her character,

therefore she has been degraded and born again as one of the canine race; however, she too remembers her former birth.'[1] The wise Devasmitá said to herself: 'This is a novel conception of duty; no doubt this woman has laid a treacherous snare for me;' and so said to her: 'Reverend lady, for this long time I have been ignorant of this duty, so procure me an interview with some charming man.' Then the ascetic said: 'There are residing here some young merchants that have come from another country, so I will bring them to you.'"

The wicked ascetic returns home delighted with the success of her stratagem. Meanwhile Devasmitá resolves to punish the four young merchants. So calling her maids, she instructs them to prepare some wine mixed with *datura* (a stupifying drug), and to have a dog's foot of iron made as quickly as possible. Then she causes one of her maids to dress herself to resemble her mistress. The ascetic introduces one of the young libertines into the lady's house in the evening, and then returns home. The maid, disguised as her mistress, receives the young merchant courteously, and, having persuaded him to drink freely of the drugged wine till he becomes senseless, the other maids strip off his clothes, and, after branding him on the forehead with the dog's foot, during the night push him into a filthy ditch. On recovering consciousness he returns to his companions, and tells them, in order that they should share his fate, that he had been robbed. The three other young merchants in turn visit the house of Devasmitá, and receive the same treatment. Soon afterwards the pretended devotee, ignorant of the result of her device, visits the lady, is drugged, her ears and nose are cut off, and she is flung into a foul pond. In the sequel, the lady, disguised in man's apparel, proceeds to the country of the young libertines, where her husband had been residing for

---

[1] "This contrivance," remarks Professor H. H. Wilson, "is quite consistent with the Hindû notion of the metempsychosis, and is clearly of Indian origin."

some time, and, going before the king, petitions him to assemble all his subjects, alleging that there are among his citizens four of her slaves who had run away. Then she seized upon the four young merchants, and claimed them as her slaves. The other merchants indignantly cried out that these were reputable men, and she answered that if their foreheads were examined they should be found marked with a dog's foot. On seeing the merchants thus branded, the king was astonished, and Devasmitá thereupon related the whole story, and all the people burst out laughing, and the king said to the lady: "They are your slaves by the best of titles." The other merchants paid a large sum to the chaste wife to redeem these four from slavery, and a fine to the king's treasury. And Devasmitá having received the money, and recovered her husband, was honoured by all men, returned to her own city, and was never afterwards separated from her beloved.

It will be observed that in this old Indian version the *dénouement* is more moral than in any others: instead of the lady yielding, she entraps successively the four young merchants and their go-between, and punishes all of them in the most edifying manner.

———

No. XII—p. 63.
THE PRETENDED WIDOW.

NOTHING at all resembling this fragment is found in any of the Eastern texts represented in our Comparative Table. Without the commencement it is difficult to guess at the details of the story. Perhaps the lady, in her husband's absence, had gone to the house of an old lover, under some false pretences; she is apparently disguised, and so is not recognised by him; then she gets drunk there, and discovers herself to him in her joy to be near him again, and is maltreated in consequence. She pretends to her neighbours that it is all her own doing, because of her grief for the news of her husband's death. When he comes, however, she turns the tables on him, and he pays off the debts she had incurred during his absence.

In the manuscript, on the first of the three remaining pages of the story (fol. 177), there is a painting of the "tresses" scene : A young man is seated, holding the lady's severed hair in his right hand, near his left is a wine bottle overturned, and two others are introduced to show there has been a drinking-bout going on ; the lady, with her hair cut off and her face apparently flushed and idiotic, stands near the youth ; while at a short distance is a figure which seems meant rather for that of a eunuch than an old woman, "biting the finger of astonishment." It is not very clear from the text whether by "the old companion" who "leaped into her suddenly" we are to understand the old lover, or this unsexed personage—probably the former. I should suppose the *Suka Saptatī* likely to contain the complete story, or something similar.

———

No. XIII—p. 65.
THE FATHER-IN-LAW.

THIS story is found in the 8th Night of Nakhshabī's *Tūtī Nāma* (where it is told by the 5th vazīr) and also in the modern version of its Sanskrit prototype, the *Suka Saptatī.*—Readers of Lane's translation of the *Thousand and One Nights* will probably recollect a more elaborate conversation by signs in the touching story of 'Azīz and 'Azīza, where the young man's cousin and betrothed interprets the amorous lady's symbols ; for instance : She tucked up her sleeves from her forearms, and opening her five fingers, struck her bosom with them (with the palm and five fingers) ; next she raised her hands, and held forth a mirror from the lattice, and took a red handkerchief and retired with it ; after which she let it down from the lattice towards the street three times, letting it down and raising it, and then wringing and twisting it with her hand and bending down her head ; meaning thereby : "Come hither after five days ; seat thyself at the shop of the dyer [indicated by the dipping and wringing of the red handkerchief], until my messenger shall come to thee."—Lane remarks, that "the inability of numbers of Eastern women in families of the middle classes to write or read, as well as the difficulty or impossibility existing of conveying written letters, may have given rise to such modes of communication."

Another example of conversing by signs occurs in the Story of the Minister's Son, in the Sanskrit collection entitled *Vetala-panchavinsati* (Twenty-five Tales of a Demon). The prince and his companion, the minister's son, discover a lady bathing in a tank ; and the prince and the damsel become immediately enamoured of each other. The lady took a lotus from her garland of flowers, and put it in her ear ; she then twisted it into an ornament called *dantapatra*, or tooth-leaf ; then she took another lotus and placed it significantly upon her heart. The minister's son explains these signs : the lady lives in such a place ; she is the daughter of a dentist there ; her name is Padmavati, and her heart is wholly the prince's. An old woman (as usual) acts as go-between. The lady scolds her, strikes her on both cheeks with her two hands smeared with camphor ;—meaning : "Wait for the remaining ten nights of moonlight, for they are unfavourable for an interview." A second time the old woman goes to the lady, who again pretends to be angry with her, and strikes her on the breast with three fingers dipped in red dye ;—meaning : "I cannot receive you for three nights." A third time the lady receives her more graciously, but, instead of letting her go into the street by the usual way, she places her in a seat with a rope fastened to support it, and lets her down from a window into the garden of the house, where she must climb a tree, cross the wall, and let herself down by another tree, and go to her own house ; thus indicating to the prince the way by which he was to be admitted into the house.

Cardonne, in his *Mélanges de Littérature Orientale,* gives a variant of our story, with additions, from a Persian or Turkish collection. After the father-in-law (a merchant of Agra) has failed to convince his son of his wife's infidelity, by displaying the anklets, he is still resolved to open his eyes to her true character, at whatever cost. "There was at Agra a mysterious reservoir, much admired, constructed by some wise men, who had brought water into it under the conjunction of certain planets. The virtue of the water consisted in trying all kinds of falsehood. A woman, suspected of infidelity, swore she had been faithful, and was thrown into this tank, called the Tank of Trial; if she swore falsely, she instantly sank to the bottom, but if truly, she swam on the surface. The enraged father-in-law cited the lady to this tank, according to the right of every head of a family. Conscious of her guilt, the lady studied how to clear herself in the eyes of the world. Acquainting her gallant of her situation, she begged him to counterfeit madness, and to seize her in his arms the moment she was to undergo the trial. The lover, solicitous to save the honour and life of his mistress, made no difficulty to expose himself to the eyes of the spectators, and found an opportunity to approach and embrace her, which he effected by subjecting himself to a few blows, being deemed insane by those who did not know him.

"The suspected wife advanced to the edge of the tank, and, raising her voice, cried: 'I swear that I have never touched any man but my husband and that madman who has just insulted me. Let this water be my punishment if I have sworn falsely.' Having thus spoken, she threw herself into the tank. The water buoyed her up in the sight of all present, who unanimously declared her innocent, and she returned triumphant to the arms of her husband, who had always thought her faithful. But the old man could not give up the opinion he had formed from the evidence of his own eyes; he kept constant watch in the garden, but the lover and the lady discontinued their meetings.

"The vigilance of the father-in-law did not, however, abate. The king of India, being informed of his indefatigable care and attention, thought him a very proper person to superintend his harem, and appointed him to that responsible office. The old man discharged his duties with great severity; every one trembled before him, and his eyes seemed to penetrate the walls of the seraglio, even to its inmost recesses. One night as the unrelenting old fellow was going his usual rounds, he perceived the prince's elephant mounted by its driver. This privileged animal advanced to the balcony of the king's favourite wife, which opened, and the elephant, taking the lady upon his trunk, conducted her to his rider. After some time the lady was brought back again in the same manner, and set down in her balcony. The aga could not help laughing at the docility of the animal, the confidence of the lady, and the happiness of the guide. The adventure having taught him that the sultan was no more fortunate than his son, he took comfort, and resolved to keep the lady's intrigue more secret than he had done that of his daughter-in-law.

From a *fabliau*, possibly, Margaret Queen of Navarre obtained the material of the 45th tale of her *Heptameron*, in which an officious neighbour, looking from his window, discovers a lady and her gallant in the garden; when she sees that they are being thus watched, she sends her lover away, and, going into the house, persuades her husband to spend what remains of the night with her in the same spot. In the morning the neighbour meets the husband and tells him of his wife's misconduct, but is answered: "It was I, gossip, it was I."

<hr />

No. XIV—p. 69.

THE ROBBER, THE LION, AND THE MONKEY.

PROFESSOR Benfey has pointed out, in his *Pancha Tantra*, the resemblance between this tale—which is not found in the *Seven*

Vazīrs—and one in the *Suka Saptatī*. The fate of the officious monkey finds numerous parallels in Asiatic folk-tales. For instance: In the story of "Ameen and the Ghool," related to Sir John Malcolm by the Shah's Story-teller, Ameen having outwitted the monster, who sought to slay him, while he slept, by the same device as that adopted by our own hero Jack, of giant-killing renown, the ghūl, on finding his intended victim alive and hearty in the morning, fled from his den in great terror, upon which Ameen took the opportunity of escaping. He had, however, only gone a short distance when he saw the ghūl returning with a large club in his hand, and accompanied by a fox. His knowledge of the cunning animal instantly led him to suspect that it had undeceived his enemy, but his presence of mind did not forsake him. "Take that," said he to the fox, at the same time shooting him through the head. "That brute," said he to the ghūl, "promised to bring me seven ghūls that I might chain them and carry them to Isfahān, and here he has only brought you, who are already my slave." So saying, he advanced, but the ghūl had taken flight. (*Sketches of Persia*, chap. xvi.)

Another parallel is found in the Kashmīr folk-tale of "The Tiger and the Farmer's Wife:" One day a farmer went to his field to plough with his bullocks. He had just yoked them when a tiger walked up to him and saluted him; the farmer returned the salute, when the tiger said that the Lord had sent him to eat his two bullocks. The farmer promises that he will bring him a fine milch-cow instead; but his wife objects, and, putting on the farmer's best clothes, sets off, man-fashion, on the pony to where the tiger is waiting. She calls out: "I hope I may find a tiger in this field, for I have not tasted tiger's flesh since the day before yesterday, when I killed three." The tiger, on hearing this, turns tail and flees into the jungle, where he meets a jackal, who asks him why he runs so fast. "Because a tiger-eating demon is after me." The jackal tells him it is only a woman. But the tiger is still afraid, and the jackal and he knot their tails together, so that one should not escape at the other's expense. When the woman sees them, she calls out to the jackal: "This is very kind of you, to bring me such a fat tiger; but considering how many tigers there are in your father's house, I think you might have brought me two." Upon this, the tiger flies off in a fright, dragging the jackal after him, and the latter is killed by being bumped against the stones. (*Indian Antiquary*, 1882.)

No. XV—pp. 71-73.
The Peri and the Devotee.

It may possibly interest some students of comparative folk-lore to know that in the Persian version of this story the First Wish of the devotee is similar to that in the old Castilian version, *Libro de los Engannos et los Asayamentos de las Mugeres*, appended to Professor D. Comparetti's most valuable *Ricerche intorno al Libro di Sindibād*. And it is perhaps worthy of note that the Turkish rendering of the story agrees, in this respect, with the Persian and old Castilian versions; which seems to show that the Ottoman translation of the *Thousand and One Nights* was made from a different text from the Calcutta or the Būlāq.

No. XVI—pp. 73 and 198.
The Concealed Robe—The Burnt Veil.

An error in the translation of the story of the Concealed Robe falls to be corrected in this place: pp. 76, 77, "One day the vile hag," etc.,—it is not the old woman who visits the lady at her mother's house, after she ran away from her husband's violence, but the same "effeminate one" who concealed the robe, and who not only conducts her to her lover, but also makes peace between the husband and wife. The only part the old woman takes in the intrigue is to engage the services of the "effeminate one"—in the original, *mukhannas*, which means a hermaphrodite, and has another signification, which need not be here explained—for, although she "had now cleared her hands from the affairs of the world, she had formerly managed many such matters." (I may as well mention that I had originally suppressed the circumstance of the want of sex on the part of the individual employed by the old woman, and, somehow, neglected to alter the terms in pages 76, 77.)—The wretched being who is so comically described in the text would doubtless readily obtain access to the women's apartments of any house in Persia or India; and as Eastern tales of common life are considered to faithfully reflect the manners and customs of the age in which they were composed, it may be concluded that eunuchs and epicene individuals were formerly employed in those countries as go-betweens in affairs of gallantry. It is hardly to be supposed, surely, that the author of the *Sindibād Nāma* deliberately substituted this hermaphrodite go-between for the conventional old woman of the same story as found in other versions. But I shall not take upon myself to say whether this peculiar turn of the story in the Persian text is evidence of its greater antiquity. I may add, that it will be observed that in the Persian version of the story the cloth, or robe, is not burnt, nor is the lady divorced, apparently, as in the Arabian and other texts; and perhaps the most remarkable difference is, that it is the young man himself who suggests that the husband should be reconciled to his wife. The story is so differently told in the Persian text from the Greek, Arabic, and other versions, that Falconer could only have cursorily looked at it in the MS. when he referred his reader to the tale as given in Jonathan Scott's *Seven Vazīrs*. Professor Comparetti has stated, in his "Researches," that the Story of the Burnt Cloth is not in the Persian text of the Sindibād. He was, perhaps, misled by the French translator of Falconer's analysis, in the *Revue Britannique*, who may have omitted the brief allusion which

Falconer makes to the story, in these words: "The vazír
[*i.e.* the sixth] next relates the Story of the Stratagem of the
Old Woman with the Merchant's Wife and the Young Man,
which, being told in the *Seven Vazírs* ('Tales,' etc., p. 168),
need not be here repeated."—As this is one of the "secondary"
tales of the vazírs, which Professor Comparetti conceives was
added when the tales of the Libertine Husband and the Old
Woman and the She-Dog were fused together, it is of some
importance to find it in the Persian text, and told so differently, as well as these two stories separately.

In some of the Arabian texts of the *Seven Vazírs*, the story of
the Burnt Veil is followed by the tale of

The Lady in the Glass-Case,

which is almost identical with the well-known story in the introduction to the *Arabian Nights*. The original is perhaps found in
the *Kathá Sarit Ságara*, section seventh, to the following effect:
Two young Bráhmans travelling are benighted in a forest, and
take up their lodging in a tree near a lake. Early in the night a
number of people come from the water, and having made preparations for an entertainment retire; a Yaksha (or genie) then
comes out of the lake with his two wives, and spends the night
there; when he and one of his wives are asleep, the other, seeing
the youths, invites them to approach her, and, to encourage them,
shows them a hundred rings received from former gallants, notwithstanding her husband's precautions, who keeps her locked
up in a chest at the bottom of the lake. The Hindū story-teller
is more moral than the Arab: the youths reject her advances;
she wakes the Yaksha, who is going to put them to death, but
the rings are produced in evidence against the unfaithful wife,
and she is turned away with the loss of her nose. —The story is
repeated in the next section with some variation: the lady has
ninety and nine rings, and is about to complete the hundred,

when her husband, who is Naga (or snake-god) wakes, and consumes the guilty pair with fire from his mouth.—*Dr. H. H. Wilson.*—There is a variant of this story in the Persian romance of *Hatim Taï* (a pre-Islamite chieftain, renowned throughout the East for his unbounded generosity and liberality): A king, on a hunting excursion, loses his way and is separated from his attendants; he comes to a beautiful garden, in which is a palace, and an artificial lake, sits down, and, as he is performing his ablutions, catches hold of an iron chain in the water, pulls it towards him, and behold, it is attached to a chest, which opens, and discovers a woman of surpassing beauty. After conversing with her, the king takes a ring from his finger and offers it to her as a memento, but she tells him that she has already a string of rings, of which she cannot tell the number, nor can she recollect which lover gave her a particular ring.—Forbes says there is a similar tale in Nakhshabī, near the beginning, but I have failed to find it in that work.

———

No. XVII—pp. 80 and 144.
THE LION'S TRACK.

THIS story is told by the first vazīr in all the versions, save the Persian *Sindibād Nāma*, where it is related by the seventh vazīr, and two of the Arabian texts, namely, Scott's MS. and the Rich MS. in the British Museum, where it is, not inappropriately, told by the Damsel, since it tells rather against men than women, the king being the aggressor, and the "wile" of the lady being in defence of her own virtue.—As an instance of the "hashy" manner in which the *Book of the Thousand and One Nights* has been put together, it may be mentioned that in the Calcutta printed Arabic text (which hardly differs at all from that printed at Būlāq), this tale of the Sultan and the Virtuous Wife is also related separately from the *Seven Vazīrs*—Night 404.

A variant of the story is found in a Turkish collection, entitled

'Ajā'ibu-'l-Ma'āsir, Marvels of Memorials (*i.e.* of Traditions, etc.), which Cardonne translated, under the title of "La Pantoufle du Sultan," in his *Mélanges de Littérature Orientale*. This version differs in some particulars from that of Scott. The sultan sends the vazīr a written order to proceed on some business to a distant place. The vazīr, in his haste to depart, leaves on the sofa the sultan's order. Instead of the lady giving the sultan a book to read while she prepares supper for his entertainment, she recites to him two distichs, to the effect that the lion would scorn to devour what the wolf leaves, and deigns not to quench his thirst in the river which had been polluted by the dog. "These words immediately convinced the sultan that he had nothing to hope for there; he retired greatly disconcerted, and in his confusion forgot *one of his slippers*. The vazīr, in the meantime, having in vain searched for the prince's order, recollected that he had left it on the sofa, and was obliged to return home for it. The sultan's slipper, which had lain till then unperceived, gave him a too clear conviction of the monarch's real designs, and his motive for sending him away. Tormented at once by ambition and jealousy, he concerted means to divorce his wife without the loss of his dignity. Having despatched his business, he returned to give the sultan an account of his commission, and pretended to his wife that, as the sultan had just given him a sumptuous palace, it was necessary for her to pass a few days with her father, in order that he might have leisure to furnish it, presenting her at the same time with a hundred pieces of gold." The rest of the story agrees with the Arabian and other versions.

Boccaccio has adapted the first part of the Arabic version for the 5th Novel, Day i, of his *Decameron*. The Marchioness of Monferrat, while her husband was absent—being engaged in the crusade against the Turks—was visited by Philip, King of France, who had become enamoured of her from the accounts he had heard of her beauty and virtue. The lady, suspecting

R

his designs, bought up all the hens she could, and caused them to be dressed in as many different ways as possible. When the king perceived the uniform character of the fare, he said: "Madam, are only hens bred in this country?" "Not so," the lady replied; "but women, however they may differ in dress and titles, are the same here as in other places." The king felt the force of the rebuke, and presently departed.

No. XVIII—p. 83.
The Wiles of Women.

THE Persian version of this story differs very materially from that in *Syntipas*, where the woman, having learned of the young man's book of wiles, tells him the following tale:

"A certain man possessed a house and a prudent wife, and was always disparaging all woman kind. 'Abuse not all women,' his wife said, 'but only the bad.' 'All,' retorted he. 'Speak not thus,' the wife replied; 'since you happen not to be united with one of them.' 'Had I fallen in with one of them,' he then said, 'I should have cut off her nose.' After his own fashion, he also held up to obloquy some quarrelsome female neighbours. The wife then said to her husband: 'What do you purpose doing to-day?' And he answered: 'I am going into the field, and, at your leisure, cook something and bring it thither, that I may dine.' The wife then going forth met with, on her way, and purchased some fish, and scattered them in the field where her husband was to plough. When he discovered the fish, he said to his wife: 'Have you prepared aught for us to eat this evening?' And she replied: 'I have cooked neither flesh nor fish, nor anything else.' Thereupon he said: 'Behold the food I found in the field, and cook it.' Upon this she took the fish and concealed them. The table having been laid out, the man said to his wife: 'Where is the fish?' 'What

fish?' she demanded. 'Thou fool,' said he, 'did I not bring
some fish just now, which I found in the field?' The woman,
scratching her face with her nails, cried out: 'O listen to me,
neighbours!' And the neighbours having assembled, the wife
said to them: 'Listen, O my masters! My husband bids me
cook fish which he brought from the field.' The men asked the
husband: 'What sayest thou?—that you found fish in a ploughed
field?' He replied: 'O my masters and brethren! the food I
found there; but how it happened to be there, I know not.'
His wife then cried out: 'This man has a devil!' And the
neighbours then put iron fetters on his hands and feet, and
the whole night through the wretched man continued to say:
'Did I not find the fish, and, bringing them to this jade, bid
her cook them? Why have they, then, bound me with fetters?'
At the dawn of day the wife again raised a cry; upon which the
neighbours reassembled, and asked: 'What has happened?' and
the unfortunate man once more repeated the truth. 'He is possessed of a devil!' cried the woman; and the neighbours, believing
her, said: 'Verily, the man is suffering somewhat.' After the
third day, the woman said to her husband: 'Art thou hungry?
May I give thee somewhat to eat?' And he answered; 'Yea;
and what hast thou to give me to eat?' She said: 'Cooked
victuals, in the frying-pan.' 'Thou sayest well, woman. Are
not those the same that I brought to you from the field?' The
wife then exclaimed: 'O Christian masters! the evil spirit still
possesses this man, as he continues to talk about the victuals.'
But on his declaring, 'I no longer maintain what I uttered
before,' she gave him a portion and he ate of the food, without
saying a word about it. But she asked: 'Dost thou not
remember the food?' He replied: 'I know not what thou art
talking about.' She then released him, and said: 'O husband,
all that thou hast uttered is true; but wherefore abusest thou
not only the bad but also the good women? And I said to thee:
" Be silent;" but thou repliedst: " If I had such a wicked wife,

I should slay her." No longer vainly boast of being superior to womankind.'"

Having put the youth off his guard by this artful story, the woman makes advances to him, and then makes a great outcry, which brought the neighbours, who asked the cause of her exclamations. The youth by this time had taken his seat at the table, and the woman said in reply to the neighbours: "This stranger, who is received kindly by us, eating at our table, was suffering grievously, and was in great danger of being choked, in consequence of a morsel sticking in his throat; but I, quickly seeing what had happened, and fearing the death of a guest, shouted out as you heard me. But now the help of God has saved him from the danger of choking, and granted him health," and the neighbours went away. The woman, then approaching the stranger, said: "Hast thou written down all I have related to thee, and all I have done?" The stranger answered: "By no means." She then said: "In vain, O man, have you sustained labours and outlays;—despite your endeavours, you have accomplished nothing, and never fathomed the machinations of women!" And the stranger immediately took the records of the wiles of women, and threw them into the fire, and, marvelling, said: "No human being is able to know the knaveries of women." After this, hesitating, and not realising what might happen, he discontinued the investigation of woman's evil-craft, returned to his native land, and married a wife.

This story is not found in the *Mishlé Sandabar* or the *Seven Vazírs*, and the subordinate tale, related by the woman, as above, is peculiar to the Greek text. The woman's own wile is also found in the *Bahár-i Dánish*, or Spring of Knowledge, by Ináyatu-'lláh of Delhi, a work which is avowedly derived, all but the frame, from ancient Indian sources; and in the 8th Night of Nakhshabí's *Túti Náma*, where it is told by the fourth vazír.—The twenty-first vazír's story in the Turkish book of *The Forty Vazírs* is not remotely related to the same tale.

Mr. E. J. W. Gibb has favoured me with the following translation of it, from a printed text procured at Constantinople:

"There was in the palace of the world a great king, and he
had á beautiful wife, such that many a soul dangled in the
tresses on her cheek. That lady had a secret affair with a
youth; and she used to hide the youth in a chest in the palace.
One day the youth said to the lady: 'If the king were aware of
our work, he would slay the two of us.' The lady said: 'Leave
that thought; I can do so that I shall hide thee in the chest,
and say to the king: "Lo, my lover is lying in this chest;" and
then, when the king is about to kill me, I will make him re-
pentant by one word.' While the youth and the lady were
saying these words, the king came, and the lady straightway
put the youth into the chest and locked it. The king said:
'Why lockest thou that chest in such haste? What is in the
chest?' The lady answered: 'It is my lover; I saw thee
coming, and put him into the chest and locked it.' Then was
the king wroth, and he bared his sword, and thought to slay
him who was in the chest, when the lady said: 'O king, art
thou mad? Where is gone thy understanding? Am I mad,
that I should advance a strange man to thy couch, and then
say to thee: "Lo, he is in the chest?" In truth, I wondered
if thou wast sincere in thy trust of me, and I tried thee, and now
I know that thou thinkest evil concerning me.' Then did the
king repent of what he had done; and he begged and besought
of his wife, saying, 'Forgive me.' And he gave her many
things, and craved pardon for his fault. When the king had
gone out from the harem into the palace, the lady took that
youth forth of the chest, and said: 'Didst thou not see what
a trick I played the king?' and they gave themselves up to
merriment."

In another Turkish collection, according to Cardonne, a
philosopher who had compiled a book of the tricks and devices
of women is concealed in a chest by an Arab woman on the

appearance of her husband. It seems the man and his wife had been for some time playing a game, which consists in receiving nothing from the person one is engaged to play with, without pronouncing the word *Diadestè*, or Touch-stake, from which the game derives its name. The woman, to the terror of the concealed philosopher, coolly tells her husband that she has a lover locked in the chest, upon which he furiously demands the key, which she gives him, and then calls out to him: "Pay me the forfeit —you have lost the *Diadestè!*" The husband, happy to find no cause for his jealousy, returns the key to his wife, and goes away, and the philosopher on being released from his confinement is advised by the woman to enter this contrivance in his book.

The trick played by the wife on her husband with the fishes in the ploughed field, which is interwoven with the Story of Woman's Wiles in the Greek text, finds parallels in other collections of Eastern fiction. For instance: In the tale of the Bang-Eater and his Wife (vol. vi of Jonathan Scott's edition of the *Arabian Nights*), the man having discovered a hidden treasure, his wife fetches it away, and he, being a very honest fellow, threatens to inform the chief of the police of her having appropriated the gold; upon which, in order that his story should be discredited, she scatters pieces of cooked meat around the house outside, and then awakes her husband, who was sleeping off the effects of a dose of his favourite bang, and tells him that it had just rained these pieces of food. He believes her; but next day he goes to the chief of police, and acquaints him that his wife has taken away some money which had been concealed in a heap of earth. The magistrate asks the woman if her husband told the truth, and she desires him to inquire of the foolish man what day it was that she took the money; he replies that it was the same day that it rained cooked food, and the magistrate causes him to be confined as a lunatic. Some time afterwards his wife persuades him to say that nobody ever knew of it raining anything but water, and he is set at liberty.

So, too, in the story of the Foolish Sachalī, in Miss Stokes' *Indian Fairy Tales*, the simpleton meets with a strayed camel, loaded with rupees, and takes it home; his mother conceals the treasure, and, while he is out of the way, scatters comfits outside the house. On his return home she tells him that the comfits have fallen from the skies, and the foolish Sachalī informs the neighbours that his mother had concealed a large quantity of rupees, which he found the same day that it rained comfits.—In an English story, it rained raisins, and in Campbell's *Tales of the West Highlands*, there are showers of milk-porridge and pancakes.

In the Calcutta text of the *Thousand and One Nights* there occurs (Night 394) what seems an absurd variant of the trick with the fishes: A man gives his wife one Friday a fish to cook; while he is out, her lover comes, and, putting the fish in a jar of water, she goes off with him, and is absent a whole week. On the following Friday she comes home, and her husband (who had sought for her everywhere), reproaches her, but she brings out the fish *alive* from the jar, to show that she could not have been absent at all; she then assembles the neighbours, who, considering him mad, load him with fetters.

<hr>

No. XIX—pp. 88 and 213.

THE POISONED GUESTS.

WE have in the Persian text of this ancient tale a curious parallel to a custom which prevailed in Europe during the Middle Ages. The house of the bountiful man is represented as having "neither door, nor lock, nor *porter*." In the *Mabinogion*, we read: "If it should be said that there was a porter at Arthur's palace, there was none;" on which Lady Charlotte Guest remarks: "The absence of a porter was formerly considered as an indication of hospitality, and as such is alluded to by Rhys Brychan, a bard who flourished at the close of the 15th century:

> The stately entrance is without porters,
> And his mansions are open to every honest man."

The original form of our story of the Poisoned Guests seems to be found in the 13th of the Twenty-five Tales of a Demon *(Vetála Panchavinsati).* The wife of a man named Harisvámin having been stolen from him one night by a Vidyádhara prince, he gave away all his wealth to the Bráhmans, and resolved to visit all the holy waters, and wash away his sins, after which he hoped he might find his beloved wife again ; and the story thus proceeds :

"Then he left his country, with his Bráhman birth as his only fortune, and proceeded to go round to all the holy bathing-places in order to recover his beloved. And as he was roaming about, there came upon him the terrible lion of the hot season, with the blazing sun for mouth, and with a mane composed of his fiery rays. And the winds blew with excessive heat, as if warmed by the breath of sighs furnaced forth by travellers grieved at being separated from their wives. And the tanks, with their supply of water diminished by the heat, and their drying white mud, appeared to be showing their broken hearts. And the trees by the roadside seemed to lament on account of the departure of the glory of spring, making their wailing heard in the shrill moaning of their bark, with leaves, as it were, lips, parched with heat. At that season Harisvámin, wearied out with the heat of the sun, with bereavement, hunger and thirst, and continual travelling, disfigured, emaciated and dirty, and pining for food, reached in the course of his wanderings a certain village, and found in it the house of a Bráhman named Padmanábha, who was engaged in a sacrifice. And seeing that many Bráhmans were eating in his house, he stood leaning against the door-post, silent and motionless. And the good-wife of that Bráhman named Padmanábha, seeing him in this position, felt pity for him, and reflected :ʼAlas, mighty is hunger! Whom will it not bring down? For here stands a man at the door, who appears to be a householder, desiring food, with downcast countenance; evidently come from a long journey, and with all his senses impaired by hunger. So is not he a man to whom food ought to be given?' Having gone through these reflections, the kind woman took up in her hands a vessel full of rice boiled in milk, with ghee and sugar, and brought it, and courteously presented it to him, and said: 'Go and eat this somewhere on the bank of the lake, for this place is unfit to eat in, as it is filled with feasting Bráhmans.'

"He said: 'I will do so,' and took the vessel of rice and placed it at no great distance under a banyan-tree on the edge of the lake; and he washed his hands and feet in the lake, and rinsed his mouth, and then came back in high spirits to eat the rice. But while he was thus engaged a kite, holding a black cobra with its beak and claws, came from some place or other, and sat on that tree. And it so happened that poisonous saliva issued from the mouth of that dead snake, which the bird had captured and was carrying along. The saliva fell into the dish of rice which was placed underneath the tree, and Harisvámin, without observing it, came and ate up that rice. As soon as in his hunger he had devoured all that food, he began to suffer terrible agonies, produced by the poison. He exclaimed: 'When fate has turned against a man, everything in this world turns also; accordingly this rice, dressed with milk, ghee, and sugar, has become poison to me.' Thus speaking, Harisvámin, tortured with the poison, tottered to the house of that Bráhman who was engaged in a sacrifice, and said to his wife: 'The rice which you gave me has poisoned me; so fetch me quickly a charmer who can counteract the operation of poison; otherwise you will be guilty of the death of a Bráhman.' When Harisvámin had said this to the good woman, who was beside herself to think what it could all mean, his eyes closed, and he died. Accordingly the Bráhman who was engaged in a sacrifice drove out of his house his wife, though she was innocent and hospitable, being enraged with her for the supposed murder of her guest. The good woman, for her part, having incurred groundless blame from her charitable deed, and so become branded with infamy, went to a holy bathing-place to perform penance. Then there was a discussion before the superintendent of religion as to which of the four parties, the kite, the snake, and the couple who gave rice, was guilty of the murder of a Bráhman, but the question was not decided."

This forms the 16th tale of the Tamil version (*Veddla Cadai*) and the 12th of the Hindī (*Baitál Pachisí*); in the latter, the traveller, having placed the dish of food at the foot of a fig-tree, went into the tank to wash his face and hands; meanwhile a black snake, gliding from the roots of the tree, thrust its venomous mouth into the food, and then went away.—An incident resembling this story is found in the *Bahár-i Dánish* (Story of the First Companion): A snake bites the lip of the lady's paramour while he lies asleep, and kills him; then it dropped some of its poison into the goblet of wine, which the lady when she awoke drank, and she also died.

———

No. XX—p. 94.

The Stolen Purse and the Child of Five Years.

This is not only a familiar "Joe Miller" story, but it has been popular throughout Europe in various forms since the Middle Ages. Wright, in his elaborate introduction to the early English metrical version of the *Seven Sages* (vol. xvi of the Percy Society publications), states that he had met with it among the Latin tales of the 13th and 14th centuries. The first appearance of the story in English (taken perhaps from Valerius Maximus), so far as I have ascertained, is in the collection of jests entitled *Tales and Quicke Answeres, very Mery and Pleasant to Rede*, printed about 1535, where it is related as follows:

"There were two men on a time, the whiche lefte a great somme of money in kepyng with a maiden on this condition, that she shulde nat delyuer hit agayne, excepte they came bothe together for hit. Nat lang after, one of them cam to hir mornyngly arayde, and sayde that his felowe was deed, and so required the money, and she delyuered hit to hym. Shortly after came the tother man, and required to have the moneye that was lefte with hir in kepying. The maiden was than so sorowfull, both for lacke of the money, and for one to defende hir cause, that she thought to hange hirself. But Demosthenes, that excellent oratour, spake for hir and sayd: Sir, this mayden is redy to quite her fidelite, and to deliuer agayne the money that was lefte with hir in kepyng, so that thou wilt bringe thy felowe with the to receyue it. But that he could nat do."

The story reappears in another jest-book, *Jacke of Dovers Quest of Inquirie, or his Privy Search for the Veriest Foole in England*, 1604, under the title of "The Fool of Westchester," where two "cony-catchers," or sharpers, deposit a sum of money with "a widow woman," one of whom obtains the deposit, and decamps. When the other fellow brings the case to trial before the judges in London, the widow—without the help of "Demosthenes"—steps briskly to the bar, and offers to restore the money on the original condition, that both came together to claim it.—It is reproduced, with some variations, in *The Witty and Entertaining Exploits of George Buchanan, who was commonly called the King's Fool*, where three pedlars leave a pack with a widow, who kept an inn on the highway-side, charging her strictly, before witnesses, to deliver it to none of them unless they all came together. Two of the pedlars return, after a time, and, pretending their partner had gone to a certain fair, obtain the pack. When the third comes and learns how he had been cheated, he cites the poor woman before the judges, and "George" dons a lawyer's gown, and pleads her cause successfully.—Strange to say, Lloyd, in his *State Worthies*, has actually related the story as an incident in the early legal career of William Noy, attorney-general (1577-1634)—the case of the

Three Graziers and the Alewife, in which judgment was about
to be given against the poor woman, when young Noy, having
obtained a fee from her in order that he should be able to plead
in her behalf, starts up and informs the court that his client is
prepared to pay the money when all three are present to receive
it. This is given, on Lloyd's weak authority, in Chalmers'
Biographical Dictionary, vol. xxiii, pp. 267, 268, although the
same legal feat had been previously credited in the same work
to Thomas Egerton, Lord Chancellor (1540-1617). We have
seen that the "case" was a popular jest in England before
either Noy or Egerton was born.—A French variant is found in
the *Nouveaux Contes à rire*, 1737, under the title of "Jugement
subtil du duc d'Ossone contre deux Marchands;" and Rogers,
in the notes to his poem of "Italy," gives an Italian version,
in which a young lawyer, the lover of the old lady's daughter,
plays the part of the successful advocate.

————

No. XXI—p. 96.
THE ADVANTAGES OF TRAVEL.

FALCONER remarks, in a note on this passage of our text :
"The advantages of travel are a favourite topic with Eastern
poets. On this subject the reader will find, in the *Asiatic
Journal* for September, 1839, some verses extracted from the
Sikandar Nāma [Alexander-Book] of Nizāmī; and in the No.
for November, 1839, a *gazal* by Jalālu-'d-Dīn Rūmī; and an
Arabian poet has panegyrised travel in some verses which may
be thus rendered :

> Rise ! flee the dull monotony of home ;
> Nor fear a friend will fail where'er you roam.
> Go, wend from clime to clime your joyous way,
> And Nature's lore will every toil repay ;
> Each shifting scene enkindling new delight,
> While languor dulls the home-devoted wight.

Change—mid the starry host, or earth below—
Works every good created beings know.
Mark the glad streamlet, fresh'ning as it flows;
The joyless marsh, stagnant in dead repose!
Shone the blest Sun one long, eternal day,
Men of each clime would loathe his garish ray;
And yon pale Moon, to pensive lovers dear,
Would tire even *them*, for ever in the sphere!

If ne'er the arrow left the twanging string,
Say, would it reach the mark, or thread the ring?
If still the lion slumbered in his lair,
Would self-doomed victims to his feet repair?
Even gold is worthless, while the mine inurns,
And aloe yields no incense till it burns.
For change—in heaven above and earth below—
Works every good created beings know."

The verses from the *Sikandar Nāma* are accompanied in the *Asiatic Journal* by the following beautiful paraphrase, signed F, and doubtless by Falconer himself:

'Tis blithe to wander earth's fair face
   With wayward footsteps over,
And, as each varied scene we trace,
   New beauties to discover.
Sweet, too, at busy daylight's close,
The halting-place, with its repose.

'Tis blithe, our track as we pursue,
   To mark with curious wonder,
Each step fresh marvels bring to view
   Concealment's veil from under;
While all that meets the observant eye
Some thoughtful lesson shall supply.

And yet, for aye, it were unwise
   On distant shores to linger,
When busy Memory homeward hies,
   And becks with restless finger;
And joys—she hints—our coming wait,
Denied us in our alien state.

> And what though, far from home, we share
>   Earth's hollow pomps that perish?
> The friends, the loves, of youth are there,
>   And these the heart will cherish:
> Its strings will twine around the home
> Where we were nursed, howe'er we roam.

Of the *gazal* of Jalālu-'d-Dīn Rūmī referred to by Falconer, as above, my obliging friend Mr. E. J. W. Gibb has made the following close translation, in which he has very ingeniously reproduced the original rhyme-movement:

1 A-foot or a-wing had the tree to wander able been,
   Ne'er had it known the wound of the saw or the hatchet keen.

2 If the sun fared not on his way a-foot and a-wing each night,
   How were the world illumed at the dawn of the morning-sheen?

3 Or again, if the bitter water rose not from the sea to the sky,
   Where from the flood of the rain were the life of the flowery green?

4 The drop that has gone from its home, when next it appeareth to view,
   Having companied long with the shell, as a lustrous pearl is seen.

5 Did not Joseph set forth in tears from his father to journey afar?
   And won he not thereby weal and honour and kingship to glean?

6 And Mustafa, journeyed he not to the region where Yathrib lay?
   And found he not empire there, and a sovereign's glorious mien?

7 If to travel thou canst not avail, then journey to thine own heart,
   And e'en as the ruby-mine, be fired by the ray serene.

8 O master, journey thou forth, away from thyself to Thyself;
   For the ore of the mine turns gold by a journey like this, I ween.

9 From sourness and bitterness hence, to the region of sweetness fare;
   For that every moon from the light of the sun is with grace beseen.

Jalālu-'d-Dīn, author of the above *gazal*, was the founder of the sūfī sect of mystics, known in Europe as the Dancing Dervishes, from their gyrations in performing acts of worship. He died at Qonya (Iconium) A.H. 672 (A.D. 1273).—In the fourth couplet of this beautiful *gazal* is an allusion to the notion, common to Asiatics, that a pearl is a condensed drop of water, which

had fallen into the oyster, when its shell was open. Sa'dī
has finely versified this in his *Bustān.*—In the sixth couplet,
Mustafa is one of the names of Muhammad, and Yathrib is the
old name of Madīna (*the* city, emphatically)—the reference is
to the Prophet's Flight, *El Hijra.*—In the eighth couplet, the
second "Thyself" seems to mean God, as Mr. Gibb supposes,
the only truly existent being in the universe, and, therefore, every
man's *true* self.—The English reader will observe that, in
this *gazal*, as faithfully rendered by Mr. Gibb, the opening
couplet rhymes, and the second line of each succeeding couplet
(or *bayt*) rhymes with the first couplet.—Let me take the
opportunity of adding, that the whole of the Dervish-doctrine
(sūfīism, or Eastern mysticism) is amply set forth in the grand
poem of Jalālu-'d-Dīn, entitled, *par excellence*, "The Masnavī,"
of which the First Book has been translated into English verse by
Mr. J. W. Redhouse, and published by Messrs. Trübner & Co.

—

No. XXII—p. 106.

THE FOUR LIBERATORS.

NONE of the other texts of the Book of Sindibād represented in
our Comparative Table has this widely-diffused tale, and the
version here given differs remarkably from all others with which
I am acquainted, although the fundamental outline is identical
in them all. One of the oldest extant forms of it must, I think,
be that found in the collection of stories, in Sanskrit, entitled
Vetāla Panchavinsati, or Twenty-five Tales of a Demon, a work
which, though originally distinct and still existing in separate
form in most of the vernacular languages of India, is now included in the grand collection (so often referred to in these notes)
entitled *Kathā Sarit Sāgara.* This is how the *Vetāla* story
is related in the last-mentioned work, according to Professor
Tawney's translation :

Somaprabhā and her Three Suitors.

In Ujjayni there lived an excellent Bráhman, the dear de-
pendent and minister of King Punyasena, and his name was
Harisvámin. That householder had by his wife, who was his
equal in birth, an excellent son like himself, Devasāmin by
name. And he also had born to him a daughter, famed for her
matchless beauty, rightly named Somaprabhā (*i.e.* Moonlight).
When the time came for that girl to be given away in marriage,
as she was proud of her exceeding beauty, she made her mother
give the following message to her father and brother : "I am to
be given in marriage to a man possessed of heroism, or knowledge, or magic power; you must not give me in marriage to
any other, if you value your life." When her father Harisvámin
heard this, he was full of anxiety, trying to find for her a husband coming under one of these three categories. And while so
engaged he was sent as ambassador by King Punyasena to
negotiate a treaty with the King of the Dekkan, who had
come to invade him. And when he had accomplished the object
for which he was sent, a noble Bráhman, who had heard of the
great beauty of his daughter, came and asked him for her hand.
Harisvámin said to the Bráhman suitor : "My daughter will
not marry any husband who does not possess either valour, or
knowledge, or magic power; so tell me which of the three you
possess." He answered : "I possess magic power." Thereupon Harisvámin rejoined : "Then show me your magic power."
So he immediately prepared by his skill a chariot that would fly
through the air. And in a moment he took up Harisvámin in
that magic chariot, and showed him heaven and all the worlds.
And he brought him back delighted to that very camp of the
King of the Dekkan, to which he had been sent on business.
Then Harisvámin promised his daughter to that man possessed
of supernatural power, and fixed the marriage for the seventh
day from that time.

And in the meanwhile another Bráhman, in Ujjayni, came and asked Harisvámin's son Devasámin for the hand of his sister. Devasámin answered: "She does not wish to have a husband who is not possessed of either knowledge, or magic power, or heroism." Thereupon he declared himself to be a hero. And when the hero displayed his skill in the use of missiles and hand-to-hand weapons, Devasámin promised to give him his sister, who was younger than himself. And by the advice of the astrologers he told him, as his father had told the other suitor, that the marriage should take place on that very same seventh day, and this decision he came to without the knowledge of his mother.

At that very time a third person came to his mother, wife of Harisvámin, and asked her privately for the hand of her daughter. She said to him: "Our daughter requires a husband who possesses either knowledge, or magic power, or heroism;" and he answered: "Mother, I possess knowledge." And she, after questioning him about the past and the future, promised to give the hand of her daughter to that possessor of supernatural knowledge on that same seventh day. The next day Harisvámin returned home, and told his wife and his son the agreement he had made to give away his daughter in marriage; and they told him separately the promises that they had made; and that made him feel anxious, as three bridegrooms had been invited.

Then on the wedding-day three bridegrooms arrived in Harisvámin's house—the man of knowledge, the man of magic power, and the man of valour. And at that moment a strange thing took place: the intended bride, the maiden Somaprabhá, was found to have disappeared in some inexplicable manner, and, though searched for, was not found. Then Harisvámin said eagerly to the possessor of knowledge: "Man of knowledge, now tell me quickly where my daughter is gone." He answered: "The Rákshasa Dhúmrasikha has carried her off to his own

S

habitation in the Vindhya forest." At this Harisvāmin was terrified, and said: "Alas, alas! how are we to get her back, and how is she to be married?" When the possessor of magic power heard that, he said: "Be of good cheer! I will take you in a moment to the place where she is." He then prepared, as before, a chariot that would fly through the air, provided all kinds of weapons, and made Harisvāmin, the man of knowledge, and the brave man get into it, and in a moment he carried them to the habitation of the Rākshasa in the Vindhya forest, which had been described by the man of knowledge. The Rākshasa, when he saw what had happened, rushed out in a passion, and then the hero, who was put forward by Harisvāmin, challenged him to fight. Then a wonderful fight took place between the man and the Rākshasa, who were contending for a woman, with various kinds of weapons, like Rāma and Rāvana.[1] And in a short time the hero cut off the head of that Rākshasa with a crescent-headed arrow, though he was a doughty champion. Then they carried off Somaprabhā, whom they found in his house, and they all returned in the magic chariot.

And when they had reached Harisvāmin's house, the marriage did not go forward, though the auspicious moment had arrived, but a great dispute arose between the man of knowledge, the man of magic power, and the man of valour. The man of knowledge said: "If I had not known where this maiden was, how would she have been discovered when concealed?—So she ought to be given to me." But the man of magic power said: "If I had not made the chariot that can fly through the air, how could you all have gone and returned in a moment like the gods? And how could you, without a chariot, have fought with a Rākshasa, who possessed a chariot?—So you ought to give her to me, for I have secured her by my skill this auspicious

---

[1] Seeta, the beautiful wife of Rama, was carried off by the Rakshasa Ravana, according to the *Ramayana.*

moment." The brave man said: "If I had not slain the Rāk-shasa in fight, who would have brought this maiden back here in spite of all your exertions?—So she must be given to me." While they went on wrangling in this style, Harisvāmin remained silent, being perplexed in mind.

A variant is found in the *Tūtī Nāma* (34th night of the India Office MS. No. 2573, and the 22nd of Kāderī's abridgment), to the following effect: A rich merchant of Kabūl had a beautiful daughter, named Zohra (or Venus), who had many wealthy suitors, but declared that she would marry only a man who was completely wise, or very skilful. Three young men present them-selves before the merchant, saying that if his daughter requires a man of skill for her husband, each of them was eligible. The first youth said that his art was to discover the whereabouts of any-thing, or anybody, that was lost, and to predict future events. The second could make a horse of wood, which, whoever might mount it, would soar in the air, like Solomon's throne.[1] The third was an archer, who could pierce any object at which he might point his arrow. The merchant having reported to his daughter the wonderful acquirements of her three new suitors, she promised to give her decision next morning. But the same night she disappeared, and the unhappy merchant sent for the three youths, desiring them to recover his daughter, by the exercise of their respective talents. The first youth discovered that a perī had carried the damsel to the summit of a mountain which was inaccessible to man. The second made a wooden horse, and gave it to the third (the archer), who mounted it, and very soon reached the mountain, killed the perī, and brought away the maiden. "Each of the three claimed her as his own by right, and the dispute continued."

---

[1] According to the Muslim legend (borrowed from the Rabbins), Solomon's carpet, having on it his throne, his courtiers, and his entire army, was borne through the air by the eight winds—subject to him through his magical signet—and conveyed to the most distant regions in a few minutes.

The story must be familiar to all readers of the common English translation of the *Arabian Nights*, in the tale of Prince Ahmed and the Peri Banou : Three princes are in love with their cousin, who is to be given to him that should bring the most wonderful thing. One of them procures a magic carpet, another an ivory telescope, and the third an apple that could cure the person who smelled at it, even if at the point of death. The youth with the tube discovers that the princess is dying ; the magic carpet carries them all to the princess ; and the apple restores her to health.

The Tartar version, in the *Relations of Siddhí Kúr*,[1] is very peculiar in all its details : Six persons—a rich youth, a calculator, a mechanic, a physician, and a smith—set out together to seek their fortunes. Arriving at the mouth of a great river, each of them planted a tree of life and then separated, having agreed to meet at the same place again. The rich youth, in the course of his wanderings, marries a beautiful maiden ; but the khān takes her from him, and afterwards causes him to be put to death, and his body to be covered with a huge rock. At the time agreed upon the five other wanderers return to the spot where they had planted their trees of life, and, seeing that the youth's tree was withered,[2] the calculator by his art discovered that he was lying dead beneath a certain rock. The smith with his hammer smote the rock and broke it, and drew forth the body. Then the physician gave the dead youth a draught, and he became alive again. The revived youth having told his companions how his beautiful wife had been taken from him, and himself been slain, by the khān, they resolved by all means to recover such a pearl of beauty. Accordingly the mechanic con-

---

[1] A dead body endowed with supernatural powers.—This is the Kalmūk form of the Hindū Twenty-five Tales of a Demon.

[2] Compare with this the knife and string of pearls of the brothers in the Arabian tale of the Quest of the Singing-Tree, etc. ; and the gloves of Ivan Popyalof in Ralston's *Russian Folk-Tales*.

structed a wooden Garūda, which went in any direction, as it was guided from within. The painter then decorated the wooden bird with various colours, so that it was wondrous to behold. Then the youth seated himself within the wooden Garūda, which immediately flew through the air, and hovered above the khān's palace. When the khān discovered the strange bird, he bade the wife of the youth go upon the roof and offer food to it, which she did; and the bird descended, and the youth seated her beside him, and they flew away. Having returned to his five companions, the youth and his wife stepped forth from the Garūda, and on their beholding her beauty they began to quarrel among themselves, each claiming her as his wife, because of his share in her recovery, till at length they drew their knives and slew one another.

Such is the outline of the Tartar version of this old-world tale. The wooden Garūda here performs the part of the Enchanted Horse of the *Thousand and One Nights*, which, however, had reached Europe long before that entertaining work was composed. The contrivance in the Tartar tale was, in fact, borrowed from Hindū fiction: in a story in the *Kathá Sarit Ságara*, the hero, in love with a princess, personates Vishnū, and rides on a wooden representation of Garūda (the bird of Vishnū), guided by a pin and moving by magic—the prototype of

> The wondrous steed of brass
> On which the Tartar king did ride,

in Chaucer's "half-told tale of Cambuscan bold," and of all other self-moving machines so famed in romance.[1]—Of European

---

[1] The Enchanted Horse figures prominently in the old French metrical romance of *Cleomades*, written by Adans, or Adenis, a poet of the 13th century. *Le Cheval de Fust* is another title of this poem, which was, according to Count Tressan (who furnished an *extrait* of it to the *Bibliotheque des Romans*), originally composed in Spanish verse; and there can be no doubt that the groundwork, at least, of the romance was brought to Spain by the Moors.—Old English tradition, too, is not without its magic horse: Leland, in his Itinerary, tells of a man named Rutter, who "was

variants, the best is perhaps the well-known German fairy tale of the Four Clever Youths who rescued from a dragon the king's daughter, and were all amply recompensed for their pains.

No. XXIII—p. 112.
THE DAMSEL'S FATE, ETC.

IT is remarkable that in our Persian text the Damsel herself suggests that her tongue should be cut out, while in the Greek and the Breslau (Arabic) versions the proposal is made by the assembled counsellors, some of whom suggest various other forms of punishment : in *Syntipas*, to cut off her hands and feet, open her alive, and tear out her heart; in the *Mishlé Sandabar*, to cut off her hands, to blind her, to kill her. Replying to these cruel suggestions, the Damsel relates, in the Greek, Hebrew, and two of the Arabic texts (the Calcutta and Breslau), the tale of the Fox that preferred mutilation to death. The following is a translation of the Greek version of the story of

The Fox and the People.

O ye magnates, all your utterances against me appear to coincide with the example of a certain fox, who during the night entered into a certain city through the window of a man who curried skins, and whenever he entered into the house he gnawed the skins. The tanner perceiving the tatters made in the skins, and being satisfied the damage was through the fox, immediately fixed a solid trap. According to his wont, the fox entered through the window, and was caught in the trap. The unhappy yet crafty fox, by some well-skilled device, ran away with the trap which ensnared him, and wandered all around the city to

---

in great favour with his king, and desired to have reward of him of as much land as he could ride over in a day on a horse of wood; and he did ride over as much as is now Rutlandshire, by art magic, and was after swallowed into the earth."

find another window by which to go out. Having wandered
about the whole night, he found no place of exit, for the city
was walled all around.

On the approach of day, he said to himself: "If day should
dawn, of a certainty I shall be seized by dogs, and they would
not leave me before they had torn away my flesh; but I know
what it behoves me to do." Thereupon he laid himself near the
threshold of the gate of the city, feigning himself dead and
breathless. And while lying as if dead, the gate, as usual, was
opened by the porter at early morn. Some one upon seeing him
said to the porter: "Of a truth, the tail of this fox is well
adapted to sponge out the mill," and straightway, on saying this,
seizing a sword, he cut off the tail. The fox bore courageously
the pain of the clipt tail. Afterwards a certain other person,
seeing him, said: "If any one has a little whining child, nothing
is better as a cure than the ears of a fox, by holding them
over the child," and forthwith he cut off his ears, and the fox
nobly sustained this anguish. And still another, passing along
the same path, and seeing him as if dead, said: "I have heard
some one say, that if a person is suffering from toothache, and
should place on it the tooth of a fox, he is immediately relieved
from pain," and with these words, taking a stone, he knocked
out all the teeth, and the fox, without wincing, underwent all
these terrible pains, until the moment when another man, walking by, said: "I have heard that a fox's heart is beneficial for
every grief, and curative of every disease." The man, upon
speaking thus, taking a sword, in order to cut out his heart,
the fox, leaping up, ran away in haste through the gate of the
fortress, for the gate happened at that time to be open, and he
was saved from the death he was about to suffer. "And thus
[continues the Damsel] am I, helpless being, O king, prepared
to undergo all the suggestions thy rulers counsel thee to follow;
but I am unable to bear having my heart forcibly taken out—
for this would be a bitter and painful death."

This story, as Goedeke has pointed out, like the four tales in the introduction to the *Sindibād Nāma*, is of Buddhist origin, being No. 23 of the *Avadānas* translated by Julien. It seems to me very probable that it also occurred in the complete text of the *Sindibād Nāma*, since it would naturally follow the Damsel's suggestion that her tongue should be cut out. And the next chapter, in which Sindibād discourses eloquently to the king, which wants the commencement, may have contained the tale, preserved in the Greek text only, related by the sage in the course of his reply to the king's inquiry, to whom his son's wisdom was due. It is as follows, and may be entitled

Destiny; or, the Philosopher's Son.

There was a certain king in former times, who had in his service many philosophers, one of whom was far superior to the others, and at that king's court a certain one also who understood and professed in a high degree the astrological art. To the first-mentioned philosopher had just been born a son, and on it being communicated to the king, the philosopher was immediately summoned to the court. But the aforesaid astrologer, hearing of the birth of the son, consulted the stars concerning the destiny of the boy. When the king asked him regarding the boy's horoscope, he answered thus: "To judge, O my master, from the signs and courses of the stars, this new-born child inherits the evil destiny of thieves and wrong-doers;—he will survive many years, and in his thirteenth year he will commit an atrocious robbery." Upon the astrologer uttering these words, the father of the new-born child said to him: "Have you then made manifest to the king the whole truth concerning my child?" "Yea, O philosopher," replied he; "for I have accurately examined that which attaches to the destiny of the boy, and discovered that he will become a robber, and the most hardened of robbers." In answer to this, the philosopher said to the king: "I shall educate my boy, then, in such a manner, that he never would or could commit such a deed, but, on the contrary, I shall cause him to avoid all forbidden acts."

The child, when eight months old, discontinued suckling his mother's milk. Shut up in a secluded house by his father, he was nourished with succulent victuals, and instructed fully in literature and honourable conduct. While educating his son with such precision and accuracy, the father forbade that any one should visit, or any boy outside the house should approach him, or that he should learn or hear of any evil deed of the outside world. Brought up in this manner, he commenced his thirteenth year. The father then said to him: "To-morrow, my son, I am desirous of going to the king, and wishing to take you with me, you must know how and by what obeisance you should hail the king." In this wise the philosopher spoke to his son. The youth, however, upon hearing of the proposed visit to the king, inwardly debated over his father's speech, and said within himself: "I have never seen a king; and as my father tells me I must pay him obeisance, it is proper I should approach his Majesty with aromatic spices, in order that their sweet odour may honour and aggrandise the king. But I am ashamed to ask any details from my father, and yet it behoves me to accomplish this purpose."

Thereupon, at the approach of night, he went secretly forth from his father's house, proceeded to the palace, and, having made an opening in the wall, entered close to the royal bed. The king, waking up, was agitated on seeing him, and, being timid and alarmed, said to himself: "If this robber did not possess great strength he would never have dared to enter at midnight;—if I should resist him, he will attempt to kill me." Communing thus within himself, in silence, he afforded full license to the robber. The youth, then, extending his hand towards the linen clothes of the king, seized a linen cloth of great value, and went out of the palace. Having sold the linen cloth, he purchased with its proceeds myrrh and various perfumes.   On that night, however, the king did not recognise the robber.

On the following day the father, accompanied by his son, went into the king's presence, and both father and son prostrated themselves in obeisance to the very floor.   The son then presented to the king the perfumes and beautiful offerings he had purchased, and began to praise and eulogise his Majesty. And the philosopher said : " O king, live for ever !   Behold, I have brought into thy presence my son, concerning whom the astrologer told thee, that in the thirteenth year of his age he should become a robber.   He is now thirteen years old, and has not committed a theft.   Thy astrologer, therefore, may be, solemnly and in public, declared to be a false prophet, and from this all the words uttered by him have now been proved idle talk."   At these words the king, steadfastly and attentively fixing his eyes on the countenance of the youth and his outward form, recognised him to be the person who had broken through the wall, and the very bold and shameless robber who had stolen the linen cloth from the royal couch.   The king then, in answer, said to the philosopher : "This is the robber who entered the king's room, and this being the fact, the prognostication of the astrologer must the rather be relied upon as true."

" From this narrative, therefore, O king [continues Syntipas], it is clearly shown that at and from the birth of each individual there is a distinct and separate career of life predestined by the Deity.   It is not what a child has learned or suffered at the commencement of his growth, as happened at the birth of this thy son, but when he arrives at man's estate.   Praiseworthy and excellent deeds and prosperous days comprised and brightened his state of manhood, but odious actions and clouds of adversity darkened the mature life of the son of that philosopher whom the king had in his service."

That this tale—or one of a similar tendency—was also in

the *Sindibād Nāma* is, I think, more than likely, from the circumstance, as stated in p. 112, that where the fragment of the chapter in which it should appear begins, "Sindibād has been making some remarks on the impossibility of avoiding destiny," and at this place, as in the Greek text, he proceeds to cite the moral precepts of Farīdūn.

It has already been mentioned (note 1, p. 110) that the story of the Four Liberators is not told by Sindibād, but by the Prince; and Professor Comparetti was therefore mistaken in supposing that it had been substituted by the author of the *Sindibād Nāma* for the tale of Destiny, related by the sage in the Greek version. Moreover, the two tales have nothing in common that should render such a conjecture probable, even if the relator of the Four Liberators was doubtful, the latter having no bearing upon the question of resisting fate.

The Syriac text must have had both the story of the Fox and that of Destiny, although they are wanting in the only known copy, which breaks off at the beginning of the story of the Blind Old Man (see end of note, p. 104). There is also a *lacuna* in the MS. where the story of the Bathman should be related.

The old Castilian translation wants both the concluding stories of *Syntipas*, also the tale of the Woman and the Rice-Dealer; the latter was certainly not suppressed from motives of delicacy, since the two most objectionable of the tales proper to the Book of Sindibād are retained. It seems probable that the MS. from which the only extant text was made had lost the leaves containing these tales. A new one has been added to the four the Prince has in the Syriac and Greek texts, which is as follows, according to Mr. H. C. Coote's translation:

The Woman and the Abbot.

I have heard of a woman whose husband went away on some business, and she sent to the abbot to say that her husband was not at home, and that he should come for the night to her dwelling. And the abbot came and entered the house. And when he came it was midnight. The husband came and called at the door. And he [*i.e.* the abbot] said: How shall it be? And she said: Go and hide thyself in that apartment till daylight. And the husband entered, and threw himself on his bed. And when day came the woman arose, and went to a friar her friend, and asked him for a habit that he might get the abbot away who was in her house. And the friar went and said: What has become of such a one? And she said: He is not yet risen. And he went in and asked him [the husband] whence he came, and was there until the abbot was dressed. And the friar said: Pardon me, I wish to retire. He said: You must go, and be well. And joining the other in the apartment, the abbot went out dressed like a friar, and in that dress went with him to the convent.[1]

The author of the Hebrew version has omitted no fewer than seven tales which occur in *Syntipas*, namely: The Drop of Honey, the Bread Elephant (both of which are also not found in the Persian text), Woman's Wiles, the Poisoned Guests, the Infant in the Cradle, the Child of Five Years, and Destiny; but he has inserted four new ones, and fused into one tale the Prince and the Ghūl and the Changed Sex. He has also altered the order of the tales as they appear in the Greek version. Two of the new tales are of Jewish argument; the two others are undoubtedly of Oriental origin. The Woman, on the fifth night, adduces, as a warning to the king,

The Revolt of Absalom.

Knowest thou not, O my lord and king, that revolt will stalk with head on high under thy descendants, if, while thou art

---

[1] Comparetti remarks that, "though the text is very corrupt, and certainly mutilated in some parts, we recognise in this tale a novel of Bandello (iv, 8), which has an equivalent in the 19th Night of the *Suka Saptati* (Galanos)."

still alive and before thy gray head has disappeared, thou riddest not the country of thy son? Is it not true that if the King David had put to death his son Amnon for having out-raged his sister, Absalom would not have required to fly to Geshur, to nourish hatred in his breast, to revolt against his father, and David would not have suffered all the misfortune which he suffered? And all this occurred because his father did not wish to vex him at the time, and because he said to him, Why actest thou thus? his heart became so inflamed with pride thereby that he no more feared to offend, and abused his sister Tamar. Thou too shalt fall in the same way, and the advice of thy evil counsellors will not protect thee. Else thinkest thou that thy son is better than Absalom?

The effect of this argument on the king is counteracted by the Sixth Vazīr, who says:

The Death of Absalom.

Was it not the King David whom thy wife cited as an example? But had not that King David more sons than thou? And yet did he not pardon them their faults? When he fled with Joab, said he not to him before his people, "Behave with gentleness towards young Absalom?" Did he not weep over him when he was killed? "Alas!" he cried, "my son, Absalom! O my son, my son!" And if it had been in his power would he not have killed Joab? He spared him only to put him into the power of his son Solomon, whom he ordered to put him to death. Yet heaven and earth had been witnesses of the crimes of Absalom, whilst thy son has committed no fault against thee. Canst thou determine to make him die? Canst thou resolve to exterminate thy name, and the posterity issued from thee, and the house of thy ancestors? Then thou wilt remain without children, whilst David had several sons, and notwithstanding the loss of two of whom, there still remained others; and then

David at this time was still young, but thou—thou art old. God has favoured thee with a son in thy old age, and thou wishest to banish him for ever from thine eyes.

The Seventh Vazīr's first story is of

The Disguised Young Man.

There was a man married to a woman fair of body and face. A young man was in love with this woman, but could not obtain access to her because her husband was very jealous; and by reason of this great jealousy he always kept her shut up, and kept the key himself. This man was a merchant, and old. The young man, mastered by his passion, became sick on account of it. An old woman came and found him thus, and he told her what was the matter. The old woman said to him: "Wilt thou do all that I tell thee?" "Yes," answered he. "Then," said she, "shave all the hair off thy face and thy beard." He did so. Then she dressed him in woman's clothes, and putting on him a veil, only his eyes were to be seen. After this, the old woman went to the house of the merchant, and said to him: "I come to beg a favour, my lord. I am a widow, and I have one daughter. Now I wish to go to another town, and I have heard of the propriety that reigns in your house, and I must confess I feel some anxiety in leaving my daughter in a strange place. That is why, my lord, if it will suit you, I wish to bring her to thy house, that she may serve thy wife without any wages." The merchant was delighted at hearing this, and said to her: "I will take care of her; she has only to come to my wife." The old woman then brought her pretended daughter, and the latter remained in the house, and the husband went to travel. Then the young man discovered his face, made himself known to the young woman, and passed several days with her.[1]

---

[1] In the conclusion of the European versions of the *Seven Wise Masters*, the prince, when he has begun to speak again, exposes the queen's intrigue with a youth who is disguised as one of her female slaves. Goedeke

The vazīr then relates the story of

The Hunchbacks.

There was a woman married to an old man. As to her, she was young, fair of person and face. The husband would not allow her to walk in the street, and she submitted to this only with impatience. One day she said to her maid : "Go outside ; perhaps thou wilt meet some one who will be able to amuse us." The maid went out, and met a hunchback, who had a tambourine and flute in his hand. He was dancing and beating the tambourine, so that the people might give him some reward. The maid brought this man to her mistress, who gave him to eat and to drink, which caused him great pleasure. He then rose to dance and leap about, at which the young woman was much pleased. She dressed him in beautiful clothes, and gave him a present, and then sent him away. The friends and comrades of the hunchback saw him, and asked him where he had met with such good luck, and he told them of the beautiful wife of the old man. The hunchback's companions said to him : "If

considers this incident as having been adapted from the above tale of the Disguised Young Man (*Orient und Occident*, iii, p. 394). But in the Hebrew story the disguised youth is not discovered, and it is perhaps possible that the original of the incideut is to be found in a Persian tale, in which a young page points out to the king his favourite's paramour among her assembled female slaves.—It seems the practice of thus introducing men into the women's apartments was formerly very common in India : "By means of their female attendants," says Vatsyayana, "the ladies of the royal harem generally get men into their apartments in the disguise or dress of women. . . When a go-between has no access to the harem, then the man should stand in some place where the lady he loves can be seen. If that place is occupied by the king's sentinels, he should then disguise himself as a female attendant of the lady who comes to the place or passes by it." (*Kama Sutra,* Part v.)—The 35th tale of the *Tuti Nama* (India Office MS. No. 2573, and tale 23 of Kaderi's abridgment), of the Brahman in love with the Daughter of the King of Babylon, bears some resemblance to the story of the Disguised Young Man.

thou dost not take us with thee, we will make the whole affair
public." Now the young woman sent again for the hunchback,
that he might come to her. He said to her: "My companions
also wish to come to amuse thee." The lady replied: "Let
them come." She offered them all sorts of things; they set to
eating and drinking, and they got drunk, and fell from their
seats. Presently, the master of the house came back, and the
woman immediately rose with her maid, and carried the men into
another part of the house. There they quarrelled and fought,
and strangled each other, and died.[1] Meantime the husband,
having taken some food, went out again. Then the woman
ordered her maid to bring the hunchbacks out, but they were
dead. Then said the woman: "Go out quickly, and find some
foolish porter," and she put the dead bodies into sacks. The
maid-servant chanced to meet a black man, and brought him to
her mistress, who said to him: "Stay with me." After he had
passed some time with her, she said to him: "Take this first
sack, and throw it into the river; then come back to me, and I
will take care to give thee all that thou mayest require." The
black did so; then he returned and took the second sack, and
in that way he took them all, one after the other, and threw
them into the river.

It is generally supposed that this story of the Hunchbacks in
the *Mishlé Sandabar* suggested that of the Lady and her Three
Lovers in the *Septem Sapientum*, which is to this effect: A lady
promises her favours to three knights, unknown to one another,
for a hundred florins each, then she acquaints her husband, and
persuades him to consent to slay them for the sake of the money
they will bring with them. When the first knight arrives, and
she is assured that he has brought the money, she admits him

---

[1] In Wright's analysis of this story (Introd. *Seven Sages*, vol. xvi of Percy
Society) "the lady conceals them hurriedly in a place full of holes and
traps, into which they fall, and *are* strangled."

into the house, and he is instantly murdered; the two other knights, as they arrive in succession, meet with the same fate; and the three bodies are dragged into a private part of the house. The lady then sends for her brother, who is one of the city night guards, and showing him the body of one of the knights, tells him that her husband had slain the knight in a quarrel, and she wishes him to dispose of it at once. He takes up the body, goes out and throws it into the sea, and returns, to learn that the body has come back again, and is now shown the body of the second knight, which he also carries away and casts into the water; and on his return to the house is shown the body of the third knight as the same that he had already twice disposed of. Convinced now that he has a sorcerer to deal with, he resolves to try whether another element will not destroy him, and accordingly carries the third body into a wood, where he makes a great fire, in the midst of which he instantly tosses it. Presently a knight on horseback, on his way to a tourney, rides up and dismounts to warm his hands, upon which the man, supposing this to be the sorcerer come to life once more, seizes him and his horse and throws them into the fire, which consumes them to ashes. In the sequel the lady, in a passion with her husband, accuses him before neighbours of the triple murder, and they are both put to death.

This story, however, has been taken into the *Septem Sapientum* almost word for word from the Anglican *Gesta Romanorum*[1] (see Madden's old English versions of the *Gesta*, [xxv] p. 80), which was compiled, according to Herr Oesterley, towards the end of the 13th century, while the *Septem Sapientum* does not date earlier than the beginning of the 15th century. And if the author of the Anglican *Gesta* had for his model the Hebrew story of the Hunchbacks, it must have been a version very different in the details of the catastrophe from that which has reached us,

---

[1] Or rather, from the continental *Gesta*, which was formed from the Anglican text.

T

since in the latter no mention is made of the woman's device of persuading the man that the body had come back again. Wright, indeed, conjectured that the Hebrew story originally concluded in the same manner as the Three Knights and the Lady. This may have been so; but why suppose the original of the Latin story to be one so different in its *dénouement* as we now know it—whatever it may or may not have been—when we have another, and probably an earlier, version which it much more closely resembles, namely, the Trouveur Durant's *fabliau* of *Les Trois Bossus?* The following is the outline of this tale:

An old, ugly, and hunchbacked *chatelain* had a beautiful young wife, of whom he was so very jealous, that he kept a constant watch on her. One day three minstrels, hunchbacked too, came to the castle, and, for once, were entertained by the surly *chatelain*, who then dismissed them with a present, and he shortly afterwards went out to walk in the fields. His young wife, sitting at her window, perceives the three hunchbacks dancing and capering along the road in great glee, and sends for them to come and amuse her. They have hardly entered her chamber, when she hears her husband coming, so she pushes them into three coffers that stood in the apartment. The husband, however, having only looked in to see whether all was right, immediately goes away to resume his walk, when the lady hastens to release her prisoners, but, to her horror, finds all three dead—suffocated! What was to be done? But woman is ever fertile in expedients. She went to the gate, and, seeing a simple rustic pass, called him in, and, showing him the body in one of the coffers, promised him ample recompense if he disposed of it. The rustic stuffed the body in a sack, carried it off to the river, threw it in, and then returned for his reward. By this time the lady, with the help of her maid, had changed the position of the coffers; so she showed him the body of the second minstrel, saying it was the same that he had thrown into the water. The rustic was amazed, but disposed of it as he had done the first, and in like manner rids the lady of the third body, believing he has had to deal with a magician; after which, on his way back to the lady, he meets the *chatelain*, returning home from his evening walk. Enraged now beyond measure, "Dog of a hunchback!" he cries, "are you come back again?" So saying, he seized and stuffed him into the sack, tied a large stone round his neck, and presently the unlucky husband joined his brother hunchbacks at the bottom of the river. "I warrant me," quoth the rustic to the lady, "you haven't seen him this time." She confessed that she had not. "Yet you were not far from it," said he, and then related what had happened. The lady instantly comprehended the whole affair, smiled, and dismissed him with a handsome reward.

It thus appears that the *fabliau* corresponds with the Hebrew version in all essential points excepting the *dénouement*, and it is highly probable that both were derived from a common source. That the story came from Asia admits of no question, though I am very far from believing, with Douce and Madden, that the Arabian tale of the Little Hunchback is the original of all such stories of adventures with dead bodies. Had Douce known of the comparatively recent date of the *Thousand and One Nights*—at least, as it exists at present—he would hardly have credited that work with being the original source of tales which were current in Europe in the 12th and 13th centuries.

— — —

No. XXIV—p. 137.

AHMED THE ORPHAN.

THIS remarkable tale, of which variants were current throughout Europe during the Middle Ages, does not belong to the original Book of Sindibād, and is found in only two of the five Arabic texts of the *Seven Vazīrs* represented in our Comparative Table, namely, Scott's MS. and the Rich MS. in the British Museum.

Its earliest appearance in European literature seems to have been in the spiritual tales, or *Contes Devots*, written in the 12th and 13th centuries, under the title of "D'un Roi qui voulut faire brûler le fils de son Seneschal," from which it was probably taken by the complier of the first Italian collection of tales, *Cento Novelle Antiche*, and by the author of the Anglican *Gesta Romanorum*, both of which works were composed about the end of the 13th century; it is also found in the continental *Gesta*, translated by Swan. The 68th of the *Novelle Antiche* is to the following effect : An envious knight is jealous of the favour a young man enjoys with the king. As a friend, he bids the youth hold back his head while serving this prince, who, he says, was disgusted with his foul breath, and then acquaints his master that the page did so from being offended with his Majesty's breath. The irascible monarch forthwith orders his kiln-man to throw the first messenger he sends into the furnace, and the young man is accordingly despatched on some pretended errand, but happily passing a monastery on his way, tarries for some time to hear mass. Meanwhile, the contriver of the fraud, impatient to learn the success of his stratagem, sets out for the house of the kiln-man, and arrives before his intended victim. On inquiring if the commands of the king have been fulfilled, he is answered that they will be immediately executed, and, as the first messenger on the part of the sovereign, is forthwith thrown into the furnace.[1]

This forms the 95th chapter of the Anglican *Gesta Romanorum*, edited for the Roxburgh Club, by Sir Fredrick Madden, and No. 70 of Herrtage's recent edition, published for the Early English Text Society, in which the youth, who is an orphan and the king's nephew, is called Fulgentius, and in place of a knight is an envious steward, who tells his master that his favourite says that his Majesty has leprosy. Fulgentius hearing a chapel-bell, on his way to the lime-pits, goes in to hear mass, and afterwards (having got up earlier than usual) falls asleep in the chapel.

---

[1] Dunlop's History of Fiction, 4th Ed., p. 205.

When he awakes, he hastens to the lime-pits, inquires, as he was instructed, "Have you done the commandment of the king?" and learns that the steward had met the fate intended for himself.—Cinthio has the story in his *Hecatommithi* (viii, 6), written in the 16th century, and it is also found in the *Anecdotes chrétiennes de l'abbé Reyre*, t. i, under the title of "Les Deux Pages." From an Alsatian tradition Schiller, it is said, composed his ballad, "Der gang nachdem eisenhammer," which is well known to English readers through Mr. Bowring's excellent translation, entitled, "Fridolin; or the Walk to the Iron Foundry." Schiller's version bears a slight resemblance to our Arabian tale of Ahmed in one point : Robert the huntsman, having long cherished in vain a guilty passion for the countess, in revenge falsely accuses the page Fridolin to the Count Savern of the crime which he had been but too willing himself to commit :

> Then to two workmen beckons he,
>   And speaks thus in his ire :
> The first who's hither sent by me,
> ' Thus of ye to inquire—
> Have ye obeyed my lord's word well?
> Him cast ye into yonder hell,
>   That into ashes he may fly,
>   And ne'er again torment mine eye.

In the Turkish tales of the *Forty Vazírs*, the lady's 22nd story is another variant. Instead of a page, the favourite is a courtier, of whom another is envious. Having privately told the king that his favourite went about asserting that his Majesty was leprous, and that he could not endure his breath, the envious courtier caused a Tātār pie to be cooked, strongly seasoned with garlic, and invited the favourite to his house. They ate together of the pie, and immediately after went to the court ; on the way thither the envious man warned his "friend" not to approach too near the king because of his garlic-tainted breath. Accordingly the favourite held his sleeve close to his mouth, and stood a little way off. The king naturally thought that this confirmed the report, and gave him a letter to the chief magistrate, telling him at the same time to keep whatever he was offered. The envious man persuaded the favourite to give him the letter, for the sake of the expected present, saying that he should always have the king's countenance. The result of delivering the letter was different from the courtier's expectations;—its contents were : "Seize him who gives this letter into thy hand, and spare him not, but flay him alive, and stuff his skin with grass, and set it upon the road, that, when I pass, I may see it there." Some days afterwards the king perceives the stuffed skin of the envious courtier, and sends for his former favourite, who explains the whole affair from first to last.

There are innumerable variants of the story current in India, where, indeed, it had its origin, one of which is a Bengali folk-tale, translated by Mr. C. H. Damant, under the title of "The Minister and the Fool," in the *Indian Antiquary:* The minister, in the course of a journey, meets with the fool, and, being struck with some of his remarks, takes him into his service. One day the rāja hears three birds talking together, and requests his minister to inform him what they had been saying. The fool, knowing the speech of birds, gives his master the required information, which he at once communicates to the rāja ; but, jealous lest he should learn that it was the fool's wit which had solved his question, he determines to have the fool put to death, and accordingly gives him a sealed letter to the executioner. On his way the fool meets the minister's son, who desires him to pick a nosegay of flowers for him. The fool replies that he will do so immediately after he has delivered the letter; but the youth would brook no delay, and told him to remain in the garden and pick the flowers, while he himself delivered the message. When the minister saw the fool in the garden, and learned that his own son had done the fatal errand, he was frantic with grief.

A parallel incident is found in the *Kathâ Sarit Sâgara:* In the Story of Sundaraka, the king is persuaded by his wife, in order that he may acquire magic power, to consent to practise the horrible rite of eating human flesh. The narrative thus proceeds (Professor Tawney's translation, vol. i, pp. 162-3):

"Having made him enter into the circle, previously conse-crated, she said to the king, after he had taken an oath: 'I attempted to draw hither, as a victim, that Bráhman named Phalabhûti, who is so intimate with you; but the drawing him hither is a difficult task: so it is the best way to initiate some cook in our rites, that he may himself slay him and cook him. And you must not feel any compunction about it, because by eating a sacrificial offering of his flesh, after the ceremonies are complete, the enchantment will be perfect, for he is a Bráhman of the highest caste.' When his beloved said this to him, the king, though afraid of the sin, consented;—alas! terrible is com-pliance with women! Then that royal couple had the cook summoned, and, after encouraging him, and initiating him, they both said to him: 'Whoever comes to you to-morrow morning and says, "The king and queen will eat together to-day, so get some food ready quickly," him you must slay, and make for us secretly a savoury dish of his flesh.' The cook consented, and went to his own house. Next morning, when Phalabhûti ar-rived, the king said to him: 'Go and tell the cook in the kitchen, "The king, together with the queen, will eat to-day a savoury mess, therefore prepare as soon as possible a splendid dish."' Phalabhûti said: 'I will do so,' and went out. When he was outside, the king's son, whose name was Chandraprabhâ, came to him, and said: 'Have made for me this very day, with this gold, a pair of ear-rings, like those you had made before for my noble father.' Phalabhûti, in order to please the prince, im-mediately proceeded, as he was ordered, to get the ear-rings made, and the prince went readily with the king's message, which Phalabhûti told him, alone to the kitchen; and when he delivered the king's message the cook, true to his agreement, at once put him to death with a knife, and made a dish of his flesh, which the king and queen ate, after performing their ceremonies, not knowing the truth. After spending the night in remorse, the next morning the king saw Phalabhūti arrive with the ear-rings in his hand. So being bewildered, he questioned him about the ear-rings immediately; and when Phalabhūti had told him his story, the king fell on the earth, and cried out: 'Alas, my son!' blaming the queen and himself; and when the ministers questioned him, he told them the whole story, and repeated what Phalabhūti had said every day: 'The doer of good will obtain good, and the doer of evil, evil.'"

Closely allied to the class of stories above cited is the 20th chapter of Swan's *Gesta Romanorum:* A king, belated while hunting, takes shelter for the night in the hut of an exiled courtier, whom he does not recognise. During the night the count's wife gives birth to a fine boy, upon which the king hears a voice telling him that the child just born should be his son-in-law. In the morning the king orders his squires to take the infant from his mother and destroy him; but, moved to compassion, they place it upon the branches of a tree, to secure it from wild beasts, and then kill a hare, and convey its heart to the king. A duke, passing through the forest, hears the cries of a child, and, discovering it, wraps it in the folds of his cloak, and takes it to his wife to bring up. In course of time, when the child is grown a handsome youth, the king suspects him to be the same who was predicted to be his son-in-law, and despatches him with a letter to the queen, commanding her to put the bearer to death. On his way he goes into a chapel, and there having fallen asleep, a priest, seeing the letter suspended from his girdle, has the curiosity to open it; and after reading the intended wickedness, he alters the purport thus: "Give the youth our daughter in marriage," which the queen does accordingly.

Dr. Dasent, in his *Popular Tales from the Norse,* gives a

variant of this under the title of "Rich Peter the Pedlar;" and
Dr. A. C. Fryer presents similar incidents in the first story of
his charming little work, recently published, *English Fairy Tales
from the North Country*, in which a beautiful maiden takes the
place of the miller's son, and a sorcerer knight that of Peter
the Pedlar.—Professor Tawney has pointed out, in the *Indian
Antiquary*, the exact resemblance which a story in the *Kathākosa*
bears to the Norse tale: A merchant named Sāgarapota, of the
town of Rājagriha, hearing it prophesied that a young beggar
named Dāmannaka (he was, however, the son of a merchant
who had died of the plague) would inherit all his property,
makes Dāmannaka over to a Chandāla to be killed. The
Chandāla, instead of killing him, cuts off his little finger, and
Dāmannaka, having thus escaped death, is adopted by the
merchant's cowherd. In the course of time the merchant
recognises Dāmannaka. In order to insure his being put out
of the way, he sends him with a letter to his son Samudradatta. But when Dāmannaka reaches the outskirts of the town
of Rājagriha he feels fatigued, and falls asleep in the temple.
Meanwhile the daughter of that very merchant, named Vishā,
came to the temple to worship the divinity. "She beheld
Dāmannaka with the large eyes and the broad chest." Her
father's handwriting then caught her eye, and she proceeded to
read the letter. In it she read the following distich:

> Before this man has washed his feet, do thou with speed
> Give him poison [*visham*], and free my heart from anxiety.

The lady immediately concluded that she herself (Vishā) was to
be given to the handsome youth, and that her father had in his
hurry made a slight mistake in orthography. She, therefore,
makes the necessary correction, and replaces the letter. Samudradatta carries out his father's orders, and the merchant returns
to Rājagriha to find Dāmannaka married to his daughter Vishā.
The termination of the story is the same as that of Phalabhūti

[see p. 296] and its European parallels, the tales of Fulgentius, Fridolin, etc. The merchant Sāgarapota arranges a second time to kill Dāmannaka, whom he will send to the temple of the goddess of the city. But, as the bridegroom and bride are going to the temple of the goddess, Samudradatta, the son of the merchant Sāgarapota, meets them, and insists on performing the worship in their stead. "Having taken the articles for offering, Samudradatta went off, and as he was entering the temple of the goddess, he was despatched by Khadgila, who had gone there before."

The incident of a person being made the unconscious bearer of his own death-warrant is as old at least as the Biblical story of King David and Uriah; while classical legend furnishes a familiar example in the tale of Bellerophon; and another instance (not so well known) is found in Arabian tradition, in the story of the celebrated pre-Islamite poets Tarafa and Mutalammis, who, having offended the King of Hīra, by composing satires upon his drunken habits, were sent by him with letters to the govenor of Bahrayn, ordering him to put the bearers to death;—Mutalammis having learned the nature of the missive he carried destroyed it, and urged his friend to turn back with him, but Tarafa declined to do so, and continued his fatal journey.—But in these tales, Western and Eastern, which I have cited, there is the same fundamental outline—the same sequence of identical incidents, which indicate, without any possibility of doubt, that they have all been derived from a common source.

No. XXV—p. 154.
THE DROP OF HONEY.

A SOMEWHAT analogous story to this occurs in the Ottoman romance of the *Forty Vazīrs*; it is related by the 30th vazīr, and Mr. E. J. W. Gibb has translated it as follows:

How Two Tribes went to War because of a Goat.

An Arab of the tribe of Benī 'Aqīl took a goat to a city with the purpose of selling it. An Arab of the tribe of Benī Nefīr wished to buy that goat. The owner of the goat wanted eight baghdādās as the price ; the purchaser offered six. The owner of the goat swore he would divorce his wife if he gave it for an aspre less than eight baghdādās. And the purchaser swore he would divorce his wife if he gave an aspre more than six. Then the two of them began to quarrel. The Arab who wished to buy took up a stone and threw it at the owner of the goat ; it hit his head, which smashed like a rotten gourd. His kinsfolk heard this, and they came and smote that other man, and killed the killer. As a man of each tribe had been slain, they fell one upon another. Every one came on his horse, with his arms, to the field, and they began to fight with each other, so that hills of slain arose, and blood flowed in streams. At length the tribe of Benī 'Aqīl was victorious and put to flight the tribe of Benī Nefīr. That tribe went to the Prince of the Abyssinians and asked help. So the Prince of Abyssinia gave them 200 horsemen, and the Nefīr prince again fell upon the 'Aqīl prince, and they began to fight with one another. At length the fortune of the 'Aqīl prince was changed into disaster, and the Benī Nefīr army returned with victory and triumph.

Feuds, often originating in trifles, are still common among the desert Arabs, and this story is probably of Arabian invention, if not the narrative of an actual occurrence.

———

No. XXVI—p. 156.

THE CHANGED SEX.

IT is unfortunate that a *lacuna* in the Persian MS. text (see p. 80 of the present volume) deprives us of the whole of this story, since it probably represented a version nearer to the original than that found in *Syntipas*, which is very confused towards the conclusion : after the transformation, the prince meets with a peasant, who agrees to become a woman in his place, on condition that his proper sex be restored to him at the end of four months; the prince then proceeds to the court of his intended father-in-law, marries the princess, and contrives to evade the fulfilment of his promise to the peasant.—In the *Libro de los Engannos* the story is similarly garbled, a "devil" taking the place of the rustic.—In the *Mishlé Sandabar*, the prince, after his transformation, passes the night near the enchanted fountain; in the morning he meets in the forest a troop of girls, to whom he discloses his rank and present misfortune, and they direct him to the other fountain.—There can be little doubt, I think, that the Arabian version has better preserved the original form of the story, though, strangely enough, nothing is said of the punishment of the treacherous vazīr.

The idea of enchanted fountains whose waters produced re-markable moral or physical transformations in such as drank of or bathed in them is very ancient, and was probably borrowed from classical legends by the mediæval romancists. In chap. xiv of the *Gesta Romanorum*, a king leaves his daughter in the care of his secretary, who is warned not to allow her to drink of a certain fountain that affected all who drank of it with leprosy. The princess, in spite of all precautions, contrives to reach this fountain, and immediately after drinking of it becomes a leper. In dismay the secretary seeks advice of a holy man, who directs him to a mountain, where he will find a peculiar kind of stone, and a rod. He is to strike the stone with the rod until moisture exudes from it, then smear the affected parts of the damsel's body with the liquid, and she will be restored to health and beauty.

According to the classical legend, there were two springs in Bœotia, of which one was believed to increase, the other to take away, the memory. Cupid's two arrows—one of gold, which created love, the other of lead, which instilled hate—may have suggested the idea of the two fountains in Claudian's picture of the gardens of Venus (*De Nupt. Honor. et Mar*, l. 69) :

> Two fountains glitter in the solar beam;
> This spouts a sweet, and that a bitter, stream,
> Where Cupid dips his darts, as poets dream—

which again seems to have been imitated by Ariosto, in the *Orlando Furioso* (c. i, st. 77, 78) :

> Then, as at hazard, she directs her sight,
> Sounding in arms, a man on foot she spies,
> And glows with sudden anger and despite;
> For she the son of Aymon eyes.
> Her more than life esteems the youthful knight,
> While she from him, like crane from falcon, flies—
> Time was the lady sighed, her passion slighted;
> Tis now Rinaldo loves, as ill requited.
>
> And this effect two different fountains wrought,
> Whose wondrous waters different moods inspire.
> Both sprang in Arden, with rare virtue fraught :
> This fills the heart with amorous desire;
> Who taste that other fountain were untaught
> Their love, and change for ice their former fire.
> Rinaldo drank the first, and vainly sighs;
> Angelica the last, and hates and flies.[1]

So, too, in Berni's *Innamorato*, there are the Fountains of Love and of Disdain.—In the old Spanish romance of Diana, by Montemayor, we are told of a fountain that possessed at once the qualities of inspiring love and producing indifference: The priestess of Diana, who knew by inspiration all the misfortunes of her guests, and had traced in her mind a plan for their future happiness, conducted them to the interior of the temple, and filled three cups from an enchanted stream. This beverage having been quaffed by Sereno, Sylvanus, and Sylvania, they

---

[1] Rose's translation, and note on passage.

instantly fell into a profound sleep, in which they remained for considerable time. Sereno awoke in a state of the most perfe indifference for his once much loved Diana, while Sylvanus ar Sylvania, forgetting their former attachments, arose deeply enar oured of each other, and employed the most ardent expressio of affection.[1]

But more closely resembling the enchanted springs of our ta of the Transformed Prince are the magical streams in the Hin romance of Somasekhara and Chitrasekhara,[2] which recounts tl adventures of two princes, one of whom meets a monkey, who, his gambols, plunges into a pool, and comes out a man; th leaping into another pool, issues a monkey as before. And the Indian collection, *Sinhásana Dwátrinsati*, Thirty-two Tal of a Throne, we read of a magical well which transforms monkey into a woman, whenever a certain pious hermit com to converse with her, and again into a monkey before I retires.[3] In the *Tútí Náma* (35th Night of India Office M No. 2573; tale 23 of Káderí's abridgment), a Bráhman, in lo with the daughter of the king of Babylon, receives from a mag cian a globule, which, put into the mouth, instantly changes man into a woman, and he is thus enabled to gain access to tl damsel. In the Turkish *Tútí Náma*, a sorceress takes the pla of the magician, and gives the enamoured youth a seal instea of a globule. But this story is found in a much older wor the *Vetála Panchavinsati*, 15th tale.

---

[1] Dunlop's *History of Fiction*, 4th Ed., p. 332.—Some of the most i teresting scenes in Shakspeare's Midsummer Night's Dream, Dunl remarks, seem to have been suggested by the transference of love occ sioned by the potion of the priestess.

[2] Wilson's *Catalogue of the Mackenzie Collection*, vol. i, p. 51.

[3] I am indebted for a loan of a manuscript translation of this collecti to the courtesy of Mr. F. F. Arbuthnot, author of a very interesting litt work, *Early Ideas: a Group of Hindoo Stories*, by Anaryan (Allen & C London), which contains a compendious account, with specimens, of tl most important Indian romances.

No. XXVII—p. 166.
THE GOLDSMITH AND THE SINGING GIRL.

EASTERN fiction presents numerous instances of princes becoming enamoured of the portraits of beautiful women ;—in the *Kathá Sarit Ságara* occur two examples: the story of the handsome King Prithvirūpa (Tawney's translation, vol. i, p. 490), and the story of Sundārasena and Mandāravatī (vol. ii, p. 370). In Gomberville's romance of Polexandre the African prince Abdu-'l-Malik falls in love with the portrait of Alcidiana, and a similar incident is found in the romance of Agesilaus of Colchos. The notion, nevertheless, is undoubtedly of Oriental origin.

Our story of the Goldsmith is an Arabian variant of a tale in the *Dasa Kumara Charita*, Adventures of Ten Princes, a most entertaining romance, in Sanskrit, by Dandin, of the 6th century, according to Dr. Albrecht Weber.[1] The following translation of this tale, by Dr. H. H. Wilson, is taken from the *Oriental Quarterly Magazine*, of Calcutta, 1828, where it first appeared :

Story of Nitambavati.

In Surasena is a city called Mathura, where dwelt a youth of family, who was addicted to loose pleasures and to vicious society, and, being a lad of spirit, he was so often entangled in broils that he was called Kalaha Kataka. One day he saw, in a painter's possession, the picture of a girl, with whose charms he became violently enamoured. After some solicitation, he prevailed on the painter to tell him who the original was, and having learnt that she was the wife of Anantakirtti, a merchant of Ujjayni, and her name Nitambavati, set off in the disguise of a mendicant for that city. Having got access to the house, under pretence of soliciting alms, he obtained a sight of the lady, and found her still more fascinating than her picture.

---

[1] *History of Indian Literature*, by Albrecht Weber (London, 1878), p. 213, note.—This work is singular among the Sanskrit romances in being written in prose.

With a view to effect his projects, he solicited and obtained the care of the cemetery, and with the clothes of the dead he attached to his interests a female Sramanika, or Buddha devotee. This woman he employed to convey a message from him to Nitambavati, inviting her to come and see him, to which she sent back an angry and indignant reply. He was not discouraged, but desired his messenger to return to the merchant's wife, and say to her, as from himself: " Persons like us, who are fully acquainted with the insufficiency of life, and only desirous of final emancipation, cannot be suspected of entertaining any purpose adverse to the reputation of a woman of respectability. The message I lately conveyed to you I only intended to try your merit, as I was afraid such youth and beauty could scarcely be satisfied with a man so advanced in years as your husband. I was mistaken, and the result has so much pleased me that I am anxious to confer upon you a proof of my esteem. I should wish to see you a mother, but the planet under which your husband was born has hitherto opposed it. The evil influence, however, may be counteracted if you will be content to assist. Accompany me to a grove at night, where I will bring you a seer versed in incantations. You must put your foot in his hand whilst he conveys into it his charms; then, as if angry, kick your husband in the breast, when the evil influence will be expelled, and you will be blessed with progeny, and your husband will venerate you as a goddess: there is nothing to be afraid of."

Nitambavati, with some little difficulty, consented, and, being apprised of her intentions, the false saint awaited her at the appointed place. She came as was directed, and put her foot into his hand; he pretended to rub it, muttering imaginary charms all the time, until he had taken off her golden anklet, when, making a sudden cut at her thigh with a knife, which he had covertly prepared, he inflicted a gash in the upper part of it, and then quickly withdrew. Nitambavati, full of pain and terror, and reviling herself for her own folly, and ready to kill the Sramanika for having exposed her to such peril, returned home, and, privately dressing her wound, kept her bed for some days.

The rogue in the meantime offered the anklet to Anantakritti for sale; he knew it to be that of his wife, and inquired how the vendor had come by it; he refused to tell, and the merchant threatened him with punishment, on which Kalaha Kataka professed himself ready to communicate the truth to the guild (or committee of merchants). He was accordingly taken before them, when he desired the merchant to send for his wife's anklets. She replied that she had lost one of them; it was large, and had slipped off, but she forwarded the other. The anklet in the possession of the supposed mendicant, being compared with this, was found to correspond, and there remained no doubt of their owner. The ascetic, being then questioned as to the circumstances under which he had gained possession of it, replied as follows:

"You are aware, gentlemen, that I was employed to take charge of the graves of the deceased. As some people wished to deprive me of my fees by burning the bodies by night, I kept watch at all hours. Last night, I saw a dark-complexioned woman dragging the half-burnt fragments of a dead body from the funeral-pile, when, to punish her horrible design, I made a cut at her with my knife, and wounded one of her thighs, as she turned to escape: she ran off, however, dropping one of her anklets as she fled, and I thus became possessed of it."

The account thus given inspired all the auditors with horror. Nitambavati was unanimously pronounced a sakini, or witch. She was turned out of his house by her husband, and rejected with abhorrence by all the citizens. In this distress she repaired to the cemetery, where she was in the act of putting a period to her existence, when she was prevented by her lover. He threw himself at her feet, and told her that, unable to live without her, he had adopted this contrivance to obtain her person, and

U

entreated her to rely upon the fervour and faithfulness of his regard. His entreaties and protestations were at last successful, combined with the consciousness of her helpless situation, and Nitambavati rewarded his ingenuity with her affection.

A considerably different form of the story is found in the *Vetála Panchavinsati*, Twenty-five Tales of a Demon, namely, that of

The Minister's Son,

of which the commencement has already been given in p. 249. The prince having gained entrance into the house of his beloved Padmavati, in the way she had indicated by signs to the old go-between, he marries her by the Gandharva form (in which the consent of parents is dispensed with), and, after passing some time happily in her society, visits his friend the minister's son, who is still lodging with the go-between. While the prince is there, a great outcry is heard in the streets, that the rāja's son had disappeared; upon which the minister's son details to him a cunning plan for carrying off the damsel to their own country, which he consents to adopt. Accordingly the prince returned to Padmavati, and when she was sound asleep he marked her on the hip with an iron spike which he had brought with him for the purpose, and, taking her ornaments, quitted the house and rejoined his friend. Next morning the minister's son went to the cemetery, and there disguised himself as an ascetic; and, having made the prince assume the garb of a disciple, he said to him: "Take this necklace, which is part of this set of ornaments, and offer it for sale in the market, but ask a high price for it, so that it may attract attention; and should the police arrest you, say, 'My spiritual preceptor gave it me to sell.'" The pretended disciple is arrested by the police (who had been informed of the lady's loss), and answering them as he had been instructed, the sham devotee is at once sent for. On being asked how the necklace came into his possession, he

replied : " I am an ascetic, in the habit of constantly wandering
in the forest, and as I was by chance in the cemetery at night,
I saw a company of witches collected from different quarters.
And one of them brought the prince, with the lotus of his heart
laid bare, and offered him to [the god] Bhairava. And the
witch, who possessed great powers of delusion, being drunk,
tried to take away my rosary while I was reciting my prayers,
making horrible contortions with her face. And, as she carried
the attempt too far, I got angry, and marked her on the loins
with my trident ;[1] and then I took this necklace from her neck,
which I must now sell, as it does not suit an ascetic."—The
magistrate informed the king of this extraordinary affair, and he
concluded that it must be the pearl necklace which the dentist's
daughter had lost ; so he sent a trusty old woman to see if she
was really marked on the loins. When this was ascertained, the
king consulted the pretended ascetic as to how Padmavati should
be punished, and by his advice she was banished from the city.
" In the evening the minister's son and the prince rode out of
the city, and found Padmavati lamenting ; then they mounted
her upon a horse, and took her to their own country, where the
prince lived happily with her."

It seems strange that a prince should have required to employ
so many artifices to obtain a dentist's daughter for his wife. The
exact meaning of the Sanskrit word which Tawney has rendered
"dentist," namely, *dantaghātaka*, appears to be doubtful ; and
the name of the lady's father, Sangrāmavardhana, having, as
Tawney remarks, " a warlike sound," perhaps he may have
been, as he is represented in the Hindī version *(Baital Pachīsī)*,
a powerful rāja.

The original story may very possibly date centuries before our
era. In all the three versions, the Goldsmith, Nitambavati, and

---

[1] The trident, or three-pronged fork ; the weapon is peculiar to the god
Siva, of whom the disguised son of the minister pretended to be a votary.

the Minister's Son, the catastrophe is the same—the stealing of the ornaments, the wounding of the girl, and the charge of witch-craft, although differently brought about in each. The first and the third are alike in this respect: the youth gains entrance to the girl's chamber by means of a rope, and she is wounded and robbed while asleep. The incident of the portrait occurs only in the first and the second. We must therefore conclude that the Arabian translator derived the materials of his story from a version—perhaps Persian—combining incidents of both the Hindū tales.

No. XXVIII—p. 170.
THE FORBIDDEN DOORS; OR, CURIOSITY.

IT is a peculiarity of Fairyland that there are certain rooms which the fortunate mortal who has entered the enchanted palace is expressly forbidden to enter, or doors which he must on no account open, or cabinets which he must not unlock, if he would continue in his present state of felicity. This story of the Young Man who was taken to the Land of Women bears a very close resemblance to that of the Third Royal Mendicant in the *Thousand and One Nights*, but it is perhaps better told, at least in some texts of the *Seven Vazīrs*. Both may be compared with the Story of Saktideva in the *Kathá Sarit Ságara* (vol. i, p. 223 of Tawney's translation, now in course of publication at Calcutta): Saktideva is conveyed by a monstrous bird—one of the race of Garūda, the bird of Vishnū, and the prototype of the "Roc" of the Arabian Tales—to the Golden City, the residence of female Vidyádharas (a species of fairies), the queen of whom welcomes him as her husband. Having occasion to leave him for a time, the queen gives him strict charge not to ascend to the middle terrace of the palace. But, impelled by curiosity, he goes there, and sees much to marvel at, and coming to a lake discovers by the side of it a horse with a jewelled saddle. Saktideva approaches to mount him, but the steed kicks him into the lake, and on his rising to the surface he finds himself standing in the middle of a garden pond in his native city.

Fairyland has, among its numerous marvels, subaqueous halls of dazzling light, as we find from the following tale in the *Hito-padêsa*, in which there is also a forbidden thing to tempt curiosity (ch. ii, fab. 6—Johnson's translation):

The Queen of the Fairies.

One day, as I was in the pleasure-garden, I heard from a voyaging merchant that, on the fourteenth day of the month, in the midst of the sea which was near, beneath what had the appearance of a kalpa-tree, there was to be seen, seated on a couch variegated with the lustre of strings of jewels, a certain damsel, as it were the goddess Lakshmī, bedecked with all kinds of ornaments, and playing on a lute. I therefore took the voyaging merchant, and, having embarked in a ship, went to the place specified. On reaching the spot, I saw her exactly as she had been described; and, allured by her exquisite beauty, I leaped after her into the sea. In an instant I reached a golden city; where, in a palace of gold, I saw her reclining on a couch, and waited upon by youthful sylphs. When she perceived me at a distance, she sent a female friend, who addressed me courteously. On my inquiry, her friend said: "That is Ratna-manjarī, the daughter of Kandarpakeli, king of the Vidyádharas. She has made a vow to this effect: 'Whosoever shall come and see the city of gold with his own eyes shall marry me.'" Accord-ingly I married her by that form of marriage called Gandharva: after the conclusion of which I remained there a long while delighted with her. One day she said to me in private: "My beloved husband, all these things may be freely enjoyed; but that picture of the fairy Swarnarekhā must never be touched." Some time afterwards, my curiosity being excited, I touched Swarnarekhā with my hand. For so doing, I was spurned by her although only a picture, with her foot beautiful as the lotus, and found myself alighted in my own country. Since then I have been a miserable wanderer over the earth.

Subaqueous halls and forbidden rooms, doors, or other objects are common to the popular fictions of almost every country of Europe and Asia. Those gifted ones who can discover "a rich truth in a tale's pretence" may perhaps be disposed to regard stories of forbidden rooms as distorted versions of the Fall of Man : it is just possible, however, that their conception is due to hashish, or some other narcotic which constitutes the Paradise of Fools !

No. XXIX—p. 178.
THE LOVER IN THE CHEST.

DOUBTLESS a chest has been frequently found very convenient for concealing a gallant or for conveying him to his mistress; however this may be, or have been, it is a common expedient in tales of intrigue, Western as well as Eastern. In the Norse tale of Big Peter and Little Peter, a woman hides her lover, a priest, in a big chest on hearing her husband's knock at the door. Similar instances abound in the early Italian novels; and in Balzac's *Contes Drolatiques*, one of the canon's nephews (story of the Devil's Heir) tells him how he carries on an intrigue with the wife of a jeweller, by being shut up every night in a chest, to which she goes, under pretence of getting some *medicine*.

The story of the Lover in the Chest is in some versions of the *Seven Vazirs* followed by another, also told by the Damsel :

The Slave-Boy who pretended to know the Language of Birds.

A young slave, learning that his master and his wife were to spend the morrow in a suburban garden, went secretly there,

and buried beneath three trees some fruit, comfits, and wine.
The husband sent his wife, escorted by the young slave, before
him to the garden, promising to join her in a short time. As the
lady and the slave were walking up and down the garden, a
crow, sitting on a tree, croaked, upon which the young slave
exclaimed: "Thou sayest truly." His mistress asked him what
he meant by such a remark, and he replied that the bird had
said there was some fruit at the foot of such a tree. She desired
him to search, and he produced the fruit; and, in like manner,
when the bird croaked a second and a third time, the comfits
and wine were unearthed, with which they regaled themselves.
After this, the crow again croaked, and the slave-boy, pretending to be angry and shamefaced, threw a stone at it. The lady
rebuking him for his ingratitude to a bird that had provided
them with such good things, the slave-boy replied that it had
made a very improper suggestion to him. She insists upon
knowing what it was the bird had said this time, and after much
seeming reluctance he told her, when, to his great delight, she
very cordially approved of the bird's suggestion, but just at this
moment the husband made his appearance—and so the story
ends, lamely enough.

———

No. XXX—p. 181.

The Lady and her Suitors.

An imperfect MS. text of the *Thousand and One Nights* preserved in the Bodleian Library, Oxford,[1] has two different
versions of this story, namely, Nights 726-728, the Lady of
Cairo and her Three Gallants, and, Nights 738-743, the Lady
of Cairo and her Four Suitors. This text does not appear to

---

[1] This MS. was brought from Constantinople by Wortley Montagu, at
the sale of whose collection it was purchased by Professor White, of
Oxford, who transferred it to Dr. Jonathan Scott, from whom it was purchased for the Bodleian Library.

contain the *Seven Vazīrs*, unless it was in the missing portion, Nights 167-305. Of the first version I know nothing, but presume it is somewhat similiar to that in the present volume, since Scott has selected, in vol. vi of his edition of the *Arabian Nights*, the second for translation, though he had to suppress parts of it. In this version the lady—unlike the heroine of our tale—is described as virtuous. Her lovers are the judge, the collector-general of port-duties, the chief of the butchers, and a rich merchant. She informs her husband of her plan to punish them, and at the same time reap some profit. The judge comes first, and presents her with a rosary of pearls. She makes him undress, and put on a robe of yellow muslin and a parti-coloured cap—her husband all the while looking at them through an opening in the door of a closet. Presently there is heard a loud knock at the street door, and, on the pretence that it is her husband, the judge is pushed into an adjoining room. The three other suitors, as they successively arrive, bring each also a valuable present, and are treated in the same manner. The husband now enters, and his wife tells him—to the consternation, no doubt, of the imprisoned suitors—that in returning from the bazaar that day she had met with four antic fellows, whom she had a great mind to bring home with her for his amusement. He affects to be vexed that she had not done so, since he must go from home to-morrow. The lady then says that they are, after all, in the next room, upon which the husband insists on their being brought before him, one after another. So the judge is dragged forth in his absurd attire, and compelled to dance and caper like a buffoon, after which he is made to tell a story, which bears a curious resemblance to the Turkish tale in the *Forty Vazīrs* included in our illustrations of Women's Wiles—see page 261; only in place of a king we have here an officer, and instead of a real lover concealed in a chest, it is a conceited tailor who has fallen in love with the lady, whom she thus punishes with fright, by first arousing and then doing away her husband's jealousy.—The judge, having told his story, is dismissed. The three other suitors go through the same performance, but their stories (albeit told in presence of the "virtuous" lady) Scott found to be unfit for translation.

In the Persian tales ascribed to a dervish of Ispahān, Arouya, the virtuous wife of a merchant, entraps, also with her husband's sanction, a qāzī, a doctor, and the city governor. And in the *Bahār-i Dānish*, a lady named Gohera, whose husband is in the hands of the police, makes assignations with the kutwal (police magistrate) and the qāzī, one of whom is entrapped in a large jar, the other in a chest, and next morning she causes porters to carry them before the sultan, who orders them to be punished and her husband to be set at liberty.

In various parts of India the story seems to be very popular. Mr. G. H. Damant has published, in the *Indian Antiquary*, 1873, a translation of a folk-tale of Dinajpur, entitled "The Touchstone," in the concluding portion of which a young woman consents to receive at her house the kutwal at the first watch of the night; the king's counsellor at the second watch; the king's minister at the third watch; and the king himself at the fourth watch. She smears the kutwal with molasses, pours water on him, covers his whole body with cotton wool, and then secures him close to the window. The counsellor is hidden under a mat; the minister, behind a bamboo screen; and when the king comes, last of all, and sees the frightful figure of the kutwal in the window, he asks what it is, and she replies that it is a rākshasa, upon which king, minister, and counsellor flee from the house in dread of the monster. The kutwal is then released and makes the best of his way home in his hideous condition. (Mr. Damant gives a Bengalī variant in the *Indian Antiquary*, 1880, in the story of Adi's Wife, who entraps the kutwal, the nazīr, the vazīr, and the king in a wardrobe.)

In Miss Stokes' amusing *Indian Fairy Tales* (No. 28), a merchant's clever wife, during his absence, takes four hanks of thread to the market to sell, and is accosted, in turn, by the kutwal, the vazīr, the qāzī, and the king, to each of whom she grants an interview at her house, at different hours, and contrives to entrap them into chests. In the morning she hires four stout coolies, who take the chests on their backs, and proceeding to the houses of her suitors, disposes of them to their sons for various sums of money, telling each that the chest contained something he would value far beyond the sum she asked.

The oldest extant form of this wide-spread tale is found in the *Kathá Sarit Ságara*, of which the following is a translation, by Dr. H. H. Wilson:

Upakosā and her Four Lovers.

Whilst I was absent, my wife, who performed with pious exactitude her ablutions in the Ganges, attracted the notice and desires of several suitors, especially of the king's domestic priest, the commander of the guard, and the young prince's preceptor, who annoyed her by their importunities, till at last she determined to expose and punish their depravity. Having fixed upon the plan, she made an appointment for the same evening with her three lovers, each being to come to her house an hour later than the other. Being desirous of propitiating the gods, she sent for our banker to obtain money to distribute in alms; and when he arrived he expressed the same passion as the rest, on her compliance with which he promised to make over to her the money that I had placed in his hands; or, on her refusal, he would retain it to his own use. Apprehending the loss of our property, therefore, she made a similar assignation with him, and desired him to come to her house that evening at an hour when she calculated on having disposed of the first comers, for whose reception, as well as for his, she arranged with her attendants the necessary preparations.

At the expiration of the first watch of the night, the preceptor of the prince arrived. Upakosā affected to receive him with great delight; and after some conversation, desired him to take a bath, which her attendants had prepared for him, as a preliminary to any further intimacy. The preceptor made not the slightest objection, on which he was conducted into a retired and dark chamber, where his bath was made ready. On undressing, his own clothes and ornaments were removed, and, in their place, a small wrapper given to him, which was a piece of cloth smeared with a mixture of oil, lamp-black, and perfumes. Similar cloths were employed to rub him after bathing, so that he was of a perfect ebon colour from top to toe. The rubbing occupied all the time till the second lover (the priest) arrived, on which the women exclaimed: "Here is our master's most particular friend! —in, in here, or all will be discovered," and hurrying their victim away, they thrust him into a long and stout wicker basket, fastened well by a bolt outside,[1] in which they left him to meditate upon his mistress.

The priest and the commander of the guard were secured, as they arrived, in a similar manner, and it only remained to dispose of the banker. When he made his appearance, Upakosā, leading him near the baskets, said aloud: "You promise to deliver me my husband's property?" And he replied: "The wealth your husband entrusted to me shall be yours." On which she turned towards the baskets, and said: "Let the gods hear the promise of Hiranygupta!" The bath was then proposed to the banker. Before the ceremony was completed the day began to dawn, on which the servants desired him to make the best of his way home, lest the neighbours should notice his departure; and with this recommendation they forced him, naked as he was, into the street. Having no alternative, the banker hastened to conceal himself in his own house, being chased all the way by the dogs of the town.

So soon as it was day, Upakosā repaired to the palace of

---

[1] In Professor Tawney's translation the lady gets a *large trunk* made, with a fastening outside, in which her lovers are entrapped.

Nanda, and presented a petition to the king against the banker,
for seeking to appropriate the property entrusted to him by her
husband. The banker was summoned. He denied having ever
received any money from me. Upakosā then said: "When my
husband went away, he placed our household gods in three
baskets; they have heard this man acknowledge his holding a
deposit of my husband's, and let them bear witness for me."
The king, with some feeling of surprise and incredulity, ordered
the baskets to be sent for, and they were accordingly produced
in the open court. Upakosā then addressed them: "Speak,
gods, and declare what you overheard this banker say in our
dwelling. If you are silent, I will unhouse you in this presence."
Afraid of this menaced exposure, the tenants of the baskets immediately exclaimed: "Verily, in our presence the banker
acknowledged possession of your wealth." On hearing these
words, the whole court was filled with surprise, and the banker,
terrified out of his senses, acknowledged the debt, and promised
restitution.

The business being adjusted, the king expressed his curiosity
to see the household divinities of Upakosā, and she very readily
complied with his wish. The baskets being opened, the culprits
were dragged forth by the attendants, like so many lumps of
darkness. Being presently recognised, they were overwhelmed
with the laughter and derision of all the assembly. As soon as
the merriment had subsided, King Nanda begged Upakosā to
explain what it all meant, and she acquainted him with what
had occurred. King Nanda was highly incensed, and, as the
punishment of their offence, banished the criminals from the
kingdom. He was equally pleased with the virtue and ingenuity
of my wife, and loaded her with wealth and honour. Her family
likewise were highly gratified by her conduct, and she obtained
the admiration and esteem of the whole city.[1]

[1] The device of the virtuous Devasmitā, in punishing the four young
libertines (see p. 246), bears some analogy to this exploit of Upakosā.

By whatever way this story may have journeyed to Europe, it was turned into a humorous but, in some of its details, very objectionable *fabliau* (interesting, however, as an illustration of manners) in the 13th century, under the title of Constant du Hamel, ou la Dame qui atrappa un Prêtre, un Prevost, et un Forestier. In this version a lady is importuned, as its title indicates, by three suitors, who, on her refusal, persecute her husband. To put a stop to their active malice, she consents to receive them, one somewhat later than another, so that by the time the first is stripped for the bath, the second arrives, and, pretending it is her husband, she hides him in a bin full of feathers, and so too with the second and third; in the end they are ignominiously bundled out of doors, well feathered, and hasten home, with all the curs of the town barking and snapping at their heels.—This is the only version that agrees with the Hindū original in the incident of the bath.

The old English metrical tale of the Wright's Chaste Wife (written by one Adam of Cobsam, 15th century), if partly borrowed from, is certainly a very great improvement on, the *fabliau*. This is an abstract of it:

The Wright's Chaste Wife.

A wright marries the daughter of a poor widow, whose only dower is a garland that will remain fresh while she continues chaste, but will wither when she becomes unfaithful. After a time the wright, thinking it likely that men would come to tempt his wife when he was from home, constructs in his house a lower room, the walls of which he makes as smooth as a mirror, and in the floor above a crafty trap-door, which would give way the moment a man touched it with his foot, and precipitate him into the pit below, out of which it was impossible to escape. Just at this time the lord of the town sent for him to build him a hall— a job of two or three months. The lord observes the wright's garland, and, learning that it is a proof of his wife's chastity, determines to visit her. He goes accordingly, and offers her forty marks. She asks him to lay the money down, and then conducts him to the room with the trap-door, and he no sooner puts his foot on it than down he tumbles into the room below. He begs and prays the dame to have pity on him, but she says: "Nay; you must wait till my husband sees you." Next day he asks for some food, but she tells him he must first earn it. "Spin me some flax," says she. The lord consents; so she throws him the tools and the flax, and he works away for his food. The steward next sees the wright's garland, and he too must visit the goodwife, whom he offers twenty marks, which she pockets, and then leads him into the same trap, where, after suffering some days' hunger, he spins flax for his meat. Then the proctor, seeing the wright's garland, asks him all about it, and in due course, after depositing twenty marks with the dame, he joins the lord and the steward in the wright's crafty trap for men of their sort. There all three spin and spin away, as if for their very lives, until at length the wright has finished his three months' job, and comes home. His wife tells him of her prisoners, and sends for their wives, and each takes away her own shamefaced and penitent spouse.

· We have here a parallel to the Hindū story of the virtuous Devasmitá, as related in the *Kathá Sarit Ságara:* Guhasena, a young merchant, is compelled to leave his wife, Devasmitá, for a short season, on business matters. The separation is painful to both, and the pain is aggravated by fears on the wife's part of her husband's inconstancy. To make assurance doubly sure, a couple of divine lotus flowers of a red colour are obtained in a dream, the hues of which, the married pair are told, will fade should either prove untrue.[1] Guhasena falls in with boon com-

---

[1] Some such marvellous indication of unsullied honour is exceedingly common in European romance. It is not always the same. In Ariosto the test is a cup, the wine of which is spilled by the unfaithful lover who attempts to drink from it; this device also occurs in the romances of

panions, who, learning the purport of his lotus and the virtue of his wife, set off to put it to the proof. *(Wilson.)*—The rest of the story is already detailed in pp. 244-247.

A somewhat similar tale occurs in Nakhshabī's *Tūtī Nāma* (4th Night of the India Office MS. No. 2573), as follows: A soldier's wife, on his taking leave of her to enter the service of a nobleman, gives him a nosegay, which, she says, will remain fresh so long as she preserves her chastity. The nobleman, marvelling that any one should be able to procure a fresh nose-gay every day in the middle of winter, inquires of the soldier how it was, and learns that its perennial freshness is a token that his wife continues faithful. The nobleman sends one of his cooks to try to form an intimacy with the soldier's wife, but she craftily entraps him; and the second cook, being next despatched to see what has become of his chief, meets with a similar recep-tion. Finally the nobleman himself, with his attendants—among whom is the soldier—proceeds to visit this paragon of virtue. The soldier's wife receives him courteously, and his two cooks, dressed as female slaves, wait upon him at supper. The happy soldier then returns his wife the nosegay, still fresh and blooming.

A curious variant is given in Narain Sawney's *Select Tamil Tales*, Madras, 1839, in which Ramakistnan (the Scogin of India) entraps the rāja and his domestic chaplain, whom he persuades to disguise themselves as women, on the pretence

---

Tristram, Perceval, and La Morte d'Arthur, and is well known in La Fontaine's version, "La coupe enchantee." Spenser has derived his Girdle of Florimel from these sources, or more immediately from the *fabliau*, "Le Manteau mal taille," an English version of which is pub-lished in Percy's *Reliques*, "The Boy and the Mantle." In the *Gesta Romanorum*, the test is the whimsical one of a shirt which will require neither washing nor mending as long as the wearer is true. There are not wanting, however, instances of such a test as this of the lotus in Somadeva. In Amadis de Gaul it is a garland [as also in the Wright's Chaste Wife]; in Perce Forest, it is a rose, which, borne by a wife or a maiden of immaculate virtue, preserves its freshness, but withers if the wearer is unchaste.—*Dr. H. H. Wilson.*

that he will introduce them to the beautiful wife of a man who has lately come to lodge at his house. The jester having locked them, as they successively arrive, in the same room, when they recognise each other, they are heartily ashamed, and softly request to be let out, but this the jester does only after he has extracted from them a solemn promise that they would forgive him a hundred offences every day.

To return to English variants. The well-known tale of the Monk and the Miller's Wife belongs to the same cycle of stories, in which a woman punishes objectionable wooers by entrapping them and exposing them to public ridicule :

The Monk and the Miller's Wife.

A monk having visited, with amorous intent, the virtuous wife of a miller, during her husband's absence, she affects to be pleased to see him, and they sit down together to a plentiful supper. But hardly have they eaten a mouthful when footsteps are heard approaching the house, and the monk, in dismay, asks what that can be. The wife answers that it is probably her husband come back unexpectedly, and bids him get into the great chest in the meantime, which he loses no time in doing, and the goodwife fastens it down upon him, and keeps him confined there in fear and trembling all the long night. In the morning she causes the miller's men to carry the chest into church at the hour of mass, where she opens it, and discovers the monk in presence of all assembled.

From the 1st Novel, Day ix, of Boccaccio's *Decameron*, John Lydgate (*circa* 1430) perhaps borrowed the idea of his metrical tale of

The Lady Prioress and her Three Wooers.

A knight, a parish priest, and a merchant are suitors to a lady prioress, who thus gets rid of them all. As the condition of her

love, the knight is to lie, like a dead body sewed in a sheet, in
the chapel in the wood, with two tapers burning beside him.
She next tells the priest that she has a cousin lying dead in the
chapel; but as he died in debt, his burial is forbidden [because
the debtor had arrested the body]; therefore she has sent for
him, in order that, if he would win her love, he should bury her
kinsman. The priest accordingly goes to the chapel, with
mattock and shovel, and says the dirge at the feet of the knight,
who had duly assumed the part of a dead body. The lady
prioress now sends for the merchant, tells him the dead man
lying in the chapel owed her a sum of money, and she wished
him to prevent the burial [to see whether his relatives would not
pay the debt], which the priest was to perform that same night.
"Shame would it be for us to lose our money, as we shall do if
he is buried before it is paid." She therefore proposes that the
merchant should dress himself up like the devil, and, when the
priest is about to bury the body, leap in at the choir door like a
fiend. The merchant consents, and, duly dressed up, goes to
the chapel door, and "roars as devils seemed to do." The
priest, in mortal terror, rushes through the window, breaking
both it and his head. The knight can endure this no longer,
so he rises up, at which the "devil" also runs away; while the
"corpse," equally frightened, flies off in another direction, and
the three suitors spend a wretched night, hiding from each other.
Next morning, the priest tells the lady prioress of all his mishaps,
how the devil appeared, and the body rose up. " I wis," quoth
she, "I never yet had a lover who died a good death." "Then,"
says Mass John, "that will serve for ale and meat; thou shalt
never be wooed by me." When the knight came, she told him
that he did not brook the bargain; so he, too, went away. She
threatened the merchant that she would tell his wife and all
the country of his wickedness; but he purchased her silence by
giving twenty marks to the convent, and after his death endowed
it in fee for ever.

X

A parallel to Lydgate's tale is found in Thorpe's Netherland-ish story of the Wicked Lady of Antwerp.—The Norse tale of the Mastermaid (Dr. Dasent) is the only version, so far as I know, in which magical arts are employed in punishment of the suitors. The heroine of this tale takes shelter in the hut of a cross-grained old woman, who is killed by an accident, and she is thus left alone. A constable, passing by and seeing a beauti-ful maiden, falls in love with her, and bringing a bushel of silver, she consents to marry him; but at night, when they are about to go to bed, she says that she has forgot to make up the fire : this the dutiful bridegroom undertakes to do himself, but no sooner has he taken hold of the shovel, than she cries out: "May you hold the shovel, and the shovel hold you, and may you heap burning coals over yourself till morning breaks." So there stood the constable all night heaping hot coals upon himself till day-break, when he was released from the spell and ran home, dancing with pain, to the amusement of all who saw him on the way. In like manner, on the second night, the maiden casts her spells over the attorney, who is made to hold the handle of the porch-door till morning; and on the third night, the sheriff is compelled to hold the calf's tail and the calf's tail to hold him till morning breaks, when he goes home in a sorry plight.

———

No. XXXI—p. 192.

PRINCE BAHRAM AND PRINCESS ED-DETMA.

NOTHING is more common in Oriental romance than for a beau-tiful, spoiled, and self-willed princess to impose certain hard conditions on her suitors: they must solve dark riddles; or answer knotty questions; or undertake a perilous journey to the confines of the earth—nay, even into jinnistān, the land of the jinn, or genii—in order to procure some wonderful talisman upon which the lady has set her heart.

The present story calls to mind the classical legend of Atalanta, who would marry only him that should outstrip her in a foot-race, but all of her competitors whom she overtook were to be killed on the spot by the dart with which she had armed herself; and who was ultimately vanquished by Hippomenes, who threw in the course, at some distance from each other, three golden apples from the gardens of the Hesperides, which Atalanta stopped to pick up, and thus enabled Hippomenes to reach the goal before her.—This tale is reproduced in Berni's *Orlando Innamorato*, where the daughter of the King of the Distant Isles makes the same condition with two suitors, Ordauro and Folderico; the latter, an old man, wins the race by the device of the golden apples.

Morier, in his *Second Journey to Persia*, relates a similar tradition, the conclusion of which is, however, tragical (he does not seem to have observed its affinity to the classical story of Atalanta): In former days a king of Persia promised his daughter in marriage to any one who would run before his horse all the way from Shīrāz to Ispahān. One of his running-footmen nearly accomplished the feat, having reached to the eminence now marked by the Shatir's Tower, when the king, fearful that he should be obliged to keep his promise, dropped his whip. The ligatures which encompassed the footman's body were such that, in the state he then was, he knew for certain that if he stooped to the ground to pick up the whip his death would immediately follow; therefore he contrived to take up the whip with his foot, carried it to his hand, and presented it to the king. This trick having failed, the king then dropped his ring, upon which the footman, who saw that his fate was decided, exclaimed: "O king, you have broken your word; but I will show you my submission to the last," so saying, he stooped, picked up the ring, and died.—The Shatir's Tower was, it is said, afterwards erected on the spot where the footman fell dead, to commemorate his exploit and his fidelity to the king.

Amazon princesses are favourite characters in old romances. In the *Nibelungenlied*, Queen Brunhilda did battle with all her suitors, and was finally conquered only by the aid of magical power. In Berni's burlesque *Innamorato*, Marphisia, a young Indian queen, made a vow never to lay aside her armour till she had taken three kings captive, namely, Charlemagne, Gradasso, and Agrican. In the Arabian story of 'Omar Bin Nu'man, a princess wrestles with the hero, and throws him, more by the *weakening* power of her fully-developed charms than by her personal strength and skill, though she possessed both these necessary qualifications of an athlete. The same lady after- wards, disguised as a knight, and armed *cap-à-pie*, encounters her lover in single combat—an incident which seems imitated from an episode of the Arabian romance of 'Antar:

Story of Jaida and Khálid.[1]

Muhárib and Záhir, the fathers respectively of Khálid and Jaida, were brothers. Muhárib was chief of the tribe of Zebíd, and Záhir was his counsellor. The brothers quarrelled, and Záhir struck his tents, and cast his lot with the kindred tribe of Sa'd. Záhir's wife becoming pregnant, he said to her that if a son were born, he would be most welcome; but if a girl, she was to conceal the fact, and let it appear to the world that they had a male child, in order that his brother should not exult over him. In due course a daughter was born, and was called in private Jaida, but Júdar in public, that it might appear she was a boy. About the same time Muhárib had a son born to him, whom he called Khálid. The daughter of Záhir was brought up as a boy, and taught to ride on horseback; and she soon became famous in all the exercises befitting a noble warrior, accompanying her father to battle, in which she ever took a prominent part.

---

[1] From my epitome of this celebrated romance in *Arabian Poetry for English Readers*.

Khālid was also one of the most illustrious horsemen of the age, universally acknowledged as an intrepid warrior and a valiant hero.

The fame of his cousin Jaida (Jūdar) having reached him, Khālid, after his father's death, visited his uncle, and spent ten days in jousting with the horsemen of the family. Jaida became deeply enamoured of him, and her mother, on learning this, revealed the secret of her sex to Khālid's mother, and suggested that their children should be united in marriage. But when Khālid was told by his mother that his cousin was a woman, he was greatly chagrined, slighted her love for him, and hastened back to his own tribe.

Jaida, enraged at finding herself thus scorned, resolved to be revenged on her cousin, and, disguising herself, set out for the land of Zebīd. Arrived there, she entered a tent of public entertainment, close-visored, like a horseman of the Hijāz. After proving her superiority to the best cavaliers in the course, she encountered Khālid for three days in succession, without either of them obtaining any advantage, when she discovered herself to her cousin, whose hatred was now suddenly converted into love. But Jaida rejected him, and returned home.

Khālid hastened to his uncle and demanded Jaida in marriage. His cousin at length consented, on the condition that he should provide for slaughter at her wedding feast a thousand camels belonging to Ghashm, son of Malik, surnamed the Brandisher of Spears. These Khālid procured by plundering the tribe of 'Āmir; but on his return Jaida imposed a further condition— that her camel should be led by the captive daughter of a prince. Khālid again set out with his horsemen, and, assailing the family tribe of Mu'āwiyya, son of Nizal, took captive his daughter Amīma; and his marriage with Jaida was immediately celebrated, when the daughter of Mu'āwiyya held the bridle of her camel, "and the glory of Jaida was exalted among women and among men."

In another Arabian romance, Delhama, of which Lane has given an account in his *Modern Egyptians*, two amazons figure prominently. One of these is a woman called Esh-Shumsta, or the Grizzle, "whom the heroes of her time held in great fear on account of her prowess and strength." The Emīr Dārim resolved to attack her. She mounted her horse in haste, on hearing of his approach, and went forth to meet him and his party. For. a whole hour she contended with them; killed the greater number, and put the rest to flight, excepting the Emīr Dārim, whom she took prisoner, and led in bonds, disgraced and despised, to her fortress. His ten sons, hearing of his misfortune, set forth with their attendants to rescue the Emīr, but they are taken prisoners and most of their followers are slain by Esh-Shumsta, who, however, is in the end overthrown and put to death by El-Gūndūba, the adopted son of the Emīr. Afterwards El-Gūndūba in the course of his adventures encounters in single combat another amazon, called Kattalet esh Shugān, or the Slayer of Heroes.

Richardson, in the Dissertation prefixed to his Arabic and Persian Dictionary, relates some curious historical anecdotes of the bravery of Arabian women in turning the tide of battle against the Greeks. —There can be no doubt that Europe has owed much of its institutions of chivalry to the Arabs, and an interesting chapter on this subject might be complied from authentic Arabian history, as well as from their romancists and poets.

No. XXXII.
THE SEVEN WISE MASTERS.

⁎ ALTHOUGH the Western versions (or imitations, rather) of the Book of Sindibād, known generally under the title of the Seven Wise Masters, possess but little in common with the Eastern texts, besides the outline of the connecting tale, yet a brief analytical account of one of the old English metrical texts may perhaps add somewhat to the usefulness of the present work. This version, entitled the *Seven Sages*, is believed to have been composed—probably from the French—about the end of the 14th century, and has been printed, from a MS. in Cambridge University Library, in the publications of the Percy Society, vol. xvi, with an interesting introductory essay by Thomas Wright. An analysis of another version, in the famous Auchinleck MSS., is given by Ellis, in his *Specimens of Early English Metrical Romances*, and the text was after-wards printed in Weber's *Northern Romances*. "Few works," remarks Dunlop, "are more interesting and curious than the Seven Wise Masters, in illustrating the genealogy of fiction, or its rapid and almost unaccountable transition from one country to another."

Introduction.

IN Rome was a renowned emperor, "as the book tellys us;" his name was Diocclecius; and he had a wife, called Helie. He had one only son, and when the child was seven years old, he was entrusted to the care of Seven Wise Masters, who undertook to instruct him in the space of seven years. They took him from the city into the country, in order that he should not learn any wickedness; and at once began to teach him the seven sciences, by means of lessons which they painted upon the wall of his chamber.[1] Thus when the prince lay on his bed he might con his lesson upon the wall. Ere the seven years were gone he was master of the seven sciences—"there was none but he had good

---

[1] The "seven sciences" anciently were: astronomy, arithmetic, music, medicine, logic, grammar, and rhetoric—"good sense" being, according to Pope, "worth all the seven."—The method of teaching the prince by means of lessons painted on the walls is identical with that described in the Eastern texts (see pp. 22, 23 and pp. 130, 131).

skill in." Then said the masters to each other: "This child
waxeth very wise. Let us therefore prove him." So they
secretly placed beneath each of the posts of his bed four ivy
leaves. And in the morning the prince said to them: "Of a
surety, either the roof of my room has become lower, or the
floor is risen." "He is a wise man, I wis," they exclaimed.

Now while the child was thus with his masters, his mother
died—"as we schalle alle dye." And soon after she was dead,
the emperor's courtiers urged him to take another wife; and as
he was "jolyf of blode," he desired them to seek out for him a
fitting wife, which they did, and the emperor was married to the
woman according to the law, and for some time he lived in great
solace with her.[1] One day she was told of the child, the emperor's
lawful heir, how he was so comely and so wise, and she began
to hate the child from that hour, and resolved to have him put to
death. So she bribed a magician to contrive that if the prince
should speak a word during seven days and seven nights he should
instantly die.[2] After this, "in a merry morning of May," she said
to the emperor that she longed to see his son, whom she loved
as if he was her own, though she had not yet beheld him; and
the emperor promised to despatch messengers at once to bring
his son to court:

> But the emperour wist nought
> What was hire wickkyd thought—
> An evyl deth mot scho dey!

The messengers arrive at the house of the Seven Wise Masters,
and command them, in the emperor's name, to bring the prince
to court within three days. They go into an arbour in the

---

[1] In another English MS. text, in Cambridge University Library, the
mother of the prince died before he was entrusted to the masters; and
the emperor, who was "old and hoar," by advice of his bold barons, and
"covetyse of heritage," married again.

[2] In the *Septem Sapientum*, the stepmother does not employ magical
arts to effect her wicked purpose.

evening, "for solace," and there one of them discovers from the aspect of the moon and stars that the prince's stepmother has by magic planned his death. The prince himself takes an observation of the heavenly bodies, and perceives the danger he should be in if he spoke during the next seven days and seven nights, and proposes that each of his masters should, by their wisdom, save his life one day, to which they readily agree.[1]

When the prince appears before his father he is dumb. His stepmother comes with her maidens, and welcomes him, but he utters not a word. She then obtains leave to take him with her into her own chamber, where having tempted him in vain, she accuses him to the emperor of having sought to dishonour his couch.[2]—During the seven following days the Queen and the Seven Wise Masters by turns relate tales to the emperor, who alternately condemns to death and reprieves his son, according as he is moved by the arguments of the accuser and defenders.

I—The Queen relates the story of

The Tree and its Branch,

that is, a creeper, which had gradually absorbed all the vigour of the tree, so that it died.

II—The First Master relates the story of

The Knight and the Greyhound,

for which see a prose version above, pp. 237-239.

---

[1] In the *Liber de Septem Sapientibus* the danger to the prince is foretold him in a dream, which is interpreted by his tutors, after consulting the stars.

[2] According to this version, the prince was only fourteen years old when he was solicited by the queen, since he was seven when placed under his tutors, and had "finished his education" in less than other seven years. In the *Septem Sapientum* he is sixteen years under the tutors.—See above, note 1, p. 134.

III—The Queen relates the story of

The Boar and the Herdsman,

a prose version of which will be found in pp. 242-244.—It is
stated, in p. 242, that this form of the story was taken into the
Historia Septem Sapientum Romæ from the *Mishlé Sandabar*, but
it occurs in earlier Western texts, such as, for instance, *Les Sept
Sages* and the *Liber de Septem Sapientibus*. Des Longchamps
thought this story was suggested by the classical legend of the
Boar of Erymanthus, slain by Hercules, to which it certainly
bears some resemblance.

IV—The Second Master relates the story of

Hippocrates and his Nephew;

the latter having cured the son of the king of Hungary, and
induced the queen to confess that the child's real father was a
foreign prince who had been on a visit to her husband, his uncle
Hippocrates, envious of his skill and fame, slew him in his
garden after his return home.

The incident of the discovery of the spurious son occurs in the
Cento Novelle Antiche (nov. 2), where a Greek king is found to
be the son of a baker; in the Arabian Tale of the Sultan of
Yaman and his Three Sons (vol. vi of Jonathan Scott's edition
of the *Arabian Nights*), where a certain sultan is proved to be
the son of a cook; and in the Lady's 2nd tale in the *Forty Vazírs*.

V—The Queen relates the story of

The Robbery of the King's Treasury.

A certain king's counsellor, having wasted all his wealth and
become reduced to great straits, with the assistance of his son,
breaks into the royal treasury and takes away a large quantity

of gold. The king, having discovered the robbery, sets a large
vessel filled with pitch close to the place where the breach had
been made in the wall, in order to entrap the robber when he
next came there. The counsellor, having once more fallen into
poverty, went again one night with his son to procure a fresh
supply of gold, and on entering the treasury, through the opening in the wall, instantly fell up to the neck in the vessel of
pitch. Calling to his son, he warned him not to enter and
attempt his release, for it was impossible; but desired him to
draw his sword and cut off his head and carry it away, so that
he should not be recognised and his family disgraced. The son
accordingly cuts off his father's head, carries it home, and
recounts the whole particulars of the misadventure.

In the *Septem Sapientum*, the robber of the king's treasury is a
knight, who had spent all his wealth at tourneys and similar idle
sports. After the son had taken home his father's head, the
king is informed of the headless body found in his treasury, and
orders it to be drawn at the tails of horses through the principal
streets to the gallows, charging his soldiers to bring before him
any persons whom they observed affected with excessive grief.
As the body was being drawn past the knight's house, one of
his daughters uttered loud cries of sorrow, upon which the son
quickly drew his knife and wounded his hand, so that the blood
flowed freely. The soldiers entered the house, and inquired the
cause of the loud cries they had just heard, when the son, showing his wounded hand, said that his sister had been alarmed at
seeing his blood, upon which the soldiers, satisfied with this
explanation, quitted the house.

This story has been adapted from Herodotus, who relates it of
Rhampsinitus, King of Egypt, and his architect, who in building
the royal treasury left a stone loose, but so nicely fitted in that it
could not be discovered by any one ignorant of the secret: his
two sons, after his death, frequently enter the treasury by this

means, until at length one of them is entrapped, as above. A similar legend is found in Pausanias, B. ix, c. 37, relating to the treasury of Hyrieus. It occurs also in the *Kathá Sarit Ságara,* eighth section, in the tale of Ghata and Karpara, which bears a very close analogy to the leading incidents of the story in Herodotus, especially the device of drugging the soldiers that guarded the body. From the *Seven Wise Masters* it was probably taken by Ser Giovanni (Day ix, Nov. i), and by Bandello (Par. i, nov. 25). The story is also found in an old French romance, *L'Histoire du Chevalier Berinus,* in which Herodotus has been imitated in the concluding incident, of the king's daughter's attempt to discover the clever thief; and it forms one of the exploits of the Shifty Lad in Campbell's *Tales of the West Highlands.*

VI—The **Third Master** relates the story of

The Husband Shut Out.

The wife of a certain old man was in the habit of stealing out at nights when he was sound asleep, and meeting her lover. It happened one night that the husband awoke, and, missing his spouse from beside him, at once concluded that she was unfaithful; so he rose up, and securely bolted the outer door. A little before daybreak the truant wife returned, and finding the door fast, she

> Bygan loud to crye,
> And badde the devle hys neke to breke
> That the doore hadde steke.

The goodman, however, was not to be moved by her entreaties or threats, and bade her begone, adding that in the morning he should expose her to all their friends and relations, yea, and to the whole town. In vain she continued to beg to be let in; the justly incensed husband was obdurate. At length she declared that she would not live to suffer such disgrace, and taking up a great stone she plunged it into the well, and then stole quietly close to the door. The husband, supposing the plash he had heard to be caused by her throwing herself into the well, began to relent, for he was doatingly fond of her, in spite of her levity and misconduct ; so he hastened to undo the fastenings of the door, and went to the well to draw her forth if possible. Meanwhile the artful wife quickly slipped into the house, bolted the door, and went up stairs to her warm bed—"an evyl deth mote scho dee!" The poor man, having fruitlessly searched into and all round the well for his wife, returned to the house, to find himself in turn shut out. Now there was a law in that town that all husbands found in the streets after a certain hour were to be taken up by the watchmen and severely punished. The husband therefore knocks repeatedly at the door, but his wife bids him return to his leman, with whom he has passed the night. The noise of their altercation attracts the watchmen, who come up, and ask what it is all about, to which the wife from the window replies, that it is her husband come back from spending the night with his leman—she had endured his misconduct too long, and now they may take him away and punish him. So the poor man is arrested, and thus "thorow his wyf he was schent."

This tale seems to have been taken into the *Liber de Septem Sapientibus* from Alphonsus (Fab. 13), who probably derived it from the Arabian story-tellers. It is one of the *fabliaux* of the Trouvères (Le Grand, iii, 143), and the 4th novel, Day vii, of the *Decameron*. Dunlop says it is "the origin of the *Calandra* of Cardinal Bibbiena, the best comedy that appeared in Italy previous to the time of Goldoni ; it also forms the groundwork of one of Dancourt's plays, and probably suggested to Moliere the plot of his celebrated comedy, *George Dandin*."—It has also suggested the plot of one of the plays of Hans Sachs, *Das Weib im Brunnen*.

VII—The Queen then relates the story of

The King and his Seneschal.

A certain king, whose body was all swollen, or leprous, desires his seneschal to procure him a mistress, and, on being reminded how repulsive his person was to women, tells him to take from his treasury whatever money might be necessary for the purpose. The seneschal's cupidity induces him to introduce his own wife to the king at night—having terrified her into compliance with his drawn sword. In the morning the seneschal repeatedly knocks at the door of the king's chamber, and is told to go away; at length he informs the king that the woman is his wife, upon which the king, having opened the window and discovered this to be the fact, declares that he will not part with her now, upbraids the seneschal for selling his virtuous wife for a paltry sum of money, and orders him, on pain of death, to quit the kingdom immediately.

This story is similiar to that of the Bathkeeper, which occurs in nearly all the Eastern texts of the Book of Sindibād, where, however (especially in the Arabian versions), it is related with some very objectionable details. In the Seven Wise Masters it is put into the mouth of the Queen, as it is made to tell solely against men; but in the Eastern texts of the *Sindibād*, it is related by one of the vazīrs, the woman being represented as yielding a not unwilling consent—though even thus its appropriateness as one of the vazīrs' tales is questionable. In the *Historia Septem Sapientum Romæ*, and its derivatives—English and Scottish, Spanish, Armenian, Russian, etc.—this story is rather clumsily joined with another. It does not occur in *Dolopathos ;*—I was induced to state, in note, p. 61, that the story is found in this old text by Goedeke's comparative table of the versions of the Wise Masters (*Orient und Occident*, iii, pp. 422, 423), where I mistook "senes" for "senesc." (senescalcus). In

:he same table the story does not appear in the contents of Rolland's Scottish version, though it forms part of another tale, as in the *Septem Sapientum.*

The form which the tale of the Seneschal in the Wise Masters and that of the Bathman in the Eastern texts of the Book of Sindibād assume in the *Hitopadēsa* (Book i, fab. viii and ix) is to the following effect: A young and wealthy prince, becoming enamoured of the blooming wife of a merchant, employed an old woman to solicit her to grant him an interview, which she refused, saying that she was devoted to her husband. The old woman, after reporting the failure of her mission, advises the prince to enter the service of the merchant, who confides to him his most important affairs. One day, at the suggestion of the 'old woman, the prince, being anointed fresh from the bath, said to the merchant that he must perform a vow to Gaurī for the space of a month, and, beginning that day, requested the merchant to bring him every evening a young woman of good family, and she should be honoured by him in due form. Accordingly, the merchant, having brought a young woman of that description, presented her, and afterwards concealed himself to watch what he would do. The prince, without so much as touching the young lady, having done homage to her at a distance, with vestures, jewellery, perfumes, and sandal, dismissed her immediately in the care of a guard. On seeing this, the merchant became confident; and his mind being biassed by the lust of gain, he brought his own wife and presented her—the result, however, was very different from his expectations, and he was overwhelmed with grief.

VIII—The Fourth Master relates the story of

The Wise Old Man and his Foolish Wife.

There was a certain wise and prudent knight who, in his old age, married a young and foolish wife. The lady, being dissatisfied with her spouse, fell in love with a priest. She told her mother of her lover, and the mother advised her to hold fast to the old knight; but if she was determined to do such a thing, she should first prove her husband. So the young wife caused the gardener to cut down a pear-tree, of which the knight was very fond, and lay it in the hall. When the husband discovers the tree, he inquires of her where it came from, and she tells him it was cut down by her orders in the garden. "Well," says he, quietly, "now that it is hewn down it can't be helped." The lady returns to her mother and relates how her husband was not angry at her cutting down his favourite tree. "Try him again," says the mother; "you do not know what he thinks of the matter." The foolish young wife next slays the knight's favourite hound, and tells him that she did so because it had lain on her dress. "Dame," quoth he, "thou mightest have drawn thy clothes together, and let my dog live: slay no more, though he lie on thy clothes; if thou dost, I shall certainly be wroth." Once more she repairs to her mother. "Old men," says the mother, "will endure much wrong; but try him again." Soon after this the knight has a noble company assembled at his house; and when all are seated at table, his wife fastens the keys suspended from her girdle to a corner of the cloth, and then suddenly rising, "drow doun coppys and dyschys ilkone," making a sad mess of the clothes of the guests. At this the good knight was full wroth, and after the guests were gone, he led his wife into a chamber, where, with the help of his brother, he bled her in the arm,[1] leaving only so much blood in her body as would keep in life, and then laid her down on a fair bed. When she recovered from her swoon, he gave her meat and drink, and said to her: "Dame, lie thou still. Thou shalt have meat and drink at will. But whenever thou waxest mad again, thou shalt be let blood." "Mercy, my lord," she cries, "and I will surely anger thee no

---

[1] In the *Septem Sapientum* the old man, more appropriately, employs a barber.

more." "If so," says the wise and prudent old man, "then do
I forgive thee thy three offences."

> Than wald scho no more
> Lever of the clerkis lore,
> For fere to be let bloode ;
> But heldir algat trew and good.

Keller, in his introduction to the *Roman des Sept Sages*, refers,
among other parallels to this story, to the Fabliau De la femme
qui voulut éprouver son Mari (Le Grand, iii, 177), and to Boccaccio's tale of Lidia and Pyrrhus (*Decameron*, Day vii, nov. 9).
It also occurs in the *Contes et joyeux devis* of Bonaventure des
Périers, and in the *Contes*, etc., of the Abbé Prévôt.

IX—The Queen relates the story of

Merlin's Pillar.

In the city of Rome a pillar was set up by the enchanter Merlin,
on the top of which was a mirror that shone over all the town,
and gave the people warning of any approaching foreign invasion.
Two clerks undertake to destroy this safeguard of the city, in
order that the King of Apulia should march upon it unawares.

Virgilius is substituted for Merlin in some texts, and, in place
of a mirror, two brazen images, which threw a golden ball to
each other as a warning to the citizens that an enemy was
advancing to attack the city.

Vincent of Beauvais, in the 13th century, describes Virgil's
magical tower, which is also the subject of a chapter in the
legendary history of Virgilius—see Mr. William J. Thoms'
Early Prose Romances, vol. ii, pp. 20-22. This story, with some
variations, is reproduced in the *Pecorone* of Ser Giovanni; it was
very popular in Europe during the Middle Ages: numerous
parallels are referred to in Keller's edition of the oldest German
text of the Wise Masters—Einleitung, pp. 57-59.

Y

X—The Fifth Master relates the story of

The Burgess and the Magpie,

which is similar to the tale of the Merchant and his Parrot—pp. 31, 141, and 222.

XI—The Queen relates the story of

The Seven Evil Counsellors,

who had, by their magical arts, contrived to render the king blind whenever he went out of his palace, in order that they might increase their own wealth by defrauding him and the people. The child Merlin advises the king to put his seven evil counsellors to death, after which his sight would be restored; this the king does accordingly, and afterwards raises Merlin to the highest offices of state.—The tale is taken from the romance of Merlin.

Wright has remarked that this story is of Indian origin, and is found in several Eastern collections, but he does not specify any of them.

XII—The Sixth Master relates the story of

The Widow who was Comforted.

There was a knight, a rich sheriff, who was doatingly fond of his wife. One day as he sat with her, and they jested together, a knife which he had in his hand chanced to wound her slightly, at which he was so much grieved that he died the next day. His widow, distracted with grief, vowed that nothing should part her from her husband, and so took up her abode beside his grave. At nightfall she made a good fire, for it was the cold winter tide, and she continued to weep and wring her hands, lamenting the loss of her loving spouse. Now near this place

were the bodies of three thieves that had been hanged, and a
certain knight had to watch that they were not stolen, as quit-
rent of his lands.

> Than the knyght was both zong and bolde,
> He was swith sore a-colde,
> And at the chappel fyer he sawe light,
> And rode thyderward ful ryght.

He dismounted from his steed and approached the fire, saying
to the widow: "Dame, by thy leave I will warm myself." The
lady answered: "Yea, sir, welcome art thou, if thou thinkest
no evil, but to sit and make thee warm." This knight was
without a wife, and he thought the lady would suit him very
well, so he began forthwith to woo her, and her heart inclined
towards him, for she saw he was a comely and a manly knight,
and he soon won her love. After a while, the knight went to
see whether the bodies of the three thieves were still on the
gallows, when, behold, one of them was stolen; so he returned
to the widow, and told her that in consequence of this he should
lose his lands and heritage.

> Sire, quod the lady, tho [then],
> There-fore he nought wo,
> Ne make thou dole there-fore,
> Ne schal nouzt thy lond be lore.
> To thys berial we wyl goone,
> And dyggyn uppe the cors anone,
> And hangye hym in his stede,
> As fayer as the othyr dyde.

"But," says the knight, "the thief had a great wound on his
head, and if your husband's body were examined and found without such a wound, still should I lose my lands." "Let not that
trouble thee," quoth she; "thou hast both sword and dagger:
with either of them do thou give him such a wound as the thief
had." "Assuredly," answers the knight, "I could never smite
a dead man." Then the lady drew a knife from her sheath,

" that was keen and sharply ground," and wounded the head of her husband, and putting up the knife, she said, "Now, sir, shall we be gone?" But the knight recollects that the thief had lost two of his front teeth, and the lady, without hesitation,

> In hyr hond scho took a stoon,
> And knockyd out twa teeth anoon !

She then advises the knight to hang her husband's body on the gallows, before day begins to dawn, which is done accordingly.

In the *Septem Sapientum,* and some other versions, the knight, after these proofs of the widow's affection for her dead husband, sternly upbraids her, saying that her husband had loved her so much that he died because he had inadvertently shed a little of her blood, but she had not scrupled to mutilate his body : he would therefore have nothing further to do with such a wanton — a more appropriate conclusion of the story, the sole object of the relator being to illustrate the levity and heartlessness of women.

This tale is identical with the episode of the Widow of Ephesus in Petronius Arbiter, which Dunlop had little doubt was originally a Milesian or Sybarite fable. However this may be, it is found in the Talmud, forming one of the supplementary paragraphs which are scattered through the Mishna and Gemara (see Hershon's *Talmudic Miscellany,* p. 28). It also occurs in the *Cento Novelle Antiche* (nov. 56), the author of which may have taken it either from the *Liber de Septem Sapientibus* or from the Fabliau De la Femme qui se fist Putain sur la fosse de son Mari. For many other parallels see Keller's *Roman des Sept Sages,* Einleitung, clix-clxvii.

Davis, in his work on the Chinese (ch. xiv), relates a somewhat similar story, which he thought was the original of the tale of The Nose in Voltaire's *Zadig:* A philosopher observed a widow fanning the earth over her husband's grave, and, inquiring the reason for such a strange proceeding, was informed by the sorrowing lady that she had promised her dying husband not to

marry again before the earth on his grave was perfectly dry:
"And now, as it occurred to me that the surface of this ground,
which has been newly tempered, would not very soon dry, I
thought I would just fan it a little." The philosopher approved
of her plan, and obtained her fan as a souvenir. Returning
home, he told his wife of this adventure, and showed her the fan,
which she snatched from him and tore into shreds, declaring the
woman to be a heartless hussy;—for her own part, were he to
die, she should never marry again. Shortly after this the philosopher was taken suddenly ill, and died. The lady was incon-
solable. Preparations were made for the funeral; friends and
acquaintances assembled, amongst whom was a young and very
handsome student, attended by his servant. He informs the
lady that he had purposed becoming a disciple of the late philosopher, and had come to attend his obsequies. The widow falls
in love with him, and conveys this to him through his old
servant. After several objections which the student raised had
been removed by the amorous widow, he consents to marry
her, but suddenly falls into convulsions. His servant tells her
the only remedy is the brain of a man, recently dead, dissolved
in wine. Quoth the lady, readily: "My husband has been dead
only a few days; open his coffin, and take the remedy from
thence." The coffin was immediately opened, when, to the consternation of the widow, the philosopher rose up, for he had only
been pretending to be dead, and had created all the scene by
magical arts.—In Voltaire's story, a lady had vowed not to
marry a second husband so long as the rivulet continued to flow
past the grave of her lately deceased spouse, and was now busy
contriving to turn its course in a different direction. Zadig's wife
tells him of this, and professes disgust at such heartlessness.
Zadig, not long after, pretends to have died suddenly; his intimate friend visits the sorrowing widow, makes love to her, falls
suddenly ill—the nose of a dead man applied to the part affected
is the only cure; so the lady immediately takes a sharp knife,

and repairs to her husband's tomb, intending to cut off his nose, but Zadig arises, and scoffs at his wife for her hollow professions of affection.

Our old English jest-books abound in satirical tales of "widows' tears, which shrink, like Arno, in the summer." The tenth jest in *Mery Tales and Quicke Answeres*, a collection of facetiæ which has been more than once cited in these notes, is as follows:

"There was a yonge woman, the whiche for her husbande, that laye a dyenge, sorowed oute of all measure, wherfore her father came often to her and sayde: daughter, leaue your mourn-inge; for I haue prouyded for you an other husbande, a farre more goodly man. But she did not onely continue in her sorowe, but also was greatly displeased, that her father made any motion to her of an other husbande. As sone as she had buryed her husbande, and the soule mass was songe, and that they were at dyner, betwene sobbynge and wepynge she rowned [*i.e.* whispered] her father in the eare, and sayde: father, where is the same yonge man, that ye said shuld be min husband?—Lo, thus may ye se, that women sorowe ryght longe, after theyr husbandes be departed."

Of the same class is the jest in *A Hundred Mery Tales*—the book referred to by Beatrice, in Much Ado about Nothing, when she says to Benedick: "Will you tell me who told you that I was disdainful, and that I had my good wit out of the Hundred Merry Tales?"—of the woman who followed her fourth husband's bier and wept; not because of his death, as she told a gossip, but because she was not this time, as on former occasions, sure of a new husband; and another in the same collection, of the woman kneeling at the mass of requiem, while the corpse of her husband lay in the chapel, and a young man whispering "that he myght be her husbande," she replied: "Syr, by my trowthe, I am sory that ye come so late, for I am sped all redy. For I was made sure yesterday to another man."

XIII—The Queen's seventh and last story is of

The Siege of Rome.

The city of Rome was besieged by three Saracen knights, and its defence undertaken by seven wise men, one of whom (named Janus, or Genus, in some of the versions) devised a stratagem with a mirror, or two glittering swords, which caused the Saracens to decamp in mortal terror.

This stupid story is not found in the *Liber de Septem Sapientibus*, but occurs in the *Roman des Sept Sages*.

XIV—The Seventh Master now appears before the king, and, having predicted that on the following day the prince will recover his speech, relates the story of

The Two Dreams; or, the Knight of Hungary.

A certain noble knight of Hungary dreamt of seeing a very beautiful lady, but knew her not; and it so happened that the lady whom he saw in his dream that same night dreamt also of him. Next day the knight of Hungary took horse and arms, and proceeded in quest of the lady. Three weeks and more did he ride, sorely sighing for his lady-love, till he came to a town, where was a fair castle, strongly fortified. He takes up his lodging at the inn, and, questioning mine host regarding the castle and its owner, he learns that it belongs to a lord who has a fair jewel of a wife, of whom he is so jealous that two years ago he built a strong tower at one end of the castle, in which he confines her, with one maiden as her companion; and he always carries the key of the tower, which is never opened save when he himself visits her. The knight had already seen the lady looking out of the tower window, and recognised her as the object of his dream. He goes on the following day to the castle, and offers his services to the old lord, who heartily bids him welcome; and the knight, being a good and valiant warrior, conquers all his enemies, so that the old man loved him fondly, and made him steward of his lands.

One day, when the steward chanced to be under the tower, the lady perceived him and recognised him as the same she had seen in her dream, and contrived to communicate with him by means of a rope made of rushes let down from the window. The knight now planned a crafty device by which he should enjoy the society of his lady-love unknown to her husband. He built a tower at some distance from the castle, and caused an underground passage to be made, leading direct from it to the lady's chamber. When all was completed, he visited the young wife, who gave him a ring as a keepsake, telling him, should her husband see it and appear suspicious, to bring it back to her at once. The old lord recognises his wife's ring on the steward's finger, "as he sat at meat," and, after examining it, hastens to the tower; but the steward having reached the lady's chamber by the private way and restored the ring, on the husband demanding to see the ring, she at once produces it, to his great satisfaction.[1] At length the lovers resolve to elope, and the lady counsels the steward to tell the old lord that, having slain a great man in his own country, he had been banished, and that his lady-love was coming to him with some tidings regarding his heritage. The old lord would, of course, ask to see the lady, and she herself would play her part. The knight accordingly

---

[1] In the *Septem Sapientum*, a king takes the place of the old lord, and he and the knight, on a hunting excursion, having dismounted during the noontide heat, the king recognises the ring on the knight's finger while the latter is asleep. On awaking, the knight suspects from the king's countenance that the ring has betrayed him, and, feigning illness, obtains leave to return home. This incident may be compared with the legend of Kentigern (or St. Mungo) and the Ring, in which the queen's gift to her paramour is discovered by the jealous king under similar circumstances—but here the likeness ends: the finding of the ring in the stomach of a fish belongs to another cycle of folk-tales.

tells his lord this story, and invites him to a banquet at his own
tower. Before he arrives, his wife, dressed in the costume of the
knight's country, has reached the banqueting hall by the secret
passage, prepared to enact the part of the crafty knight's leman.
The old lord, on seeing her, thinks she is remarkably like his
own wife ; but then he recollected the affair of the ring, and
there might also be two women exactly alike.   At this juncture
the lady pretends to swoon, is taken out, and returns with all
speed by the private way to her chamber, where, having changed
her dress, she is found by her husband, whom she embraces with
every token of affection.   He was "blythe as bird on bough,"
and remained with her all night.   On the day following the
crafty knight sends all his property on board a ship, and
goes to take leave of the old lord, as he is to return at once,
with his lady-love, to his own country.   The knight and the old
lord's wife—who has resumed the character of the supposititious
lady of Hungary—are accompanied by the deceived husband
"into the sea a mile or two, with mynstrelsy and many manner
of melody," and then he bids them farewell.   On his return
home, he proceeds, as usual, to the tower, and finds his bird has
flown :

> Than sayed he, walaway !
> That ever was he man boren !
> Than was all hys myrthe lorne,
> He lepe out of the tour anoon,
> And than brake hys neke boon.

Wright says that this story appears to be taken from some
Eastern collection, since a similar tale is found in Von Hammer's
supplementary tales of the *Thousand and One Nights.*—Berni
has adapted it, in the *Orlando Innamorato*—omitting the incidents of the two dreams : Folderico, the old knight who gained,
by the artifice of the golden balls in the foot-race (see above,
p. 323), the daughter of the King of the Distant Isles, shut her
up in a tower where he kept his treasure, and Ordauro, the un-

successful suitor, who is beloved by the lady, plays the part of the crafty Knight of Hungary.—Dunlop has pointed out that the tale of the Two Dreams corresponds exactly with the plot of the Miles Gloriosus of Plautus; the Fabliau Le Chevalier a la Trappe (Le Grand, iii, 157); a tale in the fourth part of Massuccio; and the story Du Vieux Calender in Gueulette's *Contes Tartares.*

The notion of two young people simultaneously dreaming of each other, though total strangers, is essentially Oriental, and numerous instances might be cited from Asiatic fiction. In the Hindū romance of *Vāsavadattā*, by Subhandu (7th century), as analysed by Colebrooke in vol. x of the *Asiatic Researches*, Candaspacētu, a young and valiant prince, saw in a dream a beautiful maiden, of whom he became desperately enamoured. Impressed with the belief that a person such as seen by him in his dream had a real existence, he resolves to travel in search of her, and departs, attended only by his confidant Macaranda. While reposing under a tree in a forest at the foot of the Vindhya mountains, where they halted, Macaranda overhears two birds conversing; and from their discourse he learns that the Princess Vāsavadattā, having rejected all the suitors who had been assembled by the king her father for her to make choice of a husband, had seen Candaspacētu in a dream, in which she had even learnt his name. Her confidante Tamālika, sent by her in search of the prince, has arrived in the same forest, and is discovered there by Macaranda. She delivers the prince a letter from the princess, and conducts him to the king's palace. He obtains from the princess the avowal of her love, and her confidante reveals to him the violence of her passion. The subsequent adventures of the lovers have nothing in common with the exploits of the Knight of Hungary.—In another Indian romance (now known chiefly, if not solely, through the Persian translation) Prince Kāmarupa dreams of Kāmalata and she dreams of him, having never seen or heard of each other before.—In the 39th tale of the *Tūtī Nāma* (33rd of Kāderi's abridgment), an emperor of China dreams of a beautiful damsel, and being sorely smitten with love for the creature of his dreaming fancy, he can find no peace of mind. One of his vazīrs, who is an excellent portrait painter, receiving from the emperor a minute description of the lady's features, draws the face, and the emperor acknowledges the likeness to be very exact. The vazīr then goes abroad with the portrait, to see whether any one can recognise the original of it. In the course of his wanderings, he meets with an old ascetic, who at once recognises the portrait as that of the Princess of Rūm, who, he says, has an unconquerable aversion for men, ever since she beheld, in her garden, a peacock basely desert his mate and their young ones, when the tree on which their nest was built had been struck by lightning : she believed that all men were equally selfish, and was resolved never to marry. The vazīr returns to his royal master and recounts to him these interesting particulars regarding the object of his affection, and undertakes to conquer the aversion of the princess, which he does, by exhibiting before her a painting of a male deer sacrificing his life for the safety of his mate and their fawn.—The frame of the Persian Tales ascribed to a dervish of Ispahān seems to have been adapted from this story of the *Tūtī Nāma*, in which, as Gerrans has remarked, in the preface to his incomplete translation, the nurse " Sutlumene ransacks her invention to combat the obstinacy of the princess Farrukhnaz, who, from the impression of a dream, had formed as unfavourable an opinion of men as the Sultan of the Indies [in the *Arabian Nights*] had preconceived of women. "

Next day the Prince presents himself before his Majesty and relates the particulars of his stepmother's wickedness towards himself. And here in the *Septem Sapientum* and its derivatives is interpolated the incident referred to in note, pp. 286-7, of the discovery of the queen's paramour disguised as one of her female attendants : the prince requests that the queen be summoned, with all her maidens, and when the latter have been ranged in such order that every one of them could be distinctly seen, according to Rolland's old Scottish metrical version[1]—

> Than said the Childe : Father, lift up zour Ene,
> Behald how lang that ze haue blindit bene
> With zour Emprice that is zour Maryit quene,
> And that zoung wenche that all is cled in grene,
> Quhilk is bour Mayd[2] unto zour awin Empres,
> Quhome scho hes mair in fauour and kindnes,
> Than euer scho had, I dar weill tak on me,
> Sen thay first met than to zour Maiestie.
> Quhome I desire, gif it plesit zour grace,
> To be uncled[3] befoir zow in this place.
> That being done, richt weill ze sall persaue,
> Sic ane bour Mayd, and sic Emprice ze haue.
> To quhome answerit this Nobill Empreour :
> Thou knawis, sone, it is not my honour,
> It will be schame to me and to vs all,
> Ane naikit Mayd befoir us for to call.
> Than said the Chylde : ane Mayden gif scho be,
> All the greit schame thairof beis laid on me ;
> Gif scho be not ane zoung Mayd as ze tell,
> Than let all schame remane still with her sell.
> The Empreour than commandit that be done :
> The officers thay unbecled[3] hir sone.
> The clais of tane,[4] it weill appeirit than
> It was na Mayd, bot alwayis was a man.

XIV—The Prince then relates the story of

The Ravens.

A knight and his son row over to an island where only a hermit lived. Three ravens are conversing together, and the

---

[1] *The Sevin Seages translatit out of Prois in Scottis Meter be John Rolland.* Written in 1560, printed in 1575.—The original spelling is here reproduced (the letter z represents y—*zour,* your); but to facilitate the reading of this passage, I have inserted a few commas.

[2] Bower maiden.   [3] Undressed.   [4] The clothes taken off.

father remarks to his son that it would be interesting to know
what they were talking about. The youth, who understood the
language of birds, replied that he could tell, but was afraid of
giving offence to his father by the communication. Being
assured that he might speak freely, the youth then said that
the ravens had prophesied that he should become a great man,
and that his father should one day hold a basin of water while
he washed his hands, and his mother should wait upon him with
a towel. Incensed at this, the father cast his son into the sea,
but the lad, being able to swim, contrived to reach the shore,
and was taken up by a fisherman, who sold him to the warden
of a castle. In course of time, it happened that the king was
much annoyed at being followed constantly whenever he went
abroad by three ravens, who kept up a loud chattering as if in
hot dispute. The king offered the hand of his daughter in marriage to any one who would explain the meaning of the three
ravens always following him, and the youth, being introduced to
his Majesty, explained that the ravens were two males and one
female ; that during a time of scarcity the female bird's mate had
driven her away, and she had been fed and supported by the
young male raven; but now the old male bird had returned to
claim his mate, and the female would have none of him, but
elected the young male that had befriended her in adversity for
her mate. The king then ruled that the old male bird should
depart and trouble the happy pair no more. On hearing this
decision the birds flew away. After this the youth married the
king's daughter, and ruled the kingdom jointly with his royal
father-in-law. Years passed on, and the youth's father having
fallen into poverty, he and his wife, for shame thereof, quitted
their native country, and came to the land where their own son
was become so eminent. He hears of this, and visits them, with
a grand retinue, at their humble abode. The aged couple, not
knowing him, of course, make haste to receive him with all
reverence, and the father holding the basin of water, and the

mother the towel, thus was the ravens' prophecy fulfilled. The youth then discovered himself, embraced his parents, and made them comfortable for the remainder of their lives.

In the *Septem Sapientum* and its derivatives, such as our old English prose and Rolland's Scottish metrical versions, this story is greatly amplified by the interpolation of a series of adventures which form the plot of the romance of *Amis and Amiloun.*—It is found in the *Cento Novelle* of Sansovino, (Day viii, nov. 4), and in the novels of Lope de Vega, El pronostico cumplido ; and many other parallels exist in Asiatic and European fiction ; for instance : in the Arabian tale of the Second Royal Mendicant ; in the *Bakhtyār Nāma*, story of the King of Persia and his Son ; in chapter 79 of the Anglican *Gesta Romanorum ;* in the classical legend of Danae; in the *Bāgh o Bahār*, story of the Second Darvīsh ; in Ralston's *Tibetan Tales*, story of the Ful-filled Prophecy; and in *Syntipas*, story of Destiny, or the Son of the Sage—pp. 280-282. This last, though undoubtedly of Eastern origin (as is evident from the incident of the youth breaking through the wall of the king's palace, the common practice of Asiatic thieves since the days of Job—xxiv, 26), may yet be considered as faithfully reflecting the universal belief in Europe during the Middle Ages, based upon such scripture texts as inculcate faith in an overruling Providence, directly control-ling the destinies of every human being.

Conclusion.

The prince having related the story of the Ravens, his stepmother acknowledged her wickedness, through the fiend's incitement, and she was put to death. And thus was the child's life saved, and the emperor rewarded the Seven Wise Masters who had told the tales against the vile traitoress the child's stepmother. The emperor remained a widower for the remainder of his life, for he durst no more deal with women, lest they should work further evil.

The following is a comparative table of the tales in (1) the two early English metrical versions of the *Seven Sages,* 13th and 14th centuries, edited by Weber and Wright; (2) the French metrical *Roman des Sept Sages,* about 1284, edited by Keller; (3) the Latin prose text, *Liber de Septem Sapientibus,* edited by Goedeke;[1] and (4) the Latin prose version, *Historia Septem Sapientum Romæ,* Geneva, 1492, and its derivatives:

SEVEN WISE MASTERS. Ellis, Weber, Wright.		ROMAN DES SEPT SAGES. Keller.	LIBER DE VII SAP. Goedeke.	HIST. VII SAP. Copland, Rolland.
Queen 1	Tree and Branch ...	Id.	Id.	Id.
1st Sage	Dog and Snake	Id.	Id.	Id.
Queen 2	Wild Boar	Queen 3	Id.	Id.
2nd Sage	Hippocrates	Id.	Id.	5th Sage
Queen 3	King's Treasury ...	Queen 5	Id.	Id.
3rd Sage	Husband Shut Out	Id.	4th Sage	2nd Sage
Queen 4	King and Seneschal	Queen 2	Id.	Queen 6
4th Sage	Wise Old Man	Id.	3rd Sage.	Id.
Queen 5	Merlin's Pillar	Queen 7	Id.	Id.
5th Sage	Burgess and Magpie	Id.	Id.	3rd Sage
Queen 6	VII Evil Counsellors	Id.	Id.	Queen 4
6th Sage	Widow Comforted...	Id.	Id.	7th Sage
Queen 7	Siege of Rome	Queen 4	...	Queen 6
7th Sage	Two Dreams	Id.	...	Queen 7
Prince	Ravens.................	Id.	Id.	Id.
...		...	{ Queen 7, Daughter 7th Sage, Stepmother	...
			...	{ 6th Sage, Three Lovers

It will be observed that our old English versions have the same stories that occur in the *Sept Sages,* though not all in

---

[1] *Orient und Occident,* iii, 385-423.

the same order; while the *Liber de Septem Sapientibus* has, in place of the Siege of Rome and the Dreams, two tales which reappear in several other texts represented in Goedeke's comparative table, and are as follows:

The Spoiled Daughter.

There was a soldier, who, having a pet daughter, disdained to correct her in youth. At length she became pregnant by a shield-bearer; and the soldier, not daring to take vengeance upon him, beat his daughter almost to death. When recovered, in her father's absence, she fled to a distant land. At last she was followed by her father, and found in the house of a certain prince. When the daughter observed this, she approached the lady of the land and the prince in whose friendly abode she sojourned, and said, concerning her father, that he was a low character, who had followed her through various countries to corrupt her. Then the wretched father was taken and hung from a gibbet. Observing that her father was now dead, she secretly went off to her own country, where she continued her evil life.

The Bad Stepmother.

There was a certain citizen, who had a son by his former wife. His stepmother hated him, and, that she might accomplish his destruction, she stole a golden vessel entrusted to the young man to keep, and concealed it in the straw bed in the youth's room. Some days after, the stepmother stirred up her husband to examine the bed in the young man's room. On this account, as well as on account of other misdeeds falsely alleged by the stepmother, the youth was drowned on a charge of attempted parricide. When the relatives of the drowned youth knew this, they slew the stepmother. The relatives of the stepmother slew the citizen, and thus son and stepmother and father died.

In the *Historia* a new story has been inserted, namely,

The Three Knights and the Lady,

for which see above, pp. 288, 289, and, to make room for it, the tales of the King and his Seneschal and the Siege of Rome have been very clumsily joined together.

Wright says that the Latin *Historia Septem Sapientum Romæ* "appears to have been translated direct from the Hebrew (*Mishlé Sandabar*), and it served as the groundwork of all other mediæval versions." It is surprising how he could make such an assertion, since he has given, in the same essay in which it occurs, an analysis of the Hebrew text of the Sindibād, from which the *Historia* differs as much as it does from all the other Eastern texts. It is true that four of the tales of the *Historia*—namely, the Dog and the Snake, the King and his Seneschal (first part of the Siege of Rome in this version), the Wild Boar, and the Burgess and his Magpie—are variants of tales belonging to the original Book of Sindibād, but they are also found in much earlier texts of the Wise Masters; and if it be conceded that the story of the Three Knights and the Lady is adapted from the Hebrew tale of the Hunchbacks (which is not at all probable—see p. 289; and observe that the *Historia* dates about the end of the 15th century), it is surely very slight ground on which to base the theory of the Hebrew version being the source of this Latin prose text. As to the *Historia* forming the groundwork of "all other mediæval versions," the comparative table in p. 351 shows that precisely the contrary is the fact—that *it* was based upon mediæval versions. The cause of this mistake, in which Wright is far from being singular, can now be explained:

In the 13th century a French metrical version, entitled *Dolopathos*, was composed by a trouvère named Herbers, from a Latin work by a Cistercian monk, Johannes de Alta Silva. It

z

was supposed by Des Longchamps and other investigators that
the work of this monk was the *Historia Septem Sapientum Romæ*,
and therefore that the variations occurring in *Dolopathos* were to
be ascribed to Herbers. But Montaiglon, the editor of *Dolopathos*, among others, did not accept this view; he assumed two
Latin sources: the *Historia*, by an unknown author, and the
lost work of the monk of Alta Silva (Haute Seille). And Mussaffia has rendered this last view certain; the work of Johannes
de Alta Silva having been discovered by him, in 1864, in the
Imperial Library at Vienna, and found to be quite different
from the *Historia*, but to correspond exactly with the *Dolopathos*.
Johannes dedicates his *Opusculum de rege vel Septem Sapientibus*
to Bishop Bertrand of Metz. Now Haute Seille at its foundation, in 1140, was assigned to the see of Toul, and in 1184 was
transferred from Toul to Metz. Bertrand occupied the see of
Metz from 1179 to his death, in 1212; and as Johannes would
naturally dedicate his work to his own bishop, it would fall
between 1184 and 1212; and probably wishing to commend
himself to the new bishop, who was a lover of study, when the
cloister passed to Metz, he wrote his work.[1]

An Italian version, entitled *Erasto*, based upon current European texts, was printed, at Mantua, in 1558, of which a French
translation, *Histoire Pitoyable du Prince Erastus*, was made in
1572. From the French it was rendered into English, under
the title of *History of Prince Erastus and the Seven Wise Masters
of Rome*, in 1674, by Francis Kirkman, a voluminous scribbler.
This version comprises some tales which are not found in the
earlier texts, but occur in the Italian novels and other collections.

The mediæval romance of the Seven Wise Masters must have
been one of the most popular books in England during the 16th
and 17th centuries; and even, among the common people, until
comparatively recent times; judging from the numerous editions

---

[1] Goedeke, in *Orient und Occident*, iii, 395.

of the prose version which are preserved in our great libraries.
The Latin *Historia* seems to have been translated into English,
perhaps from a French rendering, in the beginning of the 16th
century, and first printed by Wynkyn de Worde. A copy of this
editio princeps in the British Museum commences thus:

Here begynneth thystorye of ye vii Wyse Maysters of rome conteynynge
ryght fayre and ryght ioyous narracons and to ye reder ryght delectable;

and the colophon :

Thus endeth the treatyse of the seuen sages or wyse maysters of Rome.
Emprented in flet strete in ye sygne of the sone by me Wynkyn de worde.
[4to, black letter, 80 leaves, with several page woodcuts : *circa* 1505.]

According to Ellis, the Seven Wise Masters was "translated
from the French into English, first printed by W. Copland,
without date, but between 1548 and 1567." It would appear,
however, from the title of Copland's edition (only one copy of
which was known to exist, and it disappeared many years ago;
I do not know whether it has turned up again), that it was a
reprint of Wynkyn de Worde :

Here beginneth thystorye of the seuen wyse Maysters of Rome con-
teyning ryght faire and ryght ioyous narracios, and to the reder ryght
delectable. [Col.] Thus endeth the treatyse of the seuen sages or wyse
Maysters of Rome. Imprinted at London in Flete Strete at the sygne of
the Rose Garland, by me William Copland. [8vo, black letter, *circa* 1550.]

The black letter copy in the Glasgow University Library, which
I have made use of occasionally in the course of these notes, is
supposed to be a reprint of Copland's edition, by Sanders, one of
the early Glasgow printers, about the end of the 17th century.
It has been well thumbed, and wants three leaves at the beginning, and probably one leaf at the end.

Besides the *editio princeps* of Wynkyn de Worde, there are
copies of twelve other prose editions of the *Seven Wise Masters*
in the British Museum, viz.—London, 1671, 8vo; 1684, 12mo;
1687, 8vo, B.L.; 1697, 8vo, B.L.; Glasgow (Robert Sanders, son

of the printer above mentioned), 1713, 8vo; Newcastle, ? 1760, 12mo; London, ? 1780, 12mo; Boston, 1794, 12mo; London, ? 1750, 12mo; ? 1785, 12mo; ? 1805, 12mo; and Warrington, ? 1815, 12mo: the four last are chap-books. The Bodleian Library, Oxford, has two prose editions, 1653 and 1682; and a curious metrical version entitled: *Sage and prudente Saynges of the Seuen wyse Men*, by Robert Brenant, with a comment, London, 1553, small 8vo, black letter.—In 1575 was printed at Edinburgh John Rolland's Scottish metrical version, but it was written in 1560. There are imperfect copies of this work, dated 1620, in the Advocates' Library, Edinburgh, and in the Glasgow University Library. It was reprinted (in black letter, 4to), with an Introduction by David Laing, for the Bannatyne Club, in 1835.

A wretched catchpenny imitation of the Wise Masters was published in 1663, under the title of *The Seven Wise Mistresses of Rome*, which was reprinted as a chap-book, within quite recent years, at Dublin.

No. XXXIII.
DOLOPATHOS; OR, THE KING AND THE SEVEN SAGES.

⁎ HAVING furnished some account of the group of Western texts of the *Seven Wise Masters*, as they are fairly represented by our early English metrical versions, I now present, in conclusion, an abstract of another and very different text—moreover, the earliest form in which the romance appeared in Europe—entitled *Dolopathos; sive, de Rege et Septem Sapientibus* (the work of Johannes de Alta Silva, referred to in p. 354, above), edited by Professor Hermann Oesterley, and published at Strassburg, 1873; of which no description has hitherto appeared in English.[1]

Introduction.

THERE was formerly in Sicily a wise and just king, called Dolopathos. The Roman emperor Augustus having bestowed on him Agrippa, the sister of the empress, the result of their union was a son. Before his birth it was declared by "the diviners and mathematicians" that the child would be a son; that he would become a great philosopher, suffer many evils from snares laid for him, but rule in his father's place, and become a worshipper of the true God. The child was named Luscinius, and left seven years with the nurses, after which the task of his education was undertaken by Virgil. The great wisdom and learning of Luscinius caused him to be envied by those who could not equal him, and he was invited to a banquet where they designed to poison him. He went, accompanied by Virgil, and when the poisoned cup was presented, Luscinius at once declared its nature, and challenged his enemies to taste it. They knew they must now die of poison, or be accused by Virgil to Cæsar, and slain; so they drank the cup, and died.

Luscinius looks one day into the astronomical books, and suddenly falls senseless on the floor. By the aid of Virgil and

---

[1] This text forms part of a miscellaneous MS. volume preserved in the Library of the Athenæum at Luxemburg.

others the prince recovers, and informs his tutor that he found from the astronomical rules that his mother had died, that his father had married again, and that ambassadors were then on the way to convey him home from Virgil;—these events had caused him sorrow, and he had swooned. Virgil comforts him, and induces him to promise that, after leaving him, he would speak to no one on the way home, or in his country, or to the king or the queen, or to the princes, or to any one until he again saw him (*i.e.* Virgil). The messengers arrive, and take Luscinius away with them. Discovering that he is dumb, they fear the king's wrath, but he keeps them from suicide by signs, and by writing that by-and-by he should recover the use of his tongue.

Meanwhile Dolopathos makes great preparations for the reception of his son, who at length arrives, and is greeted with loud strains of music, but it is not discovered that he is dumb. Next morning the king has a private interview with his son, whom he proposes to crown in his own stead, but the prince does not reply. The king is angry; Luscinius shows signs of affection, upon which the king rages against Virgil and the messengers. Luscinius writes that he is dumb through grief at his mother's death. The king's counsellors advise the use of music, the company of girls, wine, good food, pleasant objects, etc. The queen enters, and undertakes to carry out this plan. In the queen's apartments the immodest bearing of the damsels towards the prince failing to shake his constancy, the queen herself tempts him, with amorous gestures, but has finally to confess to her maidens that she has also failed, and they advocate revenge—propose to accuse him of attempting to violate the queen: "varium et semper mutabile femina!" So they scratch and disfigure themselves before Luscinius, tear their clothes, and the queen rushes with clamour into the king's council-room, and accuses the prince—her maids attest the truth of her complaint, and Dolopathos expresses his grief, sorrow, and anger.

Luscinius is brought forward, and is still dumb and unmoved. Sentence is demanded by the queen's relatives and friends. Dolopathos calls upon the assembled grandees to decide. At first they say that the laws do not provide for such a case, but being urged, they pronounce sentence of death by burning, which is ratified by Dolopathos. A great fire is accordingly kindled next day, but the people, captivated by the appearance of Luscinius, murmur at the severity of the sentence, and no one is willing to obey the king's command to throw Luscinius into the flames. Just then one of the Seven Wise Men, by chance, comes riding up on a white mule, and, ascertaining the cause of the great assemblage, remonstrates with the king on his credulity and injustice, and relates the story of

The Dog and the Snake,

which is common to all the Western and most of the Eastern texts. The king then remands his son to prison. But N e x t D a y the counsellors again sentence him to be burnt, and when a great fire was prepared and a crowd had assembled to witness the execution, another of the Seven Wise Men opportunely comes to the spot, and obtains a reprieve for Luscinius by relating the story of

The King's Treasury,

which reappears in later Western texts (see p. 330), but is here related with variations: After the king discovers that his treasury has been robbed, he takes counsel of a wise old man, who had formerly been himself a great robber, but, though now deprived of sight, often gave the king excellent advice. The old man suggests that a quantity of green grass should be taken into the treasury and placed on a fire; then, closing the gate, the king should walk round the building, and observe whether smoke escaped through any part of the walls. This the king does, and perceiving smoke issuing from between stones which were not cemented, the precise place where the robbers had gained entrance was at once ascertained.—The youth's device of stealing his father's body (omitted in other texts, but occurring in Herodotus and in the Indian story of Ghata and Karpara— see p. 332) is peculiar: The king, still acting by the old man's advice, causes the corpse to be guarded by twenty horsemen in white armour and twenty in black. The youth disguises himself, one side in white and the other in black, so that he is mistaken as he rides past the two lines of horsemen by each as belonging to their own party.

On the Third Morning the king and his princes assemble as before; a great fire is kindled and the king's son is about to be cast into it, when, lo, an aged man of reverend aspect, on a black horse, and bearing a green olive branch, advances to the king. On learning the cause of the concourse, he says: "I am a Roman by nation, and am called one of the Seven Wise Men. Out of the treasury of my heart I offer things new and old to the kings and princes of the world. Seeing chance has brought me hither, if thou wilt hear me, I will tell thee a story—old, indeed, but perhaps new to thee." The king commands silence, and the wise man begins the story of

The Best Friend.

In the early days of Rome, a king, dying, left the throne to a young son. A protracted siege soon followed; the city was oppressed by famine; and the king, acting on the advice of counsellors of his own age, ordered all the old men and women to be slain, as they consumed food, but were useless for defence. All who concealed their parents were also to be put to death. Thus the sons became more cruel than the enemy to their fathers. One wise old man was concealed in an underground cave by his son, whose wife was aware of the fact, but promised

with an oath to keep the secret. By-and-by peace was concluded. The young king had no advisers skilled in law and
wisdom. His young counsellors drew him into every wickedness;
vice ran riot in the realm, the impious triumphed, and the
innocent suffered. The country now had cause to remember
the saying of the wise man : " Woe to the state whose king is a
boy, and whose princes feast together till morning." But the
youth who had concealed his father brought before him all causes
referred to him. The old man pointed out the proper decisions,
and thus the youth came into favour, was able somewhat to
restore order and law, and was made chief counsellor. Hence
arose hatred towards him, and plots were laid by his former
associates. They suspected that his father was alive and taught
him this wisdom. Openly they durst not say so. They persuaded the king to appoint a time for plays, games, and feasts,
and to order every one to bring forward (1) his best friend, (2) his
worst enemy, (3) as good a mimic and (4) as faithful a servant
as he had. This was agreed to. Some brought as the friend a
father, others a wife, and so on. But the youth, instructed by
his father, who detected the evil design, brought forward a *dog*,
an *ass*, his little *son*, and his *wife*. At the noise of the people
and the sound of the music, the stolid ass became excited, and
made the palace echo with his braying. Soon all were attracted
to the spot. Ridiculed by the wits, the youth, when questioned
by the king, said :

" My dog is my best friend. He does not fear to accompany
me wherever I go, encountering with me the danger of streams
and robbers, and the sharp fangs of wild beasts. For me, he
despises even death itself, and often refreshes me and my guests
with the excellent game he captures. Away from me, he is
never happy, beside me, never sad. Truly, O king, I have
nowhere found so faithful and sincere a friend, nor do I think
you have any better.

" I have brought forward to you my ass, the most faithful

and patient of servants. For he, every morning, going out to the forest, returns thence laden with firewood ; when this is removed from his back, he carries corn to the mill, and brings it back ground; then he sets off with the buckets to the well, and returns with them full. Although he does all this day by day, without murmur or reluctance, he demands no costly dress, or expensive food, but is satisfied if a little hay or chaff follows his daily toil. I ask, O king, where shall I find such a servant? Clearly, nowhere.

"But whom, as a mimic, could I bring forward better than my little son? For he daily shows me new sports, and, while he attempts to imitate what he sees or hears, puts on comic expressions, mumbles the words he cannot utter plainly, and when he completely fails to say what he thinks, expresses it by signs and bodily gestures. In the same hour, we find him joyful and sad, weeping and laughing, and that not artificially, as with others, but he acts simply, incited by his nature and age, and looking for no reward from me.

"Finally, I have brought here my wife, the greatest enemy I have." But the wife, seeing she had been reserved for this indignity, remembering the confidence, pity, and humanity exercised towards her husband and his father, was goaded into fury, and could scarcely allow her husband to finish the words. "O worst and most ungrateful of men," said she, "who, unmindful of the kindness and pity which I have shown for many years now towards your father, withdrawn from death and kept in a cave—now to regard me before the king and all the people as an enemy!" But the young man replied:

"You see, O king, that what I said concerning my wife is true, who, for a single word, both betrays my concealed father and brings me under sentence of death. So a certain very wise old man, instructing his son, commanded him to be especially on his guard against her who lay in his bosom, that is, his wife, wishing it to be understood that she was a false friend. For against open enemies it is easy to be on the watch, but no one can avoid a wife, or fair-faced friend, who is always about, because they pretend to inordinate love by their words, and plan snares in their hearts."

But the king, having admired the skill of the young man, and understanding the truth of his words, anticipated his accusers: "Go," said he to him; "you and your father are safe; delay not to bring him to the games." The old man was therefore led from the cave, and on account of his surprising wisdom, the king appointed him a judge and father of the city and country. In a short time he restored the ancient condition of things, expelled vice, implanted good, restored quiet, and, dying, left behind him many followers of virtue.

"Hear then," adds the wise man, "my story ends, and going away, O king, I ask from thee nought else but that you grant your son his life for this day, knowing that something is concealed which, if you knew, will free you from murder and your son from punishment."

This story, found in different forms in mediæval works, and probably of Talmudic origin, is reproduced, with variations, in the *Gesta Romanorum*, Tale 124, to this effect : A certain noble knight, having offended his king, is to be pardoned on condition that he enter the royal hall of audience on foot and riding at the same time, and bring with him his most attached friend, the best jester, and his most deadly foe. One evening a pilgrim comes to the knight's castle to claim his hospitality, and after he has retired, the knight, saying to his wife that pilgrims often carried much gold about with them, proposes to rob and murder their guest, which has the lady's approval. But the knight, rising early next morning, dismisses the pilgrim, and, killing a calf, he cuts it into pieces, and puts them into a sack, which he then gives to his wife, desiring her to hide it, saying that only the head, legs, and arms of the pilgrim were in the sack—the rest he had himself concealed in the stable. On the day appointed, the knight proceeds to the king's palace, accompanied by his dog, his child, and his wife. He enters the royal hall, with one leg over his dog, as if he was riding. The king is amused with his ingenuity, and then asks him for his best friend. The knight, drawing his sword, wounds his dog, who runs away, howling with pain; but on the knight calling him back, he immediately returns, and fawns upon him. "This," says he, "is my true and faithful friend." Then the king asks for his worst enemy; upon which the knight strikes his wife a severe blow. Enraged at this affront, the lady exclaims: "Why dost thou smite me? Dost thou forget that thou didst slay a pilgrim in thy house?" The knight then gave her a second blow. "Wretch!" she cries, "dost thou think I cannot tell where I placed the sack containing parts of the murdered man, and that the rest of him lies in the stable?" Messengers are despatched to search the places indicated by the woman, and they return with the flesh and bones of the calf, upon which the king bestows great gifts and honours on the knight, and ever after held him in great esteem.

On the Fourth Morning the prince is again led out to be burnt, when an aged man, robed in a toga, and seated on a mule, presents himself before the king, and relates the story of

The Hard Creditor.

There was once a nobleman who had a strongly fortified castle and many other possessions. His wife died, leaving him an only daughter, whom he caused to be instructed in all the liberal arts, so far as wisdom could be acquired from the discipline and books of the philosophers, in order that she might thus know how to secure her inheritance. In this hope he was not deceived. She became skilled in all the liberal arts, and also acquired a perfect knowledge of magic. After this it came to pass that the nobleman was seized with an acute fever, took to his bed, and died, bequeathing all his goods to his daughter. Possessed of her father's wealth, she resolved she would marry no man unless his wisdom was equal to her own. She had many noble suitors, but, denying none, she offered to share her couch with any one who should give her a hundred marks of silver, and when the morrow came, if they were mutually agreeable, their nuptials should be duly celebrated. Many youths came to her on this condition, and paid the stipulated sum of money, but she enchanted them by her magical arts, placing an owl's feather beneath the pillow of him who was beside her, when he at once fell into a profound sleep, and so remained until at daybreak she took away the feather. In this way she spoiled many of their money, and acquired much treasure. It happened that a certain young man of good family, having been thus deluded, resolved to circumvent the damsel, so, proceeding to a rich slave [freedman?], whose foot he had formerly cut off in a passion, he asked him for a loan of one hundred marks, which the lame one readily gave, but on this condition, that if the money was not paid within a year, he might take the weight of one hundred marks from the flesh and bones of the young man. To this the youth lightly agreed, and signed the bond with his seal. With the hundred marks he went a second time to the damsel, and removing by accident the owl's feather from under his pillow, thus did away the spell, and, having accomplished his purpose, he was next day married to her in presence of their friends.

Forthwith prosperous times came to the young man, he forgot his creditor, and did not pay the money within the appointed time; whereupon the lame one rejoiced that he had found an opportunity of revenge. He appeared before the king, who was then on the throne, raised an action against the youth, exhibited the bond as evidence, and demanded justice to be executed.

The king, though horrified at the bargain, had no alternative but to order the youth to come before him to answer the action of the accuser. Then the youth, at length mindful of the debt, and afraid of the king's authority, went to court, with a very great crowd of his friends, and plenty of gold and silver. The accuser exhibited the bond, which the youth acknowledged, and, by order of the king, the chiefs pronounced sentence, namely, that it should be lawful for the lame one to act as specified in the bond, or to demand as much money as he pleased for the redemption of the youth. The king therefore asked the lame one if he would spare the youth on receiving double money. He refused, and the king was attempting for many days to prevail upon him to agree, when, lo, the youth's wife, having put on man's attire, and with her countenance and voice altered by magical arts, dismounted from a horse before the king's palace, and approached and saluted the king. Being asked who she was, and whence she came, she replied that she was a soldier, born in the most distant part of the world, that she was skilled in law and equity, and was a keen critic of judgments. The king, being glad at this, ordered the supposed soldier to be seated beside him, and committed to her for final decision the lawsuit between the lame one and the youth. Both parties being summoned, she said: "For thee, O lame one, according to the judgment of the king and the princes, it is lawful to take away the weight of one hundred marks of flesh. But what will you gain, unless indeed death, if you slay the youth? It is better that you accept for him seven or ten times the money." But he said he would not accept ten times, or even one thousand times, the sum. Then she ordered a very white linen cloth to be brought, and the youth to be stripped of his clothing, bound hand and foot, and stretched thereon. Which done, "Cut," said she to the lame one, "with your iron, where ever you wish your weight of marks. But if you take away more or less than the exact weight by even the amount of a needle's

point, or if one drop of blood stains the linen, know that forthwith thou shalt perish by a thousand deaths, and, cut into a
thousand pieces, thou shalt become the food of the beasts and
the birds, and all thy kin shall suffer the same penalty, and
thy goods shall become state property." He grew pale at this.
dreadful sentence, and said : "Since there is no one, God alone
excepted, who can be so deft of hand, but would take away too
much or too little, I am unwilling to attempt what is so un-
certain. Therefore I set the youth free, remit the debt, and
give him one thousand marks for reconciliation." Thus, then,
the youth was set free by the prudence of his wife, and returned
in joy to his own house.

"Who, then," adds the sage, "may not hope, O king, that
this youth may be freed by skill? Wishing that you may be
warned by this example, I ask that you will prolong the life of
your son till to-morrow." And the king grants his petition.

We have here, in all probability, the oldest European version
of the story of the "pound of flesh," which forms part of the plot of
Shakspeare's Merchant of Venice. The tale of the bond is
of Eastern origin, and may have come into France by way of
Italy, or through the Moors of Spain. Ser Giovanni has adapted
it in *Il Pecerone*, Day iv, Novel 1, a work written about 1378,
but not printed till 1558. In this Italian version, in place of
the magical influence of the owl's feather, the lady drugs her
suitor's wine with soporific ingredients, and a Jew lends him ten
thousand ducats on the same condition as the cripple in the
above. When the stipulated period has elapsed, the Jew refuses
to accept ten times the money, and at this crisis, according to
Dunlop, "the new-married lady arrives, disguised as a lawyer,
and announces, as was the custom in Italy, that she had come
to decide difficult cases ; for in that age delicate points were not
determined by the ordinary judges of the provinces, but by
doctors of law, who were called from Bologna and other places

at a distance." The pretended lawyer decides that the Jew is entitled to his pound of flesh, but should be put to death if he drew one drop of blood from his debtor.—The story of the bond occurs in a somewhat different form in the Anglican *Gesta Romanorum*, and also in the old ballad of Gernutus, or the Jew of Venice. It is the 13th of the Pleasing Stories in Gladwin's *Persian Moonshee*, and forms the leading incident of the Persian tale of the Qāzī of Emessa ;—in the latter the debtor is a Muslim merchant, and the hard creditor is a Jew, enamoured of the merchant's virtuous wife.

On the Fifth Morning, the queen having renewed her complaint, accusing Dolopathos of being dilatory, unjust, and unworthy of the name and honour of king, for having allowed so shameless a youth to live so many days, the prince is again about to be burnt, when another of the Seven Wise Men appears, and relates the story of

The Widow's Son.

There was a certain Roman king once advancing with his army against his enemies, who had seized a very large part of his kingdom ; and it happened that his army passed through a certain village. There a poor widow, with an only son, had a little house, one only of the many in the world. She had a little hen ; and as the army passed before the house, the king's son, a mere boy, let fly the hawk, which, after the manner of the nobles, was perched on his hand, at the widow's hen. The hawk was choking the wretched little creature with its crooked claws, when the widow's son ran to aid the little bird, and killed the hawk with a stroke from a stick. On this account the king's son was indignant, and raging in his fury, in revenge for the hawk, he thrust through and killed the widow's son. What then could the poor widow do, deprived of her only son, and her only property ? In her excitement, she ran after the king, followed him with tears, and demanded with her voice and sobs that her son unjustly slain should be avenged. The king, being of a mild and pitying disposition, was greatly affected. Stopping, therefore, he pleasantly and quietly advised the widow to await his return from the enemy, saying: "Then, as you wish, I shall avenge your son." But the widow said: "And what will happen if you fall in war? Who will avenge my son?" "I shall entrust that to him who shall succeed me in the kingdom." "And what reward," said she, "wilt thou receive, if another avenge him who was slain when you were alive and reigning?" "None," said he. Then said the widow: "Do you, therefore, what you would command to others, so that you may acquire praise from men and reward from the gods." The king, moved as well by the argument of the widow as by pity, put off the war, and returned to the city. When it was known that his son was the murderer of the widow's son, "Thy hen," said he, "as I think, was fully compensated for by the death of the hawk. But for the dead son, I give thee choice of two things: For either, if you wish, I will slay my son, or, if you rather decree that he should live, I give you him in place of the dead son, that he may cherish you as his mother, adore you as queen, honour you as lady, and may serve you all the days of your life." So she, deeming it more useful for her that the king's son should live than die, took him instead of the dead one, and was transferred from the hut to the palace, and exchanged her rags and apron for purple robes.

"See, O king," adds the sage, "imitate the action of this most just and pious monarch; consider how you can hold to the rigour of justice, and yet by your prudence save your son. But if you do not wish to alter the sentence of your chiefs, this at least I may obtain from you, that you allow him the space of this day. For to-morrow, as to-day, you can easily find woo and fire with which to burn your son."

2 A

A similar tale to this last is related of more than one Oriental potentate. Several of the khalīfs are represented by historians as being equally strict dispensers of justice, and the incident is probably a historical fact.

On the Sixth Morning, the prince is once more about to be thrown into the fire, when "a certain old man of venerable hoariness, dressed in a Roman toga, passing with gentle step through the centre of the crowd of men and women, and admired of many, came to the king." After learning the occasion of such a large assemblage of people, he related to the king and his grandees the story of

The Master-Thief.

A very famous and cruel robber, having amassed much wealth, settled down to a quiet and orderly life; but finding his three sons resolved to follow the same profession, he refused to grant them a farthing of his money. The youngest son, concealed in a bundle of fodder, is introduced into the royal stables, and makes off at night with the queen's celebrated steed and his valuable trappings, but is observed and followed. He and his brothers are caught. The father refuses to ransom them; but the queen offers to set them free if the old robber will relate some of the most terrible incidents of his former career.

He relates how he and his comrades were captured by a giant whose abode they had plundered; how the giant ate them one by one; how he himself blinded the giant while pretending to cure his sore eyes, and how he eluded the giant for several days by now clinging to the beams of the roof, now taking refuge among his flock of sheep, from which he selected one daily for his food. At length the giant threw him a ring, which he put on his finger, and which caused him to shout, "Here I am! here I am!" thus betraying his whereabouts. As the ring could not be removed, he cut off his finger, and the spell ceased.—Escaped at length,

he comes upon the bodies of three robbers who had been lately
hanged. He reaches the hut of a poor woman, whom ghūls
had ordered to cook her son for their revels; he takes away one
of the dead robbers and gives it to the old woman as a substitute for her son, and then occupies the place of the body he had
removed, to conceal the trick. The ghūls came, however, and
seizing him, were about to devour him, when, lo, a sound as of
a loud rushing wind caused them to vanish, and thus he escaped
a second great peril.

A remarkably close parallel to this story is found in Campbell's
Popular Tales of the West Highlands, vol. i, pp. 145-148, in the
Tale of Connal, but the sequence of the incidents is curiously
changed: Connal saw, in the upper part of a cave, a fine fair
woman, "who was thrusting the flesh stake at a big lump of a
baby, and every thrust she would give the spit, the babe would
laugh, and she would begin to weep. Connal spoke, and he said :
'Woman, what ails thee at the child without reason?' 'Oh,'
said she, 'since thou art an able man thyself, kill the baby and
set it on this stake, till I roast it for the giant.' He caught hold
of the baby, and he put a plaid that he had on about the babe,
and he hid it at the side of the cave. There were a great
many dead bodies at the side of the cave, and he set one of
them on the stake, and the woman was roasting it. Then was
heard under ground trembling and thunder coming, and he would
rather that he was out. Here he sprang in the place of the corpse
that was at the fire, in the very midst of the bodies. The giant
came, and he asked : 'Was the roast ready?' He began to eat,
and he said : 'Fiu fau hoagrich! It's no wonder that thy own
flesh is tough; it is tough on thy brat.' When the giant had
eaten that one, he went to count the bodies; and the way he
had of counting them was, to catch hold of them by the two
smalls of the leg, and to toss them past the top of his head; and
he counted them backwards and forwards thus three or four

times; and as he found Connal somewhat heavier, and that he was soft and fat, he took that slice out of him from the back of his head to his groin. He roasted this at the fire, and he ate it, and then he fell asleep. Connal winked to the woman to put the flesh stake in the fire. She did this, and when the spit grew white after it was red, he thrust the spit through the giant's heart, and the giant was dead." We have here a distorted version of the exploit of the Master-Thief of our tale—the blinding of the giant, which, again, is evidently taken from the similar adventure of Ulysses with Polyphemus. The man-eating giant, or ghūl, may be compared with world-wide legends of dragons and rākshasas that devoured citizens—preferably beautiful maidens, at the rate of one each week or month;—the oldest extant form being found in a beautiful episode of the *Mahābharata*, which has been rendered into graceful English verse by Dean Milman, under the title of the Brāhman's Lament.—To return to the Tale of Connal: "Then Connal went and he set the woman on her path homewards, and then he went home himself. His stepmother sent him and her son to steal the white-faced horse from the king of Italy. . . A company came out, and they were caught. The binding of the three smalls was laid on them straitly and painfully. 'Thou big red man,' said the king, 'wast thou ever in so hard a case as that?'" Connal then relates his adventures, being promised pardon if he could tell of his having been in a worse plight during his past career.

On the Seventh Morning, the execution of the prince is prevented by the appearance of another old man, who, after the usual questions and replies, relates, as an example of the malice of women, the story of

The Swan-Children.

A young man, in eager pursuit of a stag white as snow, chased it into a deep and distant forest, where it escaped. In attempting to retrace his way, he came upon a fountain in which a beautiful nymph was bathing. In her hand she held a golden chain, wherein lay her power. Snatching away the chain, the youth seized the nymph, and she was constrained to become his wife. During the night she awoke her husband, being ashamed at learning the fact from the stars that she had conceived six sons and a daughter. He comforts her, and brings her home to his castle. His mother dislikes the wife, and plots her ruin; but being unable to accomplish it at once, she contrives a horrible scheme. The wedded nymph gives birth to six sons and a daughter, with golden chains, like collars, round their necks. The grandmother sends the infants away to be killed by a trusty servant, whose conscience smites him, and he leaves them un-harmed at the foot of a tree, where they are found by a philosopher, taken to his cave, and fed for seven years. The grandmother presents to her son seven little whelps as the off-spring of his wife. In horror, he orders his wife to be degraded, and exposed to all indignities at the hands of the people. For seven long years she is thus treated, until she becomes as ugly and wretched as she had formerly been fair and happy.

When out one day hunting in the woods, the father observes seven children with golden chains on their necks. He pursues them, and they suddenly disappear. He reports the strange sight, and his mother in alarm questions the servant, who con-fesses that he had not killed the babes as he had promised. For three days this servant is sent by her to scour the woods for the children, but in vain. On the fourth day he finds the six boys, transformed into swans, at play in a river, and their sister on the bank holding their golden chains. While she is watching the frolics of the swans, the servant steals up to her and snatches away the chains, but she escapes with her own chain. On his return, the joyful grandmother takes the chains to a goldsmith, and requests him to make a little cup out of the gold. In vain the workman tries fire and hammer; the chains yield to neither, save that a link of one of them appears a little battered. The goldsmith weighs them, takes the same quantity of other gold, makes it into a cup and gives it to the old woman, who conceals it and keeps it unused.

By the loss of their chains it becomes impossible for the swans to resume their proper form. They lament their condition, and, with their sister, now also transformed into a swan, they fly away to seek some lake or river suitable for a permanent abode; and select the lake beside which their father's castle stands. The nobleman is delighted with their beauty and the sweetness of their music, and gives strict command for their protection. Food is also daily thrown to them. But their sister, resuming her human form, goes every day to beg at the castle, like an orphan. She divides the alms with the wretched nymph, her mother, who is kept degraded and loathsome at the castle; she weeps over her and pities her, still ignorant of their relationship. Other portions of the alms she divides with the swans, her brothers, who ever meet her with joyous demonstrations. At night she returns to the castle, and sleeps with her wretched mother. It soon begins to be whispered that the orphan is like the nobleman's wife, and, questioned by him, she confesses that she knows not her parents, but tells the story of the swans, her brothers. The grandmother becomes again alarmed, and at her order the servant follows the girl to the side of the lake, where he attempts to kill her with a sword. At this juncture the noble-man, who is returning from the field, comes up, and strikes the sword out of the servant's hand. In his fear, the servant relates the whole story of the exposure of the children, the theft of the chains, and so on. The grandmother is compelled to produce the cup; the goldsmith is sent for, and the chains are restored. The swans now resume the human form, excepting the one whose chain had the battered ring;—he continued still in the form of a swan, and is the same, so celebrated in story, who, with his golden chain, draws the armed soldier in the little boat.

Thus the father recovered his children, and the children were restored to their father. The degraded mother was restored to dignity, and, with care, in time recovered her former beauty, while the wicked old crone was condemned to suffer the lot she had devised for her unfortunate but innocent daughter-in-law.

This beautiful fairy tale, under the title of Helyas, the Knight of the Swan, and considerably amplified and modified, was one of the favourite romances during mediæval times. The golden chain which the damsel wore round her neck having been obtained by the young nobleman, and thus compelling her to submit to his will, may be compared to the feather dress of the fairies in the Persian tale of King Bahram Ghūr and the Perī Hasn Bānū, and in the better-known Arabian tale of Hasan of Basra. In like manner, in Ralston's *Russian Folk Tales*, a youth discovers on the sea shore twelve birds which turn into maidens, and he steals the shift of the eldest, who must, in consequence, become his wife.—In the Farö islands it is still believed that the seal casts off its skin every ninth night, and becomes a maiden; should her skin be stolen she must continue in human form. And in the Shetland islands the superstition is current (according to Hibbert) that when mermaids wish to visit the upper world, "they put on the *ham*, or skin, of some fish, but woe to those who lose their *ham*, for then are all hopes of return annihilated, and they must stay where they are."—The six children of our tale who were deprived of their chains immediately became swans, but could not return to human form until their chains were restored; yet the damsel caught bathing in the fountain, when the nobleman took possession of her chain, underwent no transformation—a piece of inconsistency common enough in fairy tales.

This tale of the Swan-Children and of the inveterate malice of their grandmother may be a Western survival of a myth which was the common heritage of the whole Aryan race. In Miss

Frere's *Old Deccan Days*—a very entertaining collection of modern versions of ancient Indian fictions—the story of "Truth's Triumph" presents a curious parallel to the leading incident of our tale: The twelve wives of a rāja, envious of his new wife, who had borne him one hundred boys and a girl, at one time, resolve to destroy them. A nurse is bribed to throw them on a dung-heap to be devoured by rats, and put stones in their cradles. They persuade the rāja that his favourite wife has given birth to stones. The rats foster the children, but some years afterwards they are discovered and thrown into a well, and so on. Ultimately they are restored to the rāja, who puts all the envious rānīs to death.—In the Norse tale of "Twelve Wild Ducks" (who are so many princes thus transformed), the old and spiteful queen, jealous of her son's young wife Snow White and Rosy Red, takes away her baby, and accuses her to her son of having killed and eaten it. She does the same each time the princess has a baby. At length the children are discovered in a well.—And the Arabian tale of the Three Sisters who envied their Youngest Sister must be well known, in which the three baby boys and the baby girl are successively delivered to a servant to be destroyed, but are providentially preserved.

On the Eighth Morning, the king, having been again bitterly reproached by his wife for listening to the idle tales of old men, and allowing his son to live, declares that he will throw him into the flames with his own hands, if others are still unwilling to do so; but, just as he is about to commit this terrible crime, the philosopher Virgil rides up, is greeted by his pupil Luscinius, and relates the story of

The Husband Shut Out,

which differs from the old English metrical versions in the catastrophe: instead of leaving her husband to be taken up by the watchmen, the woman admits him, after he has solemnly promised to allow her to go out whenever she wished. (See p. 332.)

Conclusion.

Having ended his story, the sage orders the prince to be un-fettered and richly robed, and Luscinius then informs his father of the cause of his silence, of the lascivious conduct of the queen and her maidens, and why they had plotted his destruction. The king commands his wife and her damsels to be thrown into the fire prepared for the prince. Dolopathos and Virgil die the same year; the ashes of the king are inurned at Palermo, and those of the philosopher at Mantua. Luscinius ascends the throne, governs his subjects well and wisely, and finally is con-verted to the Christian faith.

No. XXXIV.

ADDITIONAL NOTE.

The Tank of Trial—p. 250.—I understand, from Professor Comparetti's note on Nakhshabī's story of the Father-in-Law (*Researches*, etc, p. 41), that the 15th tale of the *Suka Saptatī* is similar to the version I have cited from Cardonne's *Mélanges* in the incident of the "water trial," to which a close parallel is found in the legendary "life" of Virgilius, as follows (from Thoms' *English Prose Romances*, ii, pp. 34-36):

Than made Virgilius at Rome a metall serpente with his cunnynge, that who so euer put his hande in the throte of the serpente, was to sware his cause ryght and trewe; and if hys cause were false he shulde nat plucke his hande out a geyne; and if it were trewe they shulde plucke it out a geyne without any harme doynge. So it fortuned that there was a knyght of Lum-bardye that mystrusted his wife with one of his men that was moost set by the conseyte of his wyfe: but she excused hyr selfe ryght noblye and wysely. And she consented to goo with hym to Rome to that serpent, and there to take hyr othe that she was not gylty of that, that he put apon hyr. And therto consented the knyght: and as they were bothe in the carte, and also hyr man with hyr, she sayd to the man; that when he cam to Rome that he shulde clothe him with a foles-cote, and dysgyse hym in such maner that they shulde nat knowe hym, and so dyd he; and when the day was come that he shulde come to the serpent, he was there present. And Virgilius knowinge the falsenes of the woman by his cunnynge of egromancy, and than sayd Virgilius to the woman: "With drawe your othe and swere nat;" but she wolde nat do after hym, but put hyr hande into the serpentes mouthe: and when hyr hande was in, she sware before hyr husbande that she had no more to do with hym than with that fole that stode hyr by: and by cause that she sayd trowthe she pulled out hyr hande a geyne out of the throte of the serpent nat hurt: and than departed the knyght home, and trusted her well euer after. And Virgilius hauing therat great spyte and anger that the woman hade so escaped destroyed the serpent: for thus scaped the lady a waye fro that great daunger. And spake Virgilius, and sayde: that the women be ryght wyse to enmagen ungraceousenes, but in goodnes they be but innocentes.

"It is curious," says Mr. Thoms, "that at this day there is a chapel at Rome called Santa Maria, built in the first ages of the church, which is likewise denominated 'Bocca della verita,' on account of a large round mask, with an enormous mouth, fixed up in the vestibule. Tradition says that in former times the Romans, in order to give a more solemn confirmation to oaths, were wont to put their hands into this mouth, and if a person took a false oath his hand would be bitten off."

INDEX.

476

GLASGOW :
PRINTED BY JAMES CAMERON, 45, WEST NILE STREET.